RIDERS OF THE DEAD

'REGROUP THE LINE! Regroup!' Gerlach yelled into the uproar and the smoke. Another enemy rider broke towards him, riding downfield with his sword circling. The iron blade made a whooping noise as it swept around.

Calmly, Gerlach slid his spent pistol back into its holster and drew its twin. It banged out a little cloud of hot smoke as he fired it and unhorsed the Norther.

His charge had run out of steam. Around him he saw the demilancers fighting with sabres, saddle to saddle with the enemy riders. He saw friends and comrades torn down, gutted, thrown by wounded horses.

Gerlach drew his sabre and spurred Saksen forward, blade and standard raised high. 'For the company! For the company! For the Emperor!' he yelled.

· GAUNT'S GHOSTS ·

*Colonel-Commissar Gaunt and his regiment the Tanith
First-and-Only struggle for survival on the battlefields
of the far future.*

The Founding
FIRST AND ONLY
GHOSTMAKER
NECROPOLIS

The Saint
HONOUR GUARD
THE GUNS OF TANITH
STRAIGHT SILVER
SABBAT MARTYR

· THE EISENHORN TRILOGY ·

*In the nightmare world of the 41st millennium, Inquisitor
Eisenhorn hunts down mankind's most dangerous enemies.*

XENOS
MALLEUS
HERETICUS

· WARHAMMER FANTASY NOVELS ·

HAMMERS OF ULRIC (with Nik Vincent and James
Wallis)
GILEAD'S BLOOD (with Nik Vincent)

A WARHAMMER NOVEL

Riders of the Dead

Dan Abnett

For Emma and Peter Abnett
and about time too.

A BLACK LIBRARY PUBLICATION

First published in Great Britain in 2003.

Paperback edition published in 2003 by
BL Publishing,
Games Workshop Ltd.,
Willow Road, Nottingham,
NG7 2WS, UK

10 9 8 7 6 5 4 3 2 1

Cover illustration by Adrian Smith,
Map by Nuala Kennedy.

A CIP record for this book is available from the British Library.

ISBN 1 84416 019 X

Distributed in the US by Simon & Schuster
1230 Avenue of the Americas, New York, NY 10020, US.

Printed and bound in Great Britain by
Cox & Wyman Ltd, Reading, Berkshire, UK.

See the Black Library on the Internet at
www.blacklibrary.com

Find out more about Games Workshop
and the world of Warhammer at
www.games-workshop.com

THIS IS A DARK age, a bloody age, an age of daemons and of sorcery. It is an age of battle and death, and of the world's ending. Amidst all of the fire, flame and fury it is a time, too, of mighty heroes, of bold deeds and great courage.

AT THE HEART of the Old World sprawls the Empire, the largest and most powerful of the human realms. Known for its engineers, sorcerers, traders and soldiers, it is a land of great mountains, mighty rivers, dark forests and vast cities. And from his throne in Altdorf reigns the Emperor Karl-Franz, sacred descendent of the founder of these lands, Sigmar, and wielder of his magical warhammer.

BUT THESE ARE far from civilised times. Across the length and breadth of the Old World, from the knightly palaces of Bretonnia to ice-bound Kislev in the far north, come rumblings of war. In the towering World's Edge Mountains, the orc tribes are gathering for another assault. Bandits and renegades harry the wild southern lands of the Border Princes. There are rumours of rat-things, the skaven, emerging from the sewers and swamps across the land. And from the northern wildernesses there is the ever-present threat of Chaos, of daemons and beastmen corrupted by the foul powers of the Dark Gods. As the time of battle draws ever near, the Empire needs heroes like never before.

Come out, young man! The spirits sing
And see what war has bred
The grave mounds of the living
And the riders of the dead.

– from a Kislevite banner song

DEMILANCE

I

VATZL TO DURBERG, Durberg to Harnstadt, Harnstadt to Brodny, in one furious week, in one laborious gallop, a double line of helmet cockades and lance banners bobbing and fluttering.

A rest stop at Brodny, then out, into the edges of the oblast itself. After Brodny, all the place names began to change, for there the Empire slipped away behind them like a flying cloak cut loose.

The sparse haunches of Kislev lay before them.

To the west, the dogtooth line of the Middle Mountains, receding into violet haze. The sky, light and clear like glass. Endless acres of green crops, hissing in the wind. Grasslands riven with gorse and thistle. Larks singing, so high up they were invisible.

Brodny to Emsk, Emsk to Gorovny, Gorovny to Choika, through numerous oblast villages that no one had time to name, tiny hamlets where rough wooden izbas clustered around lonely shrines.

On the track, the massed columns of infantry under standards, each trailing behind itself a long baggage train like the tail of a comet. Ox-teams, kitchen wagons, tinkers with barrows, victuallers with heavy drays of kegs and barrels, muleteers, war carts piled with pike-shafts, stakes, firewood and unfletched arrows, all plodding north. The convoys of engineers, hauling the great gun carriages and the pannier trucks of shot and powder with oxen and draft horse, struggling with block and tackle where iron wheels fouled in the mud. Halberdiers and pikemen, in file, looking from a distance like winter forests on the move. Marching songs. A thousand voices, making the oblast ring. A hundred thousand.

The Empire was lowering its head and squaring up for war.

For that was the spring of the Year That No One Forgets. The dreadful year of waste and plight and hardship, when the North rose as never before and plunged its several hordes like lances into the flanks of the World. It was the two thousand five hundred and twenty-first year marked on the Imperial calendar since the Heldenhammer and the Twelve Tribes founded the Empire with sinew and steel. It was the age of Karl Franz, the Conclave of Light – and Archaon.

* * *

II

AT CHOIKA, WHERE the river was wide and slow, they rested their horses a day. The people there regarded them in a sullen manner, unimpressed by the sight of fifty Imperial demilancers jogging two abreast into the town square. Every horse was a heavy gelding, chestnut, black or grey; every man dressed in gleaming half-plate and lobster-tail burgonet. A light lance stood vertical in every right hand. A brace of pistols or a petronel bounced at every saddle.

The clarion gave double notes with his horn, long and short, and the troop flourished lances and dismounted with a clatter of metal plate. Girths were loosened, withers patted and rubbed.

The company officer was a thirty-two year old captain-of-horse called Meinhart Stouer. He removed his burgonet and held it by the chinstraps as he knocked grass burrs out of its comb of feathers.

Thus occupied, he barked sidelong at the clarion. 'Karl! Find out what this town is called!'

'It's Choika, captain,' the young man replied, buckling his gleaming silver bugle back into its saddle holster.

'You know these things of course,' smiled Stouer. 'And the river?'

'The Lynsk, captain.'

The captain raised his gloved hands wide like a supplicant and the lancers around him laughed. 'May Sigmar save me from educated men!'

The clarion's name was Karl Reiner Vollen. He was twenty years old, and took the teasing with a shrug.

Stouer wouldn't have asked if he hadn't expected Vollen to know.

The company's supply wagons, with their escort of six lances, rattled belatedly into the square and drew up behind the lines of horse. Stouer acknowledged their arrival and limped over to the well fountain. He was stiff-legged and sore from the saddle. He tucked off a leather riding glove, cupped it in his hand, and splashed water from the low stone basin over his face. Then he rinsed his mouth and spat brown liquid onto the ground. Beads of water twinkled in his thick, pointed beard.

'Sebold! Odamar! Negotiate some feed for the mounts. Don't let them rob you. Gerlach! Negotiate some feed for us. The same applies. Take Karl with you. He probably speaks the damn language too! If he does, buy him beer. Blowing that horn and thinking hard is thirsty work.'

Gerlach Heileman carried the company's standard, a role that earned him pay-and-a-half and the title of vexillary. The standard was a stout ash pole three spans long. The haft was worked in gilt and wrapped in leather bands. On its tip was a screaming dragon head made of brass, from the back of which depended two swallowtails of cloth. These symbolised the Star With the Pair of Tails. Under this astrological omen, the great epochs of the Empire had been baptised. Some said it had been seen again, in these last few seasons.

Beneath the brass draco was a cross-spar supporting the painted banner of the company, a heavy linen square edged in a passementerie of gold brocade. A leopard's pelt hung down behind the banner and parchment extracts from the Sigmarite gospel were pinned by rosette seals around its hem. The banner's fields were the red and white of Talabheim, and it showed, in gold and green, the motifs of that great city-state: the wood-axe and the trifoil leaf, either side of the Imperial hammer. A great winged wyrm coiled around the hammer's grip.

Gerlach kissed the haft of the standard and passed it to the demilancer holding his horse. Removing his helmet and gloves, he nodded over at the clarion.

The pair walked together across the square, their half-armour clinking. Long boots of buff leather encased the legs of every demilancer to the thigh. From there to the neck, they wore polished silver suits of articulated plate over a coat of felt-lined ringmail. The horse company was a prestigious troop, recruited from the landed nobility, unlike the levies or the standing armies of the state, and so each demilancer was required to provide for his own arming. Their armour reflected this, and the subtle nuances of each rider's status. Gerlach Heileman was the second son of Sigbrecht Heileman, a sworn and spurred knight of the Order of the Red Shield, the bodyguard of Talabheim's elector count. Once he had served his probation in the demilance company, Gerlach could expect to join his father and elder brother in that noble order. His half-armour matched those rich expectations. The panels were etched and worked to mimic the puffed and slashed cut of courtly velvet and damask, and his cuirass was in an elegant waistcoat style that fastened down the front.

Though outwardly similar, Karl Reiner Vollen's half-armour was much plainer and more traditional. He could trace his lineage back to the nobility of Solland, but that heritage had been reduced to ashes in the war of 1707. Since then, dispossessed and penniless, his family had served as retainers to the household of their cousins – the Heilemans. Gerlach was two years Karl's senior, but they had grown up within the same walls, schooled by the same tutors, trained by the same men-at-arms.

Yet a world of difference existed between them, and it was about to get much wider.

III

THE PINE DWELLINGS of Choika-on-the-Lynsk bore roofs of grey aspen shingles that overlapped to give the appearance of scales. There had been a town here for a thousand years. This incarnation had stood for two centuries, since the razing of the previous version in the time of Magnus the Pious. Dry and old and dark, it would burn quickly when the hour came.

Vollen and Heileman walked under low gables into the gloomy hall that served as the town's inn. Ingots of malachite were inlaid around the door posts, and the lintel was hung with charms, sprigs of herbs, and aged, wooden-soled ice skates.

Under its roof of smoke-blacked tie-beams, the hall was dark. The compressed earth floor was strewn with dirty rushes, and there was an ill-matched variety of benches, stools and trestles placed about. Wood smoke fouled the close air, and twisted in the light cast by the window slits. Vollen could smell spices and spit-meat, vinegar and hops. Heileman couldn't smell anything that didn't offend his nose.

Three long-bearded old men, grouped around a painted table, looked up from the thimble cups of samogon they were warming in arthritic hands. Their hooded eyes were deep-set in their crinkled faces, and utterly noncommittal.

'Hail and met, fathers,' said Heileman, perfunctorily. 'Where is the inn host?'

The eyes continued to twinkle without blinking.

'I said, fathers, the inn host? Where is the inn host?'

There was no reply, nor any sense that they had even heard his words.

Heileman mimed supping a drink and rubbing his belly.

Karl Reiner Vollen turned away. He had little time for Gerlach Heileman's arrogance, or his condescending pantomimes. He saw a huge broadsword hanging on the wall and looked at that instead. Its blade was mottled with rust. It was a Kislev weapon, a double-edged longsword of the Gospodar, deep-fullered and heavy-quilloned. A shashka, he believed they were called.

'What is you here?' asked a deep voice. Vollen turned back, expecting a man, but saw instead a heavy, sallow woman who had emerged from the back room, hugging a round-tipped serving knife to her streaked apron. Her eyes were permanently narrowed to slits by the ample flesh of her face. She stared at Gerlach.

'Food? Drink?' Gerlach said.

'Is no of food, is no of drink,' she told him.

'I can smell it,' he insisted.

She shrugged, humping up the slopes of her thick shoulders under her shawl.

'Is wood burns.'

'You miserable old mare!' snapped Gerlach. He tore a kid-skin pouch from his belt and emptied it onto the floor. Silver Empire coins bounced and skittered in the dirty rushes. 'I've sixty-two hungry, thirsty men out there! Sixty-two! And there's not a wretch in this ditch-town fit to clean the boots of any of them!'

'Gerlach…' Vollen said.

'Get off, Karl!' A blush was rising in Heileman's neck, the sign of his ugly temper. He closed on the flabby woman, then suddenly stooped and snatched up a coin. Holding it between finger and thumb, he pushed it at her face.

'See there? His Holy Majesty Karl Franz! On his orders we've come here, to take up arms and save this bloody backwater! You'd think you'd be grateful! You'd think you'd be happy to feed us and keep us warm so we might be fit and ready to guard your souls! I don't know why we didn't just leave you to burn!'

The woman surprised Gerlach. She didn't recoil. She lunged at him, slapping the coin out of his hand so hard it pinged away across the inn. She shouted a stream of curses into his face; a torrential proclamation in the harsh language of Kislev.

As she did so, she waved the serving knife expressively.

Gerlach Heileman backed away a step. He reached for his dagger.

Vollen interposed himself between them. 'Enough!' he snapped at Gerlach, pushing him backwards with one hand. 'Enough, mother!' he added, waving at her to calm down.

Gerlach walked away with a dismissive oath, and Vollen turned squarely to face the woman. He kept his hands raised and open to reassure her.

'We need food and drink, and we will pay for both,' he told her slowly.

'Is no of food, is no of drink!' she repeated.

'No?'

'Is gone all! Taked!'

She beckoned him with a rapid, snapping gesture and led him into a little side room where sacks of rye were piled up. There was a wooden coffer perched on the sacks. She lifted the lid and showed Vollen what was inside.

It was full to the brim with Empire coins. Enough to make the chests of most company paymasters look meagre.

She raked her fat fingers through the silver. 'Taked!' she repeated firmly.

'Tell me how,' he said.

* * *

IV

IN THE COURSE of the previous week, seven Imperial units had passed through Choika. The first had been another company of demilancers, and from her description, they were the Jagers of Altdorf. The folk of Choika had welcomed them and seen to all their needs: meat, sup, bedding, fodder. They had welcomed all seventy of them like brothers.

Two days later, an infantry column of nine hundred men from Wissenland arrived – pikemen mostly, but a fair number of arquebusiers. On their heels, two hundred more pikes from Nordland, and a train of cannon from Nuln. That night, the population of Choika had almost doubled.

Barely had these gone when another infantry mass marched in. Archers, arquebusiers and halberdiers, wearing yellow and black, she said, so that probably meant Averland.

Then sixty great fellows from Carroberg, shouldering their massive hand-and-a-half swords like polearms. After them, nigh on fifteen hundred Imperial levies, who drank so much they almost rioted.

A day behind the levies, thirty Knights Panther. These were the most impressive, she admitted, tall and armoured like princes. They were courteous and deserved much respect but, by then, the novelty had worn off.

Choika had been wrung dry.

'There's barely enough food left to see the town until harvest,' Vollen said. 'Wave as much damn money as you like, there's nothing to buy.'

They were standing out under the gables of the inn. Heileman turned slowly to face Vollen.

'I smelt cooking. It was rank, but it was food.'

Vollen shook his head. 'They're cooking for the town. Pooling what they have left. Our advance has even taken most of their firewood. What you could smell was supper for the entire place, roasting over the one fire they can afford.'

'We'll take that, then,' said Gerlach simply.

'You want them to starve?'

'If we starve, they'll be dead. Burned and split and raped when the Northers come in, with us too empty-bellied to stop it.'

Vollen shrugged.

'I'm not going to say anything to the captain, not this time,' said Heileman.

'What?'

'In respect of our association. I won't say anything.'

'About what?' Vollen asked.

Heileman's eyes narrowed. 'Damn you, Vollen! You showed me disrespect in there! I am vexillary! Second officer! No junior horse shows me up like that! You forget yourself, sometimes, and I'm man enough to appreciate why.'

Vollen reined himself in. He knew better than to push it. 'I am honoured by your kinship, vexillary. I will mind my place.'

Heileman bit his lip and nodded, shifting away. 'Good, Karl, that's good. I'd hate for you to forget you're only here because of me.'

Karl Reiner Vollen felt himself tense. It took considerable will to fight back the desire to swing for Gerlach Heileman. The conceited bastard...

Captain Stouer hallooed them from across the square. They walked together, over the cobbles, to rejoin him.

V

HANDING OVER THE reins of his gelding to one of the troop, Stouer watched as Heileman and Vollen approached him from the inn.

Stouer knew his vexillary looked forward to great things in his future. Heileman had the blood for it, after all, and the connections. Another summer or two and he would be a Knight of the Red Shield, or spurred to some other great order at least, part of an elector's life company. He looked the part. Heavy set and over two spans tall, with fair hair shaved short and a trimmed beard that grew white-blond. Noble of bearing and hazel-eyed, he had exactly the frame you expected to see filling a full suit of silver-steel plate, exactly the face you hoped to find behind the close-helm's visor.

The clarion, though. Ahh, Vollen. Like Heileman, a gifted horseman, and just as tenacious. But his future was not so bright. It was all down to blood. Vollen didn't have the lineage, or the connections. He might make captain of a state troop eventually, but that was about it. But for the recommendation of Herr Sigbrecht Heileman, Vollen wouldn't even have got a position in the demilancer company.

Vollen was a head shorter than Gerlach Heileman, and as dark as Heileman was fair. He was clean-shaven, like a boy, and his jaw jutted forward pugnaciously. His eyes were as blue as a summer sky. He was the most learned soldier Stouer had ever had the pleasure of commanding. Even the most noble-born sons riding in the horse troop were only partially literate, and Stouer had never had much of letters himself. Vollen had studied hard under his tutors and it showed. It was probably an effort to compensate for his lack of status.

'Say it as it is,' he instructed as they came up.

'There's no victuals here, captain,' Heileman replied. 'The town's been picked bare by the companies that have preceded us. They have some food cooking, but it's the last dredgings of their larders. We should look to our own supplies rather than deprive these people.'

Stouer nodded.

'Karl was all for taking the food by force, but I think we owe it to these kind folk to be respectful.'

Stouer glanced at Vollen.

'That true?'

The clarion stiffened, and looked like he wanted to spit. He said simply, 'My appetite got the better of me, captain. The vexillary is right.'

Stouer scratched an ear. He knew full well there was more to it than that, but he wasn't really interested. There was never any sense pampering soldiers. If what he'd been told at the Vatzl garrison was true, there were hard times ahead for all of them. Stouer had seen service in the oblast before, five summers previously. It was a hard country, more brutal in climate than any part of the Empire, and it seemed to go on forever. The people were by turns dour and hearty, though he'd never had much time for any of them. Their great, harsh territory, only partly conquered by civilisation, formed a natural buffer between the Empire and the Northern Wastes. He'd heard Kislev men state emphatically that they were the true protectors of the North, keeping the Empire's border secure. That was nonsense, of course. The Empire had the greatest army in the world, and when it moved north in times of invasion-threat, as now, it usually ended up saving the skins of the Kislevites too. But for the grace of Sigmar they held this land, and but for the army of the Emperor they would lose it.

And now the Northern tribes were rising again. Rising as never before. Thick and dark, like ants upon the tundra, spilling south. There had been omens, prophecies, signs. Even if the threat was exaggerated, it was going to be a hard year. Stouer had certainly never known the Imperial army to dispose a force of this size into the north, nor bind itself to so many allies. Bretonnian heavy horse, trained bands from Tilea, and from the damnable Old Races too. Everyone was taking this seriously.

The captain walked over to his saddlebags and took out a scroll-case. 'Karl! Your eye, please!' he said. Gerlach and the clarion were still regarding each other poisonously, and Stouer knew they needed a distraction or two. Like siblings, the pair of them. Constantly locking horns.

Stouer opened the case and unrolled a small chart. 'This is Choika, yes?'

Vollen examined the map and nodded. 'Yes, sir.'

'Here, the river. The crossing, here.' Stouer traced lines with his fingertip in a general way. It was all inky scratches to him, but he didn't want to betray his lack of learning.

'This is the Lynsk,' Vollen said, pointing. He was well aware of the captain's lack of letters, and knew that Stouer often used him as a clerk. 'Here's the crossing. About a league upstream.'

The captain studied the map and nodded sagely as if it made perfect sense. 'Our orders are to join up with Marshal Neiber and the Wissenland pike north of the crossing by noon tomorrow. At a place called Zhedevka. Now then, Zhedevka… Zhedevka…'

'There, sir,' Vollen pointed.

Stouer straightened up and took a deep, thoughtful breath. 'Still a few hours of light left. Gerlach, take three horse and scout the crossing. See what you can see. And be back by nightfall.'

'Yes, sir,' Heileman said. He pulled on his rein-worn gloves. 'Sebold? Johann? You too, Karl.'

Stouer bristled slightly. His intention had been to keep Gerlach and the boy apart and occupied. What the hell! If they were busy, they couldn't fight each other.

VI

FIELDS OF UNRIPE barley and rye stretched out from the trackway east of the town, and to the north, jumbled marshes and thickets of bulrushes clustered in the sodden flood plain of the river. The sky had clouded over and turned a peculiar, flat shade of white, though it was still bright. Where the track ran beside the river, damsel flies darted through the air, bright and exquisite as living jewellery.

Their lances slung secure in saddle-boots, the four demilancers hacked up the river trail and broke into a gallop where the track widened. All had their stirrups cinched short, as per regulations, so that when they rose, heads lowered for the chase, there was a good hand's breadth between them and their saddles. Gerlach led the way on his big grey, a seventeen hand three-year old called Saksen. The companies favoured young horses for their spirit and energy, though they could be skittish and difficult, and Saksen was unruly at the best of times.

Vollen came behind, alongside Sebold Truchs, a long-faced man who, at twenty-nine, was about the oldest trooper in the company besides the captain himself. Truchs was considered something of a veteran, and the younger men looked to him because of his experience. He rode a big chestnut gelding with a star on its brow. Vollen's mount, Gan, was a black of sixteen hands with a ferocious spirit, but more even tempered than Gerlach's grey.

Johann Friedel rode at the back of the group. He was nineteen years old, the third son of a merchant baronet, and as boisterous as his young black troop horse. For all of them except Truchs, this was their first experience of war. Real war. Their careers thus far had been spent in training and cavalry schooling, manoeuvres and ceremonial duties. They were all eager and scared in equal measure, but they showed only their eagerness.

Truchs had seen action four times: two border disputes and two scourge campaigns against the bestial filth in the Drakwald Forest. His colourful stories were numerous and, to be fair, contradictory. For though he had seen action, as the phrase went, he hadn't actually seen much action. A shield wall, at a distance, through the rain. A border town shelled by Imperial cannon, from the vantage of a windy hill three leagues away. An aborted charge and rally into what turned out to be an empty wood. And four dead bodies in a dry field outside Wurschen, terribly split and twisted by sword cuts. That was an image that still woke him some nights.

But still, his stories were good, all the better for the constant embroidery. And whatever he had done or had not done, it was more than any trooper in the company – except the captain, who had been in a real war once. Sebold Truchs would have been quite content not to have ridden north that summer, preferring to linger in the spartan enclosure of the Cavalry School at Talabheim, training and drilling and practising.

For there was one thing he knew for certain about this deployment to the bitter north: there was a real war waiting there for all of them, and their days of monotonous practice were gone forever.

The river was fast and high from the spring melt. Its headlong rush sounded like jingling coins. The track following it bent north in a long, slow curve. They came to the crossing: a broad timber bridge raised out of the water on five stone piers. Gerlach didn't break stride. He just nosed his grey on, and pounded across the boards, spitting sideways from the saddle to avert the ill fortune of iron hooves on wood.

The other three did the same, though Vollen merely did it out of custom. Gerlach's spittle, flying back in the slipstream, spattered across Vollen's cuirass. The vexillary could have aimed his mouth aside, but he hadn't bothered. Vollen said nothing and wiped it off.

They came off the bridge into the reeded banks of the north side, standing upright in the stirrups to urge their steeds up the sodden slope. Open grassland lay before them, wide and flat, vaster than any landscape Vollen had ever seen. Under the flat, white sky, it looked like a grey sea, the stalks rippling in the wind like waves. To the north-west, several leagues away, the horizon swelled up in a great mound, a curve rising proud of the grass like a pregnant bulge.

Gerlach reined in, and paced his excited, snorting mount. The others drew up behind him.

'Zhedevka? Over there?' he asked.

'It lies on the grasslands near a mound of the Old People,' Vollen said. 'So… yes, I'd say.'

'Old People?' Johann Friedel called out. 'You mean… the Slight Ones?'

He meant elves. Just say it, Karl Reiner Vollen thought. In this modern age, it was preposterous for a man to be coy about saying a simple word. Mentioning them by name was said to bring bad luck. And men still believed that, damn them for fools.

'Not elves,' Vollen said, and Johann jumped in his saddle at the word. 'The Scythians, the horse warriors of old. The Gospodars – and therefore the Kislevites – trace their ancestry back to them. They ruled here once, before Sainted Sigmar came. These lands were theirs. They built the towns whose ruins are said to haunt the Steppes. They raised the kurgans.'

'The kurgans?' Truchs said with alarm.

'That's a kurgan,' Vollen said mildly, pointing to the distant mound.

'Where? Where, damn it?' Truchs turned his horse in an agitated circle.

'Be still!' Gerlach snapped. 'Karl's playing with you. Using his damned education again, eh, Karl?'

The clarion sat back against his saddle rest and shrugged.

Even the most poorly schooled son of the Empire knew the word kurgan. It was the name of the bogeyman, the term for the dark tribes who lurked in the north under the Shadow. Kurgans were the very monsters they had come there to fight.

'A kurgan,' said Vollen, 'is a man-made hill, a burial mound from the early times. The vile tribes of the North are known by the term. Presumably…' he smiled, 'presumably because they want to hide the bones of all of us in the south under similar hills.'

Truchs touched the iron of his sword-hilt to ward against evil charms, and spat again. There was too much loose talk and bad luck in the air for his liking.

They rode north-west at a hard lick, Friedel just in the lead now. The cold wind was fierce in their faces and made them breathless.

As they got nearer to the mound – and realised just how huge it truly was – Johann Friedel pulled up sharply and called out a warning.

There were riders on the track ahead of them. A dozen horsemen emerged from the long grasses, silent and slow. Their horses were small, rangy mares, brown and bay, little more than ponies, with full, heavy tails and shaggy manes. The men were swaddled in cloaks, furs and blankets. Barbarian riders, there could be no doubt.

Gerlach slowed to a trot and moved to the fore. The shabby riders halted their horses and watched them approach, unmoving. Gerlach Heileman suddenly felt vital and proud of his gleaming armour and his sleek charger with its braided mane and docked, bound-up tail.

He stood in the stirrups again as Saksen pulled slow, glancing back past his shoulders at his outriders.

'What do we do? What do we do?' gabbled Johann.

'Hail them, vexillary,' advised Vollen.

'Hail them? Look at them, Karl! They're Northers! Raiders! Why should I hail them?' Gerlach unclasped the pistol holsters on his saddle-bow, and quickly cocked the firelocks of the ready-primed pieces. Then he drew his cavalry sword. It was a basket-hilted weapon with a straight, double-edged blade a span long. It had two deep fuller grooves down the length of the blade, and its tip was pointed like a spear. It was made for thrusting, as outlined by regulations.

'No,' said Vollen quickly, in disbelief. 'Oh no… vexillary…'

'Rise in the saddle to address!' Gerlach called out. Truchs and Friedel fell into step with him, and walked their horses forward, their sword blades resting upright against their right arms. Ahead of them, the riders remained motionless.

Vollen lagged behind, his sword still in its scabbard. Gerlach, Truchs and Friedel increased their pace to a brisk trot, their sword-hands now steadied on their right thighs with the sword points inclined slightly forward.

'Gerlach!' Vollen shouted.

'Get into line, clarion!' Heileman yelled back. 'Damn you! Get into formation or the captain will hear about this!'

The brisk trot was turning into a gallop. They were less than eighty lengths from the stationary horsemen.

'Present and charge!' Heileman howled. Three sword arms lifted, the swords pointed towards the enemy and carried crosswise to each rider's head.

The shabby horsemen stirred. Their horses wheeled around and there was a dull flash in the flat light as sabres were uncased and flourished.

Vollen tore his bugle out of its case and blew hard. A quadrille. Short-long-long-short. He did it again.

The three demilancers broke their gallop, swords waving, confused. The enemy horsemen spread wide, to either side of Gerlach's abortive charge. One of them raised a bone horn and returned Vollen's hoot.

Vollen spurred Gan forward and rode up to position himself face to face with the heathen men. Gerlach, Friedel and Truchs were riding out in a wide turn to come around.

The warriors were caked in mud and dirt, and Vollen could smell the sweat and soil of both horses and riders without trying. They sheathed their thin, curved blades and closed around him, curious. Raw, mustachioed faces glared at him from the folds of furs and grease-heavy cloaks.

'Imperial?' asked one. He was a big man whose bulk seemed to be crushing his ragged pony. His front teeth were missing.

'Yes,' nodded Vollen. 'The Second Company Hipparchia Demilance, ridden out of Talabheim. Hail and met.'

'You? You is leader of men?' pressed the toothless giant.

'No,' said Vollen. 'I'm clarion.'

'Klaaryen?'

Vollen gestured with his bugle.

Gerlach and the other demilancers galloped up and reined hard to stop. The cluster of filthy steppe riders broke to let them through.

'What the devil are you doing, Vollen?' Gerlach roared.

'Vexillary Heileman, may I present...' Vollen looked expectantly at the gap-toothed brute on the shaggy pony.

The big Kislevite pursed his lips and then said, 'Beledni, rotamaster, of rota of Yetchitch krug, of Blindt voisko, of Sanyza pulk, of Gospodarinyi, syet Kislevi.'

'They're on our side,' Vollen said to the vexillary, as if it wasn't clear enough. 'They're Kislevite lancers. Allies.'

'El-ays, yha!' the Kislevite leader of horse cried, and bowed low in his worn saddle to Gerlach, doffing his fur hat. His head was entirely shaved except for a long, braided top-knot and his drooping moustache. His men called out, and rattled the staves of their lances together. Each one had three spears slung in long canvas boots against the fore of their saddles: two short, slim javelins with long, sharp tips and one long pole, thicker and tipped with a narrow blade and a crossbar.

'These heathens?' asked Gerlach, incredulously.

'Heeth-eyns?' Beledni echoed, looking at Vollen for clarification.

'We show only respect,' said Vollen, slowly and carefully. Beledni thought about this and then nodded heavily.

Gerlach spat contemptuously. 'They don't even talk our tongue,' he said.

'Yurr tung?' said Beledni.

'They speak our tongue better than you speak theirs,' Vollen ventured.

Gerlach glared at him. 'Apologise,' he said.

'Apologise?' Vollen repeated.

'Yes, dammit! For our mistaken attack.'

Vollen paused. Unblinking, he returned Gerlach's gaze for a moment. 'You ask a lot of me, sometimes.'

'Are you refusing?' the vexillary asked. His face was flushed.

'Of course not,' Vollen replied. He took a breath and looked across at Beledni. The big man and his riders had been trying to follow the exchange between Vollen and Gerlach.

'Rotamaster, we are most sorry for our mistaken challenge, and uh...'

Beledni used the tassels of his riding crop to chase away a marsh fly that was buzzing around his face and made an odd little gesture with his other hand. It was a dismissive slight turn of the wrist as if he was spilling out a handful of corn. 'Is of no matter,' he added with a careless, almost theatrical frown.

'We meant no disrespect, sir...'

The gesture again, the down-turned corners of the mouth. 'Is of no matter,' Beledni said once more, and walked his shabby little horse ahead a few steps so that he drew level with Vollen. Beledni patted him on the arm, an informal, avuncular action. 'We will all live,' he said sagely. Then he leaned forward, his lips to Vollen's ear, so close Vollen was assailed by the smell of body sweat and rank breath. 'Vebla?' he said, and indicated Gerlach with his crop.

'Vebla, yha?'

Some of the Kislevite riders heard this, and snorted out chuckles.

'What did he say?' asked Gerlach sharply.

'I don't know, vexillary. I don't know the word.'

Heileman sat back against his saddle rest. He was annoyed. They were laughing at him, these heathens. Making him the butt of some crude joke.

He'd heard many stories of Kislev lancers, stories that described them as triumphant, spectacular, armoured in finery and feathers, masters of horse, as magnificent as Imperial knights. Someone had once told him that the lancers often scared their enemies from the field by the sheer splendour of their wargear, which attested to their prowess by all the riches they had won.

Not these dogs. It seemed that every story about the North was a lie. There was no magnificence in its landscape or its people, and their famous lancers were positively squalid.

'Zhedevka,' he said to Vollen. 'Just ask him where Zhedevka is.'

VII

WITHOUT COMMENT OR ceremony, Beledni's little troop of lancers led them another league north until the great kurgan was behind them. Zhedevka lay on the plains behind it, looking out across undulating grasslands and the distant shadow of a forest. Small patches of woodland dotted the landscape around the town.

It had ceased to be much of a town at all, now the Imperial army had arrived. Acres of tents and pot fires, great assemblies of pikes and halberds, musters of horse. In the fields north of the town, cannons had been drawn up behind sod-built palisades and wicker gabions, and stakes had been driven into the earth, facing the forest.

A fine drizzle came down from the east, pattering against their armour. The Kislevites drew their matted furs tighter. They rode into the town.

Gerlach tried to estimate the numbers there. He counted at least fifteen standards, all Imperial, as well as artillery banneroles, and colours flown by two sections of Tilean foot. That meant, even at a conservative estimate, six thousand men-at-arms.

This was what an army should look like, Gerlach thought. This was Imperial might. Combined with other forces that were now assembling along the Lynsk, they would scour the North and turn the rising darkness back.

As they rode down the muddy, tracked-up thoroughfare, he felt unashamedly proud. Here were marching halberdiers in clean, brightly coloured tunics: blue, red, gold and white. There, pikemen with spotless surcoats and glittering steel sallets. A cantering file of demilancers from another unit, cockades and banners rippling as they came past. Fork-bearded men in gaudy velvet puff-breeches and polished hauberks, sweeping whetstones along the white-steel blades of great swords. Pipers, fifers, drummers and horn blowers, the daylight gleaming off kettledrums and the long trumpets of field clarions. Archers in leather caps and long shirts, drilling with yew longbows against straw targets.

At a crossroads, they reined up as six Knights Panther rode by, followed by their squires and lance carriers. Huge destrier chargers, with shaggy feathering on their mighty hooves were dressed in embroidered caparisons of purple, lilac and gold, their riders giants in full plate, leopard skins draped over their shoulders. Now that was glory and splendour.

Gerlach was annoyed to see Beledni and his men didn't seem at all impressed. Some of them even sneered at the gigantic knights. The only thing that seemed to take their interest was a crude wooden standard, a shield on the top of a ragged pole, hung with a red and white snake of banner cloth. The severed wing of an eagle was nailed, spread out on the shield front. This standard marked a field where the levies of the Kislev confederates were camped. More filthy men in furs, their dirty ponies wandering loose between their stretched hide tents. No discipline, no order, no sign of any pride.

Beledni gave a half-hearted wave, more to Vollen than the other demilancers, and turned his riders away towards the Kislev muster.

Glad to be rid of them, Gerlach rode on to the town hall, or the zal as it was called. It had a shingled roof shaped like an onion, and was the tallest structure in Zhedevka.

Marshal Neiber had made his quarters here.

Gerlach left Friedel and Truchs outside with the horses, and brought Vollen in with him as his escort. Neiber's trabanten of six swordsmen, two drummers and two fifers sat listlessly in the outer atrium of the zal, passing a bottle between them. They were all richly dressed in extravagant silk pludderhosen, broad hats puffed with heron feathers, doublets artfully slashed to reveal the conspicuous damask linings. None of them gave the two marching demilancers more than a passing look as they went by.

Neiber, field marshal of the entire host, was a heavy, sagging man with a bulging face that had been scored in early life by a duelling scar. His beard was square-cut and fierce. The field marshal's well-fed weight seemed to bow him down, and it was helped by the wine he had been drinking. A large fire had been banked up in an open grate, and the demilancers could smell poultry fat and onions.

Neiber was sipping wine out of a tiny thimble glass that he refilled regularly. The glass was from an expensive gentleman's travelling case that lay open on a side table, its leather straps draped open to reveal the satin-lined caskets that held the glasses. The case had a drawer for silver cutlery that was engraved with his heraldic crest. It was etched on the glasses too.

'Who the shit are you?' Neiber asked bluntly as they came up and saluted, their helmets tucked under their left arms.

'Second Company Hipparchia Demilance, ridden out of Talabheim, sir,' said Gerlach.

'Schott! Schott? Where are you, you noxious little leper?'

A short, balding man appeared, with an attitude that reminded Vollen of a mule that had been beaten once too often. He was wearing the doublet and surcoat of a staff aide.

'Here I am, my marshal.'

'Where the shit were you hiding?'

'I was supervising your dinner. As instructed.'

'Shut the shit up.' Neiber sat down on a low-backed chair by the grate and aimed the soles of his feet alternately at the fire. He was wrapped in a fur coat and damp hose clung to his feet and legs. The baton of his rank lay across his lap.

'Are my boots dry?' he rasped, swigging his drink and holding it out for a refill. Schott hurried to oblige.

'I'm working on that, my marshal,' the man answered as he poured.

'Second Company Hippos… demilancers… what the shit was it again?'

'Second Company Hipparchia Demilance, sir,' Gerlach repeated.

'That's it. Who's their commander, Schott?'

Schott crossed over to the mass of log books, patents of muster and orders of battle laid out on a nearby bench.

'Are you the commander?' Neiber asked, squinting at Gerlach and pointing the baton at him.

'No, sir. I'm vexillary, sir.'

'Well, where the bloody shit is your commander?'

'Stouer, my marshal,' Schott called out.

'Where's Stouer? Where the bloody shit is Stouer?'

'With the company, at Choika, sir.'

Neiber belched and got up. His baton fell on the floor and rolled under his chair. 'Not here?'

'No, sir.'

'What the hell's the point of them being at Choika? I mean, what the shitting hell is the point of that? There's no war down there!'

'We… we were ordered to report here to you by noon tomorrow, sir. The captain sent me ahead to make contact.'

'Did he? Did he indeed? Stupid arse. Refill!' Neiber waved his glass. Schott was still busy with records and patents.

'Refill! You, boy!' Neiber looked at Vollen. 'Get the bloody bottle!'

Vollen started forward, took the bottle from the side table, and refilled Neiber's glass.

Neiber emptied it. 'And another, while you're still hanging around like a spent fart.'

Vollen did as he was told.

Neiber looked at Gerlach. 'There's all kinds of shit in the forest out there, did you know that?' he remarked suddenly.

'No, sir.'

'All kinds of shit. I know that from the scouts I sent out.' Neiber tapped the side of his nose with his finger. It took a moment, as he missed the first time. 'Not all of them, mind. I sent out fifty and got five back. Five! Shit me out Sigmar, five! The foe is right on us. A day's ride from here, there's a horde of the heathen scum mustering in the woodland. And they'll be coming. Soon, mind you. Coming for us all. Boy!'

Vollen was already there with the bottle. Neiber drank, licked his lips, and sat down again. He looked tired and his voice dropped. 'All kinds of shit's coming. Bigger and harder and wilder than any of the idiots back south realise. They're meant to be over a fortnight away, but no. Oh no, no, no.' Neiber snorted hard and spat phlegm into the fire. He glanced at Gerlach. 'So having your company sat on their arses in Choika is no use to me. This Stouer must be a particularly stupid shit. Get back on your horse and go and tell him I said so. And tell him he better be here by dawn, or I'll ram a cannon up his arse and light the powder-touch myself.'

'Sir.'

'Where are my boots, Schott?' Neiber roared.

'Still drying out, my marshal.'

'You useless shit! I ought to have you shot. Hah! Ha ha! Shot! Have Schott shot! Ha ha ha!'

'Your wit is truly formidable, my marshal,' said Schott.

'Yeah, well shit on you too!' Neiber spat and threw his glass at the aide.

'You can go now,' Schott told Gerlach and Vollen, shooing them on out.

'Refill! Schott! Get me a refill! And... and another bloody glass!'

'Yes, my marshal.'

VIII

OUTSIDE IT WAS getting dark, earlier and faster than they had anticipated. Braziers had been lit all across the camp, flickering like earthbound stars in the twilight. As they rejoined Friedel and Truchs, Gerlach and Karl could hear camp songs being sung.

'Vexillary!'

Schott called them back to the porch of the zal. He held out a wax-sealed parchment to Gerlach.

'Tell your captain to advance and join us with all speed. Your company is to take order in the right wing. I've marked the place on this plan. The water meadows east of the town, to ride in support of the Sanyza pulk.'

'The who?'

'The marshal wants strong demilance companies interlaced with the local regiments.'

'The Kislevites? Very well,' said Gerlach, not liking it at all.

'Move up and take position. With all haste as you can. Then have your captain report to the marshal here. We're not expecting a fight for at least three days, but get yourselves up and ready.'

'We'll ride directly,' said Gerlach. He paused. 'The marshal… is he all right?'

'He's drunk,' said Schott, matter-of-factly.

'Is that… usual?'

'No,' said the aide. 'He's drunk because he's scared. He has a good idea what's coming.'

'It can't be that bad–'

'Can't it? Have you fought a border war before, vexillary?'

'No.'

'Then, to be frank, you don't know what the shit you're talking about.'

IX

THEY RODE SOUTH in the gathering darkness, the Imperial drums beating behind them in the camp at Zhedevka. Night was falling, sheathed in heavy rain. Over the receding tattoo of the Imperial drums, Karl Reiner Vollen thought he heard another drumming.

Darker, deeper, slower, throbbing from the forest.

ZHEDEVKA

I

CHOIKA TO ZHEDEVKA took ninety minutes of hard riding.

Captain Stouer got the company up and ready at midnight, in cold, driving rain. The four riders who had gone to Zhedevka and back had only been in their beds – bales of foetid straw in the barns – for three hours. Karl felt his joints aching with damp, and Friedel complained loudly, his eyes red from too little slumber.

The town square was bleak and deserted. It was so black they could see nothing much except what was illuminated in the flickering glow of their wagons' lanterns. No one, none of the townsfolk of Choika, came out to see them off or hold torches to light them as they prepared. The troops fumbled in the dark, struggling with chill armour, heavy tack and nervous horses.

Stouer's face was set grim, partly from lack of sleep and partly from his vexillary's gloomy report of Neiber's humour. He had listened intently as Gerlach recalled the field marshal's remarks about the gathering enemy.

He mounted up, leaning forward over his mount's neck to whisper reassurance in its ear, then called out to Gerlach. The vexillary walked his horse forward, and raised the standard.

'Company order?' asked Stouer.

'Company ordered and presented for travel, captain.'

At a nod from Stouer, Vollen blew the note for advance, and they moved out, splashing up the trackway in the pitch dark. He knew Captain Stouer was keen to get them in place by dawn. Stouer wanted to make a clean fist of things with the marshal.

It was surprisingly decent going. The rains ebbed and a watery moon came out. It seemed to be bouncing off the apex of the great kurgan. Mists rose and draggled the landscape.

Dawn should have been an easy mark to make, but the rain had mired the roads, and the company supply wagons were lagging behind and becoming bedded in. The horse troop turned back and dismounted to work them free.

By the time they had cleared the worst of it, a grey stain of light was spreading across the sky from the east. Dawn was less than an hour away.

Stouer dropped back and fell in beside Gerlach Heileman. 'We're going to be pushed to make it. Take them forward, vexillary,' he said.

'Captain?'

'Take them forward and get them into place. You know the plan. I'll ride on to Zhedevka and make report. It'll save time.'

Surprised by the prospect of locum command, Gerlach tried to hide his enthusiasm. 'Are you sure, captain?'

'The last thing I want to do is piss Neiber off.'

'I honestly doubt he'll be awake this early…'

'Whatever. Dawn, he said. Can you manage it?'

'It'll be an honour, sir,' replied Gerlach, hoisting the standard.

'I'll take outriders. See you in a few hours.'

Stouer broke west, following the track. He took Friedel, Anmayer and the clarion with him as flank riders. Regulations said that the clarion should accompany a field commander in his duties anyway, but Karl knew he was there because the captain anticipated having to look at charts and patents.

The vexillary led the main force away into the eastern part of the line.

II

THE CHRONICLES OF the Year That No One Forgets are extensive and thorough. It was a time, as Anspracht of Nuln memorably wrote, of 'living history', by which he meant that the daily turn of events was so significant that the future survival of the Empire might depend upon the details of a few hours. History was being shaped at such a rate it could be witnessed. This was not the long, placid drip of time that transmuted destinies so slowly that its progress was imperceptible to those living through it. This was a moment struck out hard and hot on the anvil of fate.

Every detail and particular is recorded somewhere, by Anspracht, Gottimer, the Abbess of Vries, Ocveld the Elder, Teladin of Bretonn and innumerable others, including the scribes and chroniclers of the Old Races.

Yet the Battle of Zhedevka warrants little mention in the compended histories of the time. It is a footnote in Anspracht, a passing reference in Ocveld. For it was just a small part of a much wider process called the Spring Driving. This mendaciously mild, general term encompasses a decisive horror – an onslaught from which the Empire barely recovered. It is notable that though the place name Zhedevka features infrequently in the general texts, it is woefully commonplace on tombs, memorial stones, chapel plaques and family lineages throughout the Empire.

For lives ended at Zhedevka. A great many of them.

It began in the pre-light of dawn, that peculiar time when bodies are cold and slow. The chaplains were still preparing for daybreak prayers, and the cooks had yet to start heating the breakfast pots. There was rain from the east, washing away all trace of the setting moons. The land was dark and streaked with mist.

There was virtually no warning.

* * *

III

AT THE CANNON-SET, along the north face of the town, a junior artillery observer from Nuln, sitting on picket duty by the earthwork, noticed that the faraway shadows of the forest seemed to be moving and flowing. He hurried to the tent of the master gunner, but the officer was looking for a mislaid love-token that his wife had given him, and made the junior wait.

In the interim, a sentry pike to the east of the gun-set saw the same signs, and immediately rang a handbell. Two more sentries picked up the alarum, and rang their own bells too, drawing the men of their company up out of sleep. In the tented field beyond them, a section of archers were similarly roused. The master of the watch came running at the sound of the bells, and a report was made to him. Runners were sent to the marshal's quarters, to the field commander of horse, and to the horn blowers camped near the town granaries.

Inver Schott, the marshal's aide, informed the runners that came knocking that the marshal was indisposed. When made aware of the urgency of the alert, he went to the horn blowers himself. They flatly refused to take orders without a command from the field marshal in person. The field commander of horse, also uncertain, sent his own runners to the marshal's quarters for confirmation, confident that the horns would sound if danger really was imminent.

No one, it is apparent from the records, believed a surprise attack was coming. Though raids and skirmishes might be staged without warning, battle and surprise were two concepts that simply did not go together, not when large armies were being fielded. Wars were just not fought that way.

Even when fighting the brute savages of the North, there was a protocol, a custom of battle. It was crude, but it was understood by both sides. Armies assembled on the field, faced each other, dug in, bellowed and taunted – sometimes for hours or even days – until a clash became inevitable. Indeed, it was often the case that the taunting and bellowing itself was the very matter of the battle. If an army was bellicose or large enough, the other would withdraw without any actual physical clash.

The root of this custom was the simple truth that armed forces of more than a few hundred men required huge motivation to attack one another. An individual unit might be rallied up to strike suddenly, but a mass of men needed firm coaxing. An army had to be worked up to a frenzy with phlegmatic speeches, insistent drumming and generous drink. It needed to be brought from the simmer to the boil. Then, and only then, would thousands of individuals attack as one mass.

And even if that impossibility could somehow be achieved without long notice, there seemed little advantage in charging, unannounced, out of the tree-line in the cold, grey wet of a spring dawn. Troops would be exhausted by the effort of such a charge, their push wasted, their strength depleted by the exertion.

It simply wasn't how battles were fought.

IV

THE FIRST WAVE of Northers hit the outer line nine minutes after the junior observer had first seen movement in the forest. They came sprinting, though they had already covered a league of rough ground from the forest line. And they were not simply fore-runners or berserks roaming madly ahead of their force. They were the front of it, the crest of a solid wave of horned shadows that flooded out of the woodland. Drum beats ruptured the daybreak air, their hammers pulsating through the raw din of the charging foe. It was, survivors said, the most awful sight, the most awful sound.

A nightmare, brought to life. An impossibility.

The cannon-sets were overrun before any of the great mortars and bombards of the Nuln Schools could be primed, let alone fired. The wicker breastworks were crushed flat by sheer weight of numbers. The observer who had first seen the rising was also amongst the first to die, hewn into pieces by war-axes and double-edged swords. The master gunner never lived to find his wife's love-token. Tents and wagons were set on fire.

At that time, the Wissenland pike, with their supporting cousins in the archery company, were the only Imperials on the field to have mobilised to any real effect. They staged a desperate defence of the north town line, raising a bristling pike wall. The tide of the enemy broke around them as waves broke around the prow of a galley, and washed in from the sides. Men were systematically beheaded. Their dripping skulls were spiked on the ends of their own pikes and carried forward by the horde as grisly trophies, like flotsam borne along by breakers. The archers, having felled several score with their first volleys, were overrun and maimed, left to die on the mud with their hands purposefully severed.

By then, the horde had swept into Zhedevka itself, and the massacre was under way.

At the west end of the Imperial order, around the cluster of granaries, the master of the watch managed to rally two companies of Nordland pike and halberd, and a fahnlein of arquebusiers clad in the yellow and black surcoats of Averland. They had been awoken by the tumult, but were milling around, confused and disjointed. Many were only partially dressed. The conscripted levies and the recruited patents had already fled in terror, leaving clothing and possessions scattered in their wake.

The master of the watch, along with a dazed sergeant major, quickly marshalled the Nordland pole-troops into pike blocks along the northern face of the granaries. The shorter, axe-headed halberds were laced between the much longer shafts of the pikes. The arquebusiers were lined up a little to the south. Smoke and mist billowed across the skirts of the town, filling the cold dawn air.

The pole-troops stiffened, tense, clammy hands clenching the hafts of their weapons, as a hellish noise rolled in through the smoke and became a solid line of charging figures. This was the first sight the Imperials had got of the foe. Ragged, hairy men with painted faces, draped in furs, black chainmail and leather armour. Teeth and bones and other trophies were strung in their tallow-stiffened hair, and their bare arms were wrapped in iron trophy rings beaten from the weapons of victims. Most wore horned or spiked helmets, and carried war-axes or thick swords. They came running. All of them were howling. They were terrifying.

Part of the Nordland block broke and scattered. The remainder held around their ensign and took the brunt. Northmen, in row after charging row, died against the pike block, but the weight of the dead bore the long hafts down, shattering many. The arquebusiers fired a crackling series of dull blasts, then reloaded and fired again. Their two volleys accounted for three dozen victims and created a wall of dense, white smoke.

They were reloading for the second time when they were consumed by the ravening force. Some fell back, drawing their S-hilted katzbalger swords and fighting a rearguard towards the edge of the pike block.

The field commander of horse had raised up sixty men, most of them demilancers. This troop, at full charge, came west across the main town highway and drove into the enemy's right hand flank with horse lances, for none had had time to prime their handguns. It was a bravura action that gave the Nordland pike's block a moment's renewed confidence. They pushed forward, pole-shafts dressed and lowered the way the drill repetitions had taught them. Chanting and pushing, they ground the enemy back about twenty paces.

But there was a roaring from the west now. An entirely separate flood of Northers spilled from the lowland mist, axe-heads whirling. They crushed in to meet their comrades like the jaws of a farrier's pincer. The master of the watch managed to sustain his block long enough to form them into a pike square, but they had been eroded by then, and their desperate resistance lasted about four minutes before the square shattered. They were butchered to a man.

The field commander of horse turned his demilance troop in a wide circuit around the stables behind the granaries and ordered them out with sabres raised, for many had lost or broken their lances in the first sortie. Several of the men pleaded with the commander to quit the field, but he kept on with the turn and charged the enemy mass, standing in the stirrups, sword raised crosswise to his face. His men followed, every one. They killed upwards of forty before their charge ran out of momentum and space.

Then they were wrestled over and dragged down, man and horse alike, and hacked to death with sharpened iron blades.

V

'WHAT'S THAT SOUND?' Truchs asked, suddenly.

Gerlach pulled up, and listened. The company was still a quarter league shy of the east line where they had been instructed to report. He could see little in the early gloom, but Truchs was right.

There was a distant rumble. A vibration in the air and earth. A ghostly din of voices and drums.

An instinct took over in Heileman's mind. 'Rise in the saddle to address!' he yelled. The men around him scoffed and laughed.

'Do it!' he bellowed. One by one, they demurred as the sound of screams carried to them through the distant murmur.

Stouer's orders had been to link with the Kislev pulk at the east line. Gerlach would be damned if he failed in that. With a brisk wave of his fist, he ran his demilancers out in a line formation, and bawled at those who were slow drawing their swords.

They moved ahead, in line, blades against their right shoulders.

'Steady to the front, and make do to fire in!' Gerlach shouted. He wished he could draw his own sword or prime his pistols, but his job was to hold the standard proud. The horse troop gained speed. A trot, a canter, now a gallop, riding into the mist, into the invisible world. Part of the company line was straggling, and Gerlach impugned their horse-skills. 'Tight! Keep it tight!' He was at such a speed now, the wind was beginning to swoop through the brass throat of the standard's draco, making a basso, bull-horn noise. The swallowtails of the standard were flowing out behind him.

Suddenly, horsemen were coming against them, riding out of the mist. Gerlach thought they were the enemy for a moment. Then he recognized them as ragged Kislev riders, belting away from the front, running scared on frightened ponies. 'Cowards!' he shrieked at them as they fled past, cutting holes in his company's already imperfect line.

The Second Company Hipparchia Demilance pressed on. Their hooves were so loud now he could no longer hear the ominous rumble, nor discern if it was drums or hooves or feet.

The demilancers drove down into the water-meadow basin, drawn by his hooting draco, and there met the enemy head on.

Enemy horses. Horned raiders, dark as twilight, mounted on heavy steeds with feathered hooves, none of them less than seventeen hands. They were already racing to drive out the Imperial order before them, and now they lashed their horses and rose into the charge.

Fifty horse lengths, thirty, head to head in a wide line. The Northers were wailing out an ululating roar that drowned the wet percussion of the hooves, but Gerlach couldn't hear it above the deep whooping drone of his draco.

At ten horse lengths and full stretch, the company behaved exactly as per drill and fired in. Some demilancers had paired wheel-lock pistols, one in each hand. Others fired petronels, the butts braced against the centre of their breastplates. The volley of shots was merciless. Enemy horse and enemy rider alike stumbled and sprawled, screaming. The demilancers went through them, over them, trampling many.

'Sword and lance!' Gerlach yelled, fighting to keep the heavy standard raised. Odamar and Truchs were either side of him, forming his vanguard, their war lances now drawn and lowered.

They were into the second wave. A series of bruising impacts and heavy thwacks, men tumbling from saddles. Odamar speared a Norther right off his steed with his lowered lance and the spray of blood fanned back to spatter Gerlach.

Then Odamar disappeared. There was a blur and a crunching yelp, and Odamar's gelding ran on, riderless.

Gerlach glanced sideways frantically and saw a tall, brass-helmed barbarian riding across his left flank, blood drizzling from his rising axe blade. Gerlach dropped his reins, drew one of his pistols and shot the brute through the forehead. The man's heavy, beringed arms flapped up as if in praise as his head snapped back. He fell sideways, and his horse staggered, unbalanced, then shed its dead rider and galloped on.

The body lay on the wet mud at Gerlach's feet, back arched and one arm bent clumsily under the torso. There was a scorched crater in the white flesh of the brow, a sooty dent with blood at the centre.

I have killed a man, thought Gerlach. The idea seemed preposterous to him. His entire mind concentrated into that glittering bloody spot in the middle of the sooty dent. I have killed a man. I have taken a life in battle.

Saksen bucked and turned loose now the reins were dragging. The sudden movement startled Gerlach out of his strange reverie. He fought to regain control, struggling to keep the standard upright and visible. He came to a stop.

'Regroup the line! Regroup!' he yelled into the uproar and the smoke. Another enemy rider broke towards him, riding downfield with his sword circling. The iron blade made a whooping noise as it swept around.

Calmly, Gerlach slid his spent pistol back into its holster and drew its twin. It banged out a little cloud of hot smoke as he fired it and unhorsed the Norther.

His charge had run out of steam. Around him he saw the demilancers fighting with sabres, saddle to saddle with the enemy riders. He saw friends and comrades torn down, gutted, thrown by wounded horses.

Gerlach drew his sabre and spurred Saksen forward, blade and standard raised as high as he could lift them, steering his trotting horse with his knees.

'For the company! For the company! For the Emperor!' he yelled.

Two Northers came for the vexillary, riding hard, standing in their saddles, heads and swords low. Gerlach turned Saksen in time to slash one across the back, and then reeled as a sword-edge smashed into his right arm's plating.

The company standard tumbled from his hand and stuck base-first in the ground, tilted at an angle. Cursing, Gerlach wheeled his gelding around and exchanged sword strikes with the Norther. Steel on iron, a furious ring.

Gerlach sliced a line down the enemy's cheek and, as he cried out, he speared him through the chest with his sword tip.

The enemy's corpse slumped out of its saddle, and Gerlach had to fight to break the suction and rip his sword loose before he lost it. Saksen whinnied and kicked back, terrified, and by the time Gerlach had fought for and regained control of his horse, he was some paces from the leaning standard.

Truchs galloped in and plucked it out of the ground, shaking it high for all the demilancers to see.

Gerlach made a quick mental note that Stouer should rightly honour Truchs for this moment of courage and virtuous display.

Then Truchs began writhing and screaming. It was a terrible sound, a distortion of a human voice. A barbed lance was projecting out of the man's belly, squirting scarlet blood in all directions. Truchs clawed at it, shrieking, and fell sideways off his horse.

And the standard fell too.

VI

STOUER AND HIS flank riders rode into Zhedevka just as horns started to sound. The southern part of the town seemed oddly empty and there was a strange murmur in the air, a throb.

'Drums,' said the captain, with great certainty. Karl nodded. He was still trying to make sense of the horn signals they'd just heard. Rushed, frantic, badly mouthed and poorly phrased.

A riderless horse came galloping towards them down the main roadway, eyes wild. It was an Imperial troop horse, and its reins were dragging. They had to draw their own horses over to avoid it. It kept running past them, and went on south out of the town gate.

The demilancers cantered forward behind Stouer, alert. They could smell smoke now and the throbbing was louder. Anmayer drew his sabre.

'Put that away!' Stouer snapped.

'Where is everyone, captain?' Friedel asked.

'Firearms,' Stouer growled. He pulled one of his wheel-lock pistols from its saddle holster. Anmayer and Friedel did the same. All three of them carried a pair, one on each side of the pommel. Instead of such a brace, Vollen carried a single petronel in a kidskin boot against the right block flap of his saddle, allowing him space for his bugle holster on the left. The four men checked their weapons were primed, and wound the wheels with their turnkeys to tighten the mainspring.

'Lay your dogs,' said Stouer. They all lowered into place the dog arm cock that held the lump of pyrites, from which the wheel would draw sparks.

A man suddenly appeared, running their way. His arms were held out wide and he was making an odd, mewling sound. By his garb, he was a handgunner or arquebusier from Averland. His surcoat was yellow and black. He was missing a shoe. One of his feet was clad in a wide-toed cut-out shoe, but the other was bare and the grey hose torn. His steps were oddly short and quick, so he tottered like a child that had just begun walking.

He came straight for Stouer, mewling, hands outstretched.

'Sigmar!' Anmayer suddenly said. There was a dark shape under the man's chin that they had all taken to be a goatee. It was not. It was the fletching of a black-feathered arrow. As the man turned to Stouer, they could see the rest of it – an arm's length of shaft – sticking out of the back of his neck.

The Averlander clawed at Stouer, who recoiled and shied him away, his horse jumping in distress. Then the man vomited blood in a great torrent down the shoulder of the captain's horse and fell against it, sliding down against the slippery flank.

He ended up on the ground, face turned to one side, his heels drumming and bubbles forming in the blood around his mouth.

Stouer made the sign of Shallya, and Anmayer spat and touched iron to ward off ill fortune. Vollen and Friedel stared at the man.

'Ride!' Stouer yelled. 'Karl, lead off! Take us to the marshal!'

Karl spurred Gan forward and they ran down the roadway towards the zal. The onion dome rose above the line of the other roofs.

Clearing the nearby buildings, with the zal in sight, they suddenly saw the battle raging at a distance through the northern edge of the town. What they saw mostly, in fact, was billowing smoke, but there was absolutely no doubting what it was they were looking at, even for men who had never seen battle before.

To Karl Reiner Vollen who, like Gerlach Heileman, had spent most of his life wishing to be a soldier in war, it seemed bizarre. It was messy and disjointed, difficult to track what was happening, with only odd details becoming evident. A horse turning in circles without a rider. A man kneeling, covering his head with his arms, sobbing. Dark horses with dark, horned riders moving past, so fast they caused weird eddies and curls in the drifting smoke. A seated corpse, legs out straight, torso lolling forward as far as the spear fixed through it would allow. A man on fire, walking slowly away from the edge of the turmoil.

It looked nothing like the tapestries in the Heileman house, nor did it resemble the woodcuts in the military histories he had pored over in his youth. It was, he realised, utterly real. The smoke, the confusion, the deranged behaviour of men caught up in a living nightmare, their minds lost to terror or pain or both.

'Forward!' Stouer bellowed. Horned riders were sweeping in and assaulting the zal, some of them dismounting and hacking at the doors with long handled axes.

'Give fire!' Stouer yelled as they rode down on the tails of the raiders. Some turned, howling. One thumped backwards out of his saddle, his throat blown open. Karl felt a dull tingle in his breastbone, the echo of an impact, and realised he had fired his petronel. He had killed the man. His lead ball had blown out that throat.

There was no time to reload. He pushed the petronel back into its boot, and rode down another raider, breaking the man under Gan's hooves. By then, Karl had his sabre loose.

Stouer and Anmayer had both fired and killed with their pistols in puffs of cracking white vapour, and were now engaged with sword. Friedel had missed. Two of the enemy riders slewed round and galloped for him, and he screamed in fear, losing his grip on the reins. His horse threw him and he landed hard.

Karl wheeled Gan about, leapt him over the dazed Friedel, and met the riders head on. The clarion's sabre was extended, tip forward, and it sliced through the reins and cheek-flesh of one of the men, almost by accident.

The man clutched his face and fell off his horse. The other sailed a longsword at Karl, and the clarion felt his head twisted brutally by the impact against the side of his burgonet.

He tried to turn, sweeping his sword, all blade-schooling forgotten. Gan was frenzied and ready to buck or flee. The air was thick with the smell of powder smoke, blood and dung.

Karl managed to get Gan around, though in the process he took another glancing blow across his helmet and Gan was gashed in the flank. His adversary was a massive man, his torso and shoulders rippled with muscle, a bearskin tied around his ribs flapping out behind him. Warrior rings, dozens of them, were coiled around his arms and he wore a horned helmet wrought from black brass with a full face visor shaped like the snout of a wolf. His horse was nineteen hands high, black as charcoal, with a billowing mane.

Karl jabbed with his sabre, his thrust rebounding off the warrior rings on the man's left arm. The longsword, a span and a half of razored iron blade three fingers wide, sliced around and Karl ducked. He felt a wrench at the nape of his neck and suddenly the air was full of fluttering feather scraps. The longsword had sliced off his cockade.

Desperate now, Karl hauled on his reins, wrenching Gan back a pace, and cutting out with his sabre. The horned Norther, howling through his wolf-face visor, deflected the chop with his sword and hacked in, leaving a bruising dent across Karl's right vambrace. Pain shuddered up his arm and he nearly dropped his sabre.

Instead, he tucked down and spurred forward, taking another whack across his backplate. The Norther's blow actually cut through the steel and was only stopped by Karl's mail undershirt. He felt broken rings of mail slithering down his back into his hose.

He turned and thrust again. The sharp tip of his sabre sank into the wolf-face's bare shoulder to the depth of a palm. Blood spurted out with the blade as he pulled it free. The huge Norther cried out and lost control of his massive horse. It galloped away, the wounded rider jerking in the saddle as he tried to cling on.

Karl tried to straighten up. His back and his right forearm both felt like they were broken.

Then Gan toppled sideways, hurling him off onto the ground.

Karl rose. Gan was on his side, his legs kicking wildly. Blood was splashing in every direction. The gash the wolf-face had given his horse was far more serious than Karl had realised.

There was nothing he could do. Gan kicked and kicked, head back and teeth bared, blood gushing out of him. In less than a minute, Karl's beloved gelding was dead.

Aware that tears of rage were streaming down his face, Karl ran over to Friedel and dragged him towards the porch of the zal. Friedel was moaning and sobbing. His bowels had loosened.

'Get out your sword! Your sword!' Karl shouted.

'I've fouled myself! I am so ashamed, Karl! I have fouled myself!'

'Shut up, Johann!' Karl yelled, trying not to gag on the stink of shit. 'Get your sword out and up!'

Anmayer was dead. He lay face down in the mud, his forearms, shoulders and scalp sliced in a dozen places from the relentless sword blows that had killed him as he shielded himself with his arms. Stouer had dismounted, a sabre in one hand and a spent pistol in the other. He was surrounded by enemy warriors, fighting like fury, bleeding from a dozen wounds. His left pauldron was hanging off by its straps.

The last time Karl had stood on that porch, just a day earlier – though it seemed like months before – he had been with Gerlach and they had been called back by the field marshal's aide Schott.

Schott, by some eerie coincidence, was there again, in precisely the same place. But this time he was dead, his body split to the backbone by a blade-blow.

The gaudy warriors of Neiber's trabanten were fighting a rearguard around the doorway of the hall.

Two of the ten men had already fallen, but the others were battling hard with their swords.

As befitted a field marshal's life company, the men of the trabanten were elite fighters. The distinctive blades they were wielding were called katzbalgers: wide, round-tipped short-swords with double-curved quillons. The opulent finery of their clothing reflected their high status. They had slain upwards of a dozen raiders already.

Karl fell in with them. He'd utterly lost contact with the whining Friedel, though he kept calling out his name. Karl found himself beside one of the trabanten, an older man in rich wargear and multi-coloured hose. They chopped at the enemy press. Karl felt his sabre cut through something soft and realised he had just killed another man.

One of the trabanten squealed as he was dragged under a mass of pushing enemy warriors and run through.

'What's your name?' the swordsman next to Karl shouted.

'Karl Reiner Vollen!'

'Get in there, Karl! Get inside! Find the marshal and watch over him!'

'But–'

'For the love of Sigmar, we can't let him die! I've sent a man to draw horses to the western door. Get him there! Get him clear! We'll hold the door!'

Karl faltered. The man was covered in blood, and his katzbalger was just a hacking blur.

'Please…' pleaded the struggling swordsman.

Karl broke and ran into the zal.

It was suddenly quiet. The din from outside was just a dull roar. He walked across the outer hall, past a lute that had been shattered when it was dropped. He heard a plink plink plink and saw it was the blood dripping off the fuller of his blade onto the paving.

He tore off his burgonet and tossed it aside.

'Marshal? Marshal Neiber? Sir?'

In the main hall, the fire had died back. It was cool and still. Every now and then the beams shook from a crash outside. The gentleman's travelling case lay open, with two glasses missing now from the satin rests.

Karl put his sabre down on the table, took out one of the engraved thimble glasses that remained and filled it from an open bottle of musket. He swigged it down and felt better. The beams shook again.

He set the thimble glass down and retrieved his sabre.

'Marshal Neiber?'

Karl pushed back a velvet door hanging with his sword tip and looked inside.

Empty.

He moved on, using his sword to poke open a scullery door. The kitchen was empty, and smoke floated out from the dying hearth.

He went forward into the state bedroom, and there was Neiber.

The field marshal was dead. Naked except for his hose, he lay on his back on the bed. He had been choked with his own field baton. His face was swollen and black.

Karl walked towards the bed. He laughed out loud at the idiocy of it. The trabanten band was fighting to the last outside to keep this man alive, and here he was, already dead.

Karl stiffened suddenly. This death wasn't self inflicted. Neiber had been killed.

He whipped around, his sabre rising, in time to smash aside the attack of the warrior who was pouncing at him from the shadows. A lithe, naked shape clad in leather swathes, its head covered in a brass bull-mask, with three twisted horns rising asymmetrically from the helm cap.

Caught across the snout of his helmet, the Norther tumbled away, and then sprang up again, a stabbing knife in each fist. He seemed at once ridiculous and terrifying to Karl. His head was armoured in the horned, brass mask, and he was draped in leather strips, and strings of shell-beads and bone-shards. But his feet, chest, arms and groin were exposed. All the vulnerable parts a man would usually armour with metal and modesty were bared, yet the head was locked in a metal cover. The Norther lunged at Karl, his bare feet padding on the tiles, his beads jingling.

Karl gripped his sabre and put both shoulders into the cut. His sweeping sabre hit the side of the Norther's helm and knocked him over into the shadows, the knives clattering out of his hands. A string of shells and bones broke and scattered their little, hard particles across the floor.

Karl ran. He ran towards the western door. The trabanten swordsman had said that horses would be there.

Karl wrenched open the door.

The Norther warrior with the wolf-face helm stood there, framed in firelight, blood running from his shoulder. He had an axe now. He lunged in through the doorway, smashing Karl off his feet and down on to his back. Then he swung the axe straight down to split Karl's head.

VII

THE DAWN SKY was as black as a funeral swathe. Palls of dark smoke swirled out across the oblast, driven sideways like fog banks by the wind. Zhedevka was burning.

From the eastern fields, Gerlach Heileman could see the bright flames leaping and lashing along wall posts and roof beams. The fire consuming the aspen shingles of the zal's onion dome was almost blue-white.

This image of the burning town came and went as the tide of smoke draped itself to and fro across the fields at the whim of the winds. The smoke smelled of timber, rusted iron and spoiled meat. It tasted of salt.

Gerlach realised it didn't taste of salt at all. He was tasting his own tears. He had been weeping for some minutes without knowing it.

Saksen was stamping and shuddering, foaming at the bit. Gerlach pulled the big horse round and cantered through the waves of black smoke. Bodies littered the trampled grass. Men, horses, broken wargear, splintered lances. Horses without mounts fled past like phantoms in the coiling darkness.

Gerlach had tried to fight his way back to the standard, but all he had found was Truch's skewered corpse.

In the distance, he could hear the sporadic bang of firearms.

Linser and Demieter suddenly appeared, riding hard. Linser had lost his helmet and Demieter was blood-stained and lolling awkwardly in his saddle. They pulled up when they saw him.

'Vexillary!' Linser cried.

'Where stands the line?' Gerlach demanded.

Linser shrugged his narrow shoulders and wiped a glove across his face. His hand left a smudge of blood where it had touched.

'Line?' he asked, as if the word was new to him.

'We have to rally the troops and reform–' Gerlach began.

'There is no troop,' said Demieter softly. He was clutching his arms to his belly and his face, framed in the steel of his burgonet, was ash-white with pain. 'Sigmar, you bloody fool! There is no troop! It's broken!'

Kaus Demieter was one of the quietest and most respectful men in the demilance company. To hear this new, contemptuous tone in his voice took Gerlach by surprise.

'Kaus, we have to rally. Remember our oath? We–'

'Damn you, Heileman. Gods damn you, you pompous little prig.'

'Kaus–'

Demieter spat blood and glared at the vexillary. 'If we're lucky, really lucky, we might be able to make it back to the crossing. Back to Choika. If we do, we might live until tomorrow. But if we stay here, shitting away our chances because you have some fond notion of the rules of war, we'll be dead inside an hour.'

'He's right, Gerlach,' said Linser. 'This is bloody madness.'

Shouts and screams rang from the veils of smoke. They all stiffened as horned riders pelted past, half visible in the grey haze.

'Shit!' Gerlach said. He looked at the other two.

'Can you get me out of here?' asked Kaus Demieter. 'Me and Linser? Can you get us to the crossing? I want to live, Gerlach. I want to see my girl again.'

Gerlach smacked Saksen's rump and yanked the reins. 'Ride with me!' he cried.

They rose into a gallop, passing over the jumbled bodies in the grass, veering to avoid loose horses. The wind picked up and the smoke thinned, driven clear for a moment. Gerlach saw a group of Norther horsemen turning on the flame-strewn field, riding down towards them.

'Pick it up!' he shouted. They had the edge of a lead, over thirty horse lengths. They could outrun the foe. Another demilancer appeared, riding hard on a parallel course to link with them. It was Hermen Volks.

'This way!' Gerlach hollered.

South of them, dead ahead, the smoke banks drew back sharply. A line of horsemen sat there, silent and still, blades and axe-hafts resting across their saddle bows. They were clad in black armour, ring-scale, brass, full visored helmets with long horns, all of it caked with pitch.

The enemy had the field. Now they were scouring it, systematically driving out the survivors to annihilate them. Gerlach had hunted many times in the elector's parks. He knew how to run the quarry, how to beat it up into the rise, how to block it with outriders, how to corner it for the kill.

Now he knew what it felt like to be the stag.

'Turn wide!' he yelled, and the four demilancers switched left, churning across the peaty grasses, kicking up mud and spray. The line of Northers remained still, patiently forming a barrier to their right. When Gerlach looked back, he saw that the rear end of the barrier line was now peeling away, one by one, to join up with the pack of riders at their heels. There were twenty, thirty, more.

This wasn't war at all. It had ceased to be any kind of combat Gerlach had been trained to face. It was more like some preposterous, cruel joke. The whimsy of the god Ranald perhaps, who was nothing less than a trickster and delights in the misery of man.

Captain Stouer had once told Gerlach about a nightmare he kept having. He would come to the field of war, only to find he was alone, in the wrong place. Worse still, he was naked and without his weapons. Then the enemy swooped. Death resulted, of course, the terrifying death of a man alone against overwhelming odds, but it was the ignominy that made the nightmare so awful. The fact that Stouer was as vulnerable as a man could be and couldn't even fight back. Humiliation was the demilancer's deepest dread.

This seemed to Gerlach like just such a dream. It had an unreal quality. To be trapped, outnumbered, on a field of death where the grasses smouldered and burned and to every side lay the torn and brutalised bodies of friends and comrades. And to be quarry of a hunt, stalked down and ridden to the kill by faceless creatures in horned masks.

The hunting riders forced them north again, into the meadows, away from the escape route they had sought. The four demilancers were riding headlong in a tight group, though Demieter was lagging. Gerlach felt an uncomfortable rhythm tense through Saksen's stride, as if the gelding was tiring or, worse, had run lame or thrown a shoe.

There was a stand of trees ahead, overlapping another along the lowest part of the meadow. The trees ran east and thickened until they met the edge of the forest itself.

Gerlach turned them that way, towards the trees. Behind them, closing fast, warhorns blew and blades beat upon shields.

Three Northmen on black steeds broke out of the trees and thundered down to cut them off. There was no going wide. Gerlach wrenched out his lance and charged the first of them. There was a dull crump and the Norther he had been going for wailed out and tumbled from his saddle. His foot got hooked in the stirrup and his horse dragged him through the wet meadow weed.

Volks had found the time to re-load his petronel, Sigmar bless him. But now he was fumbling with it as the other two enemy riders cut in across them.

Gerlach slewed Saksen hard to the right to return the favour and protect Volks. Lance down, and running at full stretch, he caught one of the intercepting riders side on and drove his shaft against the man's ribs. The speartip missed, but their horses rammed together. The impact smashed the Norther from the saddle and wrenched the lance from Gerlach's grip. As he came clear, he found he was barely hanging on.

They reached the stand of trees, crashing through the bare branches and the saplings, showering dew and bark splinters around them. Gerlach saw Volks to his left and Demieter to his right.

Linser was no longer with them.

Gerlach looked back. The third rider had cut Linser down, killing his gelding and spilling him onto the ground. A fair number of the hunters had stopped, drawing into a circle around the unhorsed lancer. Gerlach could see Linser on his feet, arms raised, screaming as he dodged and scurried back and forth, trying to escape the tightening thicket of stabbing swords and slashing axes. The Northers were laughing and goading, playing with their prey like huntsmen toying with a wounded boar. Gerlach saw Linser struck with a sword and lose part of his hand. His welling scream rose up like sharp ice into the smoky fog.

Oh, Sigmar! Oh, Sigmar, spare him!

'Heileman!'

Gerlach looked round. Volks was calling to him, urging him to spur on into the trees. Demieter was slumped against his horse's neck now, and Volks had taken Demieter's reins to trail him.

'Come on, Gerlach! For Sigmar's sake!'

The remainder of the chasers – those that hadn't stopped to torment Linser – had reached the tree stand and were crashing through after them. Gerlach pointed, and Volks followed him left into a maze of leafless ash and dark pine, guiding Demieter behind him.

There was a thick stench of leaf mulch and wood husk amongst the trees, and the ground was spongy and thick with a raft of rotten leaves. They were forced to ride more slowly now. Gerlach could hear the crack and splash of their pursuers in the woodland clearings behind them.

Riding slower, he had time to reload his pistols. He drove Saksen with his knees, fiddling with each wheel-lock in turn. Such work was meant to be done at a standstill. With the horse jolting, it was hard to manage. Gerlach lost a lot of powder and three shot-balls as he tried to finish the job. But by the time they had cleared the trees, both his pistols were primed and loaded, their wheels wound tight and their dogs laid down. Volks had accomplished the same feat with his petronel.

The space beyond the trees was still and grey. The stand had masked the area from the worst of the smoke fuming off the murdered town. Mist foamed the wet grasses and haunted the edge of the forest to their right.

Volks was steering his tired troop horse that way, tugging Demieter after him. He looked back at the vexillary.

'Gerlach? Come on, man! The woods!'

Gerlach wasn't listening. He was looking west, back into the burning, smoke-wrapped field of death beyond the trees. He'd as good as forgotten about the Norther riders smashing through the stand on their tail.

'Gerlach! For pity's sake!'

Half a league away west, a mass of enemy riders and foot troops was assembling around their chieftain. Many of them carried severed heads on the ends of their blades, brandishing them to celebrate his victory. Some had captured Imperial field banners and ensigns. Others were stabbing or whipping prisoners forward, ragged, bloodied figures in the rag-remnants of Imperial uniform. Gerlach could see William Weitz, Gunther Stoelm, Kurt Vohmberg...

A flash of gold. Five riders were galloping in from the north end of the field with another trophy to place at the feet of their chieftain lord.

The standard of the Second Company Hipparchia Demilance. His standard.

'Gerlach?' Volks called. 'Come on, man!'

'That's ours,' Gerlach said.

'Yes, but–'

'That's ours, Hermen.'

Volks looked at him. There were tears in his eyes.

'I know, but...'

Gerlach drew out his sabre. The enemy in the woods were scant seconds away.

'Don't be a bloody fool!' said Volks.

'Yes,' said Demieter, sitting up in the saddle suddenly. 'Be a bloody fool. There's nothing left for us now except glory.'

Gerlach stared at him. Demieter raised his arms briefly. His lower breastplate was cracked and his innards, pink and frothed with blood, were poking out. 'I'm never going to see my girl again, am I?' he said.

Gerlach shook his head.

'Let's do it,' said Demieter, carefully pulling his lance from its boot, one arm still wrapped tight to keep his guts inside him.

'Volks?'

Hermen Volks drew out his petronel. 'Come on then. Before I decide you're both mad.'

They spurred hard and charged west. They came out around the long stand of trees, out of the mist, two of them with firearms raised, one with lance extended. The hunting Northers came from cover behind them, turning to pursue.

Gerlach stood in the stirrups as Saksen gained speed, one hand to the reins, the other aiming his dexter wheel-lock. The Northers carrying their standard heard their hooves drumming the wet earth and turned.

There were cries of alarm and surprise. Sword blades flashed as they came out of scabbards.

At full charge, Gerlach fired and smacked a rider off his horse. He holstered the pistol and drew its sinister partner as Volks fired his petronel. One of the Northers recoiled and clutched at his arm, his horse suddenly bucking.

Gerlach fired his second pistol. The shot went low, killing a Northman's horse stone dead. The beast collapsed under him and threw him off. He tried to scramble clear, but the lifeless horse rolled and crushed his leg, pinning him.

Then they were engaged in a melee. Gerlach had to throw his last pistol away so he could draw his sabre. He hacked at the man carrying the standard and probably blinded him, but Saksen was driving ahead, and he overshot. A swirl of figures around him, men shouting and horses braying. Something struck him a dull blow side on, and Saksen staggered. Mud splashed up. Nearby, a wooden stave or a shaft snapped. A man screamed. Horse spittle splattered around in stringy droplets.

Gerlach manhandled his gelding round, running clear for a second, and then turned as a yelling Norther ran at him on foot, brandishing a long berdish axe. The tribesman had a red-dyed horse tail fluttering from his helmet spike and his wild eyes were black with white rims like a hound's. Gerlach wrenched forward and ran the man through the chest with his sabre – a perfect downward thrust that the sergeant majors at the Cavalry School had taught them all.

Gerlach yanked his sword out as the man collapsed. Close by, in the frantic struggle, an enemy rider crashed over, without reason as far as Gerlach could tell. A boar-spear jabbed at him, the stab too short. He sank his spurs and drove Saksen back into the press, thrusting left and right. Something made an inhuman squeal.

He saw Volks through the chaos. The demilancer had the standard by its shaft and was fighting to ride clear, dragging it behind him. A broadsword swung at Gerlach's face, and he blocked it with his sabre, grunting with effort. He could feel the sheer panic rising in the horse between his knees. The broadsworder, astride a heavy black stallion, tried to slash again, forcing his mount in against Saksen's flanks. The stallion was biting and kicking out. Gerlach struck once, twice, with his sabre, hacking with the blade edge because the melee was too close-packed to draw back for a clean thrust. He had no idea if he'd hit anything, but the barbarian with the broadsword was suddenly no longer in his field of view.

'Volks!' he yelled. 'Ride clear! Ride clear!'

He couldn't see the demilancer any more, but above the thrashing mass of bodies, the standard head appeared briefly, waving wildly, the banner flapping.

More Northers were gathering in, riding hard from their chieftain's side to join the skirmish. Gerlach hadn't seen Demieter since they'd engaged. Something hit him across the left shoulder blade, and almost simultaneously he felt a sharp pain in his right hip. The stinking, howling enemy were all around him, close and lethal, like a pack of wolves. His sabre was slick and sticky with gore.

The sun suddenly came out. It was the most peculiar thing. Perhaps the weather had turned. Or perhaps the gods had intervened for a second, commanding the elements to respond to the extraordinary moment of battle that now took place. Afterwards, that's what Gerlach felt sure it was. Ulric, fierce god of courage, pleased by the carnage he saw, or Myrmidia, goddess of war, saluting valour, or even trickster Ranald again, taking delight in spoiling the darkness of a scene that should have belonged to his dour cousin, Morr, deity of the grave.

The sun came out, bright as the armour of Sigmar. Cold spring sunlight, like bars of smoking silver, shafted down across the field through an aperture in the black smoke and the grey-cast clouds. Everything glittered: blades, sweat beads, blood, breastplates. Everything was touched by that light and the black armour of the massing foe turned blacker still, like night shadows, contracted by daybreak.

Out of the western slopes, riders were coming. They were close, almost into the fight, by the time Gerlach spotted them through the mayhem or had heard the sound of their hooves above the clatter of skirmish. There were forty of them at least, riding fast, riding hard, caught in the shafts of sunlight and lit up like angelic beings. Gerlach felt terror the moment he saw them, a more awe-filled dread than anything he had felt in the face of the Northers. The feeling hardly waned when he realised they were not the enemy at all.

They were lancers. Kislevite lancers.

Each one wore silver mail and sleeved coats of segmented lamellar plate inscribed with gold that glittered in the sun like a breaking summer sea. Their round-topped steel helms had hard peaks, long neck-guards of mail and heart-shaped visors lowered across their noses. The cloth of their clothes was crimson and blue and many were draped in the white-and-black pelts of snow leopards. Breathtaking eagle wings, each one two spans high, rose vertically from their backs, the long feathers fluttering in the slipstream of their rush. Their long lances were lowered to the horizontal and couched.

The stories Gerlach had been told of the noble, terrifying splendour of the winged lancers were true after all.

The lancers swept into the milling thicket of barbarians with such force Gerlach felt the earth shake. Couched expertly under the arm by men well braced in saddle and stirrups, the lances conducted not only the strength of the rider's arm but also the force of his charging steed. They punched through shields, through bodies, through horses, demolishing everything in their path. Northers and loose horses fled madly out of the way.

The main mass of enemy riders was riding face on to the Kislev charge when they met. Armed with hooked axes and billed swords, the Northers had no reach at all, and the first rank were dead and unhorsed by the long, relentless cavalry spears in a second.

Gerlach heard a huge voice bellowing commands, and a bone horn blew. The charge line broke with disciplined skill, the riders barely restraining their gallop, and they began to skirmish in twos and threes. Most left their long horse lances behind them, thrust tip-down and quivering in the soil as they switched to curved swords or dragged javelins from their saddle boots. The javelins, short and slim and light, flurried out like arrows, taking Northers to whatever afterworld had been prepared for them. Each lancer carried two javelins, and Gerlach gawped at the astonishing horsemanship they displayed. The lancers loosed the javelins overarm, then leant as they passed to pluck the missiles back out of the dead targets to throw again.

The melee around Gerlach had broken and the ground was covered in jumbled bodies. He looked around for Volks or Demieter – for anyone – but saw only the broken waste of slaughter that lay in the wake of the charge. A dazed Norther lumbered nearby, and Gerlach despatched him quickly. The vexillary's hands were shaking. He was dazed and breathless as he came down off the pitch of blind rage that had driven him into the fight.

The bone horn sounded again. The sun was folding back into the cloud cover and the light was failing, as if the gods had decided their display was over. The winged lancers were disengaging and turning. They had driven a deep wedge into the ranks of the enemy, but if they remained, without the pressure of the charge to their advantage, they would be overwhelmed by the sheer number of barbarians.

The lancers were sweeping back towards him now, standing in their stirrups and hallooing victory shouts. Each rider bent low to recover one of the lances they had left spiked in the earth. One of the front horsemen was brandishing a standard high for them to follow. It was the eagle wing on the shield, the long red and white stripe of banner snapping out behind it.

Gerlach saw Volks now, and Demieter, riding clear with them. Volks had the demilance standard, and was struggling to raise it up as he rode hard.

Gerlach started Saksen forward, coming across the front of the retreat, gaining speed to reach Volks. The enemy, shaken and mauled, was charging in pursuit, horse archers leading the reply, firing barbs from the saddle.

Gerlach turned hard until he was in with the lancers, riding with them. He lost sight of Volks and Demieter again, but he was close to the Kislevite leader and the man with the eagle wing standard. It was all he could do to keep his tired gelding up with the smaller, sprightly Kislev mounts. He began to lag a little.

The lead lancer, his face hidden by the heart-shaped visor that jutted down from the peak of his helm, turned, shouted something, and waved him up urgently. Black-feathered arrows hissed into the grassy mud around him. One hit a lancer to his left between the shoulder blades, and he rolled from his saddle soundlessly, hands raised.

'Go on! Go on!' Gerlach sang out to Saksen, leaning forward, straining. They were onto the eastern slopes of the meadow now, powering towards the forest line.

An arrow glanced off his right pauldron with a painful crack that jerked his whole torso round.

Gerlach fought to steady himself, but his balance had been thrown. There was a strange moment of weightless confusion and then a hideous, jarring impact. He was out of the saddle, on the ground, dazed and bruised and not quite aware of where he was.

He got up. The enemy wave was just twenty lengths behind him, down the slope. Arrows chopped the air. He looked east. Two more lancers had been brought down by the horse archers. One was the standard bearer. He had an arrow through his throat and another through his torso. His horse had come over with him, but now it was struggling up, shaking its head, rattling its silver war harness and plated bridle.

Gerlach ran towards it, hands raised to calm it. But it was oblivious to him and took off towards the trees before he could grab its trailing reins.

'Yha! Yha!' a deep voice cried. The leader of the lancers was closing on him from the right hand at a spirited lick. He had turned back, sweeping right around, and was leading Saksen by his bridle.

'Come you! Yha!' the lancer cried.

Gerlach paused for a split second and then bent down and grasped the shaft of the fallen Kislev banner. He raised the eagle wing up and ran towards the approaching lancer.

'Take it! Take the damn thing!' he shouted, thrusting the banner into the man's gloved hands. Then he threw himself into Saksen's saddle and they turned to follow the main Kislev mass into the trees.

Screaming darkness followed them.

* * *

VIII

THEY RODE INTO the trees, into the gloom. The Kislevites had all but vanished. Gerlach caught glimpses
of silver, red and gold as lancers wove in and out of
the shadows and the moss-green trunks. The sounds
of hooves and voices and jingling armour echoed
around him under the roof of leaves. Gerlach forced
Saksen on, over ragged earth, peat-black soil, clus-
ters and outcrops of rock and root mass. Branches
whipped and brushed at his face. A loop of thorn
drew blood from his cheek. The hollow acoustics of
the forest carried the dull, raucous sounds of the
pursuit.

He caught up with two lancers. One of them was
the leader, clutching the banner tight to stop it foul-
ing in the branches. Together, they leaped a stream
and turned to the right, following the leaf litter in
the bed of the winding ditch. Gerlach simply stayed
with them. He had no idea where he was going,
except that it was vaguely east.

Over the space of an hour, they began to slow,
allowing for their horses' fatigue. The sounds of the
Northers fell away behind them.

Then they broke from the forest into a crow-
haunted marshland skirted by dark trees. The
winged lancers were gathering there, watering their
horses while sentinel riders watched.

Gerlach reined up, and leant wearily across his
saddle bow. His hands were still shaking. The Kislevite leader stopped beside him, and raised the
heart-shaped visor, opened the cheek-guards and
pulled his steel helm off. He tugged off the leather

cawl after it. His head was shaved but for a long top-knot, and his moustaches were long and drooping. When he grinned, he exposed the gap where his front teeth were lacking.

It was Beledni.

'Quite a day, yha? Yha, Vebla? Quite a day!'

IX

THUNDER ROLLED ACROSS the marsh and the forest line, and lightning underscored the thickening blanket of granite-grey cloud. Some of the winged lancers touched the iron guard-bows of their swords to ward off storm magic, others boldly shouted oaths and prayers up into the sky to the Kislev thunder god.

Gerlach Heileman watched Beledni use the cuff of his glove to wipe sweat and greasy dirt from his face and shaved scalp.

'I didn't recognise you,' Gerlach said.

'Shto?' Beledni pouted and narrowed his eyes.

'I didn't recognise you... I didn't know who you were. In your armour.' Gerlach pointed to the Kislevite's intricately wrought hauberk of silver lamellae, the gold-chased pauldrons and gorget, the great, black-tipped feathers of his wings. Last time they had met, Beledni and his men had seemed like beggars in rags and furs.

Beledni smiled. 'For bittle, we dress. Dress in scale and szyszak and wings. We make our fine show when it time to fight. Dress... and shave, of course.'

'Shave? What does that matter?'

'Shto?'

'I me... never mind. Where did you come from?'

Again, Beledni frowned.

'In the battle. The battle. Where did you come from?'

Beledni thought about this. 'In bittle, we start come from to the east, with pulk.'

'What?'

'East... chast... chast... aah, word is "part", yha? East part of meadowland. Where pulk githers.'

'What? What is this word "pulk"?'

Beledni smiled and waved his arms wide. 'Pulk is... bittle...' he groped for the term, '...host. Bittle host. Rota of Yetchitch krug part of Sanyza pulk. Many rota make together pulk, many rota... one, two, more many!'

'Rota,' Gerlach murmured. He'd heard that word before too. He looked away, trying to spy Volks or Demieter amongst the gathered riders.

'Yha! Rota! Word is for it you have... "banner". Yha? Ban-ner? You much save Yetchitch banner, Vebla. Pick it up from ground when Mikael Roussa fell down to death. This honour you do for us.'

Beledni suddenly looked very serious. He held out his hand. Gerlach offered his own hand in puzzlement and got it almost crushed by the big rotamaster's emphatic paw.

A lancer – tall and slender, with a scar along his left cheek bone – cantered up and leaned to whisper into Beledni's ear. The rotamaster's face darkened.

'You come, Vebla. You come,' he said.

* * *

X

DEMIETER LAY BESIDE his horse on the black clay of the marsh bank. Winged lancers had dismounted and stood around him. Two knelt by him. Gerlach jumped down from Saksen and crouched at his side.

'Kaus?'

'Heileman? Is that you? I can't see so well. It's dark.'

'There's a storm coming in…'

'No, you're all shadows.' Demieter's belly wound was a terrible mess. The skirts of his armour were coated in blood.

'Where's Volks?' Gerlach asked.

Demieter licked his lips and swallowed before answering. 'Didn't you see him? I saw him, Gerlach. He came so close. They shot him down at the tree-line. Just as we got to the forest. Such a lot of arrows in his back.'

'And the standard? Kaus, the standard?'

A dry rattle wheezed out of Demieter's lungs. He was dead.

Gerlach got to his feet and pulled off his riding gloves. Somehow they'd managed to rescue the Kislevite's worthless banner and lose their own a second time during the fight. He felt sick to his stomach. Of the Second Hipparchia Demilance, only he remained. Not even their beloved standard had survived the field. He was alone and, as vexillary, disgraced by the loss of their colours. Better he had died on the meadow. Better the Kislev dogs had left him to die in glory.

Thunder grumbled again, twigs of light danced along the northern skyline under the black water-mark of glowering cloud. Beledni and his lancers were all staring at him.

He had to salvage something. Some scrap of honour.

'We ride,' he said to Beledni. 'To Choika, or one of the towns on the Lynsk. We must ride there. Carry a warning–'

Beledni crinkled his chin and shrugged.

'We must ride there!' Gerlach said. 'The Northers just obliterated everything at Zhedevka! They'll go south, to the river! Beyond that! Sigmar has spared us from the day's slaughter. That's a gift we must use!'

'No,' said Beledni. 'East.'

'Damn it! Armies of the Empire are still coming north to the frontier! To the river! They'll be marching straight into destruction unless we warn them!'

'No, Vebla. Is best we can go east. Run clear. Turn bick later.'

'No–'

'Is only way, yha? We take horse west or south, we die many times death. Here is death, here is death, here is death also again. Is little much we can do. But east, yha? Little and much, much by little. Like tale of man who has pebble and wants castle. With little he–'

'Shut up! Where the hell is your loyalty? Where the hell is your honour?'

Beledni frowned, then pointed to the eagle wing banner.

'To rota,' he said, as if it was obvious.

A bone horn blew. The enemy, fanning through the forests, was in sight. The lancers scattered to their horses. Beledni looked at Gerlach.

'Little and much, Vebla, much by little,' he said, and turned to mount up. He pointed to Gerlach's troop horse. Dry sweat caked Saksen's flanks.

'You ride, Vebla. Ride to live. When you can live, then you can choose how to die.'

KURGAN

I

THE WHOLE OF creation had become an unpleasant place.

It had gone dark, and compressed itself into a single, slender, vertical line of immense density that was pressing against the bridge of his nose and his forehead.

All darkness, all creation, all the composite parts of the world, all 'matter' as he had read the great scholars of the Empire were calling it these days, had channelled itself into that line, making it a thousand times harder than rock, a hundred thousand times harder than iron. Even darkness was soaked up into it. The pressure it exerted would surely cave his skull in very soon.

The only part of the whole of creation that wasn't contained in that line was a smell. And that smell was the wafting reek of shit.

Karl Reiner Vollen coughed and realised he was alive. In an instant he knew that the hard line of pain pressing down his head was the great split the wolf-head's axe had made in his skull. He didn't want to move in case his face hinged open like a book.

He clawed around with a gloveless hand. He was sprawled on his belly on a very uneven surface, and his head was tilted back because his face was jammed up against something. A rung. A bar.

He felt his face. It wasn't split, though it was agony to touch his left cheek. The slender vertical line was the bar his face was jammed against.

He opened his eyes. Flamelight, blurry. The smell of ordure remained strong, but mixed now with smoke and sweat and blood. His mouth had lolled open during his unconsciousness, and his tongue and gullet were as dry as tar paper.

He tried to move. He groaned at the effort and other voices groaned and protested too. He realised he was sprawled across a pile of bodies. Karl slithered round and sat up. His head pounded.

He was in a cage. A cage of sorts. It had been made from pikes and pole arms, each long shaft stabbed blade-down into the earth, each a hand's breadth from the next. They staked out a circle five spans across. Brass chains had been lashed around the raised shafts midway and at the top to keep them true. The cage roof was open to the swirling storm clouds.

The pole arms, the pikes... were all captured Imperial weapons, the arms of fallen men.

Outside the makeshift cage, there was nothing to see except churned mud, smoke and fire. Soot and sparks billowed up from burning buildings. Screams and drumming rolled out of the dark. Karl had no idea where he was, but he presumed he was still in Zhedevka.

Inside the cage, the floor space was packed with a mound of bodies. Men of the Empire all of them: bloody, filthy, most of them unconscious, some of them undoubtedly dead. They lay in a jumble where they had been flung. Karl realised he was lucky to have been one of the last thrown in. He'd ended up on the top of the heap. Those at the bottom had surely suffocated. Limbs curled and flopped, some of them protruding through the spaces between the bars.

A man from Carroberg lay next to him, his slashed doublet was drenched with blood, his jaw broken. Beneath him was a Wissenland pikeman with an ear hanging off and swollen blue lips. An archer, beside and under him, was either dead or unconscious. Others were too filthy or blood-stained or stripped of their wargear to identify.

Karl's own clothing and half-armour were tattered and shredded. He felt his face again and winced. That axe! Why wasn't he dead?

'What will they do with us?' asked a low, scared voice.

Karl looked around. Another Wissenland piker sat on a slope of bodies with his back pressed to the bars, staring at him. The pikeman was young, his surcoat ripped, a long gash down his chest. His hair was lank with sweat or blood.

'Demilancer? What will they do?'

Karl shook his head.

'What's your name?' asked the young pikeman.

'Karl R–' Karl began. Then 'Karl.'

'That's my name too!' the pikeman said, bright for a moment. His face fell. 'Karl Fedrik, of Wissenland. They'll kill us, won't they?'

'They haven't done yet,' said Vollen. No one built a cage, however crude, for men they were going to kill anyway. He didn't want to say it, but he had a hunch death was the least alarming of their prospects.

'What then? What?' the young pikeman stammered.

'Shut up, boy! Shut the hell up, for Sigmar's sake!'

Karl glanced around and saw a grizzled veteran from Averland curled up against the bars on the other side of the cage. He too was clumsily perched on the pile of bodies.

'Just shut up,' the man said. He had a sword wound in his arm, which made him clutch the limb stiffly against his chest. His beard had been hacked off, recently, and crudely, it seemed, from the bloody grazes on his stubbled jaw.

Karl tried to move around, but the shapes under him groaned and cried out. He was sure it was just breath being squeezed out of dead lungs. The smell of decay was stifling. Flies billowed around them all.

Two Norther riders suddenly galloped past them outside the bars, and the boy pikeman shrank down. The riders disappeared again into the choking curtain of smoke.

'It's all right,' Vollen assured the boy. 'It's all right, Karl.' He didn't believe his own words at all. This was nothing like all right.

He looked across at the Averland veteran again, in time to see the older man sliding a dirk out of his blood-stained sleeve. The man grasped the little dagger, pressed the tip to his throat and closed his eyes.

'No!' Karl lunged, oblivious to the shrieks and moans that issued from the bodies under foot. He crashed into the veteran and wrenched the dirk back from his neck. Its tip had drawn a dark spot of blood. The veteran cried out and punched at Vollen, but the clarion kept his hand clamped to the wrist of the knife hand and slapped the man hard across the face with his free palm.

The man sagged, and Vollen took the dirk away from him.

'What the hell are you doing?'

'Give it back! Give it back!' the older man whined.

'No! What were you thinking?'

The Averlander shoved Karl backwards and spat at him. 'Damn you! We're dead! We're dead here! Give me back my blade so I can slit my own throat and have done! Spare me the pain that they will inflict on us!'

'No. Shut up!' Karl growled.

'Please! You bastard!'

Karl pushed the struggling man back against the bars so hard the brass chains jingled.

'We are men of the Empire… sworn to the service of Karl Franz! When death claims us, it claims us! Not sooner – not by our own hands! There is always hope!'

The man sagged back, breathing hard. The light of the flames reflected in his eyes. 'There is no hope. Not now, demilancer,' he said softly. 'You have no idea. The heathens have penned us here simply so they might have fodder for their death games.'

'No.' said Karl. 'We'll be stood hostage t–'

The man laughed in his face. He laughed so hard, blood flew in his spittle. 'Have you fought the North before, boy?'

'No?'

'What do you know of the Northers? The brute tribes? The Kurgan?'

'I have read a little–'

'Then you know nothing!' The man's head dropped. He sighed. 'Two seasons before I have fought the Kurgan. I've seen things that… I cannot say. Acts of barbarism. They are not human, you know. They are daemons. They make piles of skulls, and stretch the hides of their enemies. And their rituals. Oh, may Sigmar spare me. Their rituals. Blood sacrifices to their infernal gods. Why do you think we're still alive?'

'I–'

'Hostages? Ha ha ha! You idiot! They want us alive so that our hearts will be beating when they offer us up to their gods!'

The young pikeman on the far side of the ghastly cage moaned aloud at the thought of this.

'Shut up!' snapped Karl, and slapped the man again. 'You're scaring the boy!'

'He should be scared...' the veteran hissed.

'Shut up, you fool!' Karl replied and delivered another slap. 'We can get out of here. We–'

'No, demilancer. We can't. We're livestock now. Livestock. If you care for a fellow's life, really care, you'll give him back his dirk. Then, when he's done, you'll use it on the boy and yourself too. That is Sigmar's mercy.'

Karl shook his head.

The man reached out his hand. 'Please? The dirk?'

'What's your name?' asked Karl.

'Drogo Hance, from Averland.'

'Drogo Hance, we will get out of here. I swear it on the honour of my company. Death is not the only escape.'

The Averlander chuckled coldly and turned away.

There was a noise from outside the cage. Three horned warriors appeared out of the smoke, dragging a man in full plate armour. One had him by the ankles, the others scooped under the armpits. The man was unconscious or dead. From his armour, it was clear he was one of the majestic Imperial Knights Panther. His wargear rattled and clattered as they drew him across the turf.

The Kurgan warriors threw him down and began to strip the polished steel plate off his limp body. They cast it aside, breaking the mail and cutting the leather straps. Pauldrons, vambraces, breastplate, leopard pelt. They pulled off his mail coat and tore away his undershift and leggings.

The man was face down now, naked. He still hadn't woken up.

Karl crawled across to the bars to watch.

One of the Kurgan warriors moved away into the smoke and returned with a wooden keg. He set it down and the other two draped the naked man across it, so that it supported his chest and his head hung down over the rim.

Another of the trio, his arms thick with muscles, drew his pallasz, a long, straight, double-edged sword.

'Hold him, seh,' he instructed. The other two did so. The knight was beginning to stir. The Kurgan with the pallasz raised his arms up to strike.

'Wait! You wait!' a voice boomed.

The horned warrior dropped his arms slackly. Three tall figures were striding into the firelight out of the smoke. One was a Kurgan bodyguard in a scale-linked mantle, a berdish axe clasped across his chest. The other two were hetmen. A slender, but inhumanly tall figure in head-to-toe black plate armour... and the massive warrior with the wolf's head helmet.

His shoulder was now wrapped in blood-soaked bindings.

'What do you do here?' the tall, plated figure demanded of the men. His ornate armour had a coating of black pitch that had been scratched and inscribed with a sharp tool, leaving an intricate etching of spirals, loops and stars in bare metal. His helmet was a barbute, similarly decorated, with a horizontal gash as an eye-slit.

'Prizing of a skull, Zar Blayda,' answered one of the Kurgan, putting his hand flat across his heart.

'This skull?'

The warrior with the pallasz put aside his blade so that he could put his hand over his heart too. 'Zar Herfil craves two more to make his trophy heap...'

'Not this one. I want him for my own sport.' The tall hetman tugged a small leather flask from his sword belt. It was stoppered with wax, through which a long, iron pin had been spiked. The hetman slid the pin out, lifted the knight's slack head by the hair, and quickly pricked the skin of the right cheekbone three times. Then he let the head drop. 'There. I have made my mark upon him now. '

'But Zar Herfil–'

The tall, black-armoured figure swung round sharply and struck the swordbearer around the face. He yelped and stumbled back.

'Don't raise a question to my word, dog-boy. Herfil may have his skulls.' The tall black shape turned and gestured to the cage. 'Take them from there instead.'

The Kurgan hurried forward, leaving the naked, unconscious Knight Panther to roll slackly sideways off the keg. One of the warriors pushed up an axe head to loose the brass chains around the makeshift cage, and the other yanked the freed poles out of the soil and tossed them aside.

'They're all dead!' one of the Kurgan warriors announced, peering in.

'There's one,' said Zar Blayda, pointing.

The Kurgan warriors manhandled Karl Fedrik of Wissenland out of the cage. He was screaming.

'Leave him alone!' Vollen yelled, clawing at them. The Northers kicked him back hard.

Karl Fedrik of Wissenland, now so terrified and so absolutely sure of what was happening to him he had soiled himself, was thrown face down over the keg. The Kurgan with the pallasz flourished it twice and then chopped down, striking off the boy's head. Blood gouted in rhythmic spurts from the neck stump.

'Him too?' Zar Blayda said, pointing at Vollen.

'No. Leave him.' The words, deep and dark, came muffled out of the wolf-mask helmet. 'I have marked him.'

'Very well, then. That one.'

The men grabbed Drogo Hance and pulled him out of the cage. Looking back at Vollen as he was dragged out backwards, Hance screamed, 'I told you! I told you, you bastard! I told you! You could have spared me this! You could have made it quick! You bastard!'

The Kurgan warriors made it quick anyway. The pallasz swept down and Hance's head rolled.

Zar Blayda picked up the two heads by their hair. Hance and Fedrik, mouths open, eyes rolled back.

'Herfil will be pleased,' he said.

The wolf-mask glowered through the bars at Vollen as the men threw the naked body of the Panther Knight into the cage and reformed it.

'You will keep for me,' said the wolf-face. Then he turned and walked away through the wide lakes of blood emptying out of the two corpses.

II

LEFT ALONE, KARL vomited. Revulsion and terror, terror and revulsion, the two things throbbed and circled in his head. He was close to panic. The iron tang of warm blood was so strong he vomited again until his retching was dry. He tried to spare the others in the cage his indignity, but there was no space. 'I'm sorry! I'm sorry!' he gasped between retches, trying to wipe his spew off the men beneath him.

It seemed though, that everyone else in the cage was dead.

Shuddering with cold and the dry spasms of his gullet, Karl curled up against the bars. Outside, in the fiery dark, a crude horn blew out a long, deep atonal note, and others joined it, some close, some far away. The horns wailed and sang for minutes and then finally died away.

Karl realised he was curled in the very space his name's sake, poor Karl Fedrik of Wissenland, had occupied. The thought… the comparison… was too much to bear. He couldn't even bring himself to look at the headless bodies slumped outside the cage. He scrambled round until he found another place to sit. His movement ushered cries and groans from the body pile.

When he settled again, he realised there was something in his left hand. Something small and cold and hard.

It was Hance's dirk.

Karl raised it up to his face, slowly. A fine little piece, tempered in the blade-forges of Averland, the palm-long blade curved and waisted like a tulip. It had a simple brass hilt, and a grip that was wound in matt black wire. A boot-knife, a belt-knife, a typical pole-armer's piece. Made for stabbing in through visor slits and armour joints once the halberd or pike had done its work and brought an armoured foe down. Pikemen called such dirks their 'true killers'. They were famed for the use of their long-shafted weapons, but their little dirks and daggers most often did the actual killing.

Karl stared at the dirk. The true killer. He realised Hance had probably been right. A little quick blade for a little quick death. Merciful, sparing. For the pain and horror that waited for him outside the rude cage was beyond imagining.

This was simple, this was honest.

Karl Reiner Vollen closed his eyes and said a prayer to Sigmar. He asked Emperor Karl Franz for forgiveness. The gods would understand, surely?

He pressed the flat of the dirk to his throat with one hand, and felt around with the fingers of the other for his neck vein. It was fat and pulsing. His heart was racing.

He turned the dagger so the edge was against his flesh. Another prayer, to remember his sisters, and his father and mother, and Guldin who had trained him to horse and–

He bit his lip.

His hand wouldn't move.

'Sigmar, please…' he moaned.

He couldn't do it. Some desperate will for life blocked him and stayed his hand. If nothing else, there was something so unseemly about an Imperial weapon being used to end an Imperial life.

'Gods damn you, Drogo Hance!' Karl sputtered, and dropped the dirk. Then, with tears welling in his eyes, he murmured, 'Gods spare you too…'

'Hello…?' a voice called.

Karl looked round. The Knight Panther, stripped bare and tossed onto the body heap, was struggling up, gazing around blankly.

'Is anyone there? Anyone? Hello… anyone…' The man's voice, rich and strong, was cracking weakly.

'You're fine. You're all right,' Karl reassured him, clambering forward across the mattress of limbs and torsos.

'Who is that? I can't see. I don't know where I am.'

'My name is Karl Vollen, sir. Second Company Hipparchia Demilance. I'm clarion. You're all right… just now, you're all right.'

The knight rolled over, vulnerable and exposed, and reached out towards the sound of Karl's voice. 'Karl Vollen? Where are you?'

'Here, sir.' Karl reached out a hand and the knight clasped it.

'I'm blind,' the knight said. There was a dark contusion on the man's temple and his eyes were rolled blankly, like loose kernels inside a husk-case.

He gripped Karl's hand tightly. 'Where are we?'

'We're in a bad place, sir, I can't lie. Captured and caged by the Northers.'

'Ahhh,' the knight nodded and sighed. 'I feared as much. They took my horse down. Poor Schalda. Then something hit me across the face. Across the head. A lance, I think. Maybe an axe. I'm cold.'

'They took all your armour and your clothes,' Karl said, wanting to add that they'd nearly taken his head too, but thought better of it.

'This is a pretty end for me,' said the knight.

Karl pushed down into the mass of bodies and found a man who was clearly dead. Dragging and straining, he managed to pull the corpse's jerkin and woollen undershirt off.

'Sir?' he said. 'Take these, and put them on. You'll be warmer.'

His eyes almost crossed in their blindness, the knight felt his way into the dirty clothes Karl had provided.

'Better,' he said. 'For this simple kindness, I am in your debt, clarion Vollen. Your demilance is from Talabheim, yes?'

'Yes, sir.'

'Are you sworn up? Are you ready for your spurs?'

The knight was asking if Karl was preparing for entry into a knightly order.

'I... my birth is not adequate, sir. I am not.'

The knight wriggled round so he was looking at Karl, even though he couldn't see him. His blank eyes glared at a point far above Karl's left shoulder.

'If we get out of this, Karl, your birth won't be an issue. It's in my power to reward you for your help.'

'I didn't do it because–'

'Of course you didn't! I meant no offence.'

'What is your name, sir?' Karl asked.

'Von Margur,' the knight replied, cradling his arms around his body.

'Von Margur? Like the great hero of Altdorf?'

Blind, looking the wrong way, the knight smiled.

'Gods!' Karl started. 'You are von Margur of Altdorf!'

'I am. Unless there is another I know not of.'

'I'm truly honoured, sir,' Karl began, and then his voice trailed off. He realised how ridiculous it was. They were penned in an enemy cage, awaiting barbarous death, and here he was hero-worshipping.

The blunt truth was that his hero was as helpless as he was. They were going to die.

'Karl? Where did you go?' von Margur called hoarsely.

'I'm here, sir,' Karl answered. He was groping into the pile of bodies to recover the dirk. His hand closed around it and he pulled it up.

And held it close to his heart.

III

AFTER A WHILE, the knight fell asleep, the deep, sick sleep of the wounded. Karl sat back against the bars, and slid the dirk into his undershirt.

He turned his head and looked out at the headless corpses for the first time. They were thick with flies.

A figure emerged from the smoke. A bull mask visor wrought from brass, three asymmetrical horns. Leather straps. Jingling strings of shell beads and polished bone. An otherwise naked body.

It was the barbarian warrior Karl had faced in Marshal Neiber's bedchamber.

The man plodded forward, his bare feet slapping the wet mud. He was short and squat of body, with a thick neck. In each of his hands dangled a long stabbing dagger.

He reached the bars of the makeshift cage and stared in at Karl. There was no doubt in Karl's mind that the horned devil recognised him. In fact, he had the distinct feeling the Norther had come to find him. There was a deep, sharp gash down the side of the Norther's helmet visor where Karl's sabre had sent him tumbling.

The man sheathed one of his daggers and reached his empty hand up to the gouge in his helmet. He slid the fingerpads back down the ragged score and cut them open on the bare metal.

With a whip of his wrist, he flicked his hand to Karl and spattered him with blood.

'I am Ons Olker, flesh,' he said, in halting but competent Imperial. 'I have blood-tied thee. For thy offence, I will take thy soul.'

Then he walked away into the smoke, shaking the blood off his hand.

IV

KARL WAS WOKEN by rain, pelting and cold. He wasn't sure when or how he'd fallen asleep. The rain – the heaviest that had fallen since they'd left Brodny – was icy. It roused many of the other penned men, including von Margur and several that Karl had supposed to be dead. With so many awake, there was no longer any space to crouch or sprawl. The prisoners were forced to stand, shivering, some moaning, on the bodies of those that would likely never rise again.

Someone was sobbing. Another was yelling out disjointed nonsense. Several joined together to recite Sigmarite prayers of deliverance and fortitude.

Karl found himself mouthing the old, rote-learned words. He was so wet and bone-cold, he could barely control his shaking. Beyond the cage wall, he could see less than four spans, so heavy was the rain. He wondered if anyone was watching them. It would not be impossible to pull up one or more of the pikes that formed the bars and make a run for it.

A run to where? An attempt to escape would surely provoke savage reprisal from the barbarians.

But still, how could anything be worse than the miserable plight they were in?

Karl took a good grip on the pole arm facing him.

'What are you doing?' hissed a man next to him. Karl didn't reply.

'Stop it!' the man added. 'They'll kill us all for sure if–'

Karl looked at him. He was a heavy-set man in early middle-age, wearing the ragged leather coat and apron of a smith or a gunner.

'They'll kill us all anyway,' said Karl.

'Karl? Is that you?' von Margur called, reaching out.

'Lad's trying to escape!' the heavy man said.

'Stop it, Karl,' von Margur said softly.

'There's no one out there, sir...' Karl began, rocking the pole shaft to work the buried head out.

'Yes, there is,' said von Margur.

'How could you know that? You can't... I mean...'

'I can feel them. I can feel them watching,' the blind knight said. He said it with such conviction Karl pulled his hands off the pole shaft guiltily.

After a few minutes, the rain ceased suddenly. The downpour had washed the smoke out of the air. What it revealed was a world in grey half-light, a kind of twilight without colour. Devastation lay all around: acres of mud, mangled fields, and the steaming black ruins of Zhedevka. Their cage of captured pikes was just one amongst twenty standing in a waterlogged pasture beside the dead city's west wall. Each cage was as full of filthy, forlorn bodies as theirs. Upwards of a thousand prisoners, penned like swine.

In the distance, great fires burned, so big even the torrential rain hadn't doused them. Mounds of timber higher than a barn, casting up huge flames into the desolate sky. Watch fires, funeral pyres, victory blazes... Karl couldn't decide what they were. He could see dark figures – just specks at that distance – ringing around the huge bonfires like worshippers. He could hear drums and chanting. Carrion crows, hundreds of them, circled the field, fluttering in the air like autumnal leaves.

One other thing, closer at hand, had been revealed by the deluge. Norther warriors with axes and boar-spears lurked around the edges of the cage pasture, watching over them all. Some had large hounds lying by them, kept on chain leashes.

'You see?' hissed the heavy man beside Karl.

'You were right, sir,' said Karl to the knight.

No one spoke after that. Even the man who had been yelling nonsense shut up. The vista before them was too bleak, too dismal, too apocalyptic for words.

Night fell, black and cold and clear. The freezing, glassy darkness of a spring night in the oblast.

They remained standing, shivering, aching from the chill. A moon rose, fuzzy and glittering like a white lamp. Stars came out, but they seemed dim and cold, and they resembled no pattern Karl could recall from his studies. He was sure that was just his imagination.

The second moon rose late, but it could not match the bright, frosty glare of the first. In the darkness of the distance, the drumming and chanting stopped and, one by one, the great fires were snuffed out.

V

KARL WOKE AGAIN at dawn, cold through to his marrow. He was shaken awake, and was still upright. He blinked round in the thin light and found that the heavy man had been propping him up so that he could sleep without falling. Karl was astonished by the man's kind effort.

'You're all right there, lad,' the man said with a nod. 'I couldn't let you fall. You'd like have been crushed.'

Karl could see from the man's drawn face and red eyes that he had been weeping. There was a tremor of cold and fear in his large, powder-stained hands.

'What's your name?' Karl asked.

'Ludhor Brezzin, of Nuln.'

'An engineer?'

'No, lad. Nothing so grand. I am a powderman and tamper, from the cannon crews. I... I was a powderman.' He shrugged his powerful arms as much as the tight pack of bodies would permit. Then he looked away and snuffled, rubbing his nose and eyes with his thick wrists.

'He has a son,' a voice whispered in Karl's ear. It was the blind knight.

'A son?'

'A boy about your age. All night he has wept for grief that he would not see the boy again.'

'He told you this, sir?' Karl whispered.

Von Margur shook his head.

Karl wanted to ask the knight how he could know such things, but the nobleman looked ashen and weak. The bruise across his temple had grown and become more discoloured. His eyes still rolled like a broken doll's, and now the left, nearest the bruise, was bloodshot. Though the blow that had felled him had not opened his head, it had done massive concussive damage, Karl was sure. Shaking the eyes loose and useless, and undoubtedly harming the brain. When von Margur opened his mouth to speak, his white teeth were outlined with blood.

'My adversary struck me hard,' von Margur said suddenly, conversationally, as if hearing what Karl was thinking. He turned his face towards the clarion, though his eyes did not look that way. 'It was the fiend in black armour, the one with the etched patterns...'

'The Kurgan called him Zar Blayda,' said Karl.

'He is a daemon,' said the blind knight. 'His thoughts are like molten iron. He fancies himself High Zar, and plots to murder Surtha Lenk.'

'Who?'

'I don't know. The words are just in my mouth.' Von Margur stopped talking abruptly, and held out a hand to Karl. The clarion took it. Von Margur's touch was like ice. Karl could see Zar Blayda's mark on the knight's right cheek. Three dark pinpricks of dried blood. The flesh around them was discoloured green.

There had been dye or ink on that pin. What had the wolf-face meant when he said he'd marked Karl too? The clarion gently felt his own face with his free hand. The left side was still a tender, swollen mass of bruise. There were numerous nicks and grazes. He felt a soreness on his own right cheek. A tiny, painful dot. A pinprick.

What did the mark mean?

'Karl,' von Margur said. 'I am afraid.'

'We're all afraid, sir.'

'I am afraid of myself. Things have got into my head. They're trying to get out. They make me see things and tell me the words for the things I have seen. I–' He stopped again, shook his head. And then he collapsed.

Von Margur began convulsing, his spine and limbs as rigid as spear hafts. A horrible drooling rattle was issuing from his throat, and pink froth was

dribbling from his clenched teeth out over his gri-
macing lips.

Karl grabbed him and tried to support his thrashing weight. The fearful prisoners all around
attempted to back off, not wanting to touch the man.

'Help me with him!' Karl yelled.

'Let him be, boy! He's touched by the curse!' one
of them warned.

'He's possessed! Got the evil of the north in him!'
another squealed.

'You bastards! You ignorant fools!' Karl shouted.
'It's just a seizure! Caused by his wound! Gods,
we're men of the Empire! We're supposed to be
civilised! Help me, you superstitious fools!'

Only Brezzin moved to help him. 'Make sure he
doesn't bite his tongue,' the bulky gunner said,
cradling von Margur securely in his powerful arms.

After a minute, the knight's body went limp and
he stopped spasming. Brezzin released him gently,
and von Margur abruptly sat up, bent over and
spewed noxious black bile onto the bodies that
formed the floor of the cage. Then he fell into a
slumber.

'I thank Sigmar you didn't share the opinion of
this ignorant rabble,' Karl said to the gunner.

'What, that he was possessed?'

Karl nodded.

'I do,' said Brezzin. 'But you needed help.'

VI

AN HOUR AFTER von Margur's seizure, the Kurgans
came en masse to the cages. There was great

excitement. Horns blew, drums thundered, dogs barked, and men laughed and shouted in the coarse dialects of the North.

The prisoners waited in apprehensive silence inside the cage rings.

A thicket of Northers closed around the cage Karl was in. They peered in, shouting taunts and poking with the tips of boar-spears. The prisoners pressed tightly together, watching the black visored faces that circled outside. Karl saw the brute he knew as Ons Olker amongst them, his asymmetrical horns distinct in the crowd.

Hooves thundered, and the Kurgan parted to let a rider through. It was Karl's nemesis, the great warrior with the wolf-face helm.

He dismounted and strode towards the cage. He still wore the bearskin and black leggings and boots, but his skin was clean and oiled to a sheen. He slapped his forearms together, making the warrior rings wrapped around them chime. This provoked a throaty shout from the Kurgan all around. Then he raised his hands and lifted the black wolf-helm off his head by the jutting horns.

His face was nothing like Karl had imagined. It was shaved clean of beard, head hair and even eyebrows. Ancient ritual scars ran in wide furrows diagonally down his cheeks, five on one side and two on the other. His eyes were bright and hard like diamonds. He was astonishingly beautiful in a feral way – handsome like a sire wolf is handsome.

He tossed the wolf-helm to one of the Kurgan and wiped his palms over his smooth, oiled scalp. 'Bring them out,' he ordered.

The Kurgan moved forward and shook the pike shafts out of the earth, pulling the linking chains down. Then with sticks and boar-spears, they herded the prisoners out of the open cage. A miserable, jumbled raft of bodies was left behind them.

Brezzin and Karl were supporting von Margur between them. Several of their fellow prisoners were sobbing and pleading. The Kurgan jostled round them, pushing in to slap and cuff the captives, pawing at them and toying with them, laughing out loud. One man fell on his knees at the feet of the wolf-face and began begging for mercy.

The wolf-face kicked him in the mouth.

'Tri-horn!' von Margur said suddenly, waking up with a start. Brezzin and Karl both looked at him in confusion. A hand grabbed at Karl's arm and he turned to look straight into the three horned bull-mask of Ons Olker. The squat, naked brute had pushed right into the press to reach him. He had one of his daggers out.

The wolf-face moved, knocking prisoners out of his way, and punched Ons Olker in the chest before he could stab Karl. Ons Olker fell, whining. Captives and Kurgan alike spread back to give them room.

The wolf-face slapped down another blow, connecting across Ons Olker's helmet with the mass of warrior rings around his forearm. The blow bent one of the horns that was already twisted.

Ons Olker whimpered like a dog. His beads rattled.

'What do you, Olker? What games do you play?' the huge wolf-face demanded.

'He owes me, zar! I have blood-tied him for he did me offence! I claim his soul!'

'Your blood-tie is meaningless. He already wears my mark, Olker. You must claim him from me, not strike behind my back.'

'I claim his soul!' the smaller man wailed.

The wolf-face kicked at him. 'Be off, dung-eater! Zar Blayda may prize you for your sight, but I do not. You are a runt and a dung-eater. Be off until your eyes peel back far enough for you to see something useful!'

Ons Olker hissed at the massive warrior, and made some warding sign with twisted fingers. He shook his bone beads.

'Damn thy charms! My shaman has already blessed me!' the wolf-face bellowed after him.

Ons Olker hooked his fingers under the rim of his bull-mask and lifted it back far enough to expose a ragged whiskered mouth of broken, brown teeth. He spat at the wolf-face.

'Curse thee, Zar Uldin! Thou owest me a soul!'

The wolf-face – Uldin – looked aside at one of his men. 'Fetch my pallasz here to me,' he said.

At that, Ons Olker turned and fled.

Zar Uldin slowly turned back and stared at Karl. His eyes were as bright and frosty as the moon that had glared at them the night before. 'You have cost me, little Southlander. This–' he touched the still-raw gash on his shoulder that Karl's sabre had dug during the fight at the zal. 'And now the curses of a war shaman. I think you may be too dangerous to keep alive.'

'You cost me my horse,' Karl said bluntly.

Zar Uldin's eyes narrowed. Then he laughed. 'You won't be needing a horse now.'

He walked away, dishing out orders to the Kurgan.

The prisoners were led up from the pasture onto the wide meadow where the battle had raged. The Kurgan herded them over to one of the great bonfires that had been burning the previous night. It was a steep stack of charred timber and ash – dry-white and smoking in the cold dawn. Karl could see that the prisoners from other cage pens were being led up to the other bonfire heaps. There was an odd smell in the air – it was smoke, but with a hanging odour like cooked meat.

Goading with boar-spears, the Kurgan forced the captives to dig in the ashes. The fire heap was still baking hot and searing to touch, and as they scooped ash-powder away with their bare hands they exposed pockets of furnace heat. In a few moments, their hands were scorched and blistered from glowing charcoal logs and glowing coals.

'What the hell are we doing?' one of the prisoners asked.

Karl scraped away at the hot ash with raw fingers and then discovered the answer. Several others made the same discovery simultaneously and cried out in horror.

They were digging up skulls. Skulls that had been burned clean. Skulls that had had the flesh roasted off them. Skulls that were chalky-white with ash and throbbed with internal heat. When they pulled them out, hot dregs of fluid dribbled out of them.

That was what the great fires had been for, to prepare the skulls of the vanquished for Kurgan victory heaps. The task of digging them out was another humiliating indignity for the captives to suffer.

VII

LAUGHING AND SHOUTING, the Kurgan made the prisoners dig up the skulls and stack them beside the fire. They made a loose heap of dusty white bone that clacked and knocked together. Some of the captives retched as they were forced to work, and one man refused. The Kurgan beat him and then stabbed him with their spears, and left him for the crows.

Zar Uldin reappeared, and some of the Kurgan began to carry the recovered skulls from the heap over to him. Patiently, like a child with building blocks, he began to stack them. His shaman was with him: a little, stunted man, wizened and as naked as Ons Olker. He wore an iron barbute with a snake inscribed around the crown, and chanted as he capered round the zar, shaking bead rattles and strings of shells and finger bones. He had marked symbols on his naked flesh with white ash from the bonfire.

Zar Uldin followed the barking instructions of his shaman carefully. He placed the first skulls in a square, thirteen to each side, all looking out, and the shaman made sure the square was aligned with one corner pointing north. Karl wasn't quite sure how he did this, though the shaman seemed to have a lightning stone and an iron needle.

Then Uldin began to stack the skulls the Kurgan brought to him inside the square, raising a pyramid. He chanted words Karl couldn't hear as he did so. The shaman hopped around him, rattling and singing all the while, and never letting his left foot touch the ground.

By then, all the captives were gut-sick and caked up to their elbows in chalk-white ash. Many were crying.

The pyramid rose. The shaman hopped and jangled his rattles and strings.

Karl pawed free another skull from the ash and dared to look about him. At every bonfire around the battlefield, the scene was repeated. Under guard from Northers, the captives were exhuming skulls from the char of each fire, and zars were building heaps with them as their shaman danced. A hundred paces away, at the nearest bonfire, Karl could see Zar Blayda in his etched black armour building a pyramid of death while Ons Olker capered around him.

Uldin's pyramid was almost complete. It was clear that the stack was built on mathematical principles. A specific number of skulls was needed to complete it.

'Three more!' Uldin demanded.

The captives had broken down the whole bonfire pile, sweating in the steam and smoulder. They dredged up two more skulls. Kurgan hurried the discoveries over to Uldin.

'Another!' he cried.

A man in the ragged uniform vestiges of a Nordland arquebusier uniform dug out the final skull. He seemed pathetically delighted to have pleased the zar so much. Uldin walked over to him, took the hot skull out of his grip, and led him by the hand over to the skull stack.

Uldin placed the final skull onto the pinnacle of the heap. Uldin's shaman whooped and yelled. The bone-white slopes of the pyramid seemed to gleam in the dank light. The eye sockets were like windows in the slopes.

All the captives stood, sombrely, and watched as the last skull clinked into place. A cold wind rose from the west and gusted white dust across the wet field.

Zar Uldin looked down at the shivering arquebusier from Nordland who had dug up the last skull and smiled in an almost friendly, reassuring way, as if the man had done him some great service.

Then Uldin took a flint knife from his shaman, grabbed the Nordlander and slit his throat.

The man was still wailing and choking and gagging as Uldin held him up over the skull heap and washed it with his hot blood.

Disgusted, Karl looked away. Some of the captives sank to their knees in woe.

Uldin threw the corpse aside and turned to his dancing shaman. He handed back the blood-wet flint knife.

Uttering some barbaric enchantment, the shaman took the knife and cut a slash down Uldin's cheek. Now he had five on one side, and three on the other. Uldin raised his massive arms and howled up into the sky.

Thunder rolled. The gods, Karl thought alarmingly, were listening. Vile gods he didn't have a name for.

The Kurgan led the captives back to the stinking pasture and caged them up again. Karl hadn't been able to count the skull heaps on the field.

VIII

IN THE NIGHT that followed, von Margur suffered another fit. When he woke up, clamped in the arms of Brezzin and Karl, he said something that sounded like 'kill me'.

'I cannot kill you, sir. I will not,' said Karl.

Von Margur shook his head. His eyes rolled slack and he smiled through the froth covering his mouth.

'No, Karl. I said… you will kill me. And you will kill Uldin. But not before you have marked the fifth scratch on his cheek.'

Then he fell asleep.

Karl Vollen hoped he would not wake up.

NORSCYA

I

FOR TWO FULL days following the slaughter at Zhedevka, the rota of Kislevite lancers rode east, and
Gerlach Heileman went with them.

The oblast east of Zhedevka was an uninhabited
hinterland of tangled forest and mud-flats where
the great open steppes of Kislev slumped down to
meet the natural barrier of the River Lynsk. The forest tracts were deep-shadowed wilds of maple, yew
and elderly poplar where spring growth was beginning to bud. Tiny, smoke-blue flowers grew in
profusion through the ground cover, forming drifts
like blue snow. Songbirds haunted the glades, and
there was a scent of rain and balsam in the air. Every
few leagues, the forest would break open and reveal
stretches of black clay that glistened in the pale

spring light. Here, the spring melt-waters had driven the Lynsk up into its flood plains. The rota crossed the mud flats in single file, a line of blurry reflections spreading out away from them on the waterlogged clay.

The lancers rode in silence, following their lank banner. They did not stop, not even once.

By day, they moved at a steady trot, by night a slow plod. Some of the men slept upright in their saddles, heads nodding, but their horses moved on, following the group.

The nights were cold and fathomlessly black. The lancers lit no lamps or tapers. Between flurries of rain, the twin moons glared at them, fuming with radiant white light. Screech-owls mocked them. Thunder occasionally grumbled.

The days seemed even harsher. Rain fell frequently and hard, raising thin mists and streaming down through the dark boughs of the forest. In the open, on the mud flats, the rain came raw, and the ground clay, covered as it was with standing water, became indistinct in the splashing of the torrent. There was seldom any sun, just a white haze of backlit vapour. Very occasionally, something pale yellow and luminous tried to swirl out of the overcast cloud, but it never succeeded. They saw herons and waders, and once, from a great distance, a brown wolf trotting down the foreshore.

Three or four lancers lagged back behind the main group permanently, watching for pursuit. Every few hours, riders from the column would swing back and relieve them. Late on the first day, the outriders bolted forward, and the rota picked up its speed for a few leagues, racing wide across a clay floodplain and into another reach of forest. But no enemy appeared.

On the third day, Beledni turned them north.

II

DEMIETER CAME WITH them. The Kislevites had wound his body in a ground sheet and lashed it over the saddle of his troop horse. Gerlach insisted on leading it, tying Demieter's reins to his cantle.

No one spoke to the vexillary, and he spoke to no one. He had nothing in him left to say. He rode, hunched and exhausted, limp in the saddle, vaguely aware of the growing lameness in Saksen's gait. Hunger gnawed at him and his bruised body ached.

When the rota turned north on the third day, it raised its pace. Gerlach realised he was slowly being left behind. He decided he didn't really care. The change of route and pace seemed to alter the demeanour of the lancers. He could hear them now chatting to each other, laughing occasionally. He wanted them to go on and leave him. He didn't want to be around them any more.

Two lancers rode back down the file to join him. They fell in either side of him, and made smiles and gestures that indicated they wanted him to catch up.

'Go on. Leave me,' he said.

The riders looked at each other, not sure what he meant.

'Go on!' Gerlach gestured wearily.

'We go on but you go on,' said one. He was a tall man with a greying top knot and deep-set eyes. His mouth was wide and full of small, evenly-spaced teeth. The tall, curved wooden frames of the wings rising from his hauberk's back were thick with hawk feathers.

'Just go,' snapped Gerlach.

'Rotamaster sayt with you come. With you come. With...' the lancer faltered. 'How it you sayt?'

Gerlach sighed.

'Is you of come to now with his!' prompted the other suddenly. He was a smaller man, just a youth really, with a wispy moustache and very blue eyes. The bright feathers of a jay interlaced between the heron quills on his wing frame.

He looked eagerly at his comrade, apparently proud of his linguistic skill. 'Eyh? Eyh?'

'Is you of come to now with his!' repeated the tall man with an enthusiastic nod. 'Is you of come to now with his!'

'Eyh?' said the boy again, pleased with himself. He looked at Gerlach. 'I tongue good you!'

'I don't think so,' Gerlach murmured.

'Eyh?'

'I said... never mind.'

'Shto?'

The older lancer looked solemn. He indicated the boy. When he spoke, a great deal of deliberation went into the choice of every word. 'Vaja is boy who... ummm... speaking most... ummmm... good word for his mouth. Is in your... ummm... ear for good also?'

The boy – Vaja – quickly hissed across at his comrade, correcting him. 'Ah!' said the older man. 'Vaja, his tongue is in your ear.'

'Eyh?' urged the boy.

Gerlach looked at him. 'It's very good. Good word.'

'You understand! Is good thing!' Vaja looked delighted, and the older man beamed like a proud parent. 'Is many time I read book. Same book. Many reads time. Is book. Oh! Is book again. So I learn.'

'Very good,' said Gerlach. He was so weary. He wondered what Vaja's book-learning would understand of the words 'get lost'.

The boy leaned over towards Gerlach. 'Vitali him. Vitali no good learn.'

Vitali looked hurt. 'Vitali speak little good,' he insisted plaintively.

The boy began to scold Vitali good-naturedly in Kislevite. They bantered back and forth. The main column had almost disappeared ahead, lost in the trees. Gerlach wished he could get them to leave him alone.

They shut up suddenly, simultaneously, and both looked over their shoulders. Behind them, the forest trail went quiet.

'Norscya,' hissed Vitali, and Gerlach needed no gloss to understand that word.

Vitali gave the boy instructions quickly and turned his horse round. He slid a javelin from his saddle boot and rested it on his shoulder, tip down.

'Yatsha!' he snarled and galloped away back down the track.

Vaja leaned forward and tried to grab Gerlach's reins. Gerlach waved him off.

'We have go! Ride!' Vaja gabbled.

Gerlach looked back. Vitali had vanished.

'We have go!' Vaja repeated.

'Oh, all right!' Gerlach replied, spurring Saksen up after the boy's cantering mare. Demieter's troop horse trailed heavily behind Gerlach.

They continued up the wet trail for a minute or so. Vaja kept looking backwards. He was agitated. There was still no sign of the company's tail-end ahead of them.

'Have you got a bugle?' Gerlach whispered.

'Shto?'

'A bugle? A horn?'

'Hawn?'

Gerlach mimed putting a bugle to his lips and blowing. Vaja nodded, and dutifully offered Gerlach his water skin.

'Sigmar spare me, no. We should warn the company. Warn the rota.'

'Rota...?'

'Warn them!' Gerlach barked. He untied the reins of Demieter's horse, and handed them to the boy. Then he pointed up the trail.

'Go tell rota. Tell Beledni.'

Vaja looked doubtful, so Gerlach smacked the rump of his mare and made him start forward. The young lancer slowly rode away up the narrow track, looking back.

Gerlach drew his sabre, and wheeled Saksen around.

III

HE RETRACED HIS route, looking for signs of Vitali. The forest had become ominously quiet. Mist drifted like campfire smoke through the bracken, and rain-water shone like diamonds on the bark of yew and larch trees. Gerlach jumped at a sound, but it was only a woodpecker drumming in the timbers nearby.

He followed the trail down into a dell where a wide pool had formed between exposed tree roots. The water was black and still, and avalanches of ivy cascaded down the clay banks and sagging trees.

Then he heard the noise. Shouting voices. Metal impacts.

Ducking under the low boughs, he spurred Saksen on, along the edge of the pool, into the sunken glade beyond.

Vitali had found the Norscya.

There were eight of them. Six ugly men on foot and two on black horses. All of them were wearing iron scale armour and horned barbutes darkened with pitch. They had surrounded Vitali, who was in the middle of a shallow stream, turning his mare in a circle and kicking up water.

There had been nine. One lay on a bank, half in the water, a javelin embedded in his chest.

The Norscya were tightening their circle around the lancer, jabbing with boar-spears and spade-tipped foot lances. One had a morning star that he was whirling in vicious, expert arcs.

Vitali had his second javelin out and raised overarm, shouting defiantly at the enemy, turning to face each aggressor that took his chance to lunge closer.

One of the riders was a partially armoured, barechested Kurgan with a sword. His helmet spikes rose high and straight, like a southerland buffalo. The other was altogether more impressive. He wore a long coat of blackened scale mail, and every single scale plate was finished with a thorny spike. His cloak was made of wolf pelts, half sewn together so they straggled around him, grey and white. His head was encased in a close-helm with a hinged visor that must have been made in an Empire smithy and taken as a trophy. It had been daubed black, and curling horns had been forged onto it. They were coiled around each other like snakes, the ends of each an open wyrm mouth. He was the leader, Gerlach knew that at once.

The snake-horned leader couched a long horse lance under his arm. It was three spans long and its black shaft was wrapped with strips of gold foil. He clearly intended to take this kill, once his men had corralled Vitali tight.

Gerlach sheathed his sabre and drew his one remaining pistol. He'd primed and loaded it the day before, and now he laid its dog and drove Saksen into the charge.

'Karl Franz!' he bellowed.

The Kurgan turned in surprise, seeing the tattered demilancer bearing down on them along the stream bed, sheeting spray up from his hooves.

The leader first, Gerlach thought. He aimed and fired.

The wheel-lock cracked, and smoke hissed out of it.

There was a distinct thtang! as the ball struck the snake-horned leader. He cried out, and was knocked out of his saddle so hard his horse came down with him. The horse lance in his hand splintered under the writhing steed.

Gerlach was two horse lengths from the nearest Kurgan foot soldier, the brute with the ball-and-chain mace. He slammed home his spent pistol and scythed out his sabre, chopping down hard with the edge and ramming the Kurgan into the overhanging ivy.

The others rushed him. Gerlach reared Saksen up, and drove its milling fore hooves at the first of them. Then, as his gelding dropped level again, he stabbed down, straight, with the point, and cut through the shoulder of another.

Vitali cried out, exuberantly galvanised by the sudden change in fortunes. He unleashed his javelin, and brought down one of the Norscya holding a boar-spear. Then he drew his Kislevite sabre, a curved sword with a beautiful slender blade and simple cross guard, and laid about himself.

They had now reached an impasse. Gerlach and Vitali had the edge of surprise and horse power between them, and were pushing the enemy group back. But the Kurgan had the reach of boar-spears and were growling and barking as they kept the horses at bay.

The remaining Norscya rider came up, broadsword swinging, and Vitali turned to meet him. The lancer's slender sabre would surely break at once under the weight of the Kurgan's heavy, straight blade.

Vitali was nimble. It was pleasing to watch. He ducked under the striking sword, came back up, and struck to the rear. The edge of his curved sword sliced into the back of the rider's neck, under the lip of his barbute. The Norther's horse carried him away into the misty woods, the man's body lolling from side to side in the saddle.

A horn blew, close and sharp in the forest confines.

Eight winged lancers, led by Vaja and Beledni, came cantering into the glade, kicking water in all directions. They had javelins in their hands as they drew up in a line beside Vitali and Gerlach. The remaining Kurgan, all on foot, backed away around the bole of an ancient oak, threatening with their boar-spears.

'Yhta!' Beledni ordered from behind his heart-shaped visor.

The lancers threw their weapons.

The cornered Norscya died, most of them pinned to the tree bole and roots by the narrow lances.

'I warn rota!' Vaja announced proudly to Gerlach.

Gerlach acknowledged this with a grunt. Vitali splashed his mare up alongside Gerlach and held out his hand. Gerlach took it. The lancer smiled and nodded. He said nothing, because he knew he didn't have the vocabulary, but the meaning was clear.

'Rotamaster!' one of the lancers cried out.

Gerlach turned.

The snake-horned leader was rising to his feet. He was spattered in clay, and his scale armour coat showed a dent where Gerlach's firearm had struck it. Gerlach wheeled his gelding round.

'Nyeh!' Beledni called out, holding off a hand sideways to block Gerlach.

He looked round at the demilancer and shook his head.

'Nyeh. Savat nyor Norscya gylyve,' he said, but Gerlach had no clue as to his meaning.

Beledni dismounted.

The lancers drew back, leading Beledni's scraggy mare with them.

The Kurgan leader had produced a long, double-edged pallasz, and stood his ground on the far bank, defiantly.

Beledni took off the slim Kislevite sabre he wore around his waist and handed it to Vaja. Patting his horse around, he reached to the saddle and slipped out the long, straight length of a shashka. Gerlach saw now that most of the lancers carried a slim, curved sabre at their belt, and a long, straight sword in a scabbard about their saddles. A saddle weapon for use when horse warfare was done; a weapon to draw on foot. Beledni's shashka was every bit as long as the Kurgan's pallasz. It had a wide, straight pair of quillons, and a looped iron bar that curled back to the pommel to surround the owner's hand. The pallasz was triple-fullered right down its length, and had an ornate cage of curled bars guarding the user's fist.

Rotamaster Beledni splashed across the stream bed, dark mud spattering up around the shins of his knee boots. He held his shashka upright, with his right hand, his left around the pommel.

The Kurgan warlord was waiting for him on the far bank, sword down. Beledni was big and squat, but his enemy was wider and far taller. Gerlach sensed that a much larger, fitter man than the rotamaster lurked inside the thorny black plate. He tensed. There was clearly some ritual honour thing going on. Leader to leader. Maybe even something that he had provoked himself by failing to kill the Kurgan lord cleanly, or simply by dint of him just being there. Beledni seemed to think he owed Gerlach for salvaging the rota's banner. Maybe this unwise single combat was Beledni's way of making things even.

The lancers seemed content to watch. Gerlach began re-priming his pistol. He would not have the rotamaster's death on his conscience too.

There was a resounding clang. Gerlach looked up from his wheel-lock. Beledni and the snake-horned leader had begun. Straight sword against straight sword. They circled, exchanging cuts, causing sparks.

It was over very fast.

The Kurgan hammered a good slice at Beledni, and the Kislevite parried, tossing the cut aside and opening his adversary's guard. Beledni put both arms into the next swing.

Gerlach knew it was going to be a deathblow. What he hadn't counted on was the force that old Beledni could muster. The shashka tore through the neck of the close helm, popping out rivets as the plates deformed. He sliced the entire skull away. Like a cannonball, the skull, encased in articulated metal capped by the twined snake horns, flew off into the bracken.

The headless Kurgan collapsed like a felled tree and made a sound like a dozen dropped cymbals.

'Gospodarinyi! Gospodarinyi!' Beledni shouted, raising both arms and shaking his bloodied shashka. He turned to face his cheering men.

'Gospodarinyi!'

IV

WHEN THE MEN had stopped whooping and slapping him on the back, Beledni issued a curt order for them to return to the rota. The lancers recovered their javelins, washing the sticky tips and hafts in the stream, but made no effort to touch or move the enemy dead. They seemed to shun them, in fact. There was no searching the bodies for trophies or coins or rings. Men of the Empire would have at least thrown the dead into a ditch or gully or, if circumstance permitted, burned them. But the Kislevites just left them to bloat and wither and decay in the glade.

But then, just before they rode away, Beledni and Vitali went to the corpses one by one and put out their eyes with their dagger tips. Beledni had to search in the bracken to find the head he had taken off to do the same to it.

It occurred to Gerlach Heileman this was a strangely bestial thing to do.

They rode up the file to find the body of the rota. Gerlach rode behind Beledni, who was chatting in a low voice to the tall, thin lancer with the scar on his high cheekbone. This man's name, Gerlach gathered, was Maksim, and he was one of Beledni's most senior, trusted men.

They were discussing the Northers – Gerlach overheard the word 'Norscya' several times.

'There are more around?' he asked interrupting.

'Shto?' They glanced back at him.

'More Northeranders? Norscya?'

Maksim seemed amused by Gerlach's badly accented use of the Kislevite word.

'Nyeh,' Beledni said with a shake of his head. 'Not so much, I think.'

'What about those we faced back there? They must have been following us for days.'

'Nyeh, Vebla, nyeh,' Beledni assured him. 'For day, maybe, not long more. Norscya pulk go on horse, many men, south. Rich lands there.'

Indeed. The more civilised provinces of Kislev. The Empire. Beledni seemed to suppose that the Kurgan were so intent on the south that they wouldn't waste men or time pursuing a small company like the rota east.

'But what about the ones back there?' Gerlach insisted.

'Kyazak,' said Maksim.

'What?'

'Raiders,' said Maksim, turning his attention back to the trail ahead as if his word explained everything.

The rest of the rota was waiting for them on the saddle of a grassy hill above the forest line. One lancer had Demieter's horse in tow.

The daylight was beginning to fade. When they crested the hill, Gerlach saw a great plain stretching out before them. An unbroken territory of grass, gorse and thistle that rolled away towards a far-off line of dim hills. The steppe grasslands of the mighty oblast.

Beledni circled his hand. They would rest here for the night before starting off across the steppe.

Gerlach dismounted and sat down in the grass. He knew he should see to Saksen, ease the gelding's saddle, rub him down. But he felt very weak suddenly. In less than a minute, he was asleep.

V

WHEN HE WOKE, it was dark and warm. Night had fallen, glass-clear, and in the sky above the hillside, a multitude of stars glittered. Someone shook his shoulder gently, and he realised that was what had woken him.

He sat up. He was lying precisely where he had sat down. Someone had thrown a cloak over him. A large fire was crackling not too far away, and it threw out a pleasant heat. Around its jumping glow, Gerlach could see the figures of men, and what seemed to be small tents.

Vitali was crouched down next to him. He had removed his helmet, hauberk and wings, and was wearing a shabby velvet coat with cut-out sleeves that he'd thrown back over his shoulders to expose arms clad in a wool undershirt. He was offering a little wooden bowl to the vexillary. Steam rose from it. The smell of hot food made Gerlach's mouth flood with saliva and his belly ache and churn.

He took the bowl. In it were some lumps of meat mixed with stewed grains in an oily wet hash. It smelled amazingly good.

Vitali beckoned him to join the figures at the fire.

'You come, Vebla. You come to krug.'

Gerlach carried the bowl over to the ring of figures round the fire. The heat was quite intense on his face, and the smoke from the wood and spitted meat was thick. He sat down, with Vitali on his right. To his left was a thickset man in his thirties, who was already eating from a bowl with his bare fingers.

Gerlach started to scoop and eat. He had no idea what meat it was, but it was delicious. He realised he had been days without food. He was quickly wiping the empty bowl with his oily fingertips. His lips shone with grease.

There was a low conversation going on round the fire. All the men had removed their armour and put on coats and furs, so that they once more resembled the ragged barbarians he had first seen. All of them were eating. Cook pots and spitted haunches of meat were standing around the edges of the fire.

The man on his left, who had also emptied his bowl, took Gerlach over to the fireside and showed him how they could fill their bowls for more.

The meat was fresh. Hare or perhaps some small buck. Some of the men had evidently been busy as they rode through the forest, taking game and gathering wood. Near the fire, one of the Kislevites was splitting boughs with a small hand-axe. He took wood from the heap piled up to feed the flames.

Gerlach resumed his place in the circle and gobbled down his second bowlful. As he ate, he watched the sparks fly up. Invisible heat rippled in the cold air above the camp, distorting some of the stars.

By the time he had finished the second bowl, he felt tired. He sat back, uncomfortable and hot, and so stripped off his half-armour piece by piece, piling it up behind his back. He settled against it, feeling every ache and bruise and cut and graze on his weary body soothed by the heat and the warmth of food in his gut.

Drinking skins were passing around the krug circle. The men were swigging and handing them on to the man on their right. The heavy man took a deep drink, smacked his lips and pushed the skin to Gerlach.

'Starovye!' he said.

Gerlach thought for a moment that it was the man's name, but realised it was a toast or hail. He took the skin, raised it to the man and said, 'Health to you!'

'Starovye!' the man repeated.

'Starovye,' Gerlach agreed, and took a drink.

It was sweet and thick, with a sour taste of old, tepid milk, but it was strong and he felt its burn immediately.

'It's good,' Gerlach nodded.

'Yha. Koumiss,' the man replied. 'Koumiss, good for soul.'

Gerlach handed the skin to Vitali.

'Health to–' he began, then corrected himself. 'Starovye.'

'Starovye, Vebla!' Vitali returned with a broad smile full of his small, even teeth. He added something more in Kislevite, but Gerlach didn't understand.

'Vitali,' Vitali said, more slowly, pointing to himself. 'Vebla,' he pointed to Gerlach. 'Do war good together. Do war on kyazak.' He took a drink and passed the koumiss on.

'My name is Gerlach Heileman,' Gerlach said.

'Shto?'

Gerlach patted his own chest. 'Gerlach.'

'Shto? Nyeh Vebla?'

'No. Nyeh. Gerlach.'

Vitali pouted thoughtfully as he considered this, then shrugged.

'What does "kyazak" mean?' Gerlach asked.

'Kyazak, yha!' Vitali said, waiting for more.

'What does it mean?'

'Shto?'

'What does "kyazak" mean?'

Vitali looked helpless.

'Uh… shto kyazak?' Gerlach tried.

'Ah! Is… is… ummm…' Vitali screwed up his face. He looked past Gerlach at the thickset man.

'Mitri!' he called, then asked something in Kislevite. Gerlach caught the words 'kyazak' and 'impyrinyi'.

Mitri thought about it. 'Means… raider,' he said, his voice gruff and deep.

'They're all raiders,' Gerlach said. 'All Norscya… raiders.'

'Nyeh,' said Mitri. 'Raiders… kyazak… small numbers. Hunt for own. Not part of Norscya pulk.'

He explained some more. Gerlach realised that 'kyazak' had a specific meaning that 'raiders' did not convey. The kyazak were reavers, freebooting bands who moved at the edges of the main host, raiding for spoils. He'd never thought about it before, even though men of the Empire talked of the Northern tribes. The North wasn't one unified place, and the Northers were not a single race. They migrated south en masse, but only because they shared a common hunger for land and loot. They had no formal military organisation like the Empire. This made it all the more extraordinary that they could operate as a unified host, as they had at Zhedevka.

What alloyed them into one mass, Gerlach wondered, what dread force?

Muzzy now, and half asleep, he reclined by the fire and watched the activity around the ring. Some men were repairing helms or hauberks, using the pommels of their daggers as hammers. Others were adjusting and dressing the feathers that attached to their wood-frame wings. Two men were singing a long, slow song of strange, entwined harmonies. The skins of koumiss circled the ring.

Gerlach suddenly remembered his horse and sprang up. He was unsteady on his feet for a moment. The drink had either been stronger than he had thought, or it had taken a firm hold on his weak, empty system.

'Vebla?' Vitali called after him.

Gerlach walked away from the fire. It was dark, and much colder away from the flames. He'd stripped off his armour and mail shirt, and now his linen undershirt and felt coat clung cold and wet to his clammy body.

The lancers had pitched tents around the fire. As he walked amongst them, he saw they were simple structures. Each man had made a tripod out of his lance and two javelins, and artfully hooked his cloak or saddle blanket over it. He could hear the horses, and smell them, but the cold clear darkness was absolute.

'Vebla?' Vitali approached, carrying a bough that he'd lit from the fire.

'My horse,' Gerlach said. 'I didn't see to it. And it was running lame...'

Vitali shrugged.

'My horse?'

Vitali took him by the sleeve and led him down a slope. The horses had been corralled in a ring of gorse, though only Saksen and Demieter's mount had been tied up. The steppe horses grazed together obediently.

There was a light amongst the horses. As they came closer, they saw it was a little tallow lamp.

Gerlach could see two lancers from the company, stripped to the waist and sweating from their exertions, rubbing down the horses with handfuls of grass. An older man, in a long beshmet tunic, stooped in the lamp light, fixing a mare's shoe with deft taps of a small steel hammer.

'Borodyn!' Vitali hissed.

The man finished the job and carried his weak lamp over. It was a little pottery dish with a wick.

Vitali explained something to the man in Kislevite.

He raised his lamp to study Gerlach. Borodyn's own face was old and weather-beaten.

He took Gerlach to Saksen. The gelding, and Demieter's troop horse, had been unharnessed and rubbed down. Borodyn lifted Saksen's forefoot and showed Gerlach where he had reshod the lame foot, and applied salve to the sore hoof.

While Gerlach had slept, his horse had been cared for like one of the Kislevites' own.

'Borodyn, he master horse,' Vitali said.

'My comrade Vitali means "horse master",' said Borodyn. 'It is my honour to hold that noble post, and be master of metal also for the rota.' His accent was thick, but he spoke Gerlach's native tongue very well.

Both Vitali and Borodyn saw the look of surprise on Gerlach's face. Vitali laughed.

'Borodyn has learning much!' he chuckled.

'Go back to the krug, man of the Empire,' said Borodyn softly. 'You need as much rest as Saksen.'

Gerlach nodded, and allowed himself to be drawn back up the slope by Vitali.

He stopped suddenly, and looked back.

'How did you know my horse's name?' he called out.

But Borodyn had gone back to his work and did not reply.

* * *

VI

BY THE TIME they had returned to the heat of the fire, the lancers had become more lively. Drink was still circulating, and the songs were faster and more robust. Several men were singing now, and one was accompanying them on a small wooden instrument like a shrunken lute. His fingers flashed as they plucked a rapid melody, and the instrument's strings gave out a hard, brittle chime. Two men were beating time on upturned cook pots. A few were dancing around the fire in circles and clapping.

Gerlach and Vitali sat back down, and Vaja joined them, with another young lancer called Kvetlai. They drank some more koumiss as it came by. Gerlach was feeling profoundly warm and sleepy.

'What are they singing?' he asked.

Between themselves, hoping to make the maximum amount of sense through a joint effort, Vitali and Vaja endeavoured to explain. They took a few words each, back and forth, comically repeating each other and overlapping. Vitali's command of Gerlach's language was far better than he realised. Young Vaja's, who kept correcting Vitali, was far, far worse than he believed. Kvetlai, who knew no Reikspiel at all, sat and watched.

The men, they explained, were giving thanks to the gods. To Ursun, the Bear Father, for protection. To Dazh, for the fire. To Tor, for victory.

Gerlach began to doze. Breathing deeply, he asked another question. 'The kyazaks. Why did you take their eyes?'

It took Vitali and Vaja a while to make sense of this. Then Vitali replied.

'Is to blind them, yha?'

'But they were dead.'

'Nyeh. Not spirits of men. Spirits will come. Angry. Looking here, looking there, looking everywhere to find men who kill them. Vitali want it to be hard thing for spirits to find him, yha?'

Gerlach laughed, and despite the heat of the flames, he shivered and touched the iron of his belt buckle as a charm.

VII

THE SPIRITS CAME for him late in the night. They came out of the forest like smoke, oozing between the black trunks, hissing the leaves. They boiled as vapour up the slope of the hill, and their passing distressed the horses in the corral.

The camp was asleep, but the fire still blazed high. Gerlach stood and watched the ghosts foam through the darkness towards him. They left frost on the grass in their tracks. They were moaning like a distant wind, groping with filmy white hands to find him, their eyes bloody holes in their white, drawn faces.

Gerlach wondered how he could fight them. His sword would not cut what was not there.

They loomed around him, a silver mist in the form of lean figures. They chided him, in sibilant whispers, for leaving them dead on the blood-stained ground.

He looked at their faces: the open mouths, the voided eye sockets, the sunken cheeks.

He knew them.

Meinhart Stouer, Sebold Truchs, Johann Friedel, Herman Volks, Hans Odamar, Karl Reiner Vollen...

VIII

HE WOKE WITH a start, cold with sweat. He was on the grass of the hill slope. The fire had died off to a meagre flicker. Men slumbered all around.

It was deathly cold. In the east, the first glimmer of dawn was stretching over the sky.

Gerlach tugged his cloak around him and tried to find sleep again.

IX

A BONE HORN was blowing a long, hard note. Gerlach stirred, and hearing it a second time, staggered to his feet. It was daylight. The fire was out and kicked over. Even the charred bones of the night's supper had gone. The tents had disappeared. He was alone by the circle of ash.

The horn wailed again. Presuming an attack, he gathered up his armour and stumbled towards the brow of the hill.

The rota had assembled on the steppe below. They stood by their horses, dressed in their furs and rags, their armour packed in bundles on the backs of their wooden saddles. The horn blower was astride his mare, head tilted back, blowing long notes into the early morning air. The eagle wing banner fluttered in the light wind off the steppes.

Beyond the rota, the sun was rising above the grassland. The sky was a diluted red, like blood in water, and the swaying grasses had turned russet and pink in the new light. Everything was still except the twitch of horse tails, the flutter of the banner and the waving motion of the endless grass. On the horizon, the distant hills were a jagged purple stripe.

Gerlach ran down the slope, stopping frequently to gather up the pieces of armour he dropped. Beledni saw him, and turned to beckon him close.

'What is this?' Gerlach asked.

'Is sunrise. Is time for goings,' said the rotamaster.

'Why didn't you wake me?' Gerlach asked, angry. Beledni shrugged. The bone horn blew again, saluting the low sun.

'We say farewell,' Beledni said.

'What? Why? Where are you going?'

Beledni shook his head and then smiled sadly and pointed. At the front of the assembled rota, Demieter's shroud-wrapped body lay over his horse's saddle.

'You say farewell, Vebla?' Beledni asked.

'What do you mean? I don't understand...'

'What his name?' Beledni asked, pointing to Demieter's corpse again.

'Kaus Demieter... but...'

Beledni raised his head and shouted out a brief but heartfelt declaration in Kislevite. The name 'Kaus Demieter' appeared amongst the alien words.

Beledni finished. The horn blew once more. Maksim smacked his hand across the rump of Demieter's gelding, and the horse took off, galloping into the grassland, the swathed body over its saddle bouncing and jerking with the motion.

'No!' Gerlach cried. 'No, what are you doing?' He threw down his armour pieces in a clatter and ran down after the departing horse, scrambling through the long grasses.

He would never catch it now.

He fell to his knees.

'It is good. A great honour,' said Borodyn, walking up behind him. 'A steppe funeral. The rota does great respect to your friend.'

Gerlach looked up at him. 'This is a joke!' he blurted. 'Kaus should have been buried with full rights from a cleric of Morr! What the hell is this? You cut his horse loose and forget about him?'

Borodyn shrugged. 'He was a horseman, yes?'

'An Imperial demilancer!' Gerlach snarled.

'Then he would want to ride. Ride forever, chasing Dazh's sky fire. Why would you wish him trapped in the clay where he is not free?'

Gerlach took a last look at the receding horse. It had almost vanished into the unbroken flatness of the grassland.

'You're heathen barbarians,' he told Borodyn. 'Heathen bloody barbarians!'

He strode back up the hillside through the rota. Borodyn patiently followed him.

Beledni was about to get on his horse.

'Rotamaster!' Gerlach shouted. 'I insist we ride for Choika or another Lynsk crossing!'

Beledni removed his raised foot from its stirrup and turned to face the vexillary.

'Nyeh,' he said.

'Don't "nyeh" me, you barbarian! I'm a demi-lancer! An Imperial demilancer vexillary! Sworn to the service of his Holiness Karl Franz! I will not ignore that oath and gallop blithely into the north or the east! The enemy is moving south! The enemy! The Norscya!'

Beledni shrugged. 'And what we do, Vebla?'

'Stop calling me that! You will address me as Sire Heileman! We have a duty… to… to Kislev and to the Empire! This is the hour of need! Why are we running?'

It took a long moment for Beledni to translate the gist of this in his head. 'Rota rides,' he said finally, pointing out eastwards across the steppe. 'You come.'

'You are an auxiliary unit of the Empire's defence and your duty is to–'

Beledni cut him off with an impatient wave of his gloved hand. He looked at Borodyn, who translated quickly in Kislevite.

Beledni nodded. 'Duty. Is funny thing,' he said.

'Is simple thing, you dullard! What are you, a coward?'

Borodyn, grim in his long beshmet, began to translate, but Beledni shushed him.

The rotamaster had a reproachful look in his eyes as he squinted at Gerlach. 'Coward?'

'What?'

'You call me "coward", Vebla?'

'If you ride into the east… yes.'

There was a murmur from the rota around them, delayed in places as men translated for their comrades.

Beledni tutted and took off his right glove. He handed it, and his riding crop, to Borodyn.

Then he punched Gerlach in the face.

Gerlach fell on his arse, blood weeping from his nose. He rolled and cursed.

'You not insult Beledni rotamaster,' Beledni said, taking back his glove and putting it on again.

Gerlach got up, and threw himself at the stout Kislevite.

They went over together on the grassy slope. Gerlach had a grip on Beledni's top knot, and the rotamaster was clawing at Gerlach's face. He had a finger in Gerlach's mouth, dragging his head aside. Gerlach bit down, and as Beledni yelped and yanked his hand back, he threw a punch that smacked Beledni's cheek. Struggling together, they began to roll down the slope. Beledni kneed Gerlach in the ribs, but the demilancer punched him in the eye.

At the foot of the slope, amid the long swishing grass of the oblast, they separated and sprang up. The men of the rota were following them down, clapping and chanting Beledni's name.

Face to face now, on foot. Punch answered by punch. They circled, jabbing and heaving at one another. Blood and spittle flew from every solid hit. Beledni was formidable, strong as a bear with a low centre of gravity. But Gerlach had huge upper body strength. He was vexillary. He had been trained to hold the heavy standard aloft for hours.

Gerlach punched Beledni in the mouth and then the ribs. Beledni recovered and snapped Gerlach's head round with a savage hook. The men formed a circle around them in the bent and trampled grass, clapping.

Gerlach took a punch to his shoulder and then to his ear. He jabbed Beledni hard in the throat, and then dealt a massive blow that knocked the older man onto his back. Gerlach threw himself onto Beledni's sprawled frame, his right hand pressed flat across Beledni's face. He rammed his head back into the flinty ground.

Beledni's hand closed on Gerlach's throat. It wasn't a tight grip, but Gerlach instinctively knew that if Beledni chose so, a simple flick would crush his windpipe. He sat back, astride Beledni.

His face bruised and bloody, Beledni glared up at Gerlach. Both were fighting for breath.

'Is man with spear,' Beledni rasped. 'Is other man with spear. They fight. One spear breaks.'

'What?' panted Gerlach.

'Is story, Vebla. One spear breaks. One man has only point of spear left. Other man still has whole spear. So…'

'So what?'

'So… does man with spear tip attack man with whole spear from front, or from back?'

Gerlach got off the sprawled rotamaster, unsteady on his feet. He staggered aside in the grass and spat blood and phlegm. His face was throbbing. It felt twice its normal size. He sunk over, his hands braced on his thighs.

Some of the rota helped Beledni upright. His face was puffy. A dark shadow circled his left eye and his mouth was seeping blood.

'Well? Answer?' Beledni coughed.

Gerlach shook his head and spat more thick blood.

'Point of spear only. Front or back?'

Gerlach rose and turned to face the gasping, battered rotamaster.

'Back,' he said.

Beledni smiled a bloody, gap-toothed smile and nodded. 'Rota will ride east,' he announced.

Beledni shambled over to Gerlach, smiling still.

'Vebla strong man,' he admitted.

Wheezing and hoarse, Gerlach shrugged.

Beledni swung a huge punch that laid Gerlach out in the grass and made him see only flashing, revolving stars.

'Vebla never call Beledni rotamaster coward again.'

X

VAJA AND VITALI gathered Gerlach up and shouldered him over to where Saksen was saddled and waiting. Gerlach retched blood, and spat out a piece of tooth.

They tried to dress him in his armour, but he shook them off and sat down, so they wrapped his wargear up in a cloak and lashed it securely to the back of Saksen's saddle in the Kislev manner.

Vaja took off his shabby beshmet and handed it to Gerlach.

'That's yours,' Gerlach said, refusing the dirty velvet coat.

'Vaja has another,' Vaja said.

Gerlach pulled the smelly coat around his shoulders.

Borodyn appeared and crouched down to face Gerlach.

Without words, he grasped Gerlach's head and turned his face to examine it. He pulled open Gerlach's mouth and looked inside, fingering the bloody teeth like he was a horse at market. Then he pulled Gerlach's eyes open wide and stared into them.

'You will live, Vebla,' he announced.

Gerlach snorted. Even snorting hurt.

Borodyn produced a small clay pot of greasy goo from the folds of his cherchesska. 'Smear on bruises. It will help.'

Gerlach took the pot and got up.

'Beledni is impressed,' said the horse master.

'Good,' said Gerlach. 'But we're still heading east.'

'North-east,' corrected the old man. 'To Dushyka. Maybe there.'

'Maybe there what?' Gerlach asked.

Borodyn shrugged.

The horn blew again, and the men of the rota climbed into their saddles.

Putting on Vaja's beshmet, Gerlach mounted Saksen.

The rota advanced, at a rising canter, down the slope and into the nodding grass ocean of the oblast, following their banner.

* * *

XI

THEY WERE SOON galloping, scything a trampled line through the whispering grass behind them. The further they rode, the more distant the hills ahead of them seemed to become. Gerlach had never known a flat space so vast.

'Where is this Dushyka?' he shouted to Borodyn as the horse master drew level with him, standing in the stirrups over his black mare.

'Three days!' Borodyn shouted back.

'But where?'

'Out there!' Borodyn pointed. 'The oblast!'

For the first time, Gerlach realised that the Kislev idea of territory and distance was utterly different from the Empire approach. They thought nothing of distances so vast that you couldn't see the destination. They simply trusted their noses and rode into infinity.

Saksen was galloping true and hard, without a hint of lameness. Ahead, the horn blew for the sheer joy of being blown, loud and into the wind. The men of the rota sent up a cry.

'What did they say?' Gerlach shouted over at Borodyn.

'They make the war cry of the rota,' Borodyn shouted to him.

'Which is what?'

'It is… Riders of the Dead!'

'What does that mean?'

'It means me and Beledni and all of us. And you,' Borodyn yelled. 'We are Yetchitch krug. We are the Riders of the Dead!'

TCHAR

I

HIS NAME WAS Skarkeetah. The stress fell upon the first syllable of his name when it was spoken. *Skarkeetah*. The Kurgan held him in awe. He was above the common rabble and filth. A man of consequence. He was the slave broker.

He appeared first out of the lingering smoke that toiled around the ruins of Zhedevka. Drums announced his approach, then cymbals. Out of the waft, thirteen horse warriors from the bitter north, their plated armour silver with a wash of pink. They held their long-bladed lances high and straight. They had whips and wound lariats hooked on their saddles.

Then the children – none of them into their second decade – danced and capered. They were

painted blue from head to foot, and clanged wide
bronze cymbals.

Then came a curtained litter of massive construction, painted maroon, with gold leaf and buttons of
pearl hammered on its hafts, and black silk drapes
floating around its frame. Twenty shaved and sweating men in skirts of fur and mail carried it along.
On either side of it rode a drummer on a white ass,
slowly thumping on the broad kettle drum that was
slung over his saddle.

Behind the litter rode Hinn.

Hinn was the slave broker's bodyguard and com-
panion. He was quite the biggest man Karl Vollen
had ever seen. His shoulders were like oak stumps
and his biceps were as thick around as most men's
thighs. He wore leggings of grey wolf skin, belted by
a heavy leather band with a large gold boss. Waist
upwards, he was naked, his extravagant muscles
oiled and scraped. A mantle of feathers lay around
his neck. The feathers were turquoise with black tips
and each was the length of a man's forearm. Hinn
wore a close-helm of gold, worked to resemble the
head of a gigantic stork or heron. The crown of the
helm seemed outlandishly tall and pointed. Huge
iron ram's horns sprouted from the helm and
curled over so far that the tips pointed at his shoulders. Hinn had a brace of pallaszs, one on each side
of his saddle.

The captives had been driven out of their pike pens
into the open, and stood in a loose huddle. In the
distance, across the fields, they could see the mounds
of trophy skulls they had been forced to erect.

At a word from Hinn, the slaves set the litter down.

Skarkeetah dragged back the black silk curtain of his litter and stepped out. He was a plump man with watery eyes and a straw-coloured beard. The crown of his head was entirely shaved, except for a patch behind his right ear from which grew a heavy, tight plait of blond hair. He wore a long, plain shift of astonishingly clean, white linen over white trews. His only decoration was a heavy gold amulet that hung around his neck on a wide, golden chain and it thumped against his chest as he moved. The amulet was the size of a man's palm. There was probably more gold in that one piece than in the state crown of any elector count. It was shaped like a single staring eye that emerged from an interwoven circle of snakes. The pupil of the eye was set with a twinkling blue stone.

It made Karl queasy to look at it. Many of the captives around him uttered low moans of dread when Skarkeetah appeared.

It was the fifth day after the Zhedevka slaughter, but the pall of smoke that clung to the countryside was so insidious and thick that little daylight had been seen in that time. None of the captives had eaten, and the only water they had taken had been rain. More had died, especially in the last day or so. The cage pasture stank of putrefaction.

Skarkeetah faced the wretched, shivering mass of prisoners, and raised his plump hands into the air. When he splayed the fat fingers, he revealed a staring eye tattooed in blue on each palm.

'Tchar!' he cried out. The word made Karl shudder, and a general ripple of apprehension and revulsion passed around the prisoners. At the sound of the word, the Kurgan warriors waiting all around howled in approval and clattered their blades and shafts against their shields.

'Tchar!' Skarkeetah yelled again, his hands still raised. Rooks and carrion birds had been circling the field since the battle, and now – chillingly – they stopped clacking and cawing and flocked down, settling all over the litter, and on the puddled clay, and all about the slave broker's feet. One perched on the left horn of Hinn's golden helmet. Half a dozen came down to roost on Skarkeetah's outspread arms. They fluttered and bobbed. Skarkeetah turned his head from one side to the other, smiling and cooing soft, inhuman words at them.

'Sigmar bless us all,' Brezzin whispered to Karl. 'We are in the presence of a daemon.'

Skarkeetah lowered his arms, and the birds hopped down onto the ground – except one, an old, ragged raven with one clouded eye, which remained on his left shoulder, chattering its dagger-like beak.

The slave lord called out instructions to his bodyguard. The plate-armoured warriors dismounted, and trudged into the prisoner mass, jostling and cracking their whips. There was a method to their work. The guards took each prisoner in turn, grabbing him by the chin, and examining his face. Then, depending on what they saw, they pushed the prisoners away either to the left or to the right.

Most men went to the left, to the Kurgan warriors waiting to corral them with ropes and spears. One in every ten was shoved to the right, where Skarkeetah waited. These few were marshaled at spear-point into a line by Hinn and a handful of Kurgans.

The drummers had dismounted. They came over to the slave lord carrying bundles of wooden staves wound together in animal hides. The litter bearers, having set down their heavy burden, busied themselves setting up a small iron brazier and an anvil, both of which they produced from a casket-box mounted at the front of the litter frame. They dragged great lengths of black iron chain and fetters from the casket too, and brought them over by the armful to the brazier. The blue-stained children tossed down their cymbals and began to play around the litter.

The drummers rolled out the hides on the ground and laid the staves out along them in neat rows. Each stave was a rod of dark wood the length of a man's arm with one side planed flat. Every one had a distinguishing knot of tassels and feathers at its top end. The drummers drew fat-bladed dirks and sharpened them on whetstones from their pockets.

By now, the brazier was flaming brightly.

The bodyguard moved roughly through the crowd of prisoners, checking each one and determining their fate. They came closer to the huddle where Karl stood with von Margur and Brezzin. Karl could smell them. Cloves, oil and a deeper reek of corruption. The pink tinge to their silver plate armour was the stain of human blood.

Whips cracked and men shrieked.

One of the bodyguard reached von Margur. He gripped the blind knight's jaw so hard that von Margur cried out in surprise. The warrior twisted the knight's face to one side, then the other, and then pushed him, stumbling, towards Skarkeetah.

The bodyguard checked two more, thrusting them away to the left and the waiting Kurgan mob. He came to Karl.

Karl's spine jolted as the brute took hold of his chin and yanked his head left and right. The vice of the mailed hand was cold and unyielding.

The bodyguard grumbled something behind his silver visor and cuffed Karl in the direction of the slave lord.

Karl looked back. Brezzin had just been examined. The bodyguard was pushing the hefty powderman away to the left. Brezzin was protesting. He looked imploringly at Karl, utterly lost.

'Lad!' he called. 'Lad!' Cursing, the bodyguard drove Brezzin back.

'Brezzin!' Karl called after him.

'Sigmar watches over you, lad!' Brezzin shouted as he was dragged away. 'Remember that! Sigmar will watch over you!'

The bodyguard's whip snapped out like a pistol shot and Brezzin yelped. Then he disappeared in the jostling throng.

Karl felt shockingly alone then. The iron tongues of spears menaced him and drove him into the line.

Von Margur was two places in front of him, standing unsteady and confused. Karl realised that every man in the queue had a pin mark on his cheek. Some had three green dots like von Margur. Others had two black dots or three red ones in a line or three blue ones in a triangle. They had all been marked by zars.

Skarkeetah was moving down the line, studying each captive's mark. With each one, he called out something to the drummers, and one or the other used his dirk to scrape a notch on one of the staves.

'Zar Blayda!'

A notch.

'Zar Herfil!'

A notch.

'Zar Skolt!'

A notch.

'Zar Herfil!'

Another notch.

Sometimes, the plump slave lord would pause longer with a prisoner and converse with him in soft tones that did not carry. When he was done with each one, the prisoners were herded over to the braziers where the litter bearers were busy. Karl could hear the tink-tink-tink of metal worked on an anvil, and he could smell hot iron and the steam of a plunge-pail.

Skarkeetah had come to von Margur.

'Zar Blayda!' he declared, and this was scored on the appropriate rod by the drummers. Skarkeetah turned his head on one side and studied the shivering knight, who was gazing off into nothingness.

'You're a fine one,' Skarkeetah told von Margur. 'Tchar has you already. Bending you to shape.'

'I am a spurred and sworn knight of Karl Franz, may his majesty shine for ever, great is his radiance,' von Margur recited, his voice wavering. 'You will have no hold over me, daemon. Yea, though I walk beneath the Shadow of Chaos I shall fear no–'

'Be silent,' said the slave lord. 'You have no idea where you are or what you are about to become. Tchar will show you real radiance. Tchar will untwist your fibres and allow you to see. You are blessed, and you do not yet know it.'

'I am a spurred and sworn knight of Karl Franz...' von Margur began to repeat, faltering.

'No, sir,' said Skarkeetah. 'You are a possession of Zar Blayda, and a vessel for the cyclops lord of serpents. Wonders beyond your feeble imagining await you.'

'You lie,' von Margur said, his voice a tiny, quiet thing.

'Alas,' said the slave lord, 'that is the one thing I never do. Move him on.'

The Kurgan bundled von Margur towards the brazier.

'Zar Kreyya!' Skarkeetah said, looking over the next man in line. 'Zar Logar!' he instructed at the next.

He came to Karl.

Skarkeetah took hold of Karl's face in his pudgy fingers and then suddenly snapped back.

'Oohhh!' he murmured, gazing at Karl. The bedraggled, one-eyed raven on his shoulder danced and chattered. 'Oohhh, but aren't you a fine thing?' Skarkeetah said in admiration. 'I thought that blind knight would be the pick of the bunch for this haul, but you… you excel even him.'

Karl said nothing.

'Zar Uldin!' Skarkeetah shouted over his shoulder. He looked back at Karl.

'Blue eyes. A perfect sign. Tchar flows in your blood.'

Karl remained resolutely silent, his lips clamped shut.

'What's your name, chosen one?'

Karl closed his eyes. Skarkeetah laughed, a long, throaty chuckle.

'Blue. Like the sky. Blue, like the mutable truth of Tchar.'

Karl opened his eyes and saw Skarkeetah's amulet. The slave lord was holding it up in front of Karl's face. Light glanced off its twisted loop of entwined gold snakes and glimmered in the heart of the blue stone set in the eye.

It was very blue. Deep blue. Deep as an ocean. Deep as a chasm.

Karl spat on the amulet. The Kurgan around hissed in dismay.

Skarkeetah lifted the heavy god amulet and deliberately licked Karl's spittle off it. Then he let go of it and allowed it to thud back against his pure white shift.

The one-eyed raven bounced and clacked.

Skarkeetah slid his hands up behind Karl's head and folded them together. Slowly, he bent Karl's head down. The slave lord kissed him on the cheek. Holding him close, brow to brow, Skarkeetah whispered,

'Tchar has a special place for you. You'll resist at first, but you will come to adore it. I envy you that closeness.'

He let go. Karl yanked his head back, revolted.

Skarkeetah smiled. 'Move him on!' he cried.

The Kurgan jostled Karl up to the brazier. One of the litter bearers was taking white-hot iron pegs from the flames with a set of pincers. They forced Karl's left leg up onto the anvil and clamped a fetter around it. Another swarthy litter bearer hammered the brass cuff closed with one of the hot pegs. Karl was now shackled to the man in front by a two-span length of chain. A similar length of iron links trailed back, waiting to connect with the next captive.

'Zar Skolt!' Skarkeetah called. Another notch. Another beat of the hammer on hot iron.

II

A PACK OF Kurgan marched the marked and chosen away from Zhedevka. The captives had to fall into step because their ankles were linked by the clinking chains. Walking out of step caused them to trip and fall. Karl was forced to adopt a halting, shambling gait, the cuff of the fetter heavy around his ankle.

The sky was smeared with smoke, and for a while Karl believed the Kurgan were leading them east.

But then they came to a river, and a broad timber bridge raised out of the water on five stone piers. They trudged across it, their feet thumping the timber boards. Some of the captives spat to avert misfortune.

It was the crossing above Choika. Karl recognised it. The last time he had crossed it, the vexillary's spit had splashed his cuirass.

He wondered, briefly, what might have become of arrogant young Gerlach Heileman. Dead, no doubt, on the smouldering fields around Zhedevka.

They tramped on. Once in a while, they had to get off the track to allow a Norther brigade to pass. Horned, black warriors at full gallop.

They came to an ashy, smoky place where the vague ruins of buildings sat in the wash of smoke and soft rain.

Karl saw a stone basin he recognised. They were in Choika, the burnt remains of Choika.

The Kurgan herded them out along the southern road. Bullrushes on either side of the track bent in the wind coming off the oblast.

All along the southern road, to either side, the folk of Choika had been crucified. The Kurgan host had passed this way, without compromise.

Karl stared at the mud in front of him. The mud and the chain. Taut, slack. Taut, slack. Taut, slack.

III

THEY WERE MARCHED for three days, pausing for a few hours every night. They followed the trail through broadleaf forest and wet woods, where the only sign of life was the movement of the Northern forces. Disorderly hosts of Norther spearmen overtook them, flocking down the track with no formal file or rank. They strode to drum beats, holding aloft wretched and often obscene banners. Some brought along warhounds or hunting-dogs with them in great numbers. Others rode in carts and wagons with stretched hide covers and solid wooden wheels. These were pulled by strings of oxen or mules.

Occasionally, enemy horsemen rode by, always heading south. Sometimes the horsemen could be seen riding through the forest itself, scorning the mire of the road. Once they were passed by a squadron of two-wheeled chariots, drawn by fast teams of four ponies each. Beside each whipping driver stood a bearded archer with a hooked, compound bow.

The days were grey and overcast, and often interrupted by periods of heavy rain. The nights were moonless and still.

There were about three-score prisoners in the marching group, all marked men from the Zhedevka battle. They were chained in six lines. About twenty Kurgan spearmen guarded them, along with three horsemen. A fourth horseman, one of the silver-armoured men from the slave lord's bodyguard, had command.

When darkness fell, the Kurgan gathered them off the track in woodland clearings and staked their chains to the ground with iron spikes. The Northers built fires for themselves, and ate and drank through the night. Only two wooden bowls were brought to each of the six chains. One was filled with rainwater, the other with ladled dredgings of meat stew from the Kurgan's cook pots. The captives in each chain quickly learned the importance of sharing.

Some supplemented their diet with stuff they could forage from the forest floor near where they were staked down: beetles, earthworms, even leaves and grass stalks. A few chewed for hours on bark or twigs, or pieces of leather from whatever belts or boots they had. The hunger was inhuman. It was a misery beyond anything Karl had ever known or could imagine. It eclipsed all the other miseries: the cold, the fatigue, their wounds, the chaffing of the iron fetters, even their predicament as vanquished captives, slaves of an enemy that treated them like animals.

Karl shook most of the time, and there was a pain in his gut like a blade wound. His fingernails had become cracked and lined, and his skin was slack and had lost its usual elasticity. His gums bled. He had been deprived of everything, including his basic dignity as a human being. But he would gladly have let it all go if he could now just have bowl of broth or a hunk of bread.

He could see the other men were in the same state. He realised they were all reaching a strange phase. Sheer desperation. It was looming. Up until then they had borne every horror and every privation, hoping that some sort of end or deliverance might come if they were patient.

Now, it was clear, it would not. Sooner or later, someone would decide that the danger of resisting or escaping no longer outweighed the terrible hunger.

On the third night, staked down in a grove of poplars, two things happened that brought them all closer to breaking point. The night was pitch black, and the Kurgan were drinking and laughing around their fires. They were late bringing the meagre offerings to the captives, and some of the prisoners had collapsed in a weak faint. Karl sat with his knees pulled up and his arms wrapped around them, trying to preserve body warmth as the temperature dropped.

All through the latter part of that afternoon, the track had been busy with massing Northers, flooding south. Word had spread that a battle was coming, and the captives discussed which burg or crossing might be its site. There were various suggestions, but none of the captives had much sense of the geography of the region, let alone where they were.

After dark, a ruddy glow underlit the sky south of them. They could see it, vaguely, through the trees. The Kurgan guards were excited by it. The promised battle. A town ablaze.

One of the captives in the middle of a chain staked out close to Karl suddenly fell sick. He convulsed and vomited violently, and wailed out. It seemed he had found some berries or forest mushrooms which, in desperation, he had foolishly ingested.

A few of the Kurgan came to look at him, but did nothing. He was most likely going to die a wracking, agonised death by poison, and they didn't care. They offered him no aid or physic. They didn't even put him out of his misery.

After about an hour, the man fell silent. Karl couldn't tell if he was sleeping or dead.

Karl began to plot how he might escape. Most likely all the captives still awake were doing the same. Karl still had Drogo Hance's true killer concealed in his mud-stiff clothes. He knew he couldn't break the fetter – and certainly not cut off a foot – but if he could get the whole of his chain to act together, they could drag out the spikes and rush the slumbering Kurgan. Karl's dirk gave them one chance. They could grab other weapons. They could–

He gave up the idea. They would be hacked to death. As far as he could tell at least two of the men on his fetter chain were too weak to fight now, and three others too scared. Then there was von Margur. Even if he was willing, his blindness was a profound handicap that would undermine them.

Karl then actually considered cutting off his own foot. Ludicrously, what dissuaded him was neither the potential pain, nor the danger of dying from blood loss, nor even the futility of trying to flee by hopping. No, it was the fact that the little dirk didn't seem to him to have enough blade to shear through something as solid as an ankle.

There was movement out on the track. Chariots and horsemen were riding past at full stretch by torch light. Hurrying, no doubt to the battle south of them.

And then another sound. Karl thought it was the wind in the treetops at first. Many of the captives looked up, curious.

A swishing, whooping noise of air. Karl had once been to the great port of Marienburg, and it sounded to him like the brisk wind of the estuary cracking and flapping the vast canvas sheets of the merchantmen and privateers in the harbour.

The Kurgan heard it too. They jumped up and immediately kicked over their fires and stamped them out until their embers were extinct. They were scared. They spoke only in whispers, and came over to insist that the captives remained silent. The insistence was reinforced by hissed threats of bodily damage and a show of drawn blades.

The flapping, swishing sounds continued, moving overhead from the north into the south. In petrified silence, they all crouched in the dark, looking up.

Karl hoped – prayed to Sigmar – that the sound did not belong to what his imagination told him was up there.

Wings. The huge, leathery wings of unnameable things flying over the forest, invisibly black against the starless sky. Feral abominations of the most distant north, swooping down to join the battle at the summons of the Kurgan sorcerers.

The captive who had eaten poison berries woke up, yelling.

He writhed and screamed out twice before the astonished Kurgan managed to react.

They fell on him and speared him to the forest floor to shut him up.

Silence returned, except for the beat of vast batwings.

* * *

IV

IN THE MORNING, at first light, the Kurgan roused them up and marched them on. It was raining again, and dismally cold and grey. The sick man they had murdered for the sake of silence was hacked out of his fetter and left in pieces under the sighing poplars.

As they shambled south, his vacant loop of iron dragged and rattled in the middle of the file.

V

KARL VOWED TO himself he would not die that way. He would not allow these barbarians to end his life so shamefully, just because they felt they owned it.

He could not escape. Not unless some miracle occurred. But he had the true killer. A small Empire-forged blade, enough for one kill. When the chance came, he would go down fighting, and he would take at least one filthy-souled man of the North with him.

As he struggled along, he absently rubbed at the sore place on his right cheek. Zar Uldin's mark. He wished he could abrade the skin away and no longer be marked as property.

The rains fell harder, torrential, turning the track to slop. The stands of woodland off the road became indistinct, so heavy was the blurring veil of the deluge. Captives, Karl included, walked with their heads turned up and their mouths open, relishing the drink the sky provided. Karl said a benediction to Taal, the hoary god of the wilds and elements, who dwelt up there and showed his children this simple mercy.

The silver-clad bodyguard, riding alongside them, was now truly silver-clad. The heavy rains had washed away the ritual bloodstains that had made his armour seem pink. That made him weaker, Karl thought, because he was deprived of the magical protection the blood afforded him.

Karl decided the bodyguard of Skarkeetah would be the one. As far as Karl could make it so, the brute slaver in the glossy silver plate would be the soul Karl took to the other world with him. That ornate, studded silver armour would be red again.

With Kurgan lifeblood.

VI

IN THE LATE morning of the fourth day, they reached a town. The rain had ebbed, and a washed-out sun tried to brighten the day.

The town was raised in a wide clearing of the forest. A clutch of izbas huddled around a fine but decayed granite temple within a wall of stone and timber.

They never learned its name.

The Kurgan host had come like wolves, burning out most of the old, frail izbas and putting the population to the sword. Then they had occupied it, to use its wells, and plunder its larders and granaries. It had become an encampment, a supply base for their armies as they drove south through the fringes of Kislev and into Karl's homeland.

The place reeked of stale smoke and dung. It was teeming with Kurgan. They had pitched their round felt gers and canvas pavilions in the pastures outside, and some in the streets of the town itself. A mighty head of horse was penned in chain corrals at the edges of the temporary town, and there were strange, new forests of stored spears, their bases stuck down in the loam.

The Kurgan whipped the captives down the track through the pastures, through the field of gers and in under the town gates. Kurgan archers manned the ramparts, their composite bows tautly strung. Sentinels with long, ox-horn trumpets stood watch over the gateway.

Inside, there had been looting and destruction. The puddles in the muddy streets were dark and cloudy. Kislevite dead had been tossed into heaps against the inner wall. Flies were everywhere.

They tracked up the main street, across a paved marketplace where singed stakes and jumbled ashes told of ceremonial burnings, and into a temple.

The great granite building, dedicated to some Kislevite deity, had been ransacked and its altars desecrated. Its heavy doors and windows had been boarded up, save the main porch. Raised in stone, the temple was the closest thing the Kurgan had to a prison.

Inside, it was dry and gloomy. Rushlights flickered. The inner space, wide and long, had been cleared, and blankets spread out on the floor. The temple smelled of aged timber, dust and sour wine.

Their guards forced them down on the lice-ridden blankets. Iron braziers were lit. After a while, they could smell food, and their drawn bellies winced.

Karl curled up in the blankets. By the firelight, he could see the main altar. Things – probably very holy things – had been cast down and smashed. On the wide basalt plinth stood an iron coffer. It had four feet in the shape of bird-claws, and stretcher handles so that it could be carried on the shoulders of strong men. On the side facing them, looking into the temple, was a single eye wrought in iron, its lids formed by wreathing snakes. A fire inside the coffer flickered in amber through the spaces cast into the eye. It seemed as if the staring eye was blinking.

They were left alone for an hour or two. Then Hinn entered the temple. His footfalls on the stone flags were loud and heavy. Nine of the sturdy litter bearers followed him. They brought the anvil with them.

Hinn bowed to the coffer, and then stood up again to remove his beaked helmet. He raised it up off his head and set it down at the foot of the altar block.

His head was hideous.

His face was small and fleshy, like a baby's. He had no beard, but he had not shaved. No hair had ever broken that soft flesh. His skull was oiled smooth, it was tall and rose in a grotesque, rounded point of distorted bone. The height of his golden close-helm had been necessary to contain its abhuman shape.

Hinn's skull had been bound from an early age. Karl had once heard about this practice amongst the most savage Northern tribes. Tight bindings had forced his soft head into this elongated shape as it grew. His skull was almost twice the height from crown to jaw as that of a normal man, and when he turned side on, it was half the depth behind the ears from brow to nape. Bare, his skull resembled an egg-like cone, high and slender, with his infant face hanging from the front.

Hinn turned to face them all. His expression was blank, almost idiotic.

'Tchar blesses you, marked ones,' he said, in a voice that was pitched high and far too frail to be the product of such a massive body.

At a clap of his hands, Kurgan with spears herded the captives to the anvil, one by one. The litter bearers used a chisel and hammer to free them. They gouged several calves and broke at least one toe before the captives were all released.

It seemed a small price to pay.

Then the Kurgan brought food.

VII

THE FOOD CAME in a series of beaten copper pots, each one so full it had to be carried crosswise on bending poles by pairs of straining men. A steaming stew of oily fish, poached in grease and mare's milk. A hot brown broth, thick with chunks of root vegetable and fatty gobs of mutton. Beans and pulses, cooked in boiled mutton stock. Accompanying these, wooden trenchers were piled with farls of fresh, warm unleavened bread.

The litter bearers set the food down in the middle of the huddle of captives. All of the prisoners stared at the feast. Some were sobbing, others were openly drooling like dogs. No one dared to move.

Hinn smiled. It was a nasty sight. 'Eat,' he said.

That... that was the kindest thing Karl ever saw a Northerner do.

The captives fell on the pots, gobbling and craving. They tore bread and used their hands, ignoring the scalds and blisters they got from dipping fingers into hot food. They ate like famished wolves, tearing into the food in a pack, burning their lips, tongues and fingertips. Some consumed so much, so fast, that they fell in faints and stupors. Others gagged and coughed.

It was the best meal Karl Reiner Vollen had ever tasted.

The litter bearers reappeared and tossed drinking skins into the scrum of feeding bodies. The skins were full of a sappy alcoholic drink like wine, and they drained them, holding the heavy hide bags for each other, pouring the sweet, strong drink into each other's mouths.

They were laughing, their faces gleaming with grease, drops of broth in their beards. Karl found von Margur and helped the blind knight to one of the pots.

As the marked men consumed the food and drink, Hinn and the litter bearers moved around the temple, sowing seedcases into the braziers. Very soon the air was full of dry, spicy smoke. Breathing it in, the feasting captives began to howl and cry with laughter. They danced around, eyes streaming with tears, mouths wide with delight. One man laughed so hard he began to choke.

The hot rasp of the opiate smoke became overwhelming. Hinn and the Kurgan withdrew. Coughing and stumbling, the prisoners milled around in an intoxicated daze. Some of them crawled on the floor, still laughing. Others lay back on the blankets and fell asleep, snoring loudly, their bellies over-full. Two men threw up violently, and collapsed. The copper pots rolled on their sides on the blankets, scraped empty.

Von Margur slumped down in a bundle and began to sigh and weep. Karl, his head spinning, sat down heavily. His eyes were welling with tears, but he was still laughing hysterically. One of the marked men, a swordsman from Carroberg, staggered up to the altar and put on Hinn's golden bird-helm. He jigged around in it, and all those still conscious laughed so hard they were in danger of rupturing themselves.

Karl got to his feet, swaying and laughing. He had the true killer in his hand, clenched inside the folds of his dirty clothes.

He started towards the door, but he wasn't very good at walking any more.

He felt so good.

'No!' von Margur growled, reaching out a hand to grab at Karl's boot.

'Get off! Get off, sir!' Karl giggled.

'No!' von Margur said, and then snorted with laughter at the pomposity of his tone.

'Let me go, sir...' Karl said.

'No... no, Karl,' von Margur said, still sniggering. His hand was clamped around Karl's shin. 'Please don't. What will I do without you?'

Karl stopped. He didn't have an answer to that. He sank down onto his knees.

'Sir? Sir? Take the knife and hold it so I can fall onto it and escape this. Please, sir. Please.'

Von Margur was asleep, semi-digested food leaking out of his half-turned mouth.

Karl got to his feet. It was difficult, and took a while. Once he was upright, he was quivering. He held the true killer out in front of him like a trowel.

Something very cold and very solid suddenly rested on his left shoulder. Karl peered down and fought to adjust his field of focus. The solid thing was shiny. A steel something.

The blade of a pallasz.

Hinn stood before him, one of his huge broadswords lowered horizontally across Karl's torso.

Karl wavered, hot and uncomfortable.

'I don't know how you came to have that pin-stick,' Hinn said, his voice ridiculously high. 'Here are your choices. Hand it to me and live. Keep it and die.'

Karl thought hard. He wanted to hack at Hinn. But he was fairly sure he would be dead if he tried to move.

Hinn kept the broadsword where it was and held out his other hand.

'Give it to me, Empire.'

Karl blinked. 'Your voice is funny,' he found himself saying.

'Funny?'

'Yes, funny. Like it's squeaky.'

Incensed, Hinn took the pallasz blade off Karl's shoulder bone and raised it up.

'There is another choice,' said a soft voice.

Skarkeetah loomed beside his bodyguard. He smiled at Karl.

'It was clever of you to have kept that dirk hidden. Put it away now and I'll let you keep it.'

That seemed very fair.

'All right,' said Karl, and tucked the dirk away in his ragged undershirt.

Then he sat down and fell asleep.

VIII

KARL WOKE UP in the early hours when the braziers had gone out, and the temple had gone cold again. Just the after-scent of the opiate smoke and the food hung in the chilly air. All of the captives were asleep.

The true killer had been taken from him.

Karl cursed, but he was too tired to care.

IX

THEY ALL SLEPT through most of the next day. At vespers, as the day was closing, the litter bearers came in with another meal and more wine skins.

The prisoners were slower to consume this offering. They were tired and muzzy.

Outside, there was an uproar: drums beating and fires glowing.

Hinn stalked back into the temple, a broadsword drawn in each hand. At some point in the night, he had recovered his close-helm. Now it shone on his head. The bird beak. The ram's horns.

He looked around for a while, and then pointed the long blade in his right hand at a well-built pikeman from Stirland who had the three green cheek dots of Zar Blayda's mark on his cheek.

'Tchar chooses you,' he said.

Then he raised the sword in his left hand and pointed its tip at Karl.

'And you.'

X

THE STIRLANDER'S NAME was Wernoff. Karl had established this as they were bundled out of the temple into the evening.

'What in Sigmar's name do they want from us?' Wernoff asked.

'I don't know.'

'Are we to be sacrifices, Vollen? Blood sacrifices?' Wernoff wondered in dismay.

'Sigmar, great be his blessings, will protect us,' Karl assured the pikeman.

As soon as they were out of the temple's doorway, they found themselves in a thick crowd of drunken, chanting Kurgan. Hinn's men dragged Wernoff away and Karl lost sight of him.

Hinn led Karl down through the crush of chanting bodies into the market square. The acre of paving stones was clear and empty, but rang with the sound of thousands of yelling Northers. Fires blazed around the edges of the square, casting a long, yellow glare over the paving.

Hinn jostled Karl to the edge of the baying crowd.

The pitch-armoured figure of Zar Blayda emerged from the far side of the multitude and walked out in the centre of the firelit market place. He stood there, drew his sword and held it up. As he brandished it, the crowd cheered and yelled.

Then Zar Uldin, in his black furs and wolf-mask, strode out to face him. Uldin ripped out his own pallasz, and waved it aloft, to more howls and roars.

The zars faced each other in the centre of the square, Blayda with his sword raised across his body, diagonal, Uldin with his vertical.

Now Karl understood, to a certain extent. Single combat, an honour match, zar against zar. He watched expectantly.

Blayda swung his massive sword. Uldin blocked it. Sparks flew from the clash. The crowd howled.

Then they stopped. The zars bowed to each other and went back into the mob on either side of the market square.

Karl blinked as Hinn shoved a pallasz into his hands. Then the brute handed him Drogo Hance's true killer.

'You might need this,' said the thin, high voice from behind the beaked helm.

Karl still didn't understand. The crowd was baying fit to break the sky. He tucked the true killer into his belt and hefted the huge pallasz.

Hinn suddenly shoved him out into the open. Sword in hand, he stumbled out into the empty square. The firelight danced. The Kurgan host yelled the moment they saw him.

Wernoff emerged from the crowd at the opposite side of the square. He staggered as if he had been pushed. He had a Kurgan broadsword in his hands.

Karl felt his soul sink. It was single combat all right. Zar Blayda versus Zar Uldin. But a duel fought by proxy, as sport. By their marked men.

DUSHYKA

I

THREE DAYS ON the empty steppe and they came in sight of Dushyka.

At least, Gerlach believed it had been three days. It seemed there were no dimensions his Imperial mind could grasp in the open oblast. The land was a flat, featureless prospect to all compass points, the sky an immeasurable arch beneath which he felt no more significant than a pin stick. There was no direction except *forward*.

If the men of the rota had told him it had been four days, or even five, he would not have been surprised. He moved in emptiness. In it, he became a nothing.

As time followed the rhythmic lurch of the horse, hour after hour, he came to a sobering revelation.

The oblast had not diminished him; it had simply showed him how he truly was. Against the busy landscape of the Imperial principalities, he was a young man of repute, vexillary of a demilance, no less, with ambitions to match: to win glory for Karl Franz, to achieve great deeds in battle, to be the sort of man who made real things happen. That was why the fires of Zhedevka had left him so hollow. The sense of failure had been so great. Why had he not turned back the armies of the North single-handed?

Out on the steppe, he saw himself as fate saw him. A tiny thing, like a single blade of grass.

He was one small man, and here the scale of the universe was revealed... well, just a part of it. His mind might reel, giddy at the thought of the whole.

There was nothing he could have done. Nothing any man could have done. The North was a primordial torrent, in the form of flesh. He could have no more stopped it than raise up his hands and halt the giant clouds that sailed, sedate as galleons, across the oblast heaven.

The fatalism shown by Beledni, and by many of his men, seemed apt now. The slight, dismissive frown, the odd little turn of the wrist as if he were spilling out a handful of corn, 'Is of no matter'. So typically careless, so typically Kislevite. They had been raised in this emptiness, and it bred in them a dismissive philosophy.

Is of no matter. For nothing mattered. For nothing was big enough to matter in the long run, except the passing centuries and the empty steppe. All the rest was just dust, spilling from a tilting hand into the oblast wind.

Dushyka stanitsa. Dushyka town. A trading post on the route from nothing to nowhere.

A long, beamed hall with a handful of izbas packed around it inside a timber stockade. It was so old the elements had worn the wood pale as snow.

It appeared up suddenly, amid the limitless grass, under a sky that was just the blue side of colourless. It surprised Gerlach to come upon it so unexpectedly. Nothing but grass, then a township. The line of hills to the north-east still seemed as far away as when the journey began.

The men of the rota had somehow been aware of Dushyka before it came into view. The pace slowed, and conversations were exchanged between the front riders.

There was no sign of life in the town, except goats and short-necked ponies that grazed outside the stockade fence. The rota reined up in a line half a league short of the town and, at Beledni's gesture, Yevni the horn blower sounded his horn.

The sound rolled away across the open steppe and was eaten by the distance. They waited, horses twitching ears and tails.

An answering note came from the stockade, strong and clear. Gerlach saw movement as the town gates opened.

'Yha!' Beledni cried, and the rota broke towards the town.

* * *

II

STEPPE LIFE, GERLACH decided, was like an islander's way of life. The grass was the sea, and the scattered stanitsas the little island communities.

The greeting at Dushyka was very different from the one the demilancers had received at Choika. The townsfolk – what few of them there were – came out onto the packed earth of their yards and rattled busy welcomes with empty pots and pans. Hellos were called out, and men strode forward to clasp the hands of each rider in turn as the rota dismounted. Gerlach found his hand shaken by a dozen people he didn't know. They greeted him with cheerful informality as if he was a cousin or a brother returning home after a short time away.

The men of the rota seemed to know the townsfolk and vice versa, but it was hard to be sure. Maybe they simply knew each other as fellow sons of Kislev. Maybe that was enough.

The ataman emerged from the log hall. He was a bearded man with a wind-scoured face. He wore an old, spiked helmet with a wide fur brim on his head, a long cherchesska tunic with rows of charges down the chest, and a fleece draped over one shoulder. His deputy, the esaul, followed him, carrying a small mace. This – the bulava – was the ataman's symbol of power.

The ataman took the bulava from his deputy and handed it to Beledni. Simultaneously, the rotamaster handed the staff of the rota's eagle wing banner to the ataman. They each touched the totem they had been given against their foreheads and gravely uttered some oath or ritual remark. Then banner and bulava were taken back and returned to the hands of the deputies. Beledni and the ataman spread their arms wide and embraced each other, laughing and smiling. After that, Beledni, Maksim and Borodyn followed the ataman and his esaul into the hall.

Outside, the men of the rota sat around in the little yard, or saw to their mounts. Womenfolk brought bowls of pickled fish and sour cream, pitchers of chalky water, cups of koumiss and baskets of small seed cakes.

Gerlach accepted some from a little woman in a headscarf. They hadn't eaten much on the journey: just strips of dry salt-meat and biscuit handed out from saddlebags. Gerlach tried to show how grateful he was. Vaja and Vitali joined him, chuckling and tutting, to teach him how to say thank you like a Kislevite. There was a ritual to be observed, though they didn't explain it well. As usual, they were contradicting each other's use of Reikspiel.

You took the water first of all. Sip, rinse the mouth of the journey's dust and spit, then drink some more. Then a modest fingerful of the fish, to be eaten with relish. Then a seed cake, torn so that some of it could be handed back to the giver. The idea was, Gerlach worked out, that the folk of the stanitsa were selflessly offering their precious supplies to the visitors, and the ritual vouched for the visitor's willingness to share. Once this had been established, the words for thanks were spoken, and the koumiss drunk.

There seemed to be no warriors resident in the stanitsa, and no sign of armour, but a row of round, hardwood shields hung on the inner wall of the stockade and most of the men carried short, recurved bows, unstrung, in eastern-style bowcases on their belts. Several spare bowstrings were looped around the cases.

His spirits lifted by the food, Gerlach followed the lead of the other riders and worked on his horse and armour. He stripped the harness and rubbed Saksen with handfuls of straw. Then he walked him to a water trough that the local boys were filling from a pump. Women were shaking out armfuls of hay.

The younger boys took great interest in the Imperial troop horse. Gerlach realised how odd Saksen looked amongst the Kislevites' hairy, squat mares. Saksen was the biggest horse by far, with a longer neck and a much more powerful build. His fine grey colouring and tightly docked tail made him look an alien in their midst.

'Byeli!' the boys said, apparently impressed. 'Byeli!'

They turned their attention to the rider of the strange horse. It seemed Gerlach's own colouring and fair hair was just as intriguing. They followed the vexillary, cautiously, as he walked back to his harness and started to lay his kit and armour out on the hardpan.

Dented and battered in places though it was, his fine half-armour was still in reasonable shape. He hadn't worn it or his burgonet since the night they had camped on the hillside. His fabric clothing was in much worse shape, all of it dirty and torn. He'd almost forgotten that the beshmet he was wearing as a coat had belonged to Vaja.

His sabre was notched, and he couldn't remember where he'd lost his lance. His dagger was still intact. One pistol remained in his possession, but with precious little powder or shot.

He went through his saddlebags, finding there wasn't much in them. The company's supply wagons had been carrying most of their personal effects. Aside from his water flask and bedroll, there was a little comb of tortoiseshell, a folding razor, a tinderbox, a whetstone, a shoe-awl, a small bottle of polishing oil, a rag, a candle, and some beeswax in a pot. There was also a curry-comb. Gerlach looked at this particular item with a frown. He'd always been so scrupulous in his grooming of the gelding, yet he'd just brushed Saksen down with straw, in the brisk manner of a Kislevite outrider, without even thinking of this comb.

At the bottom of one bag were a few scraps of twisted silver and enamel chips.

It was all that remained of a symbol of Sigmar his father had presented him with the night before he set out. He wore a smaller, gold version on a chain round his neck that his mother had given him on his tenth birthday.

His father's gift had been altogether too large to wear except for ceremonial occasions. He carried it in his pack as a trophy. It had been entirely shattered. A brief examination revealed a blackened hole the size of his middle finger in the side of the buff saddlebag. A ball of shot had passed through it. He hadn't seen any of the enemy using firing pieces, though anything was possible. This was more likely a miserable stray shot from his own side during the chaos at Zhedevka. The holy symbol had stopped the shot and been destroyed as a result. Nothing else in the bag had been touched. But for that, Gerlach would have had Saksen killed or crippled under him on the field.

It was curious. It made him feel strangely grateful and humble.

III

GERLACH SET TO work oiling his armour and edging his sword. The boys gathered round with interest. They pointed to various details – the design of Gerlach's sabre and the style of his armour – that were foreign to them, discussed them amongst themselves with almost professional concern.

Then he began to clean his wheel-lock, and they fell silent in awe.

One of them finally dared to address him. Gerlach looked up. The boy, no older than eight or nine, with fierce dark eyes and a mess of black hair, repeated his question quickly. None of them had any Reikspiel at all, and Gerlach had a passing knowledge of only a half-dozen Kislevite words.

'I don't understand you, boy,' he said at last. The boy frowned. 'I...' Gerlach pointed to himself, '...don't understand you.' He pointed at the boy.

'Douko,' said the boy.

'Dowkoe?'

'Douko,' the boy repeated, tapping his chest.

'You're Douko? Your name is Douko?' Gerlach asked, trying to do better with the name's pronunciation. This seemed to please the boy and his friends.

'Heileman,' said Gerlach, indicating himself. There had been a time, not all that long before, when vexillary Heileman would have considered chatting idly with peasant children to be beneath him. But some inner tension had relaxed, like a clock spring uncoiling, and he could think of nothing finer than wasting time under a wide blue sky.

The boy made a few struggling attempts to repeat Gerlach's name, but it was beyond him. The children urged Gerlach to repeat it so they might try again.

He did. They failed and laughed at themselves in a way that made Gerlach smile. He tried something else.

'Vebla,' he said, patting his chest.

They laughed so hard they were helpless with mirth. They repeated the word and then ran away across the yard, calling it out.

Shaking his head, Gerlach returned to his work. His pistol was clean, his sword whetted. He went back to his armour and tried to beat out the deep dent on his right vambrace. The damage had been done by the sword blow that had knocked the draco standard from his hand.

For a moment, the tension coiled in him again, as he recalled the proud anger that had propelled him through the battle. The old, arrogant Gerlach Heileman, who had ridden to war believing he could drive out the enemy was reinstated. A flush rose in his neck.

He hammered bitterly with his dagger pommel, as he had seen the Kislevites doing, but he was no armourer. Such repairs were the job of the smith who rode with the supply wagons.

Had been the job.

'Let me see to that.'

Gerlach glanced up. Borodyn, the horse master and master of metals, stood behind him. He had re-emerged from the ataman's zal, and now was going round the compound with his farrier's hammer, pliers and little anvil, making field repairs to the armour and harnesses of the riders.

Borodyn held out his hand. 'Please. I can get the dent out and stop it rubbing your arm.'

Gerlach gave him the vambrace and Borodyn put it over the anvil's nose and began to work out the twist with little, expert taps.

'They seemed to welcome us here.'

'It is the way,' replied Borodyn.

'What happens now?'

'What do you mean?' Borodyn asked, looking up at him.

'We spent three days getting here. What do we do now?'

'Rest, water our horses. Join the ataman at the Dushyka krug tonight.'

'What is a "krug"?'

'Literally? A circle. Any close circle. The circle of warriors around a fireside. The folk of a village like this gathered for a feast. And so, they refer to the band of warriors themselves, as well as the village community as a body. Tonight, the Dushyka krug – these people – welcomes the Yetchitch krug – that's us – to join them *for* a krug.'

'It's complicated. Your language is complicated. One word with so many meanings.'

'Just one meaning. The circle. It's simple. It is the world. Every journey comes back to where it starts, for the world goes round and if you ride forever you come back upon your own tracks. Every strong people is a circle. Every rota is a circle. The circle holds us in and holds us together. True circles are strong.'

Borodyn held up the vambrace and showed it end-on to Gerlach. He had beaten the dent out and, looking down into it, it now formed a perfect circle.

Gerlach smiled and took it. 'Like armour? A good illustration for your point.'

Borodyn frowned and thought about this. 'Oh, I see. I hadn't intended that symbolism.'

Gerlach shrugged. He was quite sure Borodyn had. There was something of the teacher in the armourer, even something of a priest. Implying simple things without drawing attention to them.

Gerlach slipped the vambrace on and rotated his clenched fist. 'It's good. Thank you.'

'Is of no matter,' Borodyn said, the true Kislevite.

'Where did you learn my language, horse master Borodyn?' he asked.

'In your country,' Borodyn replied, as if this was a strange question.

'You have been to the Empire?'

Borodyn nodded. 'Years ago, when I was a young man and hungry for journeys. Before Yetchitch called me home to the steppe.'

'Yetchitch. That's your home village?'

'Yes. It is where all the men of the rota come from. It is north and east of here. In the highlands of the open steppe.'

'Isn't this the open steppe?'

Borodyn chuckled. 'Of course not.'

'So I ride in the company of the *rota* of *Yetchitch krug*?'

'Yes,' Borodyn smiled.

'Because – like *krug* – *rota* means more than one thing? A banner, and the men who follow the banner? Who might also be called a *krug*?'

'Exactly. I told you it was simple.'

IV

As EVENING FELL, a slow, languid process in the open vista of the oblast, they congregated in the long, beamed zal, where fires had been burning for an hour or more to heat the place. An extensive meal was being cooked; heavy, rich smells wafted out.

The men of the rota had put on their armour again, including szyszak helmets, snow leopard pelts and the tall wing crests, so as to look digni-fied and noble for the krug. They had spent some time out in the yard in the fading light, buffing up their gold and silver wargear, helping to set and straighten crests and details of each other's trappings.

They looked impressive, Gerlach had to admit, far more splendid than anything in this meagre stanitsa.

Dutifully, he dressed in his own half-armour and plumed burgonet. The warriors applauded him loudly when they saw him so accoutred.

Before casting off their ragged travel clothes and donning their fine wargear, the men of the rota had performed an odd rite. They had unfixed the long tips of their main horse lances, sharpened them, and then shaved. Heads, cheeks, chins, everything, with painstaking care – except for their topknots and drooping moustaches. Beledni had inspected each man's face for signs of stubble. Then they wound their top knots on their bald heads, slipped their leather cauls over them to form a cushion, before putting on their helms.

Beledni had mentioned shaving before, as if it was significant. It seemed to be the only piece of grooming these habitually grubby men worried about.

The winged lancers secured their lance tips back onto the hafts, and then left the lances and their swords at the door of the zal.

Gerlach, with his full beard in the Empire fashion, simply trimmed the proud point with his knife and longed for a bowl of hot water. He walked to the doorway of the hall, and placed his demilance sabre with the other weapons in the porch.

Inside, it was dim and smoky. The zal was full. Everyone from the village was there, even the children. Bolsters and rugs and quilted blankets covered the open floor, and the guests, ducking so their huge wing crests would not strike the low beams, took their seats on the ground to the clapping welcome of the villagers. A Dushyka man was banging a tambor, and another was playing a lively tune on a horse-head fiddle.

The music and clapping died away so that the old ataman, regal in furs and a striped dolmen, could pronounce words of welcome. Beledni rose stiffly to his feet and made a formal answer. Everyone clapped.

The younger women then went around with circular trays on which heavy stemmed glasses sat cup-down beside small bowls of salt. Gerlach was surprised to see such a delicate commodity as drinking glasses in this remote place. Clearly, the ataman was entertaining his guests with his finest chattels.

The lancers each took a glass, as did the ataman. When Gerlach was offered one, he picked it up and examined it. It was old and heavy and shaped like a handbell. The stem had no base. The only way to put it down was to empty it and overturn it. A toasting glass.

'Other of you hand!' Vaja hissed at Gerlach.

He was holding the glass in his right hand and saw all the lancers had theirs in their left. He corrected the mistake.

'Now… sol!' Vaja added. Each lancer had taken a pinch of salt between the fingertips of his right hand.

The esaul went round the circle of guests, filling each man's glass with clear liquid from a tall flask. This, according to Vaja, was kvass.

With a full glass that he couldn't put down in his left hand, and a pinch of salt in his right, Gerlach waited and watched the others to see what to do.

The ataman made a toast. It was loud and furious. He raised his kvass.

The lancers – and Gerlach – raised theirs. 'Starovye!'

Now that word, at least, he knew.

As the cry went up, the lancers licked the salt from their right hands and then downed the drink. The whole glass in one swallow.

Not wishing to offend, Gerlach did the same.

Someone had filled his glass with molten lead. It burned like flaming pitch as it poured down his throat. He wasn't even sure it had gone down his throat. It felt like it had simply burned its own way down into his gullet. He coughed and spluttered, eyes streaming.

Everyone in the room cheered.

Gerlach swayed slightly. Heat washed through his limbs and blood rushed unpleasantly through his head. He gasped for air and wished it wasn't quite so hard to stand up.

The esaul returned and refilled the glasses, and the young women went round with the salt again.

'I'm fine,' Gerlach said to the esaul as he tried to pour.

The village deputy balked in horror.

'Shto?'

'Vebla!' Vaja urged. 'Rotamaster not has make answer!'

Gerlach sighed and allowed his glass to be refilled. He took another pinch of salt.

Now they raised their cups as Beledni made the answering toast. Another cry of 'starovye!' another painful moment of liquid torture.

Flush-faced, Gerlach tried to master a way of standing that didn't require support. It was a tall order.

Vaja nudged him. 'Now is esaul's turn,' he grinned.

V

BY THE TIME protocol permitted him to sit down, many toasts later, Gerlach was giggling and in no state to stand anyway. The music resumed, and the lancers removed their szyszaks, gloves and wing crests. Food circulated. Rye bread, more pickled fish and sour cream, stews of pulses and salt-meat, cured basturma spiced with peppers, slices of kolbasi sausage, and parcels of barley and goat meat wrapped in cabbage leaves. A stuffed lamb shashlik was carved off the spit over the fire and portioned out. There was koumiss and – thankfully – water.

Gerlach ate well, his belly still burning from the kvass. As the food soaked the sting of the liquor away, he looked around him. The zal was a meeting house, as well as a temple. A rectangular box of ornately worked silver sat at the head end in a sacred alcove. In other places, cured meat and herbs hung to dry on the beams. Along the flat timbers of the wall were the sooty shapes of old murals. Stylised men with wings mounted on horse shapes that were too small for them.

'Were there lancers here once?' Gerlach asked Vitali.

'They not now here, Vebla.'

'What happened to them?'

Vitali shrugged. 'They in pulk,' he said.

Gerlach pressed the point. As usual, it took a long while to make decent sense of Vitali's answers. At least Vaja, deep in conversation with Yevni the horn blower, was not butting in and complicating matters further.

As far as Gerlach could establish, every single stanitsa on the steppe put all its efforts into raising and maintaining a rota of lancers. The size of the rota depended on the size of the village and the manpower available. Yetchitch must be a place of some size to have produced a rota as strong as Beledni's, Gerlach suggested. Vitali nodded. Yetchitch was a fine and wonderful place, and the thought of it made his eyes mist over. Dushyka's rota was barely half the size.

All the wealth of the village went into the rota too. The Kislevites wanted their warriors to be the best looking of any fighting men in the world. Every scrap of gold and precious metal went into their armour, every spare coin went into buying them the best cloth, silks from Cathay, satins and linens. A stanitsa would go without to provide for its warriors, because to send shabby men out meant dishonour for ataman and krug alike.

Now Gerlach understood why the lancers only wore their beautiful lamellar armour and finest outfits for battle – they were too precious for everyday use.

In normal times, the job of a stanitsa's rota was to defend the village. Sometimes that meant joining with the rotas of other stanitsas to see off khazak or other troubles. But in times of large scale war, like now, the villages would send out their rotas to form pulks – army groups of significant size and hierarchies of loyalty too complex for Gerlach to make sense of from Vitali's enthusiastic doggerel.

All this suggested a system, a culture, of considerable size and complexity, one that Gerlach had not suspected of the oblast peoples. What he, with his southern eyes, saw as an empty region of thinly scattered villages was actually an intricate network of trade and cooperation. Once again, he chastised himself for prejudging the Kislevites as simple barbarian cousins. He reminded himself that Kislev operated on a completely different scale to his beloved Empire. These were not isolated communities, no matter how much they felt like it. After all, they were burning wood and eating fish that night. How close was the nearest forest? The nearest lake?

Vitali said that Dushyka rota had ridden for five weeks to join the pulk down by the Lynsk, ready to stand firm with the armies of the Empire. He and the men of Beledni's rota had left Yetchitch ten weeks earlier to do the same, leaving their home in the dead of winter. So far, the lancers of Dushyka rota had not yet returned home.

Gerlach took a swig of koumiss and wished them decent fortune. He had an unhappy feeling why they had not been seen again.

Vitali made his 'is of no matter' face. 'Is way of things, for riders of dead.'

'Riders of dead? That's what the horse master called us.'

'Yha! All rota lancers are riders of dead.'

Gerlach longed to know what that meant, but Vitali could not explain.

VI

THE NIGHT WAS clear like crystal, and there were more stars in the sky than Gerlach had a number for. The stars were swollen and fierce, as if they had been unleashed by the space the oblast sky provided. Back home, the stars were just fine pin-pricks in the dark.

Gerlach wandered out into the yard where the horses were resting. He breathed in the sweet, cold air of the steppe. Behind him, the zal was heady with heat and life and music and singing.

He leaned back against a beam and sighed. He had overeaten, and had been forced to drink far too much.

In the course of the night, by accident, he had discovered that koumiss was made from fermented mare's milk. That had not stopped him drinking his fill.

He was amazed at himself. He was no longer the starchy vexillary who had ridden out of Vatzl barracks with a shit-eating grin on his face.

The stockade gates were still open, a trusting symbol of embrace to the empty steppe. Gerlach saw a shadow standing under the gate. He approached.

It was Beledni. He had a skin of koumiss in his chunky fist.

'Vebla,' he said when he saw Gerlach. 'You not about hitting Beledni rotamaster again? Is not time for.'

'No,' said Gerlach. 'In fact, I'm sorry about that. About the "coward" thing. I apologise.'

'Well, that very good. Beledni rotamaster very happy. Take drink with me.'

Gerlach took the proffered skin and swigged.

'You are good man, Vebla. Strong… fighter. I saw you ride to take back standard. Take back from many Norscya. More many Norscya.'

'It was my standard, rotamaster.'

'Yha. I would do same. For rota. I see you do this thing and I…' Beledni trailed off. He didn't know the words. 'I want. Nyah! I think I do it to. Whatever. That is why Beledni rotamaster gave charge.'

'You charged the rota to save me?'

Beledni shook his head. 'Nyeh, not save. Word is… "help". I saw Vebla's spirit. Brave. Alone. I want and wish men did same if Beledni rotamaster ride like that.'

So Beledni had led his horse lancers into the fight because he had been impressed by Gerlach's effort. He'd come to his aid because that's what he hoped other men would do if they saw Beledni taking the same huge risk.

'It didn't work,' Gerlach said.

'Shto?'

'I lost the standard. My standard.'

'But you save mine. Pick it up from ground when Mikael Roussa fell down to death. This honour you did for us.'

'Maybe. I'm glad that… mattered.'

They said nothing to one another for a good few minutes. Beledni passed the skin to Gerlach a few times.

'Can I ask a favour, rotamaster?' Gerlach said at last.

'Ask it. I owe to you.'

'Let me carry the rota. I am a vexillary. A standard bearer. It's my job. I lost mine, but I saved yours, and you lost Mikael Roussa. If I'm going to ride with you, let me do the job I'm trained for.'

'Is not right,' Beledni said. Gerlach sighed. 'Is order to things,' Beledni went on. 'Rota bearer is great honour. Man must be veteran to do job. Beledni rotamaster not want and wish to insult men of rota like Maksim, like Mitri, like Sorca, like Ifan. All wait in line for honour of to be rota bearer.'

'I understand.'

'But is special case. Is right thing. Vebla should carry banner. Men of rota will understand this. Or Beledni rotamaster will strike them on head.'

'Thank you, rotamaster. I will not fail in this duty, on my honour as a…' Gerlach had been about to say 'demilancer of Karl Franz'.

Instead he said, 'A soldier.'

'Beledni rotamaster know this, Vebla. Beledni rotamaster not a stupid man.'

'Of course.'

'Or coward.'

'Absolutely.'

Gerlach took the skin and sucked a dreg of koumiss from the slack shape. 'Where do we go tomorrow?'

'Nowhere.'

'And the next day?'

'Nowhere too.'

'And after that?'

'If Dushyka rota not return in two day times, we ride to north and west, to Leblya stanitsa, where pulk was ordered to fall back if enemy too strong.'

Both moons were up now, brilliant in the dark sky. The moonlight cast shadows back from the two men under the stockade gate.

'May I ask another question, rotamaster?'

'Yha. Was that it?'

'No...' Gerlach smiled. 'What does "vebla" mean?'

'Aha! You ask Borodyn. Horse master Borodyn, master of metals, he has right words! Now you come, Vebla. Back to zal. We drink toast to you for being rota bearer.'

Gerlach sighed and followed the heavyset shadow back towards the zal.

VII

DAWN SPREAD OVER the eastern horizon like sour cream spilled into dark water. Light rose to the surface and curdled out across the blankness.

'I'm sorry about your horse,' Borodyn said to Gerlach soon after he woke. 'The children here were over-enthusiastic.'

Gerlach wandered out into the dawn and studied Saksen. The horse seemed very lively and fit. It had been made chalk-white above the belly line and blood-red beneath, and at the junction of the two colours was a carefully painted straight line. The red went up Saksen's throat.

'Your horse was a spirit thing to them. They had never seen its like,' Borodyn said. 'You should count yourself lucky. Only the great champions of Kislev get to have their horses dyed like that.'

'They called it Byeli. The children, I mean,' said Gerlach.

'Byeli. White. Without colour. I know Saksen is grey, but to them it seemed like a pale, white horse. Well, it is certainly a white horse now.'

'Not entirely white.'

'White above and blood-coloured below. A hero's horse, dyed like in the old days. The scriptures of Ursun say that death rides on a pale horse, his destruction to unfold.'

Gerlach smiled. His head was throbbing from the night's drinking. 'I like that. I feel like that.'

'Good,' said Borodyn.

The horse master stalked back to the zal.

'Horse master!' Gerlach called, hurrying after him. 'What?'

'I have a question.'

Borodyn stopped. 'Ask it.'

'Why is the rota called "the riders of the dead"?'

Borodyn shrugged. 'Once a man leaves his home village for war, he is already dead. He will die some-day, so it is better to depart for war each year mourned as if already lost. That was not the question I was expecting.'

'What where you expecting?'

'I was expecting, "what does vebla mean?"'

'So? What does it mean?' Gerlach yelled after him.

'You will find out, Vebla.'

VIII

THE ATAMAN AND his esaul performed a blessing for them on the third day of their stay. They all huddled into the zal as the ataman went to the sacred alcove and took out the silver box.

It was an oclet: a silver-wrapped box with hinged doors. An icon. The face of Ursun looked out, painted in egg tempera on the seasoned fig wood, surrounded by silver. It was a piece of heaven, wrapped in precious metal.

They all bowed their heads as it was opened before them.

IX

ON THE THIRD morning, Beledni's rota rode away into the west. Gerlach hoisted the eagle wing banner high overhead, and rode, shouting from the saddle of his painted horse, into the oblast wind.

AZYTZEEN

I

WERNOFF WAS FAST on his feet but, as a lifelong pikeman, he wasn't used to sword play. Karl had been
trained to fence. It was part of a demilancer's
instruction. Hinn's loaned pallasz was bigger,
straighter and longer than any blade Karl was accustomed to, and needed two hands to control, but he
had the edge.

He didn't want the edge. He didn't want to be
trading blows with a fellow warrior of the Reik.

Karl had expected the Stirlander to be restrained,
and throw out a few obvious strokes for show. But
Wernoff came at him with full-blooded effort,
sweeping the heavy Kurgan sword from side to side.
Wernoff had been drilled to handle five span-
lengths of shivering pike haft. The sword felt short

and light by comparison, even if he didn't know quite what to do with it.

Karl circled, his sword upright and firm compared to the other's wobbling, improvised sweeps.

Around the flame-lit square, the mobs of Northers yelled and stamped.

There was an art to using a broadsword. It is a clumsy object, and over-heavy, but it did one thing superbly well. It cut. It lacked all the finesse of a rapier or sabre, which was why its use was no longer taught in the Imperial schools. The broadsword was an archaic weapon, current wisdom believed, a weapon for savages and barbarians. With a broadsword, there was no possibility of executing the deft moves of fencing. There was no riposte, or feint, or parry, or thrust to be had. There were just three basic moves: the block, the slash, and the remaining-on-your-feet.

A pallasz was so huge and heavy that if you committed to any blow, you were forced to follow it through. If you swung it, your torso went with it. If you blocked with it, you had better have set your feet braced square, or the impact would fell you. A broadsword duel was not a delicate thing. There was no space for fancy darts or quick footwork. It was a slow, slogging effort.

Karl was weary within seconds. The pallasz was such a leaden weight. He cut at Wernoff's swings, and finally deflected one so that the Stirlander's sword tip glanced off the paving.

'Stop trying so hard!' he hissed at the pikeman.

'They said I would be free!' Wernoff retorted.

'What?'

'They told me that if I killed you, they would set me free!'

Karl ducked the next stroke.

'You believe that?'

'It's all I have, demilancer!'

Wernoff was really trying to kill him. The idea jolted Karl harder than any broadsword blow.

'They won't!' he snarled. 'You believe them? You believe what they tell you?'

'I have to believe something!' Wernoff rasped, and thrust forward, lopping a chunk of flesh out of Karl's right shoulder.

Karl yelled out and felt hot blood coursing down his arm. The crowd went berserk, chanting and bawling.

He backed away as Wernoff, eager from the first sniff of blood, closed in.

Let him kill you, something inside Karl Vollen said. Just let him do it. It's what you want and, Sigmar knows, it's the closest thing to escape you're going to manage. Let him kill you.

Karl staggered back, his pallasz trailing over the paving slabs. Wernoff's blade whooped through the air, trying to find him.

But Karl couldn't let go. He didn't want to die. Not like this, performing in the market yard of a murdered town for entertainment. Not like anything, in fact.

He wanted to live. His life mattered.

It made sense. Why else had he been unable to take his own life in the pike pen? If he was going to give his life away, it would be for a damn good reason. And he certainly wasn't going to give these roaring bastards the pleasure of his death.

'Wernoff...' he said. 'I'm sorry. May Sigmar forgive me.'

'For what?' Wernoff asked, cutting in again.

Karl brought his pallasz up and blocked the Stirlander's blow. Then he swung hard, so Wernoff was forced to back away, out of balance thanks to the heavy counterweight of his thick sword.

With a broadsword, the damage was inflicted with the long edge. The demilancers had been taught to use the tip of a sword to thrust.

Karl did the latter. He performed an inappropriate stroke with his pallasz. The tip punched through Wernoff's unguarded sternum, and the rest of the blade followed it.

Wernoff jerked, stricken, like a butterfly on a pin. A great volume of blood squirted out around Karl's hands, under pressure.

'I'm sorry,' said Karl. Wernoff gagged, and then fell down so heavily his weight plucked the pallasz from Karl's hands.

Karl turned around slowly, gazing defiantly at the Kurgan host who were howling and cheering at him. Life was the only thing Karl had left, and keeping hold of it despite everything the Northers tried to do to him was the one way he could deny them.

Zar Uldin walked out from the crowd onto the square. His wolf-mask seemed to grin in the firelight. He crouched beside Wernoff's twitching body, wetted his hands with the blood, and marked an eye symbol on his bare chest.

He rose and faced Karl. It was hard to hear him over the noise of the rampant crowd.

'You do Tchar's work, little Southlander,' he said.

'No,' Karl answered, emphatically.

'Oh, but you do. Tchar rejoices in change, and the second holiest change in the world is the change from life to death. That is what you have done for him.'

'No,' Karl repeated.

Hinn came forward and retrieved his pallasz. They led Karl back through the crowd and into the temple. Uldin's shaman danced around them, shaking his bone-beads and sistrum. Behind them, another ritual bout was getting underway.

In the temple entranceway, Uldin pulled Karl round to face him.

'By what name are you called?' he demanded.

'Karl Reiner Vollen,' the clarion replied, involuntarily.

Uldin reached up and clutched at the air, as if snatching a fly. 'I pluck the name for Tchar and give it back changed.' He opened the hand again, and shook it at Karl as if brushing a cobweb off it.

'Now you are called Azytzeen. By that name you will be known to the Kurgan. Azytzeen!'

'Keep your damn words and names–' Karl spat, touching the iron handle of the true killer in his pocket to ward against the foul charm. He had never been a superstitious man, and had prided himself on scorning such customs. But he touched the iron without hesitation. It seemed to him some magic was very real, and the Kurgan tribes oozed it.

It felt as if Uldin's words were actually stripping his name away from him and replacing it with something heavy and venomous.

'Azytzeen!' Uldin repeated, and his shaman started to sing the name, over and again, as he pranced and capered around them.

II

THE MARKED MEN remained in the temple for the next eight days. They were fed, well and regularly, and had to endure the squealing attentions of shamans who came in and performed rites at them.

All the zars sent their shamans to the temple to conduct rituals over their marked property. Ons Olker visited five times. Though he was busy with Blayda's marked souls, such as von Margur, his eyes constantly searched for Karl. Whenever he was around, Karl kept a firm hand on his true killer.

Uldin's shaman, whose name was Subotai, visited frequently, singling out Karl and other men with Uldin's mark, and daubing them with ash and body paints as he chanted and rattled. When he removed his snake-etched barbute, Subotai revealed a strange face. It was broad and flat, and his eyes were narrow. Karl had once seen a traveller's drawing of the men who lived in the farthest east, in the realm of Cathay. They had these facial characteristics.

'He is of the Man-Chu, who dwell far around the Circle, nigh on the territories of the Dreaded Wo,' von Margur said to Karl. Of course, the knight had not even seen Subotai's face. 'He was taken by Uldin as a war trophy years ago, but marked and spared because he has the sight.'

Only then did Karl notice that the shaman had three blue dots on his right cheek, a very old mark faded by time. Zar Uldin's mark. Karl knew he had the same thing on his own face.

Word of what Karl had done to Wernoff that first night spread amongst the captives the next day, and many men chose to avoid him. Though it was not the place or time for real friendships, Karl suddenly found himself short of comrades. But von Margur didn't seem bothered. Neither did a laconic cross-bowman from Nordland called Etzel, who also wore Uldin's mark, and a Carroburger called Vinnes, who sported the red dots of Zar Herfil. Both of the latter had been forced to fight – and kill – in bouts after Karl's. The four kept themselves together. They understood.

During those eight days, other men were drawn out, and some failed to return. Gradually, the number of captives halved, and all those that remained had killed in a bout. Karl and his comrades were no longer shunned, but the mood had hardened. For most of each day, the marked men sat in bleak silence, consumed by their own thoughts.

Karl was called out twice more, into the firelit square and the blood-lusting crowd. He killed once, in a fight with another Stirlander, who seemed to give up and welcome the swift death Karl granted him.

In the other bout, Karl was drawn against a young man from Middenheim who, at the last moment, broke down and refused to do battle. The Midden-heimer threw away his blade and tried to run, weeping and begging. Hinn executed him, and Karl was dragged back to the temple.

By the seventh day, only von Margur had not been called. Vinnes and Etzel couldn't understand why the Northerners were even bothering to persevere with the blind knight.

But Karl knew. He knew every time von Margur opened his mouth and said things that he had no right to know.

Von Margur had the sight. Possibly as a result of the grievous damage to his brain, he was special, and the Kurgan prized him.

III

ON THE SEVENTH night, Hinn and the Kurgan came for von Margur. A gale had come up in the darkness outside, and it moaned and whistled around the temple's stone bulk. The place was suddenly full of strange, cold drafts, and all the torches sputtered and danced.

'Help me, Karl!' von Margur cried out as he was led away. He was turning his head to and fro, eyes cast upwards, desperate to see. 'I am afraid! I am sore afraid!'

'Sigmar will save you!' Karl called out, a blasphemy that got him a hard slap from Hinn.

Etzel and Vinnes were called too, and a Reiklan-der called Brandt.

The captives waited for half an hour, hearing the distant Kurgan cheers above the howl of the wind. Karl went to the temple altar and knelt to pray for von Margur's soul. He dismissed the desecration that the Kurgan had heaped upon the altar, and steadfastly ignored their iron coffer and its flickering eye. He also cared little that the altar and temple had originally been dedicated to a Kislevite god whose worship and tenets he didn't know. All that mattered was that it was a sacred place, all the better for Sigmar to hear him.

The iron coffer gazed at him, nevertheless, as he did his devotions.

Then the Kurgan brought von Margur back. He was walking unassisted, as if he knew the way. He didn't knock into anything but simply shambled confidently back through the main hall of the temple and took a seat on the floor next to Karl. His hands were bloody.

'It isn't easy,' he said, 'is it?'

'No,' said Karl. He had no idea how the blind knight had survived for one moment.

Von Margur gazed blankly into space.

'I suppose it will get easier,' he said at last, and curled over on the rugs and matting like a child.

'What did they make you do, sir?' Karl asked.

But von Margur had fallen asleep.

Then Vinnes returned. He had been cut on the leg and the hip, and he was shaking and sobbing. The Kurgan washed his wounds with vinegar and left him. Vinnes refused to come anywhere near von Margur.

Karl went over to him.

'What happened?' he asked, offering the Carroberger a waterskin.

'They made me kill Brandt,' Vinnes sniffed. 'Gods alive, they made me gut him! He was no swordsman. He didn't stand a chance against me, but he fought like a bastard and gave me these.' Vinnes ruefully indicated his wounds.

'They're flesh cuts. You'll heal,' said Karl.

'I don't want to heal,' muttered Vinnes plaintively.

'What about von Margur? Did you see?'

Vinnes nodded.

'Dammit! And?'

'He slew Etzel.'

'No!'

'I watched it, Vollen. They were head to head, with a pair of daggers, each of them. In the square out there. Von Margur didn't even know which way to point. He kept calling out for you to help him. The bastards were jeering. Etzel – Sigmar! He didn't want to fight with him. Not a blind man. Not a bloody blind man…'

Vinnes looked round at Karl. He had managed to smear blood from his leg wound across his face. His eyes were terrible to behold. In them, fear, despair, humiliation, disgust, all in equal measures.

'I killed Brandt!' he cried out hoarsely.

'I know, I know… My friend, tell me what von Margur did.'

Vinnes swallowed and his voice dropped to a whisper. 'He fought. Suddenly, like a seeing man. Blocking every blow Etzel threw at him. Knife to knife. A sighted man who has been trained in daggerwork could not have bettered him. He seemed to know everything Etzel was going to do and parry it. All the while... all the damn while... his eyes were slack and looking the wrong way! Sigmar spare me, it was terrifying. Even the bloody Kurgan shut up in wonder at it.'

'Go on, Vinnes.'

'The daggers were flying so fast. Chink chink chink! Etzel was suddenly fighting for real, crying out in horror. Then... then, von Margur, he... he drove both his blades home at once. Both through Etzel's heart. And it was done.'

Karl gasped and sat back.

'I will not go near him, Vollen,' Vinnes announced.

'What? Why? He only did what we all have had to do.'

'I know that! But he's blind! Blind! How could he have done that if dark magic hadn't guided him?'

'I–'

'And look at him, Vollen! Look at him!'

Karl glanced across the temple at the slumbering von Margur.

Like a contented dog, the blind knight was grinning in his sleep.

IV

AT DAWN ON the ninth day, the zars came to the temple and divided the captives up according to their marks. Zar Uldin, escorted by his shaman Subotai, drew off Karl and the seven others with the blue mark, and led them away into the square.

The town was now quiet and deserted. The Kurgan host had moved on. Only trampled mud lay where their gers and pavillions had once been pitched.

Uldin's eight marked men were roped together at the throat. Across the square, Karl could see other groups of captives being led away by their respective zars. He caught a glimpse of von Margur with Blayda and Ons Olker.

Subotai led Uldin's marked men out of the town under guard into a marshy paddock west of the main gate. More than five score Kurgan were gathered there, preparing their big, black horses.

This was Zar Uldin's warband. They were all clad in scale, plate and chainmail darkened with pitch, and their round shields were painted blue with the snakes-and-eye motif. One of the largest riders, a Kurgan called Yuskel, carried the warband's standard. It was a tall pole, the upper half of which was sheathed in clattering human jawbones. The cross spar had three skulls fixed to it: two human skulls on either side of a horse's. All three were gilded. Below the spar fluttered a leathery banner, the irregular shape of which betrayed its human source. On it was painted a wolf's head with a single, centred eye.

Yuskel was mounted on a curious beast: a stout horse with skin striped with thin, vertical black and white stripes. The stripes even extended into its thick mane. It was an angry, snorting creature.

Zar Uldin rode up on his big stallion, and his men shouted a welcome.

Uldin walked his mount between his men, clasping hands and slapping backs. A wineskin was tossed around. Then, with a clap of his massive hands, Uldin ordered them forward. A Kurgan with a huge carnyx that coiled around his torso like a serpent sounded the ugly blare of command.

The warband galloped away into the wind and the trees. Five solid-wheeled wagons pulled by oxen followed the riders, and the marked captives, strung together, were whipped along after the wagons. Subotai and six Kurgan horsemen flanked them.

Turning his neck as far as the rope around it would allow, Karl looked back at the nameless, dead town where he had been forced to cast his humanity away. He thought of Wernoff and the other Stirlander. He hoped they knew, wherever they were, that Azytzeen had killed them.

Not Karl Reiner Vollen.

V

FOR TEN DAYS, they toiled south and west. Uldin's warband roamed far ahead of the trundling wagons and the captives, but each night they caught them up at the camp-fire.

The world they passed through was desolate. Burnt forests and devastated villages. Miles of arable land churned up by hooves. Pastures full of slaughtered livestock. On the track, there were bodies: the executed inhabitants of overrun towns, fleeing refugees who had been overtaken and murdered.

The cool spring air was busy with flies and circling crows.

Apart from one day of heavy rain, the weather was improving. Spring was maturing and casting out the dregs of winter. Somehow, the calm breeze and the pale blue sky made the devastation more affecting. In other years, this time would have been sweet, a growing season for the populations living on the southern edges of the oblast and the northern borders of the Empire.

Not this year. This year that no one would forget.

Spring flowers, white and blue and yellow, grew up from fields of cinders and ruined woodlands. The early green crops sprouted through the brown bones of the recently dead, scattered across the fields. The warm, fresh breezes of springtime were tainted with the scents of rot and the gas of bloated bodies.

Karl had no idea where he was, but he guessed he was not far off the territories of his homeland. If they weren't in Ostermark yet, they would be soon.

And the captives were trailing the Northers' main advance. How deep had that cut now? What part of the Empire still remained free?

Karl was plodding home, but he was very much afraid nothing of it would remain when he got there.

VI

THEY WERE TRUDGING through a thin wood of scorched poplars. It was the tenth day since they had quit the nameless town. The poplars had heat-stripped trunks, and a few feeble burned branches protruding from them. It looked for all the world as if a great fire had burned them from above. From out of the sky.

They were walking behind the wagons, flanked by Subotai on his milk-white ass and the six Kurgan riders.

And there the enemy found them. Afterwards, Karl was astonished at himself for regarding them as the enemy.

There was a rumble of hooves, shaking the fire-dried earth. The Kurgan reacted in alarm and started shouting.

Eight knights templar of the Reiksguard plunged majestically out of the gloom, with maces and swords raised in their gauntleted fists. Their leader was swinging a warhammer strung with white ribbons. They were tremendous to behold. Laurel garlands decorated the gold symbols of their illustrious order. They were clad in full suits of silver-white plate. Their thundering steeds were thoroughbred destriers: massive horses clad with shaffrons, crinits and complete bardings of articulated steel, and caparisons of rich cloth.

The lead knight ploughed into the side of the convoy first, whirling his hammer. He smashed a Kurgan warrior off his dark horse and then dug in with his long, roweled spurs – elongated things designed to reach his steed's flanks under the deep, segmented apron of the armour bard. He surged about, his hammer turning. The air was cold enough for his breath to be visible as snorted plumes escaping the slits in his polished bascinet. He lunged at Subotai. The shaman was kicking the flanks of his white ass with his bare heels, and yelling curses at the magnificent knight.

The blunt face of the hammer hit Subotai square in the forehead of his barbute. The slip-on iron helmet buckled and flattened. A bloody vapour squeezed out of the eyeslits on impact.

Subotai fell backwards off his mount, his blood speckling the ass's white coat.

Karl wanted to run, but the thong attaching him to his fellow captives snapped taut and yanked him back. All around them, Reiksguard templars were fighting Kurgan horsemen from their saddles.

And the Kurgan were losing.

'Come on!' Karl yelled at Maddeus, the man behind him.

'We can escape now! They don't care about us any more! Come on!'

Maddeus tried to run, but fell down, strangled by the rope. The man behind him had just been trampled by a side-staggering destrier.

Karl snatched out his true killer and slashed through the rope tying him to Maddeus.

He was free. Really free.

'For Sigmar's sake, Karl!' Maddeus screamed, clutching at his throat noose. 'Me too!'

Karl ran forward and cut the rope behind Maddeus's nape with the dirk.

They started to run, heads down, into the trees. Karl tripped over a cinder root, and Maddeus dragged him to his feet.

Behind them, the templars were winning the horse to horse fight. One of the wagons had caught fire.

'This way!' Karl urged, as he and Maddeus slogged through the ash-dust. In their desperation, they barged against tree trunks that looked solid but disintegrated at a touch like powder.

They heard hooves behind them. It was the leader of the knightly detachment. He saw them and spurred towards them.

'Sir! Sir, stay your hand! We are men of the Empire, sadly imprisoned!' Maddeus called out, turning back with raised hands. 'Free us, we beg you!'

Karl had no doubt the knight heard Maddeus's frantic plea. He threw himself down as the knight charged on. Maddeus hurled himself the other way.

The templar passed between them, his destrier kicking up clods of black ash. He circled round and came back for another pass.

Maddeus squealed as the warhammer broke his back.

'You bastard!' Karl howled in outrage. 'We are not the enemy!'

The templar turned his horse and began to run Karl down.

'In the name of Sigmar!' Karl yelled, trying to escape the knight by doubling back around a tree. 'In the name of Sigmar, we are loyal to the Imperial throne! Loyal, I say!'

The knight suddenly sat upright in his saddle. A black-fletched arrow had just impaled his chest.

Zar Uldin galloped in, with many of the warband racing beside him. He was letting arrows fly from his composite bow. Uldin was riding without a hand on the reins. He drew the bowstring back past his ear and charged his arrows with such force that no bascinet, cuirass or mail could stop them. Each arrow made a spitting noise as it loosed a grinding crack and punctured its target.

Transfixed with arrows, the knight clattered off his horse.

Karl cowered against a tree stump as the Kurgan stormed past. They were whooping and yelling and their heavy arrows spat through the air. Each man had a clutch of six or seven arrows gripped between the fingers of the hand that held the bow itself, so as soon as they had fired one, their drawing hand could nock another as it went to pull the bowstring back. Their fire rate was astonishingly rapid, like some mechanical device designed by the Engineers of Nuln. The Kurgan horses, smart and hard-trained, seemed to need no rein control. This allowed the Northers great independence; they could turn in the saddle and shoot arrows in passing to the side, or even to the rear. Karl gazed as a Kurgan – Barlas – put an arrow into the chest of one templar as he charged him, and then two more between his shoulderblades as he galloped past.

The proud templars, the military elite of the Empire, were overwhelmed in under a minute. One, armed with a sword and cornered, fought on against the Kurgan riders closing around him and goading him with spears. Another, unhorsed, found himself facing Zar Uldin, who dismounted to meet him, drawing his pallasz.

Karl hurried over to where Maddeus lay face down, but the man was miserably done to death. Karl made the sign of Sigmar over him, and then began to run, as fast as his legs could take him, into the shadows of the extinct forest.

VII

HE RAN THROUGH the blackened poplars and the dried rags of burnt ivy. He ran towards the light and what he hoped was the south.

When he came out of the dead woodland, he found himself at the top of a low hill. In the wide valley below, and down on the plain of a distant river, a battle was raging. Ten thousand men and horses, twenty thousand even, resembled dark shapes seething like ants from a spaded hillock. Smoke and dust rose, swabbing out the low sun. It was impossible to tell who was who, or even who was winning.

But Karl Reiner Vollen had a feeling in the pit of his stomach that this was another day the Empire would mourn for years to come.

He stopped dead. He could run all he liked, but he could never outrun this tide of death. He leaned against an old, gnarled tree, and hugged his arms around his body.

After a while, he heard horses coming up behind him and looked round. Three of Uldin's warband walked their mounts out of the woods towards him. Their leader, a hairy man in a houndskull helm, was playing out the loops of his lariat. When he saw the look on Karl's face, he simply hung the rope back

on his saddle without comment, and casually beckoned to the demilancer.

The three Kurgan turned their horses back the way
they had come, and Karl walked after them, head
bowed.

VIII

THE KURGAN WERE laying out their dead and stripping the templar corpses of their armour. The
beautiful silver-steel pieces were being collected
in a handcart. They were of such fine workman-
ship, they would be reused, altered, or used for
barter.

Seven Kurgan were dead, including the shaman
Subotai, as well as three of the marked men.

Zar Uldin saw Karl, and rose to his feet. He had
been squatting beside Subotai's crumpled body. He
had removed his wolf-helm, and his fine, shaved
head was exposed.

'Azytzeen. You tried to escape.'

Karl shook his head. He looked up at the taller
man's scarred, murderously handsome face.

'No. I fled for my life.'

Uldin narrowed his eyes.

'They were killing everybody. They killed Maddeus. I decided to run.'

The zar thought about this, and then shrugged
lightly. He believed Karl.

'But escape was in my thoughts too,' Karl said anyway.

Uldin stiffened. 'And?'

'I changed my mind.'

The zar smiled. 'Change. There, you see? Tchar is in you.'

'No,' said Karl firmly. 'He is not.'

No longer interested, Uldin walked back over to the shaman's body. The hairy man in the hound-skull tied Karl back up with the four surviving marked captives.

The gathering warband looked morose. It seemed the death of a shaman was a bad omen, and that a warband without a shaman was weak.

'Why are the bastards so grim?' whispered the captive beside Karl.

'The shaman's dead. That is misfortune for them all.'

'How do you know that, Karl?'

'I overheard what they were saying.'

The man looked at Karl nervously. 'You can understand their words?'

'Can't you?' Karl asked.

'Of course not,' the man replied, and the other three captives, listening in to the exchange, shook their heads too.

'But–' said Karl. Then he shut up because he was far too scared to think about what it meant.

Yuskel, the banner bearer, walked up to Uldin and put his hand on his heart. He said something about preparations. Uldin nodded, and gathered up the small, limp body of Subotai in his arms.

The warband felled the cinder trunks around the clearing, and raised a small wooden stockade. The work took most of the day. Some of the warriors had to ride away to locate and cut decent wood from groves that had not been scorched by the fire. The Kurgan dead were carried inside the stockade, and their weapons laid out beside them. Then the horses of the fallen men were slaughtered and gutted, Subotai's white ass along with them. The carcasses were bled, and then set upright around the paling wall. They were raised on sharpened stakes that propped them up through their slit bellies. Fresh staves were cut to support their lolling heads so they looked like they were alive and galloping.

The stripped bodies of the templars and the corpses of the three marked captives were left where they had fallen, to rot.

The warband gathered around the stockade as night fell. The drummers beat out a slow, pulsing rhythm, and the horn blower pealed long, atonal blasts into the closing dark with his serpent-coil carnyx.

Uldin, helmless, went around the stockade, whispering to each staked horse-corpse in turn and kissing its muzzle. He finished with Subotai's white ass.

Then he took a flaming tree branch from Berlas, the master archer, and set it to the stockade.

The Kurgan warband howled like wolves into the sky as the flames rose and engulfed the stockade and the bodies inside it. The horn blew, over and over, pulsing above the throbbing howls. Then the staked-up horse-corpses began to catch fire too.

Crosswinds drove the pungent smoke through the dead grove. Coughing, the captives turned away.

Karl was transfixed.

* * *

IX

AT DAWN, THE warband roused and rode away into
the valley, trailing the wagons and the guarded captives behind it. The stockade pyre was still burning:
a grim, black ring guarded by the smouldering
skeletons of eight propped steeds.

Below, the battle had ended. The cold morning air
was filled with the miserable perfumes of mass warfare: blood, faeces, charred wood, heated iron,
powdered bone. There was no relief from it.

Those that had lost the battle had been crucified
naked, alive or dead. The foul sentinels watched
over the smouldering, debris-littered landscape.
They were staked apart every few dozen spans, on
frames of spear-shafts or wagon spokes. Black carrion birds fluttered and hopped all over the wide,
wounded vista, like autumn leaves stirred by the
breeze.

They marched until noon, when they reached a
town. An Imperial burg. From the smoke trails
wisping from the stone structures inside its high
walls, it seemed clear that the Northers had taken it.
Someone told Karl it was Brunmarl. The news
made him shiver. If it was Brunmarl, then they were
in the Marches of Ostermark, inside the Empire.
Brunmarl had a famous cathedral, he knew that
much. There was no sign of a spire, though there
was a large burning building that looked as if it
might once have owned one.

Uldin led them through the great gates. Many
more zars were massing their warbands inside the
city walls. Standard bearers challenged one another

loudly as they came in sight of rival banners. Yuskel was especially good at spitting out muscular torrents of abuse at other banner bearers.

Karl glimpsed Zar Blayda's banner – a bloody swordblade on a red field – down one side street, and Zar Herfil's boar's skull standard in a market yard. The horde had come here to roost.

Uldin's band were sent to billet in an old, sandstone building that turned out to be the town's library. Karl expected to see Kurgan defecating on the pages of the precious books, but he was surprised by the truth.

Warriors were carrying the heaps of ancient tomes out of the shattered building on wooden boards, and the shamans were working their way through the pages, arguing between them about the things they found.

Just as they came to acquire land and loot and blood for their bloody gods, the Northers had come to steal knowledge and learning.

He was nudged at spearpoint into the vacant halls of the library building. Karl stooped and picked up a slim volume that had been cast aside into the brick dust. It was a treatise on fortification, written in old Tilean, the ancient language.

'Those leaves there?' asked a shaman who looked up from nearby. 'Can you read them?'

'Of course,' replied Karl, and tossed the book away. The shaman, a tall, gangly youth with antlers rising from his cap of fur, leaped up and ran to Karl.

'You can read it?' he repeated. Ropes of shell beads tinkled around his long, thin neck. Both of his middle fingers were absent, so his hands were like curious claws as they pawed the old book.

'What is this word?' he demanded.

'That... "strong"?' Karl said.

'And this one?'

'Ahhh... "gabion"...a defence term.'

The shaman looked up at Karl. His eyes were wiped with kohl, and a black line had been painted around his mouth, making it wider. The flesh of his face, neck and shoulders was dusted with white chalk. The shaman rattled his sistrum at Karl, and hopped from foot to foot.

Yuskel dragged Karl into the building.

The marked captives were thrown into an undercroft and the hatch boarded up behind them. They waited in the dark for several hours.

Then the hatch opened again, and Zar Uldin stomped down the raw wooden stairs. He looked around and pointed directly at Karl. The warriors behind him surged forward to grab the demi-lancer.

Outside, it was dark, and torches had been lit in the beckets.

'Another fight?' Karl said sullenly.

'Yes, Azytzeen.'

Karl sighed.

'This is important!' Uldin snapped, turning to face him. 'You must prove my warband is still strong. The other zars know I have lost my shaman. I must win tonight, to prove that ill fortune does not follow me and those who ride with me.'

'And if I lose?'

'My warband will be broken up and shared between the other zars,' Uldin replied.

Karl smiled. The temptation was almost too great. 'And if I win?'

'The act might be favorable, and entice a new shaman.'

'So what I do tonight makes – or breaks – your warband?'

'Yes.'

'Then at last, I have power over you,' Karl said, and walked away.

'Azytzeen! Azytzeen!' Uldin called out, running after Karl.

'What is my name, zar? What is it?'

'I forget…'

'What is my name?'

'Uhh… Kerl?'

'Karl.'

'Seh! Karl!'

'Call me that and I might fight for you. Call me that bastard name and I will do nothing but seek a quick death. Who am I supposed to fight?'

'Some dog of Zar Kreyya's mark. Then, if you triumph, one of Zar Herfil's slaves.'

'What's my name?'

'Karl is your name.'

X

THE KURGAN OF Uldin's band took him with ceremony to the pit. Yuskel carried the standard with its gilded skulls before him, and Hzaer the carnyx blower came behind, booming out threatening notes that echoed down the firelit streets. Six warriors flanked Karl, their swords drawn. One was Berlas, the archer. Another was Efgul, the hairy warrior in the houndskull. The other four were Fegul One-Hand, Diormac, Lyr and Sakondor.

Karl knew their names because they told them to him. One by one, before their march to the pit, they presented themselves to him, bowed their heads, placed their hands on their hearts, and uttered their names.

It was not, Karl recognised, an honour as such. To them he was still marked scum. But it acknowledged his importance and the vital part he was about to play in the future of the warband. They told him their true names, and he knew there was magick in that. They were giving him power over them, by speaking their names with their hands placed as heart-truth. They were giving him power.

They led him to a derelict building that had once been a farrier's workshop or an ironworker's forge. The long, stone bath had been filled with water and oil, and heated slightly. There was steam in the air, and the strong scents of balsam and ginger.

Yuskel and Efgul made him strip and climb into the hot water. They dunked him several times and held him under. When he came up at last, coughing, he was cleaner than he'd been in weeks, and his skin was soft and slippery with oil.

Karl stood naked, dripping and tense, as Berlas combed back his hair and tied it in a tail behind his neck. Lyr shaved his face with the edge of a frighteningly sharp knife. Then Hzaer dusted blue

powder over him, so that his head, neck and chest
were all stained.

'Close your eyes,' Hzaer warned, and blew black
ink through a straw into each of Karl's eye sockets.
Now he was blue-skinned, and his eyes glinted out
of jet-black circles.

They brought him brown leather trews and heavy
black boots, and fastened on iron thigh plates. Then
a chainmail breech-clout was added, supported by a
wide leather belt with a fat brass boss-buckle
inscribed with a snake. Hzaer and Berlas bound
Karl's arms with leather windings that crossed
around the base of his thumbs and tied off around
his palms.

Yuskel brought a single pauldron of black metal
and strapped it around Karl's left shoulder.

Then they stepped back. Skarkeetah and Uldin
emerged from the shadows. The slave lord seemed
luminous in his white-bear pelt. The gold and blue-
stone eye glinted around his thick neck and the
one-eyed raven was perched on his raised left wrist.
Uldin carried a black iron barbute with short,
twisted horns.

With Subotai dead, and fearing ill omen, the zar
had called upon the sorcerous slave lord for help.
Uldin had undoubtedly paid him, for Skarkeetah
was not affiliated to any one warband.

Skarkeetah made no shamanic prancing or prat-
tling. He waved no sistrum or beads. He looked Karl
in the eyes and muttered some low, dark prayer of
blessing that Karl did not understand. He didn't
need to. Every syllable made his flesh crawl. The

raven nodded and bobbed, clacking its thick, hooked beak. Then Skarkeetah held his amulet up and Karl was forced to gaze into the blazing blue stones in the pupil of the snake-wreathed eye. Light from the candles made the blue stones twinkle and spark.

'Tchar governs you now, more than you care to admit, more than you even know. Let him guide your hand tonight.'

Karl said nothing.

'Will you fight?' Uldin asked.

'I will fight,' Karl said, dismissively.

'Make it heart-truth or not at all,' Uldin replied.

Karl hesitated. Then he raised his right hand – his sword hand – and placed it over his heart. 'I will fight.'

Satisfied, Uldin placed a leather caul on Karl's crown and lowered the heavy barbute over his head. It was stifling and he could see very little.

'No,' he said, and took it off.

'You'll need it,' warned Skarkeetah.

'Not if Tchar is with me,' Karl mocked, but the reply seemed to delight the slave lord. Skarkeetah reached out and placed his plump fingers across Karl's left cheek and rested the pad of his thumb on Karl's lips.

'Tchar is most certainly with you.'

Horns, bone and metal, blew loudly in the city outside, and Karl realised there was a dull, distant roar that could only be cheering.

His Kurgan guard led him to the door. In the doorway, Yuskel paused and handed Karl his true killer. It had been taken from him with the rags he'd stripped off. Karl slid it into his belt.

Two hundred paces from the farrier's barn was a huge round drum of a building that Karl realised had once been the playhouse. Open to the sky, its wooden structure resembled a miniature amphitheatre. The stands and galleries were torchlit and groaned with stamping, cheering Northers.

They went in under the low eaves of the players' entrance. Under the seating, through the darkness of timber beams and rib supports, and into the flickering yellow light.

The bowl of the playhouse was a circle of dirt floor surrounded by high wooden panels. Tonight, the playhouse had its biggest ever audience.

Yuskel held a round shield so that Karl could slide his left arm into place. The shield was blue, with the snakes-and-eye emblem, and a black horse tail strung from the boss. Karl hefted it, and tested his arm for flexibility. Then Uldin handed Karl his own pallasz, hilt first.

Another carnyx sounded, and Uldin took a broadsword from Lyr and strode out into the dirt bowl. Zar Kreyya, a giant in spiked gold, emerged to meet him and they exchanged the ritual sword strokes.

The zars withdrew, and Karl edged out into the arena.

The host was screaming and wailing. Fists beat time on the playhouse's wooden rails.

A figure appeared on the far side of the pit. He was similarly dressed in iron and leather half-mail and armed with a sword and shield. His lean frame was painted green. Karl raised his pallasz and charged him.

Only when he was a few paces off did Karl recognise his opponent.

It was Johann Friedel.

XI

WHITE DYE HAD been rubbed into Friedel's eye sockets and into the hollows of his cheeks, and short lines had been wiped vertically on his upper and lower lips. He looked like a cadaver, like a death's head, the green pigment daubing him the colour of putrid flesh. His hair was caked to his scalp with lime wash.

'Johann?'

The figure growled.

'Johann? It's me. It's Karl.'

Friedel's deep-fullered sword came at Karl. He got the shield up and the blade crashed off it, jarring Karl's arm.

'Johann!'

Another blow to the shield. Another. Chips of blue painted wood scattered off.

'Sigmar's name, Johann! It's Karl!'

Friedel swung a cut at Karl with enough force to smack Karl's shield aside. Karl barely managed to get his pallasz up in time to fend away the follow-through.

It was Johann Friedel's body, right enough. But Johann Friedel no longer inhabited it. His eyes, framed by the white dye, were... blank. During his boyhood, Karl had owned a dog, a good game hound, that had been bitten by a rat and fallen prey to the frothing sickness. His father had been forced to kill the dog with a mattock to stop its suffering.

The look in Friedel's eyes was the same one Karl had seen in his dog's gaze just before the end. Vacant, wild, feral, deranged by pain and fear and sickness.

They circled, trading blows, sword to shield. Friedel stormed closer, and Karl put his shoulder behind his shield and barged him away. They crashed again, shield to shield now. There was a brute strength in Friedel that Karl had never suspected. He doubted it had been there the last time he'd seen the boy.

Outside the zal, just before Zhedevka fell, Johann Friedel had yelled Karl's name and begged him not to go away.

Karl was surprised by how much that fleeting memory hurt him. Surprised – and annoyed. Since his near escape in the ash wood, Karl had become hardened and composed. He had worn out his capacity to feel grief, or to feel much at all for any of the things or people he had lost at Zhedevka. It seemed the only way he could deal with the terrible events that had transformed his life was to grit his teeth and block them out. He'd already mourned Johann Friedel in his mind, convinced he was dead like everyone else.

But Friedel wasn't. He was worse than dead. He was a rotting echo of himself, lumbering out of the dark to remind Karl of his loss and rekindle his grief. To start Karl hurting all over again. And Friedel was suffering. Suffering like a dog.

It would not do. Karl would not have it so. This mocking atrocity had to end. End. End.

The crowd was screaming and booming. The noise was so great that Karl was physically shaken by it. For a moment, he forgot where he was.

He swept around, searching for his foe, and raised his sword. Blood ran slickly down the fuller groove and over his hand.

Friedel was lying on the dirt floor of the play-house bowl in pieces. He was so rent and disfigured, Karl could not bear to look at him.

Uldin strode out into the pit, and raised his heavy arms, thick with trophy rings, to accept the adulation. Efgul hurried out after the zar, and ran to steady Karl.

'Spirit of Khar!' Efgul rasped. 'You brought him death like a daemon, Azytzeen!'

'Enough! I can't... I can't...' Karl panted. He was trembling hard. Efgul shook him.

'Stay true! You're halfwise there!'

'I can't...'

'Stay true!'

'You don't understand! He was my friend!'

'Then you gave him Tchar's gift! The gift of change! Life into death! Captivity into freedom!'

'Gods help me...'

'Listen to me, Azytzeen. Krayya's warband are of the Mark of Decay! Noork'hl, the Unclean! If that flesh-body was truly your friend, then you spared him the Great Corruption That Consumes!'

Efgul spoke urgently and earnestly, as if he was telling some grim truth. It was nonsense to Karl.

'I don't understand,' Karl said, looking at Efgul's shaggy face.

'You will, if you live.'

Horns sounded, and Efgul dragged Karl around. Uldin was making the formal challenge to the pitched-black figure of Blayda. Scrabbling Northers had dragged the bloody scraps of Freidel from the ring.

They all departed. Efgul too left, taking Friedel's sword to make a new trophy ring for Uldin's arms. Karl turned to face Blayda's ritual champion.

He was a tall man, stripped down to a chainmail clout and plated armour on his limbs. His skin was painted red. He had no shield. With both hands, he gripped the long handle of a Carroberg greatsword.

For a moment, Karl thought it was Vinnes, for he was of Blayda's mark.

It wasn't.

Yet even if it had been, Karl wouldn't have held back. Not any more. There was nothing he could face now that he was too afraid to kill.

KUL

I

THEY RODE INTO the north-west for twenty days and
twenty nights. Gerlach Heileman thought his mind
had become reconciled to the infinite openness of
the steppe during the ride to Dushyka, but this journey dwarfed it. Twenty days' riding-worth of
nothingness in all directions. Gerlach began to welcome the moonrise, or the occasional buzzards that
hung in the daylight air. They were brief, precious
breaks in the monotony of grass and sky.

Until he started to notice the clouds. This was
some five or six days into the trek. He wondered
why he had not seen them before. No two were the
same. Their shapes and forms, their textures and
colours, even their speeds. Some resembled objects
– a castle tower, a grazing horse, an eagle's wing.

Gerlach had already noticed that, from time to time, the lancers would point up at the sky and make some remark that was usually greeted by chuckles or nods. Now he understood. They saw it too.

'A ram!' someone would declare as they rode along.

Others would agree, or offer suggestions of their own.

On occasions, it was more abstract. A lancer would point and laugh, 'Mitri!' The cloud, a dark lump, looked nothing like the heavy lancer... except that its solidity and gloom somehow conveyed Mitri's demeanour. Some clouds just seemed to suggest things, as if they had inherent character.

It was strange. Once Gerlach had begun to observe the clouds, the open steppe didn't seem empty at all. It was changing all the time. There was always something to see, some pattern to identify. It had just taken a while for his southern-bred mind, accustomed to complex landscapes, to be re-educated. Now, he supposed, he saw the world as the Kislevites saw it. What he had taken to be a vacant blankness had a subtle complexity all of its own, if you knew how to appreciate it.

When Gerlach pointed at a cloud and said, 'A ewe suckling lambs!' the riders seemed delighted with him.

They stopped for a few hours each night. There was no wood, but the riders had brought kindling with them. Most of it was animal bones carefully salvaged from previous meals. In a world where there was little of anything, everything had a use.

Huddled round the weak, yellow flames of the fire, the men would talk idly and reminisce. Sometimes they would even talk about the things they had seen pass by in the clouds that day. This efficient frugality governed their way of life. Every resource in this hard, pared-down existence was used and reused until it was exhausted. The bones of one meal fuelled the next. The shapes of passing clouds stopped them going crazy with boredom during the day, and the memory of them entertained them at night. It was as ingenious as it was thrifty.

At the fireside, Borodyn told Gerlach something of the lore of the sky. It had, as Gerlach guessed, a lot to do with circles. No two clouds were precisely the same, and they went on forever, making long, repeated journeys around the krug of the sky. If a man saw a cloud that he had seen earlier in his life, he knew the sky had gone full circle, and that his time was over. Sometimes, Borodyn said, a man who had seen a cloud for a second time got on his horse and rode away from his stanitsa or his rota and into the embrace of fate, never to be seen again.

Each dawn, in the cold, almost green light of the oblast daybreak, Gerlach and the men of the rota rose and rode away into the grass. Gerlach wondered if any of them would ever be seen again either.

* * *

II

IT WAS EVIDENTLY possible to derive extraordinary
amounts of information from the steppe, more
than Gerlach would ever have believed. When the
world was this monotonous – open grass, empty
sky – then any variation, no matter how miniscule,
was strikingly obvious.

Born to this life, the Kislevites were quick to read
the signs and clues the steppe gave them. And once
he'd begun to read the cloud-forms, Gerlach found
himself noticing other details too. The grasses, for
example, were not all the same, no matter how uniform they seemed at first. Old growth and new,
different types of grass, brakes of thistle and hardy
fern. One glance at the steppe grass around him
told a rider how recent the last rains had been, how
far he'd have to dig to find pockets of moisture,
which way the wind was blowing, and what time of
day it was. An experienced rider didn't even have to
look. The sound his horse's hooves made was
enough. Firm and dry, soft and damp, flat and hollow.

From the air temperature and the humidity, it was
possible to predict the weather. The riders could tell
if rain was coming, and from which compass point.
They could tell if a gale was about to rise, long
before there was any darkening of the sky. The pattern and motion of the grass betrayed wind
direction, and the fluctuation of light across the
horizon foretold the changing climate.

By the time they neared Leblya stanitsa, Gerlach
had learned enough to understand how the rota

knew they were approaching a stanitsa before it had come into view. They had smelled smoke, and other odours like animal dung and vinegar. There was nothing to see, of course, but after days in the open air of the steppe, the merest whiff of smoke from a distance was enough.

Maksim raised his hand and the rota slowed out in a long line either side of him. 'Leblya,' he said. Several men agreed. Ahead of them was some swaying grass, bleached almost white in the afternoon sunlight.

Gerlach was about to scoff, and then he smelt it too. A remote scent of charcoal and animal sweat.

'Many of men,' Beledni muttered. Gerlach wasn't sure if that was supposed to be good or bad. With a brisk 'Yatsha!', Beledni spurred forward and led them onwards.

From what he had been told, Gerlach knew that this stanitsa – Leblya – had been nominated as a suitable restaging post for the Kislevite pulk in the event of retreat or rout. Any rota or warband that had escaped Zhedevka was under oath to regroup here. Gerlach's spirits rose. If there were 'many of men' here, then perhaps the pulk could regain its strength and prepare to return into the war zone. They could assemble at Leblya, and return south to begin the counter-fight.

After another quarter of an hour's ride, Beledni pulled up again, and halted the rota. He conferred with Maksim and the hornblower Yevni.

'What is it?' Gerlach asked Vitali.

Vitali pulled a sour face. 'Blood,' he said.

'You smell it?'

'Yha. Vebla does not?'

Gerlach couldn't. Just smoke, a little stronger now.

Beledni turned to the men and shouted a curt order. At once, the men dismounted, and dressed themselves in their wargear as quickly as possible. Gerlach did the same. It was a peculiar sight. Almost sixty half-naked men standing beside waiting horses in the middle of nothing, pulling felt surcoats over their heads and buckling on corselets of lamellar plate.

As soon as their wing crests, leopard pelts and szyszak helmets were in place, the men bundled their cast-off everyday rags into ground sheets and tied them fast behind their cantles. Gerlach hurried to keep up with them.

Once a rider was ready, he gave a shout – his name – and then leapt into the saddle from a standing pose. Now that was simply showing off, Gerlach thought, a circus trick. But the brash display of horsemanship raised the confidence of the rota. Gerlach thought about trying it, but knew he'd make an utter fool of himself. Saksen was rather bigger than the rota's ponies, and he was nothing like as fit and nimble as the lancers. By the time anyone looked his way, he was already astride his horse, buckling on his burgonet and adjusting the fit of his riding gloves.

Gerlach realised he needed to be close to the front rank. He picked up the banner, and steered Saksen forward until he was between Maksim and Beledni. The rotamaster looked over at him, his deep set eyes twinkling behind the heart-shaped face guard of his szyszak.

'This matter now, Vebla,' he said. 'This time now here. It matter you carry banner.'

Gerlach nodded. Saksen pawed uneasily, he held one ear back and the other forward with uncertainty.

Gerlach patted his neck. 'Glory awaits us, byeli-Saksen, my old friend,' he soothed. His gelding was still stark and splendid with his white and red body paint.

Gerlach hoisted the banner, and the long red and white snake of cloth fluttered out behind the wing-shield in the steppe wind.

They advanced on Leblya.

III

LEBLYA WAS MUCH larger than Dushyka. There was an inner mound – an old Scythian earthwork – on which a sturdy zal stood inside a heavy stone stockade. The town clung around the skirts of the mound, a muddle of white-painted izbas and barns. About them, a second broader and lower stockade, with a wooden gatehouse.

The wide sky had gone a dusky grey-blue, and for now there were no clouds except a thin bar in the south, just above the horizon. The grasslands had turned a pale, washed-out lime colour.

Dark dots – racing horsemen – dashed around the outer stockade in considerable numbers. There were perhaps a hundred or more. Gerlach knew what they were even as Maksim said the word.

'Kyazak!'

Leblya was under assault from the horse raiders. Under siege, in fact. As they drew closer, Gerlach could see the attackers in greater detail. Men in black rags and pitch-treated iron harnesses. Their black helmets were capped with bull horns and antlers. They were using slings to pelt the stockade with flaming missiles. Wisps of white smoke rose from the outer stockade.

Beledni slowed the rota and spread them out in a line, two hundred horse lengths from the town. By now, the kyazak had spotted them. They were breaking off from their hectic circuits and massing to face Beledni's company. It was not an aggressive response, more an act of curiosity. They easily outnumbered Yetchitch krug. They seemed puzzled that this huddle of riders had not simply turned tail and run.

'Kul!' Vaja said and spat.

'Kul?'

Kul was a tribal determination, one of the most southerly – and most feared – of the Kurgan from the Eastern Steppes. According to Vitali and Vaja, they were particular brutes, seldom allied to any main Kurgan force. They were content to prowl the oblast for scraps the host left behind. They were famous for an especially unlovely method of execution they reserved for those beaten in war. Vaja tried to explain what it was. It had something to do with a man's ribcage. Language, perhaps thankfully, defeated him.

The Kul gathered to meet them. They were dismounting, and slapping their ponies away. Slowly, they assembled a wall of shields. Many of the Kul had long, berdish axes or clubs.

'Why don't they fight us on horse?' Gerlach asked. He knew for a fact that all the Kurgan tribes were bred to the saddle.

'They know us,' Beledni said. 'They see lancer wings. They fear rota charge and rota lances.'

'So they make a shield wall?'

'Yha, Vebla. They decide Lublya is theirs. Will not give it up. Will dig down, stand ground and hold land.'

'And?'

'Land belong to no one,' Maksim said. 'Land belong to holy Urzun, and Gospodarinyi live off land by his allowance. Kul will learn this. Land is not to be theirs.'

'We're going to fight them, then?' Gerlach asked.

'Yha,' said Beledni.

'We're... going to charge a shield wall?'

'Yha, Vebla,' Beledni said.

The idea alarmed Gerlach. The notion of a battle did not – but charging a shield wall? That was madness. One of the most basic rules of cavalry warfare, as his tutors had emphasised, was that horses – no matter how well trained – would not charge into an obstacle like a shield wall. It was simply against their nature. No matter how hard you drove them, they would break eventually, rather than launch into an impediment. That was why the shield wall, though ancient in terms of military ideas, was still sound in practice. Indeed, the pike companies of the Empire relied on the principle. If they stood firm and kept their pole arms squared and disciplined, they would turn aside even the most insane of horse charges.

'Not look so worried, Vebla,' Beledni said with a chuckle. 'Shield wall looks strong, but Beledni know Kul. Beledni know how Kul think.' He rapped the brow of his szyszak with a stiff finger.

'You've fought them before?'

'Yha!' replied the rotamaster, and briefly cocked his head to one side to show and tap an old scar on his neck. Maksim pulled up his left sleeve and revealed another deep, fading scar.

'We have fought Kul many times. Sometimes, we have won.'

That wasn't terribly reassuring, although Beledni was at least alive to make the claim.

'Is time,' Beledni decided. He sat up in his saddle and looked left and right, contemplating the ranks of his lancers. They all waited, poised.

He gave a cry, and they couched their long horse lances. Horses whinnied nervously. Beledni's open hand hovered for a long moment.

He dropped it.

Yevni blew a long note on his bone horn.

And the rota charged.

IV

THEY MADE THE best pace they could across the nodding gorse and saltgrass, hooves pounding the dry earth. Gerlach rode in the lead, holding the banner upright and away from his thigh. Beledni posted Vaja and Vitali to flank the banner.

One hundred horse lengths ahead, the shield wall drew tight and waited. Kul warriors behind the front line of interlocked shields cried out and waved latecomers into the mass.

A thick, strong mass. An unmovable mass.

Shield bosses glinted in the spring light. Axe blades rose. A Kul carnyx blew a long, sharp note. The Kul standard – a set of massive antlers transfixing a wolf-skull – was hefted up at the centre of the wall line. The sockets of the wolf's skull seemed to glare at them balefully as they rode in.

Ten horse lengths. Five. Mounts at full stretch, manes flying, teeth bared.

The Kul weren't just holding their ground. They were now surging towards the charge. Towards the charge! As if they welcomed it. As if they welcomed death. The discipline of their shield wall was forgotten in the eagerness to join the fight.

This was what Beledni had been anticipating.

One length. Kul voices rose in a united shriek, barring the horsemen's way with a shield of noise. Iron-shod hooves and iron-tipped lances tore the sound shield down. And then, with cataclysmic impact, they did the same to the wall of flesh and bone behind it.

The rota slammed into the dissolving shield wall, shattering it. Lances juddered as they tore into wood and bodies. Gerlach found himself churning Saksen forward through a mass of screaming, milling men. On either side of him, riders of the krug had released their lances and were cutting in with their sabres. Vitali and Vaja kept tight, protecting Gerlach's sides, but as they fought through a particularly heavy scrum, Vaja disappeared entirely.

Gerlach's right flank was exposed. A wide-bladed axe threatened him, and he dropped his reins and pulled his loaded wheel-lock out with his right hand. The point-blank shot punched off the axe man's jaw and threw him back into the scrambling bodies around him.

Gerlach recased his pistol and brought out his sword, hacking and stabbing at anything that came near him. With his left hand, he kept the banner aloft. It felt like a dead weight now, much heavier than the more considerable demilance standard had ever seemed. Vitali stayed with him, hacking and thrusting at the kyazak.

Through the frenzy of the melee, Gerlach saw Beledni cutting through bull-helms with his gleaming shashka. He saw Maksim sweeping with his curved sabre, splashing blood up into the air. He saw Mitri plunge his lance through two of the Kul at once. Borodyn, hurling a lance. Sorca, stabbing his sabre tip into the eye slit of a Kul barbute. Kvetlai, drenched in gore, cleansing his silver blade by rushing it through the air.

Vaja suddenly reappeared, fighting clear of the pack that had delayed him, howling with brutal triumph as a tribesman went under his horse's juddering hooves.

Gerlach cleaved through head armour and iron plate, and then turned hard to take off a hand clutching a knife. Jostling bodies were packing in around him, and the stench of blood, ordure and sweat was making him gag.

A Kul warrior came at him, and he used the butt of the banner shaft to bludgeon him away.

The melee was a jarring maelstrom of noise and motion and impact. Gerlach was no longer sure which way he was pointing. He was showered with droplets of blood and spit, and tiny shards of metal.

Gigantic spectral antlers rose up above the turmoil around him. For a moment, Gerlach imagined that some great steppe beast or death devil had come on them out of the dust and smoke.

But it was the Kul standard.

Yelling, Gerlach drove Saksen into the press, smacking his sabre to and fro all the while, slicing scalps and shoulders and cutting the tips off helmhorns. Vitali shouted out, trying to stay with the demilancer.

The Kul banner bearer was a short, thickset man in a mail shirt wound from heavy wire. His brass helmet was long-chinned and mounted with a single antler, pointing forward from the forehead. A witch-priest danced around him, jangling beads, strings of bones and a rattle of tin bells. The witch-priest was painted with bright crimson stripes to imitate his bones.

Gerlach hurled himself at them through the battle's chaos. The witch-priest saw him coming at the last moment, and turned to raise his rattle.

Gerlach put cross-wise power into his sword blow. He decapitated the witch-priest, and took off the gnarled hand holding the rattle as well. Screaming, the banner bearer tried to engage Gerlach, thrusting the antlers of the Kul standard at him. One of the antler tines gouged across his left shoulder plate and left a deep streak that later rusted badly.

Gerlach spurred on under the standard and hacked down both the desperate bearer and two swordsmen who ran in to defend him. Vitali and Vaja came up on Gerlach's heels and began to defend him against further attacks.

The Kul banner crashed to the ground.

He had expected the Kul spirit to be diminished by such an event. Gerlach stiffened in shock as they roared and fought on with renewed frenzy.

Then he heard the drumming of hooves. The Kul were drawing in reinforcements. For all their efforts, the rota of Yetchitch krug was about to be slaughtered.

A second force struck into the straggling line of the battle from the direction of the town itself. But they weren't another wave of Kul at all. They were horse archers, pouring out through the stockade gatehouse, thirty-five or forty strong.

Their brown, long-maned steppe ponies swept them in amongst the hindquarters of the Kul's loose battle-gang. They rained long, red-feathered arrows into the Northers' backs from short but sturdy recurve bows. The rear line of the Kul formation began to topple and fall like a row of cornstalks under a scythe.

The horse archers had great turning speed and a prolific rate of fire. Some of the lancers – Gerlach, Vaja, Vitali and a half dozen more – had swept so deeply into the Kul ranks they had almost broken out through the back. They were now surrounded by the closing enemy host. So it was that Gerlach was one of the first to see the horse archers curling past, their onslaught causing the rear files of the Kul to turn in panic to try to protect themselves.

The archers were Kislevites, wearing grubby but embroidered beshmets or sleeveless sheepskin coats over hauberks of hardened red leather. They had long aventails of mesh dangling back around their shoulders. Their helmets were simple, spiked 'tops', with wide brims of fur around the rims. They rode with short stirrups, giving themselves a forward seat that put each rider's weight over his horse's shoulders. This favoured an animal better than placing the weight in the centre of its back.

Gerlach was impressed by the power of the small, tasselled, double-curved bows. The 'self' bows of the Empire, expertly shaped from single staves of wood, had tremendous penetrative power, but were so long they could not be shot from the saddle, especially a moving one. But these recurve bows easily drove shafts clean through iron pot-helms and brass corselets.

Harried now from front and back, the Kul began to waver and break. As men turned to run, they were brought over by arrows or javelins. Lancers broke through melees to ride them down. A few masses of resistance remained, where defiant Kul warriors had closed in tight, but Beledni and Yevni regrouped a good number of the rota and split these mobs with lance and sword.

The Kul began to flee en masse now, ditching shields and even weapons as they ran for their scattered ponies. Only a very few made it. This handful galloped away into the steppe in all directions, disappearing into the grass and leaving only the sound of their racing hooves and jingling bits behind them.

Beledni raised his sword in triumph, and Yevni sounded his bone horn again and again. Shouting and roaring, the lancers dismounted, and the horse archers cantered, whooping, in wide circles around the battle site. The general mayhem had raised a vast cloud of fine dust that the steppe wind was only now beginning to disperse.

As that dust billowed around him, Gerlach hoisted the rota banner high into the air, as high as his tired arms could manage. The dismounted lancers greeted it with cheers as they set about blinding the corpses of the enemy.

V

THE LEADER OF the horse archers was a fine, tall man, and surprisingly young. He leapt down from his sturdy pony and embraced Beledni heartily.

His name was Antal, and he and his horse company hailed from Igerov, a community in the far east of the southern oblast. Beledni knew him well. The companies had fought together in the pulk on several different campaigns. Beledni's great comradeship had in fact been with Antal's father, Gaspar. From the talk going on around him, Gerlach learned that Beledni and Gaspar had been friends and battle-brethren since their youths. Gaspar had died two summers before, and his horsemen divided into two warbands, each led by one of his sons. This explained why Antal looked too young to be a commander of horse. He treated Beledni like a favourite uncle.

Antal's horsemen, along with the company led by his brother Dmirov, had assembled with the pulk at Zhedevka, and been caught up in that great military disaster. They had braved a number of desperate escapades and managed to flee at last into the open country, first west and then north-east. Antal had come away with only forty of the seventy men he had started with. He had not seen Dmirov, nor any of his warband, since Zhedevka.

Noticing the strange rider and even stranger horse that carried the rota banner, Antal walked across to meet Gerlach. He yanked off his dusty gloves and clasped Gerlach's hands as Beledni made introductions.

'Vebla,' Beledni said, and Antal chuckled.

'Is your name?' the young commander asked.

'My name is Gerlach Heileman.'

'Good!' laughed Antal, as if the name 'vebla' was something better avoided.

'How long have you been here, at Leblya?' Gerlach wanted to know.

'Thirteen days,' Antal answered. His company had ridden there with all speed, hoping to congregate with other survivors of the battle. 'For eight days, no one come. Then lancers, Novgo's rota.'

Gerlach had to struggle to keep up with the exchange. 'Novgo?'

'Comrade rotamaster,' Beledni said. 'Of Dagnyper krug. Many good men raise wings with him.'

'Not so many,' said Antal sadly. 'Only five times five lancers of Novgo's rota live after Zhedevka.'

There was some quiet muttering and oaths of dismay from the lancers.

'Where are they now?' asked Gerlach.

'Kyazak come, same day Novgo's rota arrive. Great host, more than was here under today's sun.'

The Kul raiders had arrived from the south in huge numbers, either following the straggling survivors of Zhedevka, or happening on Leblya by pure unlucky chance. There were so many of them – 'covering steppe like flies on corpse' Antal said – that it was clear even as they approached that Leblya would not withstand the attack. Novgo, with what Beledni seemed to think was typically rash courage, had ridden all he had left of his rota out of Leblya and made a dash south, partly to warn any approaching companies that Leblya was no longer a safe haven, and partly to try to draw the kyazak away from the town.

A great proportion of the Kul had turned and chased Novgo's rota away across the grasslands. Neither rota nor enemy had been seen again.

The remaining Kul had laid siege to the town, and Antal's warriors had done their level best to defend the place. It was hard. Their supplies, especially of arrows, were limited, and the horse archers could not use their own strengths and face the raiders because they were woefully outnumbered. When

Beledni's more sizeable rota appeared that morning, and engaged the Kul, Antal had seized his chance, and led his archers out in a make or break raid to finish the siege.

It had paid off. Through strength and speed of horse, and the bonus of skilled archery, Beledni and Antal's companies had defeated a kyazak warband of much greater size.

In fact they had virtually annihilated them.

The Kislevites were all flushed with relief and victory. The thrill of battle still boiled excitedly inside them. But Gerlach couldn't help feel a little disappointment. He'd been dreaming of an allied host at Leblya, waiting to surge south and exact a bloody war-price on the Kurgan advance.

Instead, just one band, forty strong, of tired and ill-supplied horse archers, and word of a diminished lance company that had since disappeared.

He kept his thoughts to himself. The Kislevites were celebrating.

'I thought you would come today,' Antal told Beledni. 'I saw a shape in the sky that reminded me of you.'

'Yha! So I come, Antal Gasparitch! So I come!'

'I was not sure. Cloud look like you, but it came riding on strange white horse, which I know not your horse.' He smiled at Gerlach and pointed to Saksen. 'Now I understand.'

VI

THE ROTA HAD not come through unscathed. Two lancers – Ptor and Chagin – were dead, and Sorca, one of Beledni's veteran seniors, had an axe wound in his hip that was obviously mortal. But almost everyone had taken a nick, graze or cut of some kind. Mostly it was bruises and scrapes they didn't even remember getting. The worst of the minor wounds was a sword-cut along the side of young Kvetlai's hand and forearm. He showed the bloody gash off proudly.

The Kislevites retired into the town, where the inhabitants sent up a great roar and clangour with pots and pans and voices, hailing the victory and their deliverance. Antal's riders gathered up all the spent arrows they could find – even broken ones and kyazak shafts, for wood was so scarce – and rode in ahead of the lancers through the gatehouse. Ptor and Chagin were draped over their horses, and Beledni himself led Sorca, lolling in his saddle.

Many of the lancers raised their hands to acknowledge the cacophony. But Beledni did not seem to notice it. His entire concern was taken up with the dying friend and comrade riding slowly beside him.

VII

THE VICTORY FEAST that night was not grand, but generous considering the extent to which the siege had depleted Leblya's larders. Sad songs were sung to the memory of the fallen comrades, and the mood was sombre.

More miserable still was the talk. Gerlach heard a good many of the lancers, and the archers too, saying that the 'journey' was over, for this year at least.

Though it was only early summer on the high steppes, and the war-season barely begun, the men seemed to agree that there was nothing left to be achieved this year. They would be better off returning to their stanitsa homes in time to help with the harvest and the winter slaughter.

Gerlach took himself apart from the others and sat alone. They had come into the ancient zal on the top of the great earthwork for the feast. It was immensely old. The roof had been replaced many times, and the body of the hall extended, but the basic inner frame and beam-work was original. It was hundreds of years old, perhaps thousands. In places, it was black from old fire damage – not the accumulation of cook-fire soot but real burn marks – and peppered with old indentations and nail holes.

He traced his fingertips over the pock-marked beam he sat against. The firelight caught the faintest traces of gold frayed into the worn timber, tiny pin-head scraps of it caught in the grain of wood, or hammered into empty nail marks.

These beams had been covered once, Gerlach realised. They had been clad in gold, wafer-thin foils of beaten gilt inscribed with the figures and symbols of their makers' divinity. These beams had stood since the time of the Scythians – since the earthwork itself had been raised. Zals had been built and razed and built again around their solid framework. The beams had worn each successive settlement's hall as a man wears a beshmet or pole staves support a canvas tent. They were older than the great cathedral temples and fortresses of his homeland.

So did great glory come and fade until it was scarcely visible any more. Cultures so rich and powerful that they could dominate the land and afford to wrap their buildings in gold leaf. But they had fled, and left only mounds, like graves, behind them.

Gerlach knew, in his heart, the Empire must surely fade too. He had grown up believing it to be permanent and eternal, by the grace of Sigmar, and pledged his life to maintaining that equilibrium. But it was for naught. The Empire would fall. Perhaps it had fallen already. Even if the great armies of his homeland had risen with effect and driven back the Northers this time, then it would be next year, or the year after that, or the one after that. But it would one day.

All any man could hope to do was delay the inevitable.

That was a calling he could believe in. To keep fighting the darkness so long as there was light to protect.

Vitali and Vaja came over to join him, worried that he had withdrawn from the krug. They brought koumiss, and were eager to celebrate their shared exploits on the field.

'We do war good together again, Vebla!' Vitali said.

Gerlach nodded and toasted them both with the fermented milk. They seemed inordinately proud of his accomplishments during the battle. He had kept the rota safe, the banner raised, he had also fought well, and taken the enemy's banner from them.

In truth, they had achieved far more than him. They had ridden loyally to keep him safe, and each of them had accounted for a great many more kyazak lives than Gerlach.

'Why Vebla face sad look it in?' Vaja asked.

'I hear the talk,' Gerlach answered the young lancer. 'You all talk of going home. As if you are done now.'

'Vebla will like much Yetchitch krug!' Vaja decided.

Vitali, as ever, seemed to grasp Gerlach's notion more soundly. 'You not want go, Vebla?' he asked.

Gerlach shook his head. 'Has Yetchitch ever been attacked? Not by kyazak, I mean. By Kurgan host, on a great invasion?'

They didn't think so, not in their lifetimes. Yetchitch was quite remote, and mainly had only bandits and raiders to fear.

'So you will ride home, and Yetchitch will be as you remember, and you will winter there and next spring, come back again to see what war there is to be fought, what glory to be found?'

'Yha!' said Vaja.

'My home is being attacked right now. Right this very minute. I am not done.'

'Shto?'

'Vebla is not yet done.'

VIII

THEIR FACES DARKENED as they thought about this. It was as hard for them to care about towns and villages to the south that they would never see, as it had been for Gerlach to give a damn about the oblast. Until, that is, he'd seen its grandeur and the spirit of its people. But for the first time, Vitali and Vaja seemed to sympathise. They had found affection and comradeship for Gerlach, and now they shared his unhappiness.

What divided the men of the Empire from the men of Kislev was Kislevite fatalism. Vitali and Vaja agreed the plight of Gerlach's home was a sad thing, but it was beyond them to do anything about it. Not quite 'of no matter', for they weren't that heartless, but far enough away for it to be a thing that made a man shrug and sigh. In Kislev, men believed they were made by fate. In the Empire, men believed they made their fates themselves.

Gerlach left them to their thoughts and their koumiss, and went to find Beledni, but the rota-master was holding vigil with Sorca and was not to be disturbed. Gerlach walked through the hall, nodding to the men who offered him greetings. He saw Kvetlai. The boy had drunk too much, probably to dull the pain in his hand and arm, and was lolling pathetically by the fire.

Nearby, Gerlach found Maksim and Borodyn seated with Antal and the ataman of Leblya: a solid, portly elder called Sevhim.

They welcomed him and gave him a cup of kvass and a bowl of salt fish.

Antal was bright and curious, and asked Gerlach many questions about the Empire, a place he'd never visited. His thoughts ran away from him, beyond his broken grasp of Reikspiel, and Borodyn translated for him.

'I understand you're all thinking of going home,' Gerlach said at length, when he'd had enough of the questions.

Maksim nodded. He was chasing flecks of food out from between his teeth, and his working tongue bulged in his lean, drawn cheeks. 'Is of best we do this.'

'Is of best?'

Maksim shrugged.

'There is little to be gained, Vebla,' Borodyn answered instead. 'We have been bested and driven to flight. We have tried to… to regroup and make another chance for us, but…' he gestured at the hall around them, indicating Leblya itself, '…there is nothing.'

'I disagree,' said Gerlach.

'That is your privilege,' Borodyn accepted. 'Beledni rotamaster has tried hard. We rode to Dushyka, to Leblya, hunting for allies, for any remaining part of the pulk. Nothing, except for Antal and his brave riders.'

Antal smiled and nodded.

'So it is better to end and start again fresh and new than prolong this misadventure.'

'Beledni thinks this?'

'Beledni would have ridden home from Dushyka if not for you,' Maksim admitted.

'What? What does that mean?'

'This season is loss! Terrible loss!' Maksim snapped. 'Only because of Vebla did Beledni press on to Leblya. To see.'

'To see what?' demanded Gerlach.

'If pulk was gathered here,' said Antal.

Borodyn took a sip of kvass. 'Beledni rotamaster believes he owes a debt to you. To be fair, we all do. You took up the eagle-wing banner when it had fallen and carried it to safety. We all respect that.'

'Is why you carry rota,' growled Maksim.

'We all respect that,' repeated Borodyn, 'and none more so than Beledni. Most rotamasters would have turned their lancers homeward after a defeat like Zhedevka. But Beledni ordered us on here, to Leblya, because there was a chance the pulk had reassembled. If any great force had been here, we would have joined it, and gladly ridden south to help you get the vengeance you deserve. But it is not the case. Beledni has been more than fair to you. But he will not risk any more men.'

'I see. What about next year? When the Kurgan are so entrenched in the south and in the Empire there is no pulk left to join and no cause left to fight for?'

'Next year is next year,' said Maksim, tipping invisible dust out of his hand.

Gerlach got up angrily and walked away. Then he stopped, and looked back at the men.

'I have two questions,' he said. 'You are the riders of the dead, yha? Already mourned and given up by your krug?'

Borodyn and Maksim nodded at this.

'Then what lives are you risking?'

Borodyn smiled and translated. Both Maksim and Antal laughed.

'You do not understand, Vebla.'

'No, I suppose I don't. I suppose I don't understand the significance of the pictures Dazh puts in
the sky, either. You saw Beledni, coming to help you
on a white horse, didn't you?' He looked at Antal.
The young man could only agree.

'Then what is Dazh telling you? To run away or
heed the signs he puts in the sky to guide you?'

'Dazh tell us what he always tell us,' said Maksim,
a little angry now. 'Follow Beledni. Follow rota.
That is the only way.'

IX

AT DAWN, THE rota buried its dead in the steppe.

It was one of the first truly warm days of summer
and the heat began to rise even from the moment of
daybreak.

The sky was blue and clear, and they could see for
many leagues across the grassland. Skylarks were
singing, far away up beyond the sight of man, and
the air was droning with horseflies and the fizzles of
newly hatched mosquitoes.

Beledni – his eyes red and his face drawn from
too little sleep and too much drink – howled the
names of Ptor, Chagin and Sorca at the rising
sun, as if he hoped he could stop it from coming
up.

Then Yevni blew his horn. The three horses took
off from the gate of Leblya and ran away into the
grass. Ptor and Chagin were bound in cloth and
lashed over their saddles. Sorca, in the last hours of
his life, was hunched over in his saddle, and pulling
his dead comrades behind him.

Sorca had seen the same cloud shape for a second time. The three were riding away to wherever Demieter had gone.

The lancers, and mourners from Antal's company and the town, turned and went back inside the stockade, one by one.

Gerlach remained beside Beledni, the banner raised in his hand, until the three horses had become dots, and the dots themselves had receded into the dawn haze and were gone.

X

As THEY WENT back into the stanitsa, Gerlach tried to talk to Beledni, but the old rotamaster ignored him and disappeared into an izba to sleep.

Gerlach carefully planted the shaft of the banner in the earth of the inner yard, and dismounted to fetch some water and find something to breakfast on.

In the great zal, up on the mound, Kvetlai was sick. His wound had become infected, and was puffy and black. He was sweating and delirious. The men of the rota didn't seem to care. They brought Kvetlai water periodically, and Borodyn dressed his wound with salves, but their manner seemed dismissive.

Just after noon, with the sun at its highest and hottest, Gerlach saw Kvetlai stagger down across the yard and drag himself on to his horse. No one tried to obstruct him. He kicked his heels into his mare's ribs and bolted out of the gate and away across the steppe.

'Why didn't you stop him?' Gerlach demanded of Borodyn. 'His injury wasn't mortal, not like Sorca's!'

'It was full of poison. He had a fever.'

'But if you'd cared for him, he might have lived!'

'Dazh will care for him. Ursun will care. The steppe also. A sick warrior rides until the sickness sweats out of him. Kvetlai will return. Or Dazh will lead him on his journey.'

Gerlach turned away, disgusted. The Kislevite way doomed every man to fend for himself. It was as if riding answered every question of life and death. We are dying... ride away! We are defeated... ride away! We are sick... then ride away and see what fate provides! Is of no matter.

The only thing they cared about was the krug, and the only thing they followed was the rota.

Everything else was left in the hands of some distant god of wide, empty spaces who was too damn far away to hear.

XI

THE ONLY THING they followed was the rota. The banner.

Gerlach woke up in the still, cool hours before dawn. The hall fires were dying, and the whole of Leblya was asleep.

He had already decided to leave, to part company with the rota and head south, though he knew there was nothing a single man could hope to do.

Zhedevka had taught him that.

But his dream had given him a new idea.

He carried his armour and belongings out of the hall, careful not to wake the slumbering lancers, and got dressed in the yard. It was cold, and his breath smoked the air. The stars were still out, bright and proud in a canopy of charcoal grey and, in the east, the first glimmer of sunrise was showing.

Clad in his half-armour, he made Saksen ready, shushing the gelding's agitation with soft-spoken words and a gentle hand across its muzzle.

Gerlach walked Saksen out into the dry, bare yard. The first long, timid shadows of dawn were stretching out. He mounted up, and took a last look at the zal, perched on its Scythian mound like a crown.

The rota banner was sitting where he had placed it, base down in the hardpan. He plucked it up with his left hand, and then ducked both head and banner as he rode out under the open gate.

The steppe was violet in the half-light. The sky was mauve, splashed with yellow along the eastern horizon. It was growing warmer, and one by one, the stars were going out.

He turned Saksen south, raised the banner, and galloped away.

AACHDEN

I

IT WAS NOW the early summer, the better part of three months since the unholy slaughter at Zhedevka in the Year That No One Forgets. The smoke of burning forests and blazing towns had clogged the northward sky permanently since the heart of spring.

The Kurgan horde had driven deeper into the south than they had ever done before. They had overwhelmed the borders of the Empire, setting proud cities like Erengrad to the torch along the way, and bathed their blades in the blood of good, pious folk. Some said the despoilers had reached as far as Middenheim, and thus all civilisation was at an end. Others vowed Karl Franz himself was riding at the head of the Empire's armies, praying to Sigmar for the chance to close with Archaon.

Archaon. That was a name made of darkness. Where it had first come from, no one could say. Spread by word of mouth, perhaps. Shrieked out in the dying breath of pitiful victims flayed by the Kurgan and swept south to sow terror instead of seeds that spring. Maybe it was heard in the chants of the encroaching hordes. Or perhaps it had just crept into the minds of kings and seers across the Old World in their nightmares.

Archaon was the name of the being who commanded the enemies of everything. The Lord of the End Times, greater even than Morkar or Asavar Kul. A man? Perhaps. A daemon? Quite possibly. Real? Well…

There are many to this day who believe Archaon was not a single being, but rather a fearsome being amalgamated from the confused identities of several Kurgan chieftains. Certainly, the Norther host itself was not one thing, but a union of many tribal armies and cult factions, each one ruled by a High Zar. Archaon was a mix of all of them, for the High Zars used his authority to reinforce their own considerable power, and attributed many of their conquests to his name.

But he was more than this, for he was real. Only a few hundred of the Kurgan knew that for sure, and only a few hundred men of the Empire had ever confirmed it by encountering him. Few survived to tell of it.

Archaon's invasion depended for its success on the High Zars who followed him, and on the zars under them. The North had sprouted a host of nigh on nineteen hundred thousand warriors, and no single commander could ever control a force that size – not even the disciplined military systems of the Empire.

Archaon, his name couched in infamy, relied on his lieutenants, the devoted High Zars, to marshal the several armies that collectively became his Great Horde.

Surtha Lenk was one of those High Zars.

Karl-Azytzeen met him face to face one morning that summer.

II

WEEKS EARLIER IN the pit of the Brunmarl playhouse, Karl had achieved more than he realised. At the time, all he knew was that he had slain two rivals whilst in the grip of a red rage. Beyond that bald fact, he wasn't sure of much at all. The men of Uldin's band had carried him from the pit, and shut him up in some dank stone room for the night.

He slept for what seemed like several years. When he woke up, the young shaman with the antler head-dress was prowling around him slowly, hunched low and muttering ugly words.

It was day. Light and rainwater seeped in through the broken roof.

The bolt was thrown back and Uldin came in. His head was bare and water ran off his bear-pelt and the short boar-spear he was carrying. He made a nod at the shaman, who bowed and scurried out.

'Skarkeetah says I should kill you,' Uldin announced.

'Then kill me,' Karl said indifferently. Uldin did not move.

Karl sat up and leant his aching back against the damp stone of the wall. 'I thought the slave lord believed me to be precious. To be touched by…' His voice trailed off. He could not bring himself to say the name.

Uldin ground his teeth thoughtfully. 'It is so. And that is why. He says a wise man in my position would kill you before you became too precious. Too… powerful.'

That made Karl smile. He was beaten, unarmed and half-naked in a dingy cell, and a Kurgan warlord with a spear was telling him he had enough power to pose a threat.

'Well, just how wise are you?' Karl sneered.

'Wise enough to appreciate value.'

'Because I won the fights? Saved your honour and your warband? Seems I got you a new shaman too.'

Uldin nodded slowly. 'When they saw the blue-eyed slave fight and win in the pit, many shamans yearned to join with my band and take Subotai's place. I chose Chegrume. He is a potent shaman, and sees special strength in you.'

'There's no mystery,' replied Karl. 'He knows I can read.'

'Words are power,' said Uldin.

'No, Kurgan. Knowledge is power. Words are just a way of getting it.'

Uldin took a few steps forward and crouched down in front of Karl. He lowered the spear and held it so that the tip was pressing sharply against Karl's chest.

'We put our mark on those men who impress us with their strength. Such men are useful in our challenges and devotions.'

'Better to waste the life of a useless slave in a sacrifice or a pit-fight than one of your own band, eh? I understand how it works. You collect up the best and the healthiest of the prisoners you take and squander them in your rituals becau–'

Uldin cut him off sharply, not even remotely interested. 'You faced me, Karl-Azytzeen, outside the zal at Zhedevka. You gave me this.' Uldin touched the scar on his shoulder where Karl's sabre had dug in. 'The first wound I have taken from an enemy warrior in eight summers.'

'My pleasure.' The spear tip dug a little harder.

'Then I had the best of you,' Uldin said.

'In the doorway. I remember.'

'I could have killed you.'

'I thought you had. I wish you had.'

'Tchar stayed my hand. Made me strike you with the flat of my blade. A man who can wound a zar is worth marking and keeping as a slave. Your life has belonged to me ever since. I could have ended it then, but I chose not to. I could end it now…'

Uldin gave the spear another little push and then took it away. 'But I chose not to. While you remember that power I have over you, you can do me no harm. You are no danger to me.'

Uldin slid a trophy ring off his arm and tossed it into Karl's lap. It was still warm. It had been worked into shape by one of the sword blades taken from the slaves in the pit the night before.

'Add to this, and my choice will not change.'

Uldin got up and walked out of the room. He left the door wide open.

After a while, Karl slipped the warm metal ring onto his right arm, and followed the zar into the daylight.

III

THE ZARS LED their warbands away from Brunmarl one by one. They headed west to join a massive host accreting around the ruins of Berdun. There, the numerous banners of the zars flocked around the great war standard of the High Zar himself: Surtha Lenk.

This Kurgan host was easily as large as the force that had taken Zhedevka, but it was only one of many that raged into the Empire as spring turned into summer. Surtha Lenk's horde sacked three towns in the Ostermark, and then forded the Talabec and drove on west into Ostland, where more towns perished to its fury.

Uldin's band saw little of the fighting. The host was so massive that often great parts of it were still arriving at a town by the time it had been razed by the front runners. Uldin chafed for glory. He wished for a battle where his band could take enough enemy heads to raise a skull-stack and earn him another victory mark on his cheek.

But by the time they reached Aachden, just eight days' march from Wolfenburg, with the

Middle Mountains in sight, Karl had won two more trophy rings.

IV

THE LAST TIME Karl saw his fellow prisoners, who were still roped together and driven along with the wagons, they didn't recognise him. They probably wouldn't have greeted him even if they had.

Uldin's men let Karl keep the garments and armour pieces they had clad him in at Brunmarl. They gave him a sturdy spear with a black horse-tail fixed behind the long tip, and an old brown mare without a saddle or a name. He rode in the band between the watchful eyes of Efgul and Hzaer the hornblower, and followed them into the fire.

V

AT AACHDEN, AN Imperial army had assembled to stop Surtha Lenk's horde. They occupied the upland fields of crops and pasture just northeast of the town, with a broadleaf forest to their north and the plain of the river Aach to their south. They were a great glittering mass in the summer light, like a patch of sea sparkling with the sun, fretted by banners of blue and gold, red and white. A huge force of professional soldiery, supported by significant sections of levies. They were dug in to deprive the host of any further advance, and to halt them dead before they reached Wolfenburg.

The countryside presented no obvious way around them, but then again going around an enemy was not the Kurgan way.

VI

ULDIN, HUNGRY FOR a share of victory, had steered his warband through to the leading edge of the Kurgan host. They had ridden overnight to get a good place for themselves, running their horses hard the moment word spread that the Empire had rallied to meet them at arms on the field at Aachden. Karl wondered if his old nag would be able to keep up with the huge, black horses of the Kurgan riders, but it was indomitable and seemed to have fathomless stamina.

Chegrume, the shaman, rode with them on an ugly, ill-tempered tarpan. Its coat was brown, its mane and tail uncombed black, and its nature so foul that the antlered shaman had to tie himself to its back. He ran wild, weaving in an out of the galloping riders, chanting spells of fortitude and protection from metal.

Chegrume seemed a curious fellow to Karl. Not that all shamans weren't curious, given their calling. But he was young and fierce, more like a warrior than a witch priest. His youth troubled Karl too. He had supposed a shaman needed age to attain the feats of lore and wisdom necessary to his office. Subotai had been an older man, and Zar Blayda's wizard Ons Olker was not young. None of the shamans he had yet seen were younger than mature middle age.

But Chegrume was little more than a boy. It seemed as if he had been born with the arcane knowledge he needed. Or maybe acquiring that weight of lore so young had cost him something: his middle fingers, perhaps.

The day was clear and warm. The sky was blue. The weather paid no heed to the death about to take place, Karl thought.

The warband pushed their horses through the gathering press to win their ranking, as rival banner bearers, shaman and zars roared out reproachful challenges. But Uldin had chosen a place near to the lea of the river where bands of infantry spearmen had congregated, and none of them cared much to oppose five score warriors on warhorses.

The glittering army waited for them just over a league away. They had the advantage of height, for the gently rolling fields had a deceptive slope.

Breathing hard, their horses sweating and panting, the warband took its place and got its wind back. Men took off their helms and drank thirstily from skins, or daubed their faces and chests with pigment. Chegrume thumped up and down the serried rank, ululating and casting. Karl had the distinct feeling the shaman's frantic activity had less to do with magic and more to do with the fact his bastard tarpan would not stand still.

Karl sat on his mare with his spear across his iron-plated thighs and gazed at the army facing them. They were so close he could make out their banner colours and the details of their standards. He wondered whose companies they were, and what lord had command, and he tried to identify symbols he knew.

The main battle standard. A white skull with a garland wreath around it on a crimson field. That was...

To its left, a figure of death, armed with a lance and a black crossed white shield, mounted on a maned and speckled cat, walking through a flame. On the turquoise field behind it, a star with two burning tails swooped down. He knew that one, certainly. It was the... the...

Karl shivered despite the balmy heat of the morning. He knew none of them. He could not recognise a single design or emblem. Where had his memory of them gone?

'What's the matter, Karl-Azytzeen?' Efgul asked.

Karl looked round, as if blinking out of a dream. The hefty, hairy Kurgan was offering him a wineskin. Karl took it and drank deeply.

'You are afraid of the Empire?' Efgul added.

Karl shook his head. 'These last days, I have fought them already,' he said, and tapped the new-wrought rings on his arm.

'Not an army such as this,' Hzaer snarled from his other side. 'You must not shy. You are not of them any more.'

'If you shy,' Efgul said, 'the zar says we must kill you.'

'I will not.' Karl handed the skin to Hzaer, and the hornblower rotated his great brass carnyx back over his shoulder so it would not slide off while he was drinking.

'Yes, I do not think so, seh,' Efgul murmured, staring at Karl.

'I've come a long way,' Karl said to both of them and no one. 'A long and bloody way, and I can only go forward because going back now would be too hard.'

Efgul nodded, and buckled his houndskull helm into place.

'I don't recognise the emblems any more,' Karl confessed suddenly. 'Not one of them. The banners of my... of the Empire. I thought I knew them, but I can't place a single one.'

Hzaer grinned. His broken teeth made the grin a leer. 'That is Tchar's doing, Azytzeen,' he said.

'What is?'

'He favours you. Great Tchar has changed your mind to make it easier to forget. Give thanks for that.'

Karl supposed he did. Memory of his old life would make the life he had now far harder to endure.

Hooves thundered up. It was Uldin, on his great black steed. His wolf-mask helmet had been polished, and his pallasz was drawn.

'Word has been given!' he shouted to the hornblower. 'The High Zar has ordered we wait for the enemy to engage.'

'Engage?' Karl laughed. 'They've got the slope on their side and they're dug in. They're waiting for us to come to them.'

Uldin glared at him. 'They will not come?'

Karl snorted. Then, seeing the disapproving looks around him, he set his right hand across his heart and spoke more deferentially. 'They will not come. They'll do nothing if we sit here. Their aim is to block our advance and look! I believe that's what they're doing already, without lifting a finger.'

Uldin thought about this, his horse turning in circles.

Finally, he pointed at Karl and said, 'Come!'

VII

So IT WAS that, on that morning in early summer, Karl-Azytzeen came face to face with Surtha Lenk.

The High Zar's pavilion was pitched behind the head of the ranked Kurgan mass. Its fabric was composed of tanned human hides, its guy ropes were plaited from sinew, and its posts calcified struts wrought from spines. It stank of decay and perfume.

Zar Uldin dismounted and pulled Karl off his mare. Karl scrambled and staggered as he was dragged towards the entrance of the battle tent.

Huge axemen with long horns rising from their heads blocked Uldin's path and it took a lot of talk to convince them to let him past. Only when Uldin had dragged Karl inside did Karl realise that the axe men at the door had not been wearing helmets. The tusk-horns sprouted directly from the bones of their distended skulls.

He felt sick.

But he was to feel sicker still, once he was inside. It was dark in the battle tent. Brass pendant lamps fumed out an acrid pall of incense. Things brushed against his skin like feathers and chittered in the dark.

The floor seemed to be composed of a carpet of snakes. Smooth, dry coils slipped around his feet.

'Welcome, Uldin,' a tiny voice said.

Uldin bowed. 'My lord.'

'Is this the changeling you have spoken of?'

'It is, lord seh.'

Karl glanced around. There were shadows everywhere, but none of them seemed like a person. He knew he had to keep his head bowed low.

'He smells of change. I like that. What did you call him?'

'Azytzeen,' Uldin said.

'Karl-Azytzeen,' Karl corrected.

'Oh! Spirited!' The miniscule voice moved closer. 'And why have you brought him here, Uldin?'

'He declares the enemy will not move, lord seh.'

A huge, armoured figure stood over Karl now, plated in crimson steel, more massive even than Hinn.

'Look at me, Azytzeen,' Surtha Lenk said.

Karl slowly turned his head up. Lenk was a giant three spans tall, plated in brass and iron.

Except he was not. A twisted, deformed thing, no bigger than a swaddling child, was strapped in a harness across the breast plate of the giant. It seemed to be all swollen face, with tiny, wasted, half-formed hands and feet sprouting from it. This was Lenk: a loathsome, slack face mottled with warts and suppurating blisters. One eye was very human and brown, the other, lower in the rugose flesh of the cheek, was swollen and glazed milky blue. The mighty horned helm of the giant carrying him had no visor piercings or eye-slits.

Dan Abnett

Karl could not stifle a gasp.

Surtha Lenk laughed. His little pink slit-mouth wobbled and let out a child's giggle.

'I find spirit usually ebbs at the sight of me. In return for my service, Tchar has been bounteous with his gifts. Am I not beautiful?'

Karl nodded.

'Nothing pleases the Eye of Tzeen so much as a man changed completely. Now... why will the enemy not move?'

'B-because they have the rising ground. They would rather deny us than battle us, so they will not give up their advantage by coming down the field to look for a fight. The basis of the Empire's might is the pike block. That strength is best used defensively. They... they will not come to us, and all the while we wait, they will stand there too, and the victory will be theirs without spill of blood, for their purpose will have been served.'

Karl's voice trailed off. Had he said too much? Too little? Surtha Lenk took another step forward, so Karl could feel the breath of the baby-thing on his face. The horned giant nursing it slid off his left gauntlet and reached out to stroke Karl's cheek with its bared fingers. The hand, though unnaturally large, looked human, but it moved as if the bones inside it were not solid. The palm and fingers writhed and curled fluidly like the feeling antlers of a slug.

Karl knew that it was the High Zar who was touching his face. The whole figure – giant and shrivelled thing combined – was Surtha Lenk.

'I have considered these things too,' Surtha Lenk whispered. 'I have fought the Old World before, and know something of its ways. My battle-shamans augur that a delay might spook the army before us, and trick them into rash action.'

The boneless hand withdrew. 'But Tchar speaks in you, and I am content to hear him. For I am restless and done with waiting. Spread word abroad. We will commence.'

The audience was apparently over. Uldin, plainly unnerved himself, hauled Karl out of the pavilion into the daylight.

Karl took a look back at the foul tent. He vowed he would never willingly go back inside it. He had imagined the High Zar to be that rare sort of man who commanded such power he could alter the face of the world and redirect the course of history. But he had imagined wrong. The High Zar was not any sort of man at all.

VIII

THE HORDE STIRRED. A clattering ripple ran through the dark ranks as spear shafts were raised and shields knocked together. Somewhere to the left line, kettledrums began a frenzied beating, then fell silent. Then they began again and did not stop.

Karl and the zar rode back to the warband. Uldin did not speak.

As they waited in rank, Karl suddenly felt cold, and the bright sunlight abruptly dimmed. The sky above Aachden and the enemy army was still clear and blue, but when he looked to his rear, he saw

broad swathes of low dark cloud spoiling in from
the east. The clouds were moving with visible
speed, racing in to cover the heavens with a pitchy
mantle. Spears of lightning blinked above the
woodland to the east. Within minutes, the light
had gone and the valley was muffled in a dead twilight. The first spats of rain began to fall, tapping
off armour-iron and shield-wood. A vapour that
was not quite a fog breathed over the land, making
it harder to see.

Up the long slope of the field, the army of the
Empire had become partially obscured. Storm
clouds hovered above them too now, and there was
no piece of summer blue left visible. An anxious
murmur seemed to stiffen the silver-steel echelons
of the Reik. Karl heard distant drums start up, and
cymbals clash. He smelt gunpowder and hot pitch
on the wet air.

Thunder boomed overhead, and the rain began
to pelt torrentially. The vapour in the air thickened. Karl glanced down the wide front line of the
horde, and realised it was moving. Not fast, but
creeping forward, like spilled oil seeping across a
floor.

Uldin called out, and they began to walk their
horses. Berlas and the other archers slid their bows
from their cases and nocked shafts to the strings.

Drums were thrashing a frenetic tempo that made
the pulse rise in every man. Then the warhounds
were let loose.

Karl saw them as they broke out from the rolling
rank and began the chase up the slope of the field.

They were dark and monstrous things, hundreds of them, loping and bounding and sending up a chilling howl.

The advance speed increased, as if the Kurgan were now keen to keep up with the dogs. Horns blew all through the host, and Hzaer blasted on his carnyx. They were cantering, with spearmen from the middle ranks running forward between the horses and baying like the hounds. The horde shook the ground as it flooded towards the standing army.

The pike walls came up, bristling in a thicket three men deep. Even to trained men, pole arms and pikes were aggravating weapons to handle. The great length of the shafts meant they wobbled under marching conditions and caused discomfort, and they were too long to be easily accommodated in close woodland or town streets. Sometimes it was even hard to find space enough to stack them out in an overnight camp.

But the nuisance they caused was worthwhile. With perfect drill, they made a lethal barrier that would stop even the heaviest cavalry. The hammer might be the symbol of the Empire, but the pike was the weapon on which its reputation was built.

As they broke into a gallop, Karl began to consider the odds. Uldin's warband was ferocious and fearless, but horse against pike had only one outcome. These pike men and halberdiers were ready and pitched square, unlike their poor brothers at Zhedevka. Kurgan blood was about to be spilled in great quantity.

And then it was spilled. There was a series of thunderclaps that was not thunder. The Imperial cannon, anchored in sets on either wing of the enemy's battle order, had fired. Pluming cones of yellow flame and mud spray burst up amongst the charging Kurgan. The bodies of men and horses were tossed into the air. Wood and steel and bone splintered. The huge shot from mortars dropped on the horde like rocks thrown from the heavens. Shrieking fire from the great cannon and the volley guns ripped horizontally down the field and tore into the front ranks.

Then the longbows, loosed from behind the pike wall, and a wave of white-feathered shafts arced over with a rasping hiss. Kurgan toppled and fell all around, struck through the helms and pauldrons and skewered from above by the long arrows. A heartbeat later, and the second wave hissed down, followed by the first massed volley of the arquebusiers and crossbowmen laced amongst the pike men in the wall. Karl felt a ball shot burn past his ear and a quarrel cracked into slivers as it came off the iron rim of his shield. To his left, one of Uldin's riders crashed over, horse and man together.

For a moment, Karl felt a twinge of martial pride for the culture that had raised him. The greatest army in the world. He would be content to die at its hands. He would ride his nameless nag into the pike wall and find his end.

The pike wall was right ahead now, and unmoving.

The hounds reached the pike wall. Hounds are not like horses, they do not quail and veer aside from obstruction. Whether this means horses are smarter than dogs, or dogs braver than horses, is hard to call. Hounds are unlike horses in other ways too: they are lower and smaller and fleeter, and much harder to strike with a pole blade four spans long. And they have the teeth of meat-eaters.

A few of the great hunting dogs were gashed and run through by the stalwart pikes. A few more were shot by handgun and crossbow and left yelping and lame on the mud. The bulk ran in under the pikes and into the men.

At once, the wall broke in several places. Men screamed and fell back, trying to dodge the ravening war-dogs. They crashed into the ranks behind them. Pikes dropped into the mire. Some parts of the rank unformed completely as frantic pike men turned their weapons too far and too suddenly to check the murderous hounds.

The Kurgan charge slammed into the Imperial front row and poured into the breaks and gaps. Men in white and red went down under the weight of horses or the thrust of horned spearmen. Once the enemy was in amongst them, the pike men were forced to abandon their shafts and equip themselves with hand weapons. They had no shields, and none of the Kurgans' momentum.

Karl crashed through beside Efgul, his mare snorting and squealing. Without saddle or stirrup, he had no brace to enable him to couch his spear, so he stabbed down with it, overarm. His first thrust went through a thigh, the second clean into the side of a sallet helm. Mud splashed everywhere, churned up by the chaos, and the roaring tumult was a concussive force. Efgul was hacking with his war-axe, cutting deeper into the slowly-giving resilience of the enemy file. All around Karl, the men of Uldin's warband, together with Kurgan spear and axe on foot, were striking and killing. A berdish axe smote down an arquebusier. A pallasz split a pike man. A crossbow bolt struck a Norther swordsman with such force his body slammed backwards and his round shield spun upwards into the air. Uldin's man Diormac caved skulls with his heavy flail, and his black warhorse kicked out its hooves. There was no room to move in the choking press, and no possibility of seeing further than a few spans in any direction.

Gathek, another of Uldin's men, suddenly rose above the turmoil of bodies. He was impaled on a pike that had lifted him, kicking, off his saddle. The pike shaft snapped, and Gathek's corpse fell back into the crush.

A sword struck against Karl's shield, and he wrenched round, burying his speartip in the swordsman's cuirass. It wedged fast, and was tugged from his hand. He was unarmed now, and forced to weather the assault of the Imperial infantry with only a shield. His only weapon was his horse, and he drove it forward, head down, so its lashing hooves would batter and break limbs.

The rain seemed as heavy as a waterfall now. Lightning seared the dark sky and whipped down into the earth, exploding the ground amongst the Empire's rear ranks. The storm, it seemed, fought for Surtha Lenk's cause too; it was repaying the bombardment of the Imperial cannon.

For a moment, Karl caught sight of other shapes through the rain and vapour. Giant shadows loomed above the height of the men: bestial night-mares that howled into the deluge and tore into the Imperial forces with talons and claws. One seemed to have wings that spread from its shoulders like sails. Another, too grotesque to comprehend, had a great bird's beak.

Karl's shield was half shredded now, and his mare's flanks were gashed and torn. He pushed on, trampling men underfoot, and at last broke clear into the field behind the Imperial array. Efgul, Yuskel and eight other riders came through with him, then came Lyr, Berlas and Uldin himself a moment later.

The men of the Empire were already fleeing. They could be seen scattering singly or in small groups down across the field in the direction of Aachden, weapons and armour thrown down in their wake. Loose war hounds were chasing some, and pulling those they caught down, screaming.

'Leave them!' Uldin bellowed. He swung the rid-ers about as still more joined them, then drove in towards the enemy's rear ranks.

'Azytzeen!' Efgul shouted. He rode up close to Karl and gave him his saddle-sword, a falchion with a wooden grip and a billed tip. Karl took it and ran his horse after Uldin's. Hzaer's carnyx boomed.

The warband hurtled north, crossing the breaking flight of the Imperial bodies. They despatched those that came in reach as they thundered through. Karl tested Efgul's cutting sword on the head of a fleeing archer and found it was not wanting an edge.

An Imperial horse troop met the warband coming the other way. The Imperial commander had sent them to staunch the flow of deserters haemorrhaging from the back files. They were demilancers, their half-armour flashing and their cockades bobbing as they rode down the field, standing in their saddles. Most had lost their lances already, but they had sabres, and some had handguns.

Demilancers...

Karl-Azytzeen howled as he followed Uldin's charge into them. Warband and horse troop met head on, at full tilt, lashing past one another. Passing cuts from pallasz and war-axes struck demilancers off their geldings. Sabres and banging wheel-locks tumbled Kurgan riders out of their saddles.

Karl lost his shield to a pistol shot, and then swiped sideways with Efgul's sword, ripping a single, grievous wound through the neck of a lancer's troop horse and then through the ribcage of the lancer himself. Then he was fore-on to a demilancer who was intercepting him with sabre raised across the face at the charge position. Karl struck the blade aside, and they turned about each other, yanking back the heads of their steeds for another exchange. The sabre thrust at Karl, and he turned it aside again. Then he swung his steel down through the man's pauldron, shoulder and deep into his trunk. The demilancer convulsed, wailing, his blood spraying into the hard rain. Karl dragged his blade out, and the lancer was gone down into the water-logged mud.

Karl glared around to engage again, horses and men crashed past him in all directions. There was a demilancer right upon him, coming from the hindquarters. This lancer had a wheel-lock raised stiffly in his left hand.

Karl saw the dog spark and the muzzle flash with fire and white smoke.

Then the shot split his head into pieces.

ZAMAK SPAYENYA

I

IN HINDSIGHT, PERHAPS it had not been the wisest thing to do.

After a day's straight gallop across the trackless steppe, Gerlach began to feel uneasy. There was nothing and no one out there. His two long rides with the rota, especially the trek to Leblya, had falsely inflated his confidence that he could cope out on the steppe and deal with its harsh extremes and painful solitude. He hadn't realised how much he had looked to the lancers for their support. And for their expertise.

He was, by the motion of the sun at least, heading due south. But after an hour or two it occurred to him that he could only presume south was the way to go. He had no specific knowledge of

Leblya's relative location. Riding south might take him back to the Empire, but it could just as well carry him to the wilds of the World's Edge Mountains. He had no map, and no honed lore of the oblast. His course might run for days, for weeks, into nothing, unwittingly bypassing stanitsas just over the horizon that the lancers would have known to go to.

His hope had been to get a good start on the rota, and maybe outrun them for two or three days. Then, when they caught up with him, he would convince them to keep going with him into the south. If they didn't kill him, that is.

But there was no sign of riders behind him all the first day, and none on the second either.

The banner became too heavy to hold, and he was forced to ride with it cradled across his knees and saddlebow. He began to feel like a shameless thief, and dearly regretted taking it. Maybe if he had just ridden off, they would have followed him anyway. They seemed to care about his welfare. That made his crime seem worse. They had been good to him – staunch allies and generous comrades – and he had robbed them of their most precious artifact.

More than once he thought of turning back. He also considered leaving the rota somewhere for them to find. Scorching sunlit days turned to bitter oblast nights. The sun glared at him contemptuously, and the stars, in their multitude, mocked him.

The fourth day came and went, then the fifth. He had never been out of sight of other humans for so long. His only company was the passing clouds, but they seemed resentful, and chose not to show him any pictures he could read.

On the sixth morning, aching and anxious, he halted Saksen and stood for a long while, watching the northern horizon for signs of movement. Surely they would be coming close by now. He kept expecting to see them rise into view: heads, shoulders, horses, shimmering in the heat haze. Several times he thought he'd seen them, but it was just the light and space playing tricks on his tired mind.

He had brought some food and water, but nothing like enough for a trek of this magnitude. Vitali – and by Sigmar, he would have been overjoyed to see that smiling warrior again! – had showed him how to dig for water, and collect dew overnight in his armour plate and helm, but it was a meagre resource, and most of it went to his gelding. Saksen was strong, but he was also used to decent, regular fodder. He was a southerner, just like Gerlach, and was not built for these conditions. The troop horse had nothing of the stamina and resilience displayed by the robust steppe ponies the lancers rode. They seemed to fare without ready water, and greedily foraged on the tough grasses when rested at camp. Saksen appeared to find the grass indigestible. But when he was with the ponies, he had seemed content to follow their lead and graze. Gerlach could not make him eat the scrub, though he tried. Saksen was ailing.

Gerlach was ailing too. Thirst and hunger oppressed him physically, and he began to feel tormented by guilt and loneliness. He had ridden out of Leblya, intent on his scheme to draw the rota back to the war. That seemed inconsequential now. The entire fate of the Empire no longer mattered to him; he wondered why he had ever cared. Why had he been so reckless to involve himself in that faraway fight? Hadn't he realised where he was and how little he mattered?

In the late afternoon of the sixth day – maybe seventh, for he was no longer absolutely sure – he saw something in the grass ahead of him. It was nothing much, but in a place as blank and featureless, any deviation from the norm stood out.

They were bones. An untidy heap of scattered bones, old and stained pale yellow by the ministry of the wind and sun. For a while he stared at the remains, and eventually decided they belonged to a horse and a man. They had fallen here together, decayed and dried, until at last their loose bones had tumbled apart like pieces of a puzzle. How long had they been here? Years, certainly. Maybe decades, or even longer. Perhaps he was the first person to set eyes on them since the hour of their death.

They weren't the bones of a traveller, lost and killed by the brutal steppe, he decided. They were the bones of a rider who had chosen to gallop away from his life into the embrace of fate. Or the bones of a warrior who had been blessed with a steppe funeral.

As he rode away from them, a sick thought invaded his mind. Was it Sorca? Or Kvetlai? Or Ptor, or Chagin? How fast did the flies and ants and buzzards of the oblast strip a body? Were those bones merely days old?

And how long before he and Saksen formed a similar heap in another lonely spot?

No one had warned him about the sounds of the steppe. Riding with the men of the rota, he had not noticed them. But alone now, strange noises came to him above the thump of Saksen's hooves, the steady tinkling of the bit and harness, and the gentle rattle of his armour.

The open air uttered odd moans and long, distant wails that he presumed were the wind. Something invisible made strange clicks as loud as wheel-locks being wound. A fretful buzzing sound came and went, growing louder and louder until he drew up to listen for it only to find that it had disappeared. There was an occasional sound of hooves that never came closer and the inexplicable rush of racing water.

At dusk each day, dull booms pealed across the steppe. He stopped and listened for them, trying to discern their source. There were no storm clouds so he knew it wasn't thunder. It sounded like a great drum, struck once every few minutes. He would wait and listen until his patience lapsed and then, as soon as he started off again, another boom would come.

There were sounds at night too: sharper wails, and strange hollow growls that seemed to circle about him in the dark. Sometimes he heard voices, so distinct that he called out to them. The moment he spoke, the voices died away. And sometimes, there was laughter.

But the daylight sounds were the worst. At night, he could imagine, with a creeping dread, that there were things in the blackness around him. But in the light, he could see for certain there were not.

Once, under the midday heat, he caught the sound of a metal hinge grinding as it swung to and fro. There was a beat behind it, like the repeating thunk of a hammer on a metal sheet.

He drew Saksen up, and the sound continued. It was coming from close by, just to his right. Saksen's ears flicked back and forth. The gelding heard it too.

Gerlach dismounted, and walked through the grass, tracking the noise. He had drawn his loaded handgun and was clutching it in his hand. With the wood and iron piece in his hand, he was at least guarded against evil spirits. The sound grew louder and more insistent. It seemed to emanate from a rock the size of a man's head that lay in the dust amongst other quartzy fragments.

He approached it, and gingerly bent down beside the rock. The shrieking hinge and hammer were so loud now, he felt like he was in a smithy. He circled the rock and the source of the sound remained stationary. Under the stone.

Gerlach reached down and lifted the rock up.

The hinge and the hammer stopped. A terrible, shrill whistling erupted out of the depression where the rock had sat. It sang up into the air and made him fall down in shock. The noise made Saksen start.

Then it stopped, and unnerving silence reasserted itself.

Gerlach threw the rock aside. He was shaking. When he looked up, Saksen, crazed and scared, was galloping away into the grass.

II

HE RAN AFTER his horse, calling its name as loudly as his parched throat could manage. Then he stopped and doubled back to retrieve the rota banner, which had fallen onto the ground when Saksen bolted. Dragging it with him, like a deranged fool, he ran after the swiftly disappearing gelding.

'Saksen! Saksen! In the name of Sigmar! Byeli-Saksen!'

The horse was gone. The buzzing returned.

Behind it, like wind through leaves, there was distant laughter.

III

HE TRUDGED FOR a long period of immeasurable time, limping against the shaft of the heavy banner. When the buzzing returned, harsh and rasping in his ears, he turned in a circle and yelled a challenge aloud.

'What are you? Where are you?'

The buzzing seemed to swoop at him, and he cried out in alarm and fired his pistol.

Silence. The white smoke of his shot billowed up into a little cloud that drifted away into the sunny air.

For a moment, the tiny cloud looked like a white horse at full gallop. Then it fumed away and dissolved into the steppe breeze.

* * *

IV

DUSK FELL. THE sky turned a dense, Imperial blue, like the air before a storm, and the grasslands went white. The wide landscape was luminous, and the heavens a dead, lightless gloom.

Gerlach saw a stark, white speck, motionless, a league ahead of him.

He stumbled on, hurrying towards it.

Saksen stood stock still, his reins trailing, his head up. His flanks were caked in dry salt. The gelding was looking south.

As Gerlach approached, Saksen turned his noble head once to look at his master, then resumed his vigil.

Gerlach cast down the banner and the spent pistol, and edged towards his horse, cooing softly and holding out his hands. He ripped up a handful of steppe grass, the greenest he could find, and offered it out.

'Byeli... Byeli... Byeli-Saksen. Steady now. Steady now, old friend....'

Saksen allowed him to get close, and even sniffed the grass, though he would not take it. Gerlach stroked and patted Saksen's neck and took hold of the loose reins.

'Byeli... Byeli-Saksen.'

Gerlach led Saksen back and collected the banner and the pistol. Saksen tugged impatiently, wanting to turn south again.

Gerlach mounted up. Once he had the advantage of saddle-height, he saw what lay in the distance.

A puff of dust, kicked up by horsemen.

Galvanised, Gerlach found his stirrups and kicked his heels.

'Yatsha!'

V

AT FIRST IT seemed as if there were a half dozen riders, chasing north-east in the grey, fading light. But as he closed, Gerlach realised they were in fact one and five. One man was riding hard, pursued by five others.

Gerlach realised he could not hope to catch them. They were too far away, and running fast.

He reined up and raised the banner, planting its tip in the soil beside Saksen.

The chased rider saw it, and turned in towards Gerlach.

Gerlach primed his pistol, and slipped it into its case. Then he drew his sabre.

The lone rider was approaching, thrashing up a wake of dust with his furious gallop. A steppe horse. A rider in rough furs and leathers.

It was Kvetlai. And behind him came five Kul horsemen.

As soon as he recognised Kvetlai, Gerlach beckoned to him furiously. He didn't like the odds, but he was committed now. Five to one, or five to two if Kvetlai was able. Gerlach vowed he would make a good account of himself.

The riders came on.

As soon as he was close enough to identify Gerlach, Kvetlai started to yell, 'Vebla! Vebla! Yha!'

Gerlach smiled grimly. He waved Kvetlai on past him, and raised the wheel-lock, braced in both hands. He used his knees to keep Saksen at a steady halt.

Kvetlai swept past him, churning up a trail of dust and grit. The Kul horsemen were heartbeats away. Three had drawn swords, one an axe and a small shield. The closest, mailed in a low, frog-brow sallet, swung a flail.

Gerlach took aim. He was the target now. The Kul were riding him down and Kvetlai had disappeared somewhere behind him.

Four lengths away, Gerlach fired. His shot took the Kul with the flail in the neck and smashed him out of his saddle. His body slammed into the dust and rolled over and over as his empty horse rushed past Gerlach.

There was no time to reload. Gerlach cased his pistol and took up his sabre. He kicked Saksen forward and raised his blade crosswise to his face in the charge position. He galloped to greet the nearest Kul.

The horseman had a sword, and was swinging it in wild loops as he came on. Gerlach spurred Saksen abruptly to the man's off-side at the last moment, and thrust in across the saddle bow as they passed. The sabre came away bloody and the Kul screamed and fell forward over his mare's neck, dropping his blade.

The next two were on him, swordsman to the left and axe man to the right. Gerlach drove between them, and avoided both cutting slashes. Head low, Gerlach passed them, and met the tail-ender. Their swords struck and sent brief sparks up into the dark blue sky.

They both turned to re-engage.

The other two were turning as well, whooping and howling.

Gerlach went at the tail-ender and traded sword blows again. They had lost all momentum, and were saddle to saddle, hacking and blocking. The other two Kul were closing.

Gerlach split the air with his sabre, trying to drive off the tail-ender's blade. He was protecting both himself and Saksen, for the barbarian saw both as viable targets.

A fifth horseman appeared. Kvetlai raced back into the melee. He had no armour or troop weapons, but he had drawn his saddle sword. It was really too long to use while riding, too clumsy for a mounted duel. But the Kul had their backs to him and Kvetlai's blade ripped through the axe man's spine.

The man fell and his horse came over with him in a flurry of dry soil. The Kul's round shield skidded away across the dust.

Gerlach locked his sabre with the blade of the Kul he was fighting, and turned the enemy's sword aside so hard the tip of it stabbed into his mount's neck. The horse shrieked and kicked back, bucking and throwing its rider. It charged away into the gathering night.

Gerlach rode forward as the thrown man began to pick himself up out of the grass and dust, and lopped his head off.

The remaining Kul rider stopped short. He lowered his dirty iron blade. Gerlach faced him, blood dripping off his raised sabre. Kvetlai closed in from behind.

With a terrified cry, the Kul took off, and rode away into the west.

Gerlach and Kvetlai sheathed their swords and trotted forward to meet each other. Gerlach held out his hand, but the young Kislevite hugged him instead.

'Vebla!' he declared. He declared a lot of other things too, but Gerlach did not understand. Kvetlai had the least Reikspiel of any lancer in Beledni's rota.

It made Gerlach smile. Starved of company, his first encounter was with a friend who spoke nothing of his tongue.

Gerlach took Kvetlai by the hands and examined his wound. The long gash on his hand and arm was oozing pink, but it was healing. Borodyn had been right. A lancer simply had to trust in Dazh and ride out until the poison sweated out of him. Kvetlai had got on his horse and healed himself.

What adventures he had experienced in the course of that healing, Gerlach did not know. He took up the banner, and tried to beckon Kvetlai.

'South!' Gerlach said, pointing. 'We must go south!'

'Nyeh!' Kvetlai said emphatically, and pointed west.

Gerlach was about to argue. Then he looked south. There were fires on the horizon. Torches clutched in the hands of six dozen horsemen. Kul horsemen.

Gerlach looked at Kvetlai and nodded. 'You're right. Let's head west.'

VI

THEY RODE INTO the west together, and into the deepening twilight. The fires followed them, flickering: bobbing specks against the almost-black land, like grounded stars. There were more than six dozen now, and they straggled right across the south-east skyline.

Kvetlai gabbled as they rode. He was excited and talkative. Though he knew Gerlach couldn't understand him, he didn't seem to care. It was of no matter. Just the sound of a voice pleased Gerlach. He recognised occasional words as they tumbled out of the young lancer's mouth. Kvetlai said 'pulk' several times, with emphasis.

'Pulk?' Gerlach asked.

'Shto?'

'Pulk?' Gerlach repeated, wishing he had a smattering of Kislevite. Kvetlai chattered something else, and Gerlach gave up.

They'd ridden for over an hour, and night had swallowed day. It was utterly black. The only way they could tell land from sky was the fact that above a certain line, there were stars. Except behind them, where low, yellow stars burned and moved.

Something vast rose before them, slowly and grandly. At first, Gerlach thought it was a rising moon, or that a piece of the bright moon had fallen onto the steppe. It was a great slab of white stone, ghostly in the starlight, at least a league across: a single, oblong crag sprouting from the flat vista of the steppe.

They approached it. It was hauntingly beautiful, and illuminated the steppe as the moon and star light reflected off its icy whiteness. It was also immense.

'Zamak Spayenya,' Kvetlai said.

They rode onto the lower slopes of clattering scree, weaving between slabs and blocks of skewed rock that time had sloughed from the high faces of the table mountain. The rocks had a warm, damp smell as if they still radiated the heat of the day. Kvetlai led Gerlach around the northern edge of the crag. He clearly knew this place. It was hardly surprising. This rock – this *Zamak Spayenya* – was so singular it had to be a well-known landmark of the endless grassland.

Still chatting cheerfully, Kvetlai located a narrow gorge in the side of the giant rock, and they rode down its steep defile, entering a cool darkness with only a ribbon of starry sky high above. The horses' hooves cracked and clicked on the bared, uprisen rock.

The slope grew steep and their mounts slowed. Kvetlai jumped down and motioned for Gerlach to do the same. They led the horses the rest of the way on foot.

The gorge opened out into a great bowl of space open to the sky. Echoes of their every move rolled around the sides. The bottom of the bowl was filled with black water, the moons and the stars reflected there in an unrippled mirror.

Kvetlai pulled off his saddlebags, pack roll and water skin, and let his pony loose. The steppe horse immediately went to the pool to drink and stirred circles out over the faces of the mirrored moons. Kvetlai joined it to replenish his water skin.

Gerlach slipped his saddle kit off Saksen's harness. The troop horse trotted over to slake its thirst the moment Gerlach slipped the reins.

Kvetlai splashed his face with water from the great cistern of rainfall, and then jumped up.

'Vebla!' he beckoned. Gerlach followed him. The boy clearly believed their horses would be safe here in this inner place.

Kvetlai clambered up the smooth, sloping surfaces of the inner rock, making his way into its upper levels. He stopped to help Gerlach with his kit, but respectfully refused to touch the rota banner Gerlach was lugging.

They left the pool basin behind them, and scaled the steep paths and slopes of scree up to the summit of the rock.

Gerlach looked out. The steppe lay below, spreading out into the dark. A cool wind ruffled his hair. This was higher than he had ever been – higher even than the steeple of the church at Talabheim. His brother had taken him up there when he was six or seven, and he'd gasped at the vista of streets and roofs and tiny people, and the pattern of fields and woods laid out beyond. Even though it was dark, this was somehow more impressive. An endless void spread out below him, and he was aware of a great depth of space. From up here, the steppe was not so much diminished as emphasised and increased.

He could no longer see the fires of the Kul.

Kvetlai took him to a deep cave high in the rock, the mouth of which overlooked the humbling emptiness. It was cool and dry inside. Kvetlai gleefully sat down in the dark and rummaged in his saddlebags. After a short time, he had coaxed to life a small fire, and fed it with pieces of animal bone that he had stockpiled for just such a purpose.

The fire rose, washing the smooth walls of the cave with shivering light. Gerlach divested himself of his kit and the heavier parts of his armour, and respectfully set the rota banner upright against the cave wall. Then he sat down opposite Kvetlai and warmed his hands at the fire.

Kvetlai recommenced his casual, unending chatter.

'Zamak Spayenya?' Gerlach asked, gesturing around them.

'Yha, Vebla! Yha!'

Kvetlai's saddlebags miraculously provided strips of dried salt-fish, wafer biscuits, lumps of cured pork and four eggs. The eggs had been hard boiled in vinegar to preserve them. Kvetlai showed Gerlach how to rub the eggs between his palms to crush off the shell. They had their water skins, and a small leather bottle of kvass that Kvetlai ceremonially unstoppered.

It was the best, most satisfying meal Gerlach Heileman would ever eat.

It grew colder as they settled back, passing the kvass between them. Kvetlai threw his last few bones onto the crackling fire, and the pieces of eggshell too. He was talking still, and from his tone, Gerlach realised Kvetlai was telling a formal tale, a traditional myth for the krug. Every now and then, apparently as part of the indecipherable story, he sat up and laughed a false, loud laugh at the shadows of the cave.

When he finished, he looked at Gerlach expectantly.

'Vebla gyavaryt,' he said.

'What?'

'Vebla… Vebla… you,' he said, nodding eagerly.

Gerlach realised it was his turn. He took a suck on his water skin and began: 'In the old times, there was a tribe of men that was called the Unberogen, and to them a child was born. His name was called Sigmar, and on the night of his birth, a star with two tails sailed across the sky…'

Gerlach told his story gently, and Kvetlai listened, rapt. Gerlach was reaching the famous part about the Black Fire Pass when something wailed in the dark and interrupted him. Kvetlai gave it no notice. Gerlach carried on, and then stopped again as the infernal buzzing and laughter that had stalked him on the steppe whispered past.

Kvetlai sat up straight and laughed his loud, false laugh at the shadows.

The noise faded.

The laughter came again, from the back of the cave, with a tiny hammer-beat mixed into it. Kvetlai turned and laughed in that direction. The sounds stopped.

Gerlach recommenced, but halted yet again as whispering voices chattered out of the jumping shadows at the edge of the fire. Kvetlai leaned over and laughed at them, making the voices ebb.

'Spirits... phantoms of the steppe?' Gerlach asked.

Kvetlai nodded, not knowing what he was nodding at.

'They have stalked me. I have been afraid of them.'

Sibilant whispers rushed in around the mouth of the cave. Kvetlai turned his head and laughed once more, hearty but false.

'Aha ha ha ha!'

'And laughing at them scares them away...' Gerlach breathed. He smiled. When a hinge began to squeak in the roof of the cave halfway through the tale of the mantling of Johan Helstrum, they both looked up and bawled out a roaring laugh.

'Ha ha ha ha!'

Kvetlai settled back. 'Johan,' he prompted. 'Johan...'

Gerlach grinned. 'As I was saying, Helstrum was thus the first of the line of Grand Theogonists...'

VII

KVETLAI WAS ASLEEP before the history of the Sigmarite Empire was done. Gerlach sat for a while, then took a burning rib out of the fire and wandered into the back of the cave. His eyes had not tricked him. There were markings on the white limestone walls.

Primitive markings, made with graphite and ochre dust. Men riding to the hunt, their charcoal-streaked

javelins wounding leaping deer and elk. Crude
though it was, the depiction of the horses was
instantly recognisable. The low, brown shapes of
hardy steppe ponies, with shaggy, black manes. The
riders were drawn naked, simple and angular, but
great eagle wings grew out of their backs.

Gerlach moved the light of the crisping bone further down the wall. Here were boars, and sheep. A
great mound surrounded by horses that looked as if
they had been raised stiff on stakes. A star with two
streaming tails of fire. Horse warriors, clad in gold.

The gold was real foil leaf, tamped against the
cave wall. Gerlach looked again, and realised he was
not looking at horse warriors at all. The prancing
figures were horse-and-man. The bodies of flying
steeds, with the torsos of men growing out where
the horse heads should have been. Their arms were
spread wide, triumphant, brandishing recurve bows
and charcoal-streak javelins.

The centaurs of myth. Men who were horses.
Horses who were also men. Or, Gerlach thought, an
ancient people whose lives had been so wholly
dependent on the horse that there was no separat-
ing the two.

His bone-light went out. The ancient drawings
vanished, as if they had galloped away into the
shadows.

Gerlach crept back to the dying fire where Kvetlai
slumbered.

He was about to sit down, when he heard a low,
welling moan. He laughed at it, but it did not fade.
He laughed again, louder and more vigorously,

but the moan remained and rose as a whispering chatter.

It was coming from the mouth of the cave.

Gerlach walked to the opening and laughed wildly and loudly into the darkness. He heard the phantom laughter wash through the night and indignantly prepared to guffaw again to see it off.

A hand closed over his mouth, silencing him.

It was Kvetlai.

The lad pointed down the slope. Far below, around the skirts of the great rock, Kul torches were moving.

VIII

KVETLAI KICKED OUT the fire and then watched the cave mouth, his saddle sword in his hand, as Gerlach dressed himself in the parts of his half-armour that he had taken off. Gerlach began to prime his wheel-lock too, but Kvetlai stopped him and patted his sword blade. His meaning was obvious. If they were going to live, they had to act quietly.

Gerlach put his handgun and its equipment aside, and followed Kvetlai out into the moonlight. He was holding his sabre, and drew his knife in the other hand.

There were flickering torch lights below them still, but other scads of flame could be seen moving up the rocks and along the gorges that cut into the table mountain.

The Kul were not moving directly towards them. There was a good chance these kyazak could spend the rest of the night searching the rock's mighty system of caves and ravines for them.

Gerlach and Kvetlai settled back in silence to wait it out, their swords gripped in their hands.

IX

THE MOONS ROSE and set. Voices and the occasional clatter of dislodged scree echoed down to them. They waited. Hours crawled by.

Below, the flames jiggled around the foot of the rock.

Gerlach woke up very suddenly. He had no idea how long he'd been asleep, but the sky was just beginning to turn pale. Kvetlai was sleeping, hunched against the far side of the cave mouth.

Gerlach was about to hiss his name when he saw they were not alone. A Kul warrior was softly approaching the lip of rock beyond the cave mouth. He could see the kyazak only as a dark shape with glittering eyes.

Gerlach waited, playing dead. Through half-shut lids, he watched the Kul coming closer. There was another one a short distance behind him. Gerlach's sabre had slid from his grasp while he slept, but the knife was still in his left hand. He kept still as the Kul crept up to him. The man had a short-hafted adze, and as he bent down, Gerlach heard him sniffing like a hunting dog.

Gerlach lunged, grabbing the Kul by the hair and ramming the knife up into his chest. The Kul squealed and struggled, but Gerlach kept him pinned. The second Kul at the edge of the rock-lip let out a guttural shout and raised a bow. The heavy arrow hissed as it flew, and splintered against the cave wall beside Gerlach's head. Gerlach fought to retain his grip on the first Kul, who was becoming limp and awfully heavy. He had to keep the man's body between him and the archer.

Running forward, the bowman fired again. The arrow smacked through the upper body of the corpse and travelled with such force that the head of it came through the other side, penetrated Gerlach's pauldron and stabbed a thumb's depth into his shoulder. Gerlach yelped out in pain. Before the archer could fire a third time, Kvetlai had sprung up and cut him through the ribs with his saddle sword.

There was movement all around them as Kul scurried to close in on the source of the commotion. The flames of several torches showed close by. Kvetlai ran to one side of the rock-lip and hacked at another kyazak, sending his body slithering away down the sloping face. A fourth appeared, and Kvetlai turned to repel him. Their swords clattered against each other.

Having fought to hold on to his human shield, Gerlach now battled to rid himself of it. The man's deadweight pulled hard and painfully against the arrowhead and made Gerlach cry out again in frustrated anguish.

The arrow snapped, leaving a small, broken, finger length protruding from Gerlach's shoulder. The body fell away sideways, Gerlach's knife still wedged in its chest. Gerlach grabbed his sabre, pain flaming down his arm. Kyazak blood was all over his left hand and down his front.

Gerlach ran forward in time to contend with two more Kul sliding down the slope onto the rock-lip from the left side of the cave. He killed one with a swift thrust, and then battled with the other, who lunged and slashed at him with a short sword and a crackling torch. Gerlach's face was singed as the rushing flames jabbed at him.

Kvetlai had slain another Kul, and now struck out at more, moving so he was shoulder to shoulder with the demilancer. Gerlach finally managed to tear his sabre against the threatening torch and send it sparking and flaring down the incline. Then he overwhelmed the kyazak's untrained sword hand with three clean, proficient blows and finished him with a body-thrust.

Between them, with frantic effort, they killed or drove off the four Kul who had managed to get onto the rock-lip. Many more were approaching, from either side and below.

Kvetlai cried out something, and ransacked the body of the first kyazak he had taken – the archer who had gored Gerlach. He got the man's bow and his case of arrows, and began to fire them into the darkness. The spitting sounds of arrows were answered, more than once, by a cry of pain.

Dawn was on them. The sky had gone slate grey, and the crag side was slowly illuminating with watery light. The steppe below remained as dark as pitch right out to the line where it joined the cold, pale sky.

The kyazak rushed them again, from below and to the left, and it took all the effort and skill of the two men to hold them off. The Kul dropped back. To prepare bows, Gerlach thought.

Kvetlai called to him in this brief intermission and gestured upwards. Pausing only long enough for Gerlach to gather the banner, they began to scramble up the steep stone slope above the cave mouth, heading for the highest part of the crag. A few wayward arrows rattled off the rocks around them, and Kvetlai paused occasionally, legs spread and braced against the sharp incline, to loose an arrow or two back.

Gerlach concentrated on climbing and avoiding slithering back down to an ignominious doom. Half-armour was not made for such an activity, and the long, heavy banner was a downright hindrance. But he could not leave it for the filthy kyazak. He crawled up the hard, dry face of the rock, sometimes using the shaft of the banner as a prop. He was sweating freely. More arrows rushed up at them, striking the rock with brittle cracks or purring past their heads like bees.

They reached the top – a small platform of rock – just about the highest part of Zamak Spayenya. The limestone sloped away on all sides of it and to reach it any bandit would have to scale the open face as Gerlach and Kvetlai had done.

They sat down and recovered their breath. The waking day was much brighter now, and the light was falling with a silver radiance. A dawn breeze blew. They could see for many leagues in every direction. Gerlach could spot no sign of life except an eagle, gliding in the thermals a long way up.

They kept a careful watch over the edge of the platform. Some of the kyazak attempted to climb after them, and were dissuaded by a few arrows and hurled rocks. But all the Kul had to do was wait. It was already warm. The summer heat would make that exposed platform as hot as a griddle. Without water and cover, and with nowhere left to run, the two men would not last for any great time. From one side of the platform, it was possible to see down into the cool, shadowy basin in the heart of the crag where they had left their horses. They looked down at the pool and its tantalising promise of an end to thirst.

The silvery dawn became bright morning, blindingly white. The rising heat of noon broiled the sweat out of them. They became so torpid that one effort by the Kul to reach them almost succeeded. Gerlach only managed to knock the kyazak warriors back down the rock face using the pole of the banner as a makeshift spear.

The scalding heat did not seem to diminish as the long day ground on into the slow afternoon. Gerlach watched the smudges of cloud pass by overhead. They were meaningless, unformed, not even suggestive of character. But the gliding eagle returned, closer now, banking above them, and shortly after that a cloud appeared that was almost a circle or a ring.

'Krug,' Kvetlai said, his lips dry. He was watching the cloud.

Gerlach got to his feet.

'Shto, Vebla?' Kvetlai asked, supposing another rush of kyazak was coming. Gerlach slowly scanned the horizon, turning full circle. It had to be... it had to be...

Dazh did not send men messages lightly.

A tiny flash, out in the north-west, right at the very brink of the visible world.

'Kvetlai! Look there!' Gerlach pointed, and the boy stood up. Their movement at the edge of the platform provoked a couple of arrows up from below.

Kvetlai didn't seem to see, yet Gerlach was sure. The flash of sunlight on silver. But so far off, and perhaps moving away.

He grabbed up the banner and raised it as high as he could, holding the shaft by its very end in both hands and swinging the head so the banner cloth itself fluttered out in the high air. It was a huge effort, and he had to set it down every few moments to ease his arms. Every time he hoisted it up again, the Kul below loosed angry arrows and shouted curses and cat-calls. A few began to try climbing again. He waved the banner like a castaway mariner trying to hail a passing ship from a desert atoll. Gerlach's notion that the steppe was like a sea where its people lived like islanders now seemed desperately apt.

The distant flash was no longer visible, as if it had gone, or had never been there. A trick of the light, a trick of the eye.

Then Kvetlai called out, and pointed excitedly. A dot. Several dots in fact. A line of dots, moving gradually towards them.

Gerlach laughed out and set to waving the banner more vigorously.

The dots became shapes. The shapes became horsemen. Galloping horsemen, over fifty of them, clad in silver. Tall wings rose from their backs.

At some point, as the lancers raced closer, the kyazak saw them too. There was a round of hectic shouting from below the platform, and then the voices of the Norscya bandits receded. By the time the rota reached Zamak Spayenya, the bandit pack had fled, riding their ponies east into the steppe.

Gerlach and Kvetlai scrambled down from the platform, slithering most of the way. They gathered up what remained of their saddlebags and possessions from the cave where the looting Kul had scattered them, and climbed down into the shadows of the rainwater basin. Saksen and Kvetlai's horse had gone, but before they worried about that, the two men plunged into the pool to cool their baked, dry bodies and slake their thirst.

They emerged from the gorge into the sunlight. Their horses, either driven off by the Kul or simply fled away from them, were grazing in the scrub between the scattered boulders around the foot of the crag. Their ears twitched as they heard the drumming of hooves.

The rota appeared, riding around the bluff of Zamak Spayenya. Beledni was at their head. Kvetlai cried out and ran towards them as they reined to a halt.

Gerlach took a deep breath, lifted the banner, and walked after him.

* * *

X

THE MEN OF the rota were silent. Kvetlai was puzzled, not really sure what was going on or why Beledni rotamaster was glaring with such venom at the outlander they called 'Vebla'.

Beledni dismounted and walked towards Gerlach. Kvetlai went to him, and began a hasty account in Kislevite. Beledni ignored him and continued striding towards Gerlach. Then Kvetlai said something that made the rotamaster stop, turn back, and fire off a series of rapid questions.

Beledni finally silenced Kvetlai's eager answers with a curtly raised hand, and turned back to Gerlach. They stood face to face in the bright afternoon light, horseflies buzzing around them and the strong steppe wind ruffling the grass. Gerlach handed the banner to Beledni. He took it, and held it beside himself, upright in his left hand.

'Vebla steal rota banner,' he said at last. His eyes were dark and dangerous behind the visor of his szyszak.

'Yes,' Gerlach replied.

'Vebla steal rota banner so rota would follow him.'

'Yes, rotamaster.'

'Follow to find pulk. To find war.'

'Yes, rotamaster.'

'Even though Beledni rotamaster say nyeh.'

'Yha, rotamaster.'

They were not really questions. It was as if Beledni wanted to make sure he had the facts straight. He glanced up at the flapping banner for a moment, then looked back into Gerlach's face.

'Vebla save Kvetlai from kyazak.'

'We saved each other, rotamaster.'

'Kvetlai make ride to sweat out sickness. He not never come back, if Vebla not help him with kyazak.'

Gerlach shrugged.

'Kvetlai find pulk at Zoishenk.'

'What?'

'Kvetlai ride back to tell this to Beledni rotamaster.'

'I… I had no idea of this, rotamaster.'

Beledni nodded.

'Yetchitch rota go to Zoishenk now,' he said, briefly. With a casual movement, he handed the banner back to Gerlach and returned to his horse.

XI

THREE DAYS' RIDE into the south brought them to the cattle town of Zoishenk. It was larger than Leblya and Dushyka, larger than Zhedevka and Choika put together. It had a large livestock market and sat at the edge of a great grass plain on the banks of a wide, shallow river called the Tobol. The Tobol flowed down from some distant oblast mountains, and the locale of Zoishenk was riven with a range of rocky hills and dense thorn-wood.

Riding out his sickness, deliriously sweating the poison from his wound, Kvetlai had come to Zoishenk almost by chance, and there found the masses of the Sanyza pulk. In the months following Zhedevka, the broken elements of the Kislevite pulk had assembled at Zoishenk instead of Leblya

because of the threat of the kyazak bandit-army
loose in the steppe to the north.

The stanitsa was teeming with soldiers. Almost
seven hundred warriors were gathered there –
three other rotas of winged lance, several bands
of horse archers, and foot companies of pike and
axe, along with the cruder assortments of levies
and partisans. There was also the remainder of
several Imperial pike companies that had fled
Zhedevka and come here under the pulk's
colours, combining their strengths to make one
full regiment. Sanyza pulk – that is to say the
army raised and recruited from the Sanyza area of
the oblast – was under the command of the
Boyarin Fyodor Kurkosk, a second cousin of the
Tzarina herself.

Additions and reinforcements – like Beledni's rota
– were being added all the time, and scouts had
been sent out to locate other scattered parts of the
pulk and to drum up new support from the neigh-
bouring regions. Word was that the Uskovic pulk,
an army of much more considerable size, was
already en route to join the Sanyza pulk. With those
sort of numbers at his disposal, the Boyarin would
advance south, perhaps even as far as the Ostermark, and engage the Kurgan horde. By the end of
the summer season, or by the start of the autumn,
they would have joined with the foe and perhaps be
driving him out of the Reik.

At long last, Gerlach had the chance to fight for
his homeland, the chance he had been craving since
the spring.

But Sigmar – or perhaps Dazh – had other plans for him.

By the time the rota reached Zoishenk, Gerlach was sick.

XII

NO ONE COULD say what filth had been caked on the tip of the kyazak arrow, and it had not helped that the barb had remained, lodged and festering, in Gerlach's shoulder for over a day. Borodyn had managed to dig it out with a flame-heated knife, but the wound was dirty. Gerlach became feverish, and his upper arm swelled so badly he could no longer wear armour around the limb. Defiantly, despite his progressively ailing state, he carried the banner all the way to Zoishenk. Vitali and Vaja were concerned he was about to pitch out of Saksen's saddle and they suggested Maksim should take the standard.

Once they had arrived at Zoishenk, Gerlach was carried to one of the livestock barns that had been converted into barracks for the pulk. He was laid out on a straw mattress. The flesh around his wound had gone black and the injury stank. He fell into a turbulent sleep, and did not regain consciousness for several days. Borodyn, Vaja, Vitali and Kvetlai took turns to watch him, spooning sips of gruel and water into his mouth and dressing his wound with salves of astringent herbs.

Like clouds across the steppe, fever dreams passed mysteriously through Gerlach's mind. In one, his father and brother came to him, both dressed in the full plate of the Order of the Red Shield, but neither would speak to him. In another, he lay helpless in long grass that knotted around him and held him down as Talabheim burned. Then he was running into the empty steppe at night, chasing a white horse that remained out of his reach. A blazing star with two long streamers of flame arching out behind it fell out of the night. The star flew at him. In its fiery heart was a staring blue eye ringed with writhing snakes.

Delirious, he became afraid. His dreaming mind recalled the fact that he and Kvetlai hadn't had time to blind the kyazaks they had killed at Zamak Spayenya. The spirits of the dead, loose in the darkness outside life, could see him and were coming to claim his soul. He cried out so fearfully and thrashed about so much, Vaja and Vitali had to hold him down for fear he would injure himself further.

After ten days, the death-fever broke. The fretful tremor left Gerlach and he woke suddenly, with apparent clarity, long enough to sip water and broth. Then he fell into a profound but untroubled sleep. Borodyn pronounced that Gerlach would live after all.

And he lived, but his recovery was slow. It took another week before he properly regained his senses, and another two before he could sit up unassisted. He was miserably weak and his under-nourished flesh clung to his bones.

Well over a month after riding into Zoishenk, just as he was able to walk around for short periods, Maksim and Beledni came to him. They both looked serious and a little uncomfortable.

'What is it?' he asked.

'Beledni need your permission, Vebla,' said the rotamaster.

'For what?'

'For Maksim to carry rota banner,' Beledni said. Maksim made a little, respectful nod of his head.

'Why?'

'The Boyarin has make decree. Pulk is to advance.'

'That's good! Good! I'm keen to get on myself, and–'

'Nyeh, Vebla.' Gerlach hadn't realised that Borodyn had been lurking in the shadows behind the lancers. 'You are not fit enough to walk across this room, let alone get up on a horse. You cannot come. You would not live a day.'

Gerlach shook his head fiercely.

'Is so, Vebla,' murmured the rotamaster. 'Beledni is sorry. You not come.'

Miserably disappointed, but knowing they were right, Gerlach looked away.

'Please to give Beledni permission for Maksim to carry rota banner,' Beledni said quietly.

'I give it,' Gerlach replied.

XIII

THE PULK DEPARTED at dawn the next day. Gerlach managed to get himself as far as the stable doorway to watch the army move out. Drums and horns sounded as the files marched out through the streets, and it was still possible to hear them a long time afterwards, as an echo from the valleys of the south.

* * *

XIV

GERLACH BATTLED TO bring himself back to fitness.
He ate everything he could get hold of to rebuild his
strength, and exercised his weak limbs to restore
decent mobility. Three weeks after the pulk's depar-
ture, he was strong enough to walk and ride. He
knew he was yet nothing like as strong as he had
been, but it was enough. He gathered his possessions, collected some saddle supplies, and prepared
to follow the pulk south.

It was late summer by then, hot and lazy. The days
were drawing out and the land had become dry and
dusty. The herders of Zoishenk were taking their grazing flocks higher into the foot hills to look for fresher
pasture, and traders were arriving with harvested corn
and grain from the farmlands in the south-east. The
Tobol was now so parched by the high summer heat
that its course was just a wide dusty track threaded by
a feeble stream. Everywhere, the withered grass
clicked with the sound of steppe crickets.

Then the pulk returned.

XV

THE BOYARIN'S ARMY had got as far south as
Pradeshynya, contesting twice along the way with
small warbands of raiders. At Pradeshynya, they
sighted a massive host of raiders three or four times
their size, undoubtedly the collective warbands of a
significant High Zar. The pulk had withdrawn
across the Tobol headwaters to avoid annihilation,
and waited for the Uskovic pulk to arrive with reinforcements.

It never came. Whether it had been delayed, or annihilated, the men of Sanyza pulk could not know. The Boyarin decided to wait two more days, but in that time the enemy made its move. A host of warbands, a large chunk of the High Zar's horde, attacked the pulk across the Tobol salt-pan. It could have been a disaster, but the pulk was well prepared. The battle lasted for about five hours, right on into the late evening, whereupon the Kurgan fell back, badly mauled and suffering huge casualties at the hands of the resilient Kislevites. The withdrawal gave the Boyarin a grace period to retreat back into the oblast before the entire horde massed and fell on them.

They were pursued for a time but, with a higher proportion of mounted troops than the Kurgan forces, the pulk outdistanced its adversaries.

Fyodor Kurkosk, in consultation with his commanders, was forced to make a hard decision. The summer was as good as over, and the hard weather of autumn and winter would be fast on them. The pulk would disband, and its constituent companies return to their own lands over winter. This gave them all time to recruit, resupply and raise more levies, and then build support from adjoining regions. Kurkosk decreed that the Sanyza pulk would reform at Zoishenk early after midwinter, preferably at the first thaw. With luck, it would be two or three times its current size. With more luck, it might be one of several pulks coordinated and drawn together over the winter season by the urgent efforts of the Boyarin warlord and his officers.

Beledni's lancers were heading home into the steppe, to Yetchitch.

'You will come, Vebla, yha?' Vitali asked eagerly.

Gerlach had a poor choice. He could hardly ride south on his own into the enemy. And he didn't fancy staying alone in a cattle town for the winter. Besides, Zoishenk had become a place of repeatedly dashed hopes for him, and he was weary of it.

He would ride to Yetchitch with the rota. Even if it did feel like running away.

CHAMON DHAREK

I

'GIVE ME A mirror,' Karl snapped.

'A...?'

'A looking glass,' said Karl. 'I know you have one. I've seen you using it in your doltish sorceries.'

Chegrume scowled for a moment. Then he reached into the roughly sewn pelts of his spirit-bag. 'It is not meant for looking in. Only for seeing in. Only shamans should–' The shaman shrugged. 'Perhaps one such as you might be permitted to use it.' He took the precious glass from the bag and held it out to Karl in his bony, long-nailed fingers.

Karl took it. It was an irregular piece of silver-backed glass fixed into a spoon-like paddle of fig wood. He held it up and stared into it.

It was the first time Karl had seen his own reflection since leaving the garrison at Vatzl, what seemed like years before. Karl Reiner Vollen no longer looked back at him.

The demilancer's pistol ball had struck him on the corner of the brow ridge over his left eye. The bone had shattered, and the whole area from the eyebrow down to the cheek was an ugly weal of distorted scar tissue. It was pinky-white and black-scabbed, but now, a week after the battle, the swelling was beginning to go down.

The injury had destroyed his left eye. Pain still throbbed in the dead socket, and he had a constant stabbing hurt in the skull above the eye. Chegrume had cleansed the wound and the ruined socket with hot iron and herbal tinctures. He had probably saved Karl's life from blood fever, but his face and sight would never be repaired.

Karl stared at his face for a long time. He was unshaven and his teeth were dirty. His black hair was so long now he wore it permanently in a tail. The three blue dots of Zar Uldin's mark looked like an old bruise on his right cheekbone.

He had been aware that all the Kurgan he had encountered since his wounding seemed to regard him with some measure of fear or apprehension, and averted their gaze whenever he was around. This seemed strange considering they were quite used to horrific injuries and mutilations. But they hadn't been showing revulsion.

Looking into the glass, Karl could plainly see what had scared them.

He had one eye. One blue eye. To make it worse, indelible powder burns from the injury had stained lines across his face, both over and under his good eye. The lines were twisted, and looked like snakes.

A single blue eye surrounded by snakes. No wonder no one dared look at him.

He handed the glass back to Chegrume.

'You should have let me die,' he told him.

II

SURTHA LENK'S HORDE had obliterated the army of the Reik outside Aachden. It was a notable victory. The town fell soon after, and many hundreds of its inhabitants, as well as men captured in battle, passed into the possession of the slave lord, Skarkeetah. Uldin, along with Blayda, Herfil and six other zars, had killed enough with his warband to earn the glory of a skull stack.

Chegrume had carved the new victory mark on Uldin's cheek. Four now, on that side.

Then Uldin gathered his warband for a victory feast – indeed all the bands in the High Zar's horde were celebrating the victory. Afterwards they would divide the spoils of war between them. Many trophy rings were made.

Wolfenburg lay close by. Uldin hoped to earn a fifth victory mark there before the last one had even scabbed over.

III

KARL-AZYTZEEN'S LEFT forearm was now wound with trophy rings from the elbow to the wrist, and there

were three more around his right arm. Once he was
well enough to walk, Uldin took him into a muddy
field behind the ruins of Aachden and offered him
his pick of the captured horses.

'I'll keep the one I have.'

'It is a poor thing, Karl-Azytzeen. Old and broken.'

'It serves me. It does not stop for anything. I will
not trade it.'

Uldin shrugged. Even the zar refused to look
directly at him. 'Then you should name it.' The Kurgan had no sentiment at all. They only gave a name
to a thing when it became important. Most horses
weren't named until they had carried their man
through at least one battle.

'It doesn't need a name,' Karl replied. 'It is old,
and has gone for this much of its life without one.
It is simply my horse.' After this blunt dismissal, the
men of the warband began to call the old nag
Horse-of-Karl-Azytzeen.

'You are due a share of gold,' Uldin informed him.

'I have no use for gold. Give me a good fur and a
saddle. I'm damned if I will fight on with a spear
and no stirrups. And a decent sword.'

These things were provided within an hour, at the
zar's orders. A good box-saddle with a brass harness, rowel spurs that Karl had nailed to his heavy
boots, a heavy brown bear-pelt and a brooch to
hold it. The brooch was Scythian gold, formed into
the shape of a long-backed, leaping horse.

Uldin himself presented Karl with a sword. A
superior pallasz, forged from steel rather than iron,
with a straight bar guard and two hands of grip. Karl

took a whetstone to its blade, and worked it until it was sharp enough to split a bough from a tree with one stroke, from either edge.

It was high summer, a time Karl had once particularly enjoyed. The weather was fine and warm, and the landscape – where it had not been touched and marred by the High Zar's massive host – was lush and green.

The horde left Aachden to rot and moved on to Wolfenburg.

IV

WOLFENBURG, THE GREAT sentinel city of Ostland's northern marches, lay in the foothills of the Middle Mountains amid vast blankets of forest. Even in the heat of summer, the mountains were white-capped and grim. Their huge blue-black shapes, fogged by cloud, dominated the skyline.

The city itself was a fortress town of ancient construction. Occupying a raised hillside above the river bend, it was well fortified with curtain walls and high, towered inner walls of great thickness. It had shut itself up in advance of the Northers' advance. Large tracts of forest outside the walls had been freshly cleared to remove available cover for an attacking force and to fill the city's stockpile of firewood.

The first warbands to reach the city made a hasty assault of the gatehouse and the south wall. But they were driven off, with costly losses, by vase-guns, hails of arrows, and scalding oil sluiced down through the murder holes above the gate.

The main part of the horde arrived and encamped around the city. More wood was cut, in great quantity, by berdish axe this time. This wood fed the camp-fires, and was also used to construct mobile shields that were pushed forward to allow the Kurgan archers with their powerful recurve bows to pepper the wall tops and the machicolations. Once the wagon train had arrived, the horde's sturdy old ballistae, trebuchets and catapults were trained on the city. The ballistae – essentially gigantic crossbows – launched savage bolts of iron-tipped hardwood two spans long at the walls. The trebuchets and catapults hurled rocks, weighted bales of burning straw, flasks of boiling oil and rotting human heads, collected from the field at Aachden expressly for the purpose.

The siege began in earnest. It was quite the dullest kind of war Karl had ever experienced. There was a feebly slow routine. The siege engines lobbed missiles at the wall, and the guns, slings and cannon of the town fired in reply, sometimes hurling the Kurgans' own projectiles back at them. This continued for days. Every few minutes there would be a sharp creak, a thump or a squeal of metal as one of the war machines fired. The drums beat continually.

The war bands were forced to bide their time. As horsemen, they had little part to play in this slow, erosive war.

Karl found himself gazing south-west across the forest for hours at a time. No more than fifteen days' good riding in that direction lay Talabheim, the home he could never now return to, unless it was to storm its noble walls and set its towers to burn.

V

THE SIEGE GROUND on for twelve weeks. There were a precious few bursts of activity. The Knights of the Order of the Silver Mountain, along with greatswords from the city garrison, made several sorties out of the gatehouse to harass the enemy. The warbands rode to meet them. Karl won two new trophy rings: one for a greatsword who almost filleted his horse, and another for a knight-at-arms whose silver plate-mail proved the sharpness of Karl's new pallasz beyond doubt.

Dismounted, Uldin's warband took part in most of the foot assaults against Wolfenburg's admirably solid walls. These usually happened at dusk or dawn. Covered by the hissing sheets of arrows sent up by the archers from behind the wooden screens, the Kurgan warriors charged the walls, hefting scaling ladders between them. Teams of straining warriors rolled up the massive timber ram under its protective portico of stretched animal hides.

The foot assaults were costly. Even if the ram reached the gates without being set ablaze, it failed to make a dent in the colossal doors. The scaling parties were decimated by the rains of arrows, rocks and pitch, or died from broken limbs and backs when their ladders were pushed away from the walls. Karl was grazed across the left shoulder by a crossbow bolt and his left hand was blistered with boiling oil. His wounds were typical of those received by the other men in the warband. Diormac lost an ear. Lyr was pinned through the leg by an Imperial arrow. Utz had his lower jaw smashed by a rock. He lived for two days, wailing and screaming, until Uldin could bear it no longer and cut his throat. Uldin was clearly upset about this, and openly blamed the High Zar for making one of his riders die ignominiously, out of the saddle. Surtha Lenk, opinion went, was not doing enough to finish this siege. There was dissent amongst the horde.

Karl filled his time between the brief periods of action helping Berlas and the other archers in the band to compose bows. It was a complex business, as the bows were fashioned from three parts. A central stave of maple or mulberry, woods which took glue well, was laminated with animal sinew on the back and horn on the front, in order to withstand the tension and compression. For special bows, Berlas used human sinew and bone. This stave, the grip, was fixed to the two arms of the bow, along which bone from longhorn cattle had been glued. Bone tips were attached, and the bows tied up tight against the shape they would be drawn to. Then the bow was left to dry, for weeks, or, if time permitted, months.

After that, more tendon sinew, beaten with a hammer into fibres, was applied in layers to the bow arms, and the bow was back-strung tightly again for more drying.

Dried, they were carefully warmed and then strung up the way they would be shot, ready for the tillering. This was a process of gentle filing and adjustment that ensured that the arms bent evenly at full draw for maximum accuracy.

Karl was not at all good at any of these stages, but Berlas was happy to have him handle each piece during the stages of construction, as if Karl's touch somehow conveyed a blessing on the weapons. They were valuable pieces, because of the effort of manufacture, and Berlas told him that, unlike swords, armour and horses, bows were never buried with the dead unless they were broken. It was too great a waste.

Once word spread that Karl was blessing bows, other men, some from rival warbands, came to him to have him touch bow components, arrowheads or even whetstones. He deeply resented the attention and what it implied, but he did not refuse any man.

Karl learned to shoot a bow. He had grasped basic archery skill using 'self' bows as a youth, but the recurve bow was a revelation. Each one imparted a draw equal to the body weight of a good-sized man with a simple, smooth pull, and suffered no stacking of power-weight at the release, as was the case with bows of a single piece of wood. He quickly found he was more accurate with the alien weapon than he had ever been with a longbow as a boy.

Berlas finessed his bow skill. He told Karl to forget the southern manner of drawing a bow with three fingers. Instead, the Kurgan drew with the thumb, and with the first three fingers locked over it. The thumb was guarded by a ring of bone or brass. Because of this, a Kurgan loosed his arrow from the right side of his bow, rather than the left as was the practice in the

Empire. A recurve bow could send an arrow over three hundred spans, but was only considered accurate over forty-five bow lengths. Any target further than that was, in Berlas's expert opinion, a waste of arrows. However, an archer could shoot 'in arcade', which was to draw and loose upwards so that the dart came down on the target from an almost vertical angle. Unlike the Imperial toxophilists, who were infantry-based and could manage a long 'self' bow, the Kurgan needed a weapon they could fire easily from the saddle. Only the smooth-pulling recurve bows were effective in this respect.

Karl was practising arcade shots from the saddle in a tract of woodland away from the main force, when the riders came looking for him. It was the fourth month of the siege, and word had spread that the High Zar, aggrieved by the dissent showing in the horde, was intending to call up the powers of the Dark Gods and end the siege.

There were twenty riders, all from Surtha Lenk's bodyguard. One of the big men with bull horns sprouting obscenely out of his skull led them. He approached Karl and handed him a human skull that had been polished to a pearlescent finish. Karl took hold of it and then the horned man took it back. The gang of riders sped away after him.

Karl laughed. Now even the High Zar was looking to him to bless his instruments of war.

VI

THAT NIGHT, THE phosphorescent flickers of the Northland Lights danced above Wolfenburg. Then a winter storm came in, barging through the summer night. The tempest was ferocious. Thick frost covered the landscape and ice weighed down the thrashing trees. Lightning struck like repeated hammer blows against the city walls. It was so savage and unrelenting that the gatehouse collapsed.

Jeering and yelling, the Kurgan entered Wolfenburg, broke it open, and put everyone inside it to the sword.

VII

AT DAWN, AS the city burned, Uldin raised his skull-stack. His warband had done well, and the favour of the High Zar was upon them. Once Uldin had anointed the skull-pile with captive blood, he called for the mark to be made. Chegrume approached with the flint knife, but Uldin sent him back and called for Karl-Azytzeen.

Karl came forward and, under Chegrume's instruction, made the fifth victory mark on Uldin's cheek. At the last moment, he tossed the flint knife away and used Drogo Hance's true killer to slash the ritual mark on Uldin's face.

VIII

'WE'RE GOING NORTH,' Uldin told them. The truth was more complex than that. Autumn was upon them, and the leaves were just turning. Outriders reported a sizeable mass of enemy soldiers developing in the north, in the skirts of the Kislev oblast. Archaon wanted them denied, and Surtha Lenk's horde was the nearest.

Surtha Lenk summoned Uldin and made him a Hetzar, placing him in command of six warbands – his own, Zar Blayda's, Zar Herfil's, Zar Kreyya's, Zar Skolt's and Zar Tzagz's. As Hetzar, Uldin was to ride north and wipe out the harassing enemy. It was a great honour, though it was clear Uldin's warband had only been chosen because of Karl-Azytzeen. Blayda and Herfil were particularly enraged and resentful.

For the second time that year, Karl found himself advancing northwards into the fringes of the Kislevite oblast as part of a horse troop. The soft, decaying touch of autumn showed in the scenery, and the villages they passed through were either ruined by war or abandoned.

The air was turning colder, and it bore the smoky odour of leaf-fall. Dawns brought the first early frosts, and wet gales beat down for many of the days. For over two weeks, they didn't see another living soul in the woods, the fields, the pastures or the open grasses.

On the afternoon of the day they crossed the Lynsk, fording it where it was wide and shallow, they sighted riders on a stretch of open plain below forested uplands. They had left the broadleaf forests of the south behind them, and these woods were still green, despite the time of year. Fir trees, oblast pine and other evergreens formed a dark backdrop to the string of horsemen in the distance.

At first, they believed they had found the first traces of the rumoured Kislevite army they had been sent to quash. The warbands urgently readied themselves for battle.

But the riders were not Kislevites. They were kyazak horse bandits, probably Kul or Tahmak from the look of them. Efgul sneered to Karl. In his opinion, kyazak – Kul especially – were vermin and cowards. 'We have the numbers, Karl-Azytzeen,' he said. 'Mark my word, they will run before us.'

But in this, the hairy Northerner was wrong on two counts. The kyazak did not run at the sight of the Kurgan war company. And they had the numbers.

'They have put the lie to you, Efgul seh,' said Hzaer, riding on Karl's other side. The horse bandits were turning and riding down the plain towards Uldin's troop with mounting speed. Uldin had six warbands – almost four hundred horsemen – at his disposal, but the kyazak, who at first seemed to be just forty strong, quickly became a hundred, two hundred, five hundred. They came pouring out of the forest, joining the men already in the open.

Uldin roared a command, and Hzaer and the other carnyx-blowers blared out battle notes. The six standard bearers raised their banners, Yuskel hefting the largest of all. Uldin's standard of the gilded skulls and the one-eyed wolf face had been supplemented by huge elk antlers strung with bead-cords of human teeth to denote his status as Hetzar. The massed warriors immediately kicked forward into a hard gallop, drawing their weapons and shouting for blood.

Their warhorses at full stretch, the two cavalry hosts met and ran in amongst each other. The collective concussion was huge, as if the rival armies were like mountain rams slamming together and locking their horns. As the charge lines came together and overlapped, Karl was surrounded by a dizzying sequence of cracks, impacts and blows. The whole world shook and thrashed violently. Spear shafts snapped, shields shattered, bones broke. Horses went over and brought down the riders racing behind them. Men were smashed out of their seats. Karl's sword-arm already ached from the six or seven jarring blows he had landed.

All around them was a constant patter of wood splinters, metal shards, flecks of mud, beads of sweat and spats of blood. Their momentum robbed by the collision, the horse armies were now at a virtual standstill. Every man fought like a demented daemon in the saddle with those enemies within reach. Karl knew his pallasz had claimed the lives of at least four kyazak, but the combat was such a blur of overloaded sensations, he ultimately lost count.

Both forces sustained their battle-fury for over a quarter of an hour, but then the kyazak, who had taken the worst of it, lost spirit. Within minutes those that were still able quit the plain had fled into the trees. The warbands of Zar Blayda and Zar Herfil broke away and chased the fleeing enemy, mercilessly hunting them into the depths of the forest. The remainder of Uldin's force rallied and pulled up, panting and shaken. The sheer effort of the brief but explosive battle had left many exhausted.

And many dead. Uldin's war-force had lost forty riders, with another dozen badly hurt. The kyazak had paid for defeat with above three hundred lives.

The Kurgan were shouting and singing their victory chants. Karl rode back into the line. Efgul, bleeding from a deep scratch across his chest, hooted and shook his fists in the air. Hzaer blew loud, discordant flourishes of triumph, even though a kyazak sword had taken the little finger of his right hand entirely away, and he was spattering blood with every movement he made. Apart from the gore of other men, Karl-Azytzeen was entirely unmarked.

After about two hours, Blayda and Herfil brought their hunting parties back and joined the victory. They had scalps and weapons for trophy rings, and news besides. They took the news to Uldin with not a little smug satisfaction.

They had encountered other riders in the forest, the advance parties of another Kurgan host. These men, who pledged allegiance to High Zar Okkodai Tarsus, said that north of the forests their High Zar had quelled the land with his mighty horde, and was now drawing south to swell the great army of Archaon. They had been driving the kyazak army before them, which explained why the horse bandits had attacked so desperately. Engaging four hundred Kurgan horse had seemed infinitely preferable to annihilation at the hands of a High Zar's ten thousand men.

There was more yet. Okkodai Tarsus had already beaten off the Kislevite army Uldin had been sent to find. This battle had taken place a week earlier, on the salt marshes of the Tobol, high in the north, and though inconclusive, it had ended the Kislevite

threat. The army of the Gospodarinyi had scattered
into the oblast, put into flight by the size of Okkodai Tarsus's great horde.

His glory denied him, Uldin flew into a dark rage.
He had little stomach for the idea of returning to
Surtha Lenk's side with no victory to show. To the
dismay of Blayda and the other zars, he insisted
they remain in the north, and push on to confirm
the stories told by Okkodai Tarsus's men.

Besides, the oblast autumn could suddenly
plunge into winter, almost overnight. Already there
was the smell of snow in the air, and the cold
Norscya winds were rising. Even if they turned back
now, they were not likely to reach Ostland and the
rest of the host before winter overtook them.

They rode north for another week and confirmed
as best they could that no Kislevite army was lurking in the north country. Neither did they see a trace
of Okkodai Tarsus's horde, which had swept away
south and east in the direction of the Kislev capital.

As the first light snows of winter began to fall,
Uldin led them west into the wild hill country
north and east of Erengrad. They would go to Chamon Dharek, and spend winter there.

IX

CHAMON DHAREK WAS a remote place sacred to the
Kurgan. It lay high up in the inhospitable hill
country, a place of pilgrimage where the sons of the
north might go to have their souls anointed by the
gods, or where a warband might gather to shelter
for the winter and make tribute to the great

Shadow of the North. As was the case with many old and sacred places, the barriers between the mortal realm and the otherworld were thin at Chamon Dharek. The name meant the place of gold and darkness.

Chegrume the shaman was especially excited at the prospect. He had been to many shrines, but not this great and secret place in the west. 'A site of wonders and secrets!' he proclaimed, hungry with anticipation.

It took three weeks to reach it, the last stages spent trudging through drifting snow into the teeth of the blizzards that had conquered the ragged hills.

On the day they came to Chamon Dharek, the blizzards suspended their force and a red winter sun rose above the white blanket covering the hills. Chamon Dharek lay in a hidden valley, cut off from the world by a narrow pass. As they came out through the gates of the pass, many men stopped to gaze in wonder at the sacred place.

Karl-Azytzeen was one of them.

It was the largest kurgan grave mound Karl had yet seen: a towering rampart of earth now coated in fresh snow. At its base was a great hall of stone and timber, two granaries, and heavy-beamed barns for horses and chariots. Smaller shapes, perhaps standing stones, stood in a ring around the base of the mound, but they were so covered in snow it was impossible to say what they were.

At the crown of the ancient kurgan mound, a great bonfire blazed, despite the snow and the cold wind. Its flames leapt up beyond the height of many men,

and licked up into the sky. The flames were white
and blue, like burning ice.

In the sky above, the crackling, shimmering wonders of the Northland aurora made patterns and
colours across the heavens.

X

THEY WERE NOT the first to arrive. Two other warbands, smaller than Hetzar Uldin's, had come to
the place to spend the ice months feasting and wor-
shipping. One was a band of Aeslings from the
Norselands in the west – exceptionally tall men
with cross-gaitered leggings, checkered surcoats and
long, hooked axes. The other was a war party of
Dolgans, nomad warriors from the Eastern Steppes.
The Dolgans were kin to the Kurgan – indeed in the
eyes of the south, the Dolgans were Kurgan. But
there were differences that Karl could easily spot.
Their style of armour and harness was lighter and
favoured polished bronze and gold where the Kurgan used pitch-coated brass and iron. Their dialect
was different too, not incomprehensible but, like
the Aesling Norse, heavily accented.

Uldin's men put up their horses in the long stable
barns, and went to the great hall. In that vast place,
beneath the high, beamed ceiling, all the people
who came to Chamon Dharek would live commu-
nally for the winter. Even with the addition of
Uldin's three and a half hundred or so, there was
more than enough space. The warm air was thick
with fire smoke, and the smell of bodies and straw
and wine. Lean hunting hounds trotted between the

benches and across the unrolled rugs of the resting places.

Chamon Dharek had permanent residents of its own: a sect of priests who maintained the shrine all year round on behalf of the tribes of the north, and provided for any visitors. These priest-warriors defended the shrine from attack, maintained its stores, granaries and larders, and officiated at all the rites and ceremonies of the place. In return for their hospitality, any visiting warband was expected to leave a tribute of their war booty.

The sect were strange folk. The priest-warriors were heavily-built men, but the rest were women and young girls. All wore long robes as white as Skarkeetah's, and their heads were covered in pointed gold helms from the brims of which hung aventails of fine gold that entirely hid their faces. From the shape of their helms, Karl was sure they – like the massive brute Hinn – had skulls elongated by binding.

Uldin and his zars made representation to the priesthood, and paid their tribute of Kurgan gold and kyazak loot. Then Uldin met with the leaders of the Aeslings and the Dolgans, and partook of the ritual drink to pledge peace between their companies for the duration of the winter.

From the moment he entered the hall, Karl felt a tingling that warned him the air in this place was crawling with magical force. And from the moment he entered, he was the focus of great and apprehensive interest. The Aeslings, who wore heavy, studded collars to show their association with the death god,

Kjorn, treated him with wary caution. The Dolgans however, who seemed to know much of the lore of Tchar, regarded him with awe.

Even the shrine-priests, who simply served and said little, seemed struck by him.

On the first night, they feasted all together, filling the hall to the rafters with a great din of singing and boasting and laughter. Only Chegrume was missing. He had hastened eagerly to the sacred shrine itself the moment they had arrived, and hadn't been seen since. Uldin, and others of the men, had already paid respectful visits to the shrine too, and most would visit every few days for the duration of their stay.

But the idea had not appealed to Karl. He was steeped in outland magic already, and had no wish to learn more about the tradition he had been made part of. Besides, the biting winter cold hurt the damaged part of his skull, and he preferred to stay in the heat of the hall.

The feast was generous and rich. Samogon and wine sweetened with honey was served in cups made out of hollowed, upturned human skulls. The insides of the head bowls were layered with gold.

'From the great mound,' Berlas said, seeing Karl was studying his cup. 'Drinking vessels made by the Scythians and hidden away under the earth in that mound.'

Karl raised his cup. Here was a skull whose owner had been dead twice as long as the Sigmarite Empire had existed.

At one of the feasting tables not so far away across the busy hall, Karl saw Zar Blayda in his scribed black wargear, drinking and laughing with the leader of the Aeslings. Where Uldin's warband followed Tchar, Blayda and his men favoured the bloody-handed god, Khar. The Aeslings' Kjorn was a different aspect of the same daemon-deity. The two warbands had much in common. Ons Olker, Blayda's tri-horned shaman, sat near to his zar. It was the first time Karl had seen him properly since becoming part of Uldin's warband. Where before Ons Olker had taken every opportunity to gaze malevolently at Karl, now he pointedly looked away. Like all the others, he was afraid of Karl's aspect, and dared not to look on it. Karl was quite sure he longed to.

'There is one to watch with a hand on your hilt,' Efgul muttered, chewing the meat of a mutton stick.

'The shaman?' Karl asked.

Efgul belched and wiped his hand across his mouth, distributing grease through his thick facial hair. 'Yes, him, Karl-Azytzeen. But more, his damned master.'

'Blayda.'

'Blayda, that's right, Karl seh. Blayda.' Efgul took a swig of samogon, and held the empty gilt skull out until it was refilled by one of the gold-masked priest-women.

'Blayda has ambition,' Hzaer said.

'Who doesn't?' laughed Berlas.

'Ambition to be High Zar one day,' Fegul One-Hand growled. 'Efgul seh is right. Blayda despises our lord for becoming Hetzar. Uldin seh is now an obstacle in his rising path.'

'He's nothing,' Yuskel the standard bearer declared. 'Uldin would take him to his grave, and he would never be warrior enough to challenge our High Zar.'

'Uldin would take him to his grave in a straight fight,' Karl said quietly. 'But Blayda seh will fight any way he can.'

The men around him fell silent and looked at Karl, until all of them realised they should not and hurriedly turned back to the food.

'You speak like you know him better than us, Karl seh,' Yuskel said.

'I do, in a way. Our zar... Hetzar now... is a fine man. A great warrior.'

They all gave a hearty cry and thumped their fists repeatedly on the feasting table.

'And a fair man,' Karl continued as the noise died down. 'Blayda is a... he is underhand. And the shaman. He has blood-tied me, for I did him offence.'

'What offence?' Diomac asked through a full mouth.

'I knocked in his head and put him on his arse,' said Karl.

The men laughed.

'He will not touch you now, Karl-Azytzeen,' said Yuskel firmly. 'Not now that...'

'Yuskel seh means,' said Efgul, 'that Ons Olker would have to look on you to strike you, and no bastard dares do that.'

The men laughed again, and thumped the table.

'Ons Olker might,' Karl said. 'He has a lot to be gained. Which of you doubt that our fine zar rose to favour because his warband contained a man touched by Tchar this way?' He put his hand up to his one good eye, and ran his fingertips along the powder-burn snakes. Not a man risked looking.

'And what might our fine zar become with Azytzeen at his right hand? I am the real threat to Blayda. Without me, Uldin might easily be overtaken as the High Zar's favourite. But with me alive and loyal to Uldin seh…'

Karl raised his skull cup and took a pledging drink. 'Which I am, let every man here know. With me alive, Blayda will never get a chance to rise in power and influence.'

The men nodded. None saw reason to deny the clear truth of Karl's remarks.

'So, though it might cost him his soul, Ons Olker will try. Before the winter is out. He will try, because he believes it is worth it to his zar. And he can always blame my death on the blood-tie I owe.'

'We will watch you, Karl-Azytzeen,' said Efgul suddenly, putting his hand over his heart.

'We will,' agreed Berlas and Fegul One-Hand nodded, doing the same.

'Ons Olker shaman will not get close to you while we are round you in the warband,' Yuskel declared, and the men raised their cups and drank a pledge, their hands making it heart-truth.

* * *

XI

LATER IN THE feast, as the merriment slowed with drunken torpor, Lyr and Sakondor brought a Dolgan over to Karl.

'His name is Broka,' Lyr said. 'He wishes very much to find the favour of Tchar, for his fortune has not been well. He seeks that favour from Karl-Azytzeen.'

The Dolgan, a powerful man in the gold and bronze wargear of a prominent warrior, got on his knees before Karl. He was very drunk, but there was a frightening earnestness in his tone.

'Give me the favour of fortune, Karl-Azytzeen. I beg of you,' he said in his thick, eastern accent. 'Give me the blessing of Tzeentch.'

'Who?' Karl said.

'It is the name they have for Tchar, Karl seh,' Sakondor whispered.

It was all too peculiar, and Karl felt uncomfortable being the centre of attention. He was about to deny the man and send him away, when the man changed Karl's mind by doing the one thing no one had done since Aachden.

He looked Karl directly in the face.

Karl stared at him, and then said, 'I think Tzeentch will favour you now.'

Tears welled in Broka's brown eyes, and he bent to kiss Karl's heavy boots before hurrying away.

The shrine-priests continued to serve wine and distribute food to those who still required it. Most of the warrior-priests had disappeared, and only the womenfolk remained... the youngest and most comely of them at that.

'Are they trying to tempt us?' Karl said.

'Of course,' Efgul slurred. 'They do not breed with their own kind here. It's a sacred thing. They keep their population alive by breeding with the best of the warriors who come to Chamon Dharek.'

'Indeed.'

'Just another pleasure and blessing of this holy place,' Berlas sniggered.

'I have a mind to sire me a splendid warrior-priest!' Efgul announced. 'What say you all?'

'I say,' announced Diormac, 'that you will whelp the hairiest warrior-priest of all time, Efgul seh.'

The men howled.

'And a fine thing that would be,' Efgul decided, taking a drink.

'You'd need to get the chance first, Efgul seh,' remarked Yuskel slyly. 'They only choose the best and the most propitious. I'd judge their interest is in one of us in particular.'

Karl realised Yuskel undoubtedly meant him.

He excused himself from the table, not because the idea didn't appeal to him but rather, in his drunken state, it did all too plainly. He walked around the hall, through the smoke, stepping over the bodies of some who had passed out, intending to go outside and clear his head. Music was playing, and some of the warriors were dancing with the women while their brethren clapped and chanted.

Moving through the crowded hall, he caught sight of a Kurgan warrior, one of Blayda's men, sitting alone with his back to a roof-post. The man's wargear was blackened with pitch and inscribed with gouged scrolls and spirals like a zar's, but Karl suddenly realised he knew him.

'Sir? Sir? It's me!'

'I know it is, Karl Reiner Vollen,' said von Margur. 'I've been watching you.'

Karl sat down beside the knight. Von Margur looked much more healthy and fit than he had the last time Karl had seen him. He was still quite blind apparently, his deadened eyes gazing into space. Von Margur smiled.

'It seems we have both changed our fortunes and remade ourselves.'

'You ride with Zar Blayda's company now, von Margur seh?' Karl asked.

'He saw favour in me, as Uldin did in you. Offered me the chance to renew my acquaintance with loyalty and courage. It was that or death. I find Tchar makes some choices infinitely simple.'

'I am pleased to see you, von Margur seh,' Karl said.

'Indeed so. Karl, please don't use that dog-speak "seh" thing. Around me. We are men of the Reik, and we should talk like men of the Reik.'

'I'm sorry–'

'Ha ha,' von Margur chuckled. 'You should hear your voice, Karl. So thick with the round vowels and hard gutturals of the Kurgan tongue. You speak their language like a native now.'

Karl halted. 'I am speaking the language of the beloved Reik, sir–' he began.

Von Margur shook his head and laughed. His broken eyes rolled in their sockets. 'No, Karl. I am speaking Reikspiel. You, I'm afraid, are speaking perfectly in the dialect of the Kurgan.'

Karl sat back beside the knight, stunned.

'Have you thought of escape?' von Margur said.

'I–' Karl bolted forward, afraid that someone might overhear.

'Of course not. It was foolish of me to suggest it,' von Margur said. 'Tchar has made too deep a mark on you. That eye. It's really something.'

'How c–' Karl began. 'Tchar has changed you too, I think, sir,' he ended up saying.

'Oh, he has, Karl,' sighed the blind knight. 'Oh, he most certainly has.'

Karl got up and excused himself. He needed to get outside into the cool air.

'It's good to see you, Karl,' said von Margur.

XII

THE WINTER PASSED by slowly. The warriors whiled away the short dark days with sleep, contests of strength and visits to the shrine. The nights were spent feasting and raising hell.

Chegrume was almost never seen. It seemed the young shaman had taken to living inside the shrine.

Karl passed his time talking with the men and practising his bowskill out in the snow on clear days. Berlas had given him a fine bow, one of the ones they had fashioned at Wolfenburg, now finished and strung. At nightfall, he joined the warband to feast and listen to their stories. On one occasion, Uldin held the whole hall rapt with a powerful account of an old Kurgan battle, the conclusion of which brought thunderous applause and a thumping of tables. The Aeslings sang their sad, keening sagas. The Dolgans danced their potentially lethal dance of swords.

From time to time, often when the samogon had the better of him, Karl gave in to the wordless advances of the silent priest-women. He never saw their faces or knew their names, for the chambers they led him to were always dark and thick with the same intoxicating smoke of burning seedcases that Hinn had used back in the murdered Kislevite town whose name Karl had never learned. Karl would wake alone, in the cool, musky air of morning with his head full of half-remembered passions.

Some nights, he would feast with the Dolgans at their tables. They welcomed him as a brother... more than a brother, for they treated him with reverential respect. They told him of their god, Tzeentch, and how he ruled through change. Karl tried to explain that he found the ways strange and unsettling because of the world that he had come from. None of them seemed dismayed to discover he had been born a son of the enemy.

'All things change,' Broka told him. 'All things change, Karl-Azytzeen. The way we perceive the truth is dependent on context. We should never hold fast to a truth or a value because it might obscure our view of the truth of Tzeentch. That which changes grows ever stronger in the world. That which remains fixed is wasted away or broken down, for it cannot survive forever.'

It seemed an understandable philosophy for a nomadic tribe that was constantly moving and never established anything permanent. Karl liked Broka and the company of the Dolgans for their generosity and their freedom of expression. He was, however, alarmed to see that by this time – it was lately past midwinter – Broka's eyes had turned blue.

When he went out to practise drawing the bow, at least one of the warband went with him. It was usually Efgul, who always brought a flask of samogon, or Berlas or Hzaer. It seemed they were taking their pledge to guard him seriously.

There had been no sign of threat from Ons Olker, but then Uldin's band had purposefully had little to do with Blayda's company. Since the first night, Karl had not even spoken to von Margur. On the few occasions he had spied him, the knight had been aloof and remote.

Uldin chastised Karl for not visiting the shrine. The Hetzar seemed quite adamant about it, as if Karl's refusal augured badly for his band. Karl promised he would go to the shrine before the first thaw came and made it time to depart.

The year end was turning. As the long nights and quick days passed, the rainbow blooms of the aurora crackled through the sky above the eternal blue flame on the grave mound. Wolves howled in the snow-bound forests surrounding Chamon Dharek.

Karl knew he would have to go to the shrine before he left this sacred place. The women had whispered it into his sleeping ear.

* * *

XIII

THEY HAD BEEN feasting, yet again. The pleasures of unstinting food and drink were beginning to pall, and Karl had started to yearn for the clean, hard life in the saddle. At the feasting table, Lyr and Hzaer were speculating how long it would be before they departed from Chamon Dharek. A week, Lyr reckoned. Two, Hzaer insisted. Yuskel and Efgul announced between them that at least another moon would swell and slim before the snows thawed enough for decent riding.

'Karl-Azytzeen!' a voice hissed from behind them. It was Chegrume. The shaman was thin and sickly pale, and he was carefully averting his eyes from Karl's face.

'What?'

'It would be for the best if you came with me,' said Chegrume.

'I'm eating, witch-priest. Can't it wait?'

Chegrume shook his head. 'You must come now. Tchar wills it.'

'You had better do as he says, Karl seh,' Uldin growled from his seat down the table. 'I have learned to trust my shaman's instincts.'

Karl got up.

'Should I come with you, Karl seh?' asked Efgul.

Karl shook his head. He buckled his pallasz around his waist. 'I will be fine, Efgul seh. Eat well.'

'And take advantage of his absence to tup one of the women at last!' Fegul roared. 'He's had them to himself all winter!'

To the sound of their laughter, Karl followed the shaman out into the cold night outside the hall. He drew his bearskin around his shoulders and fastened the gold horse brooch firmly.

It had recently stopped snowing, and the air was clear. Stars, and the wavering, fuzzy light of the aurora, burned in the blackness above them.

'Where are we going?' Karl asked, his breath fuming the freezing air.

'The shrine,' Chegrume replied, beckoning him.

'No,' said Karl simply, turning back.

'You must! You must now! Tchar is close, oh, so close, and he has told me he is coming to bless you.'

'Tchar be damned! I don't want to.'

'He will make you whole again, Karl Reiner Vollen,' Chegrume said.

Karl took a flaming brand from a becket on the doorpost and followed the shaman around the vast hall towards the dark mass of the kurgan mound. Chegrume was shivering and hunched, his animal skins pulled tight around his thin shoulders, his bare feet sinking into the deep snow.

They trudged through the darkness. Karl had presumed they would climb up the hill to the flickering bale fire that lit the night, but instead Chegrume led him to an avenue of snow-covered shapes that led towards the base of the mound.

These were the same sort of shapes that stood in the ring around the man-made hill. As they passed between them, Karl raised his guttering torch, and saw that they were horses. Dead horses, waxed and mummified, mounted on heavy stakes to guard the tomb for the rest of time. The snow hung in heavy folds about their wizened carcasses, and hoar frost clung like glass to their drawn, snarling teeth.

Uldin had raised dead horses this way around Subotai's grave.

At the end of the icy colonnade of frozen horse-mummies, they came to a broad doorway in the base of the mound, an entrance propped open with a stone lintel. Torchlight crackled inside.

'What have you been doing in here?' Karl asked, his lips numb from the winter night's cold and tears freezing on to the tip of his nose.

'Learning, wondering, dreaming,' Chegrume said. He bowed his antlered head down under the lintel and went in. 'I came to the shrine of Chamon Dharek to learn and extend my power. The voices of the otherworld have been kind, and have blessed me in many ways. I have accepted power, Karl-Azytzeen. My efforts and ordeals in the cold have been rewarded. I have become one favoured by Tchar.'

Karl walked into the entrance tunnel behind the shaman. It was several measures warmer inside, out of the frost-wind, and the floor and walls were dry earth, lit by flaming, fluttering torches. The tunnel extended into the mound.

'I'm happy for you that you've found what you were looking for,' Karl called after Chegrume, who was hurrying ahead down the dry passage, his feet pattering on the floor. 'But why me?'

Chegrume turned back and beckoned Karl. 'Because Tchar wants you. He has set this time aside to meet with you.'

'I'm not sure I want to meet him at all,' Karl said.

'Don't!' said Chegrume, with a passion that startled Karl. 'Don't make him change his mind.'

Karl followed the lanky, antlered figure down the long tunnel into the belly of the kurgan. The air was hot and close, and stifled him with the heat of the torches. Forty-five bow-lengths in, at the extent of an accurate shot, the tunnel ended and gave out into a vast buried chamber. Its sides and floor were packed earth, and the walls curved over to form a domed ceiling.

Karl had never seen so much gold. Scythian gold, white and bright, in great profusion, spread about the place. Caskets, coffers, thrones, gorytos bow cases, helms, bridles, body armour for men and for horses. All of it was worked and decorated to the finest degree with Scythian emblems, and with intricate depictions of warriors in the saddle, chargers rising to lance, ibex and goat, ravens and eagles, swords and bows, and everywhere, everywhere, horses. The treasure of the ancient barrow glowed and twinkled in the torchlight. There was the wealth of nations in this one mound, and Karl was most amazed of all by the idea that it had never been plundered by the avaricious Kurgan and Norse who came to worship at the shrine.

They had seen it, been amongst it, but they had left it untouched. That told him of the reverence – and perhaps the terror – with which they regarded this place.

It had its guards. Warriors and servants sat or sprawled, or stood supported by stakes, all around

the chamber. They had each been strangled and
then mummified like the horses without. Husk-dry
warriors sat on golden saddles, wearing golden
armour. One, whose dead fist was raised on a stake,
supported a mummified hawk with a golden hood
over its desiccated eyes. Withered servants had been
nailed and propped into kneeling poses of submis-
sion, their staked-up hands supporting golden
platters on which the offerings had long since
mouldered to dust, and gilded skull cups whose
contents had evaporated before the coming of Sigmar. Emaciated concubines lay ready and eternally
willing on golden bed frames, clad in dusty, rotting
swathes of gold-shot silk. A wilting mummy
clutched a golden carnyx, ready to blow it with his
grinning, lipless mouth. Shrivelled warriors brandished swords and round shields with musty
horse-tail decorations at their bosses. The warriors
glared sightlessly into the gloom, sentries at the
gates of the otherworld.

Karl walked forward slowly, gazing around at the
extraordinary sight. He held his torch high above
his head.

Chegrume had hurried to the centre of the chamber, where a great gilt altar was set on a heap of
earth. Some kind of lustrous fire blazed within the
golden altar, and the blue, green and white flames
licked up out of it and raged up through a hole in
the centre of the roof. The eternal fire on the mound
top, Karl realised, came from within.

'Hurry! Hurry, Karl-Azytzeen!' Chegrume called.
'Tchar is close and he wishes to find you here.'

Karl joined the shaman at the foot of the altar. The flames had no heat to speak of. He felt greater warmth from the brand in his fist.

'Look into the flames,' Chegrume said. 'Look, and you will see.'

'See what?'

'You will see!' Chegrume insisted. He gestured to the blazing flames inside the gold coffer of the altar.

For the first time, Karl noticed the shaman's hands. Chegrume had suffered the loss of his middle fingers early in his life, and his hands had been like claws as a consequence.

Now, they were truly claws. The claws of a great bird. The outside fingers remaining on either hand had fused and become a lean, mobile claw, as had the index fingers and thumbs. The flesh had taken on the crumpled, scaly quality of a hawk's skin, and the nails had been replaced by dark, hooked talons. One of Chegrume's rewards had been to have his hands transformed into the feet of a bird of prey. Sallow brown feathers were growing in a fuzz out of his wrists and forearms.

Karl looked into the flames. He had no idea what to expect, so he was not disappointed. No great visitation came to him, no rush of otherworldy power, chorused by the clacking of immense avian beaks and the flapping of giant wings; no single, gazing eye.

No hissing voice of Tchar.

He pulled back and looked at the waiting shaman. The shaman grinned with joy.

'What was I supposed to see–' he began. And stopped. He could see. He could see out of both of his eyes.

Karl reached a hand up to his face and groped for the rough scar-tissue around his ruined eye socket. The rough knots of flesh were still there, but he could see, even when he closed his good eye.

Even when he put his palm over his lost eye.

He could see without eyes.

'Your glass!' he snapped, frightened. 'Give me your seeing glass.'

Chegrume reached his clumsy bird-hands into the spirit bag and brought out his seeing glass. Karl could not bear to touch the hooked talons as he took the object.

He gazed into the glass.

His face was as broken as he remembered it. Dark twists and folds of healed tissue surrounded and covered his left eye socket. But behind the thin coating of healed-over flesh, a hard blue light glowed and pulsed in his dead socket. It backlit the drawn skin so fiercely he could see traces of thin blood vessels in it, as a man sees against his eyelids when he turns his face to the sun, eyes closed.

'What have you done to me?' he said, stepping back off the altar mound and dropping the seeing glass.

'Nothing. I have done nothing–'

'What has Tchar done to me?' Karl hissed.

'Given you sight again,' Chegrume said.

Karl was about to reply when he froze and looked suddenly at the mouth of the chamber.

The flames flurried and blazed.

'What?' asked the shaman. 'What did you see?'

'You simple fool!' Karl spat, drawing his pallasz. 'You've played into their hands.'

'What? What do you mean, Karl-Azytzeen?'

'You've got me alone out here, shaman. It's what they've been waiting for.'

'Who?' Chegrume implored.

'Blayda and his shaman.'

'But... but they dare not even look on you, Karl-Azytzeen, chosen of Tchar! How could they hope to–'

A figure walked into the chamber, dressed in scribed-pitch wargear. His sword was drawn.

It was von Margur.

'Only those who cannot see would dare to strike at me,' Karl said to the shaman. 'It doesn't take the enlightenment of Tchar to work that out.'

XIV

'WE DON'T HAVE to do this, sir,' Karl said as he walked from the altar towards the knight, his pallasz raised.

'We do, Karl, I'm afraid,' said von Margur.

'Why?'

'Because you are much too dangerous to live. An abomination.'

'I see. In the slave-cages outside Zhedevka, you told me I would kill you. Doesn't that decide this fight before it starts?'

'I said you would make Uldin's fifth mark too,' von Margur said.

'I have done so.'

'And kill him.'

'He lives.'

'So what the sight shows us can be changed. Some things remain true and some things alter, thanks to the ebb and flow of Tchar's will. I will best you now and take your life.'

'Why, sir?'

'Because I am a spurred knight from a holy order, masterfully trained in swordsmanship, and you are nothing but a demilancer.'

'That's not what I meant.'

'Because you are an abhorrence to the world and I must be true to my oath as a knight of the Empire and rid mankind of you. You are an unwitting pawn of Khaos.'

'We are both pawns of Khaos,' Karl said. 'I just know it better than you. Do not force me to make true your prophesy. Back away, so we will not fight.'

Von Margur lifted his sword in both hands. His eyes rolled back into his skull as he swept his head around. He stroked his heavy sword about himself in a rushing figure of eight, expertly.

'Karl, you're wasting time,' he said. 'I know a Khaos bastard when I see one.'

'So do I,' said Karl-Azytzeen, closing his good eye.

Von Margur ran at him then, his sword whirring round. They met, and their blades chimed together. Both men probed with blind vision to find a gap in each other's defence. Von Margur drove Karl backwards, then came down with a hammer blow that would have slit Karl from his pauldron to his hip.

But Karl saw it was coming, and blocked, causing a shower of sparks. He lunged his heavy broadsword sidelong at von Margur's head.

The knight ducked away and circled, bringing his sword upright to defend against Karl's next cross-wise stroke.

Parrying, von Margur danced back lightly, and swept his steel around to cut out Karl's belly. Karl deflected low, and shoved von Margur's sword back at him, following up with another strike towards the knight's head.

Von Margur saw that stroke's intent before it began, and landed a counter thrust that was bashed aside by the trophy rings on Karl's right forearm. It was then Karl noticed that both of von Margur's arms were solid with trophy rings from wrist to bicep.

Karl rounded and dug at von Margur with his blade tip. The knight denied this with a sure-handed parry, and then flew at Karl, his broadsword carving down at Karl's skull.

Karl stopped it dead, with another clink of sparks, then blocked and blocked again as von Margur hammered blow after vicious blow at him.

Backing up to give himself space, Karl then rejoined, his heavy, double-edged blade overlapping understrokes and overstrokes.

Von Margur stopped them all. He was more gifted than any sighted master of the heavy sword. This duel would be decided by the whim of Tchar alone, Karl knew. Which of his instruments did Tchar favour the most?

Von Margur cut at him, a slicing blow delivered to split Karl's head in two. But Karl had backed out of the lock, and threw his blade's tip up in a brutal slash.

The pallasz cut through von Margur's armpit and out of the opposite shoulder. It did this with such force of impact that the knight's turning sword flew out of his hand and winnowed away across the grave chamber, and struck a stake-raised set of golden horse armour before dropping to the ground. The two portions of von Margur fell on the dirt floor and a vast pool of steaming blood drained out of them.

Karl stared down at von Margur of Altdorf for a long time.

'Karl-Azytzeen?' Chegrume said softly, moving to approach him.

Karl ignored him and suddenly rushed into the treasure heaps on one side of the kurgan chamber. He threw aside golden chairs, stacks of gilded shields that fell with a crash, and coats of gilt mail so he could lunge into the shadows behind them. He stabbed once, and then again, as if jabbing at a rat. Then he pulled back with Ons Olker's naked, thrashing body impaled upon the length of his pallasz blade. Shell beads and necklaces of bone broke and scattered onto the chamber floor in the shaman's frenzy, and an awful gurgling wail shrilled out of the mouth-slit of the three-horned bull helm. More Scythian grave-goods crashed over as Ons Olker was dragged out of hiding.

Karl tipped his sword over, and let Ons Olker slide under his own weight off the razor-edged steel.

The shaman, convulsing, sprawled with a splash into the spreading lake of von Margur's lifeblood.

'I have done what I should have done at Zhedevka, Ons Olker,' Karl said. 'May you burn in the daemon pit.'

'Please, p-please, Azytzeen–' pleaded the shaman as he spasmed in his agonised death-throes, his roping guts coiling out of his ruptured torso, his drumming feet flecking blood into the air. 'P-please… say thee a fair word for m-my sake to Tchar–'

'Damn you,' Karl said.

Ons Olker twitched and shrieked his way to the end of his messy, painful death. When he finally fell silent, Karl looked at the doorway of the mound chamber. Chegrume followed his gaze, but could see nothing.

Karl raised his hand and pointed. 'Zar Blayda! I see you, you worm! I see you out there, cowering in the shadows!'

Blayda, clad in his black, inscribed armour, slowly stepped into the torch-glare of the chamber. He gazed down at the butchered bodies of von Margur and Ons Olker lying in the slick of stinking blood and sank to his knees with a moan of mortal dread.

'I submit to you, Karl-Azytzeen,' Blayda said, bowing his head. 'I submit.'

'Blayda…' Karl growled. 'Look at me. Look at my face.'

Hesitantly, terrified, Blayda looked up at Karl. He cried out at what he saw.

'Look at me. Look upon Tchar. Let what you see blind you forever. You will follow me until the end of all days.'

'Yes... yes! I will!' Blayda yelled, his left hand on his heart, and tears streaming from his eyes. A heart-truth.

Arrows thumped into his back, one after the other. The tips came out through his chest, one pinning his hand to his heart. Blayda pitched forward onto his face, transfixed and still kneeling.

Berlas, Diormac and Efgul burst into the tomb chamber, recurve bows drawn back and nocked with ready arrows. Behind them came Hzaer, Fegul One-Hand, Lyr, Sakondor, Yuskel, and many others, their sword blades dripping red-wet from the men of Blayda's band they had been forced to kill to gain entry to the mound.

His fellow riders had come to save him, as they had pledged. Karl-Azytzeen smiled.

'Aside! Get aside, you dogs!' a voice roared outside in the tunnel. 'Yuskel? Where are you?'

Uldin strode into the chamber, pushing violently through the gathered men and splashing into the great puddle of red. He glared down at the bodies, the blood and tumbled gold.

'What is this bloody crime, Berlas? What have you done, Diormac? A zar cut down, against the peace-pledge... and on sacred soil th–'

Uldin balked as he saw Karl clearly for the first time. He made a warding sign and, like Blayda, fell on his knees. Karl could see the Hetzar's scared eyes flashing through the slits of his wolf-mask helm.

'A Hetzar such as you should not bow to a man like me,' Karl insisted. 'My life has belonged to you since Zhedevka. You could have taken it, but you chose not to. You told me that all the while I remembered the power you had over my life, I was no danger to you. Get up, Hetzar Uldin.'

Uldin did so.

'I don't belong to you any more, Uldin. I am Tchar's now.'

'I know that,' Uldin said, his voice wavering slightly.

'And you should have listened to Skarkeetah slave lord's advice,' Karl said. He lashed out with his true killer, and the slim blade of Drogo Hance's dagger punched in through the sight-slit in Uldin's wolf mask, through his eye and deep into his brain.

Karl wrenched the knife out and Uldin fell onto his back, another bloody offering to the altar of Chamon Dharek littering the chamber floor.

Karl looked at the stunned faces of the men in the warband.

'Well?'

'Karl-Azytzeen!' Efgul yelled.

'Karl! Karl seh!' bellowed Hzaer and Yuskel.

'Zar!' Karl spat back at them, his ring-wrapped arms raised in triumph.

'Zar Azytzeen! Zar Azytzeen!' the men cried. 'Zar Azytzeen!'

VEBLA

I

THEY BARELY MADE it to Yetchitch before deep winter established its rule of raspotitsa. The word meant 'roadlessness', and referred to the period when the oblast succumbed to such a weight of snow that even the simplest of paths and tracks were lost and indecipherable.

All through the last week of their trek – the longest and most arduous Gerlach had undertaken – the snow fell, until the grass ocean of the steppe became a pure white flatness that hurt the eye.

They were in what Borodyn called the open steppe now. This great waste of plains extended across the north-east parts of the Kislev oblast, a higher and more open country than ever before. Gerlach had been awed by the vacant flatness of the steppe where Dushyka and Leblya and Zamak Spayenya lurked like little secrets, and could not imagine anywhere with a greater scale of emptiness. Level land and the surrounding horizon could surely only express so much.

But the open steppe was the wilderness's masterpiece. Even the lancers seemed humbled by its void. The sun and moons, as they cycled through the sky, appeared to have been reduced in size themselves so the landscape was vaster by comparison.

Through icy dawns and blizzarding days, they made their route, until thick snow reduced their pace to a trudge. Armour was too cold to wear, or even touch, for fear of flesh sticking fast to frozen metal. Huddled in layers of furs and beshmets, the men shivered into the frost-wind. Before departing Zoishenk, Beledni had obtained two coats for Gerlach: a sheepskin cloak, leggings and woollen hood-cap with a fur trim, all of which had seemed impractical purchases in the lazy heat of summer on the Tobol.

But Beledni knew what lay in the north to greet them.

In the final days, white hills and a hint of green forest could be glimpsed ahead of them through the fast-falling snow. This was the territory of Blindt, the hill country at the edge of the Sanyza region, the wooded highlands where Yetchitch lay.

The frozen mood of the rota thawed as they rode up at last into the deep pine forests. They began to sing krug songs with raw voices. The giant, black-trunked conifers rose around them, dusted with ice, and snow flakes fluttered down. They glimpsed elks, and flighty arctic foxes that pricked their ears at the sound of the men's voices and took away into the snow.

Gerlach could feel the rota's delight that home was close. He let Vaja and Vitali teach him the words to one of the songs, so he could join in. Their attempts were so confused, and so hindered by numb lips and muffles of fur, all three fell into uncontrollable laughter that rang out through the trees.

Ifan spied the lights of Yetchitch first and put up a cry. Yevni carefully warmed the mouthpiece of his horn, and blew a great blast that rolled away into echoes. A lonely horn sang back in reply from the stanitsa.

Yetchitch was a place the size of Dushyka. Thatched izbas huddled around a long zal, whose tiled roof was thick with snow except for the melt-hole around the chimney flue. The stanitsa had no defensive stockade, but was surrounded by a high fence of pine boards that acted as a barrier against the drifting snow. They walked their horses in through the fence gate and entered the yard.

The folk of Yetchitch flocked out in heavy clothes to greet them. There was no banging and clattering of pots, no ritual exchange of shared food and drink, just a warm, silent embrace of figures greeting lost sons. Parents and friends, siblings and, in some cases, children hurried through the snow to wrap their arms around their loved ones.

For a forlorn moment, Gerlach sat alone on Saksen, watching the wordless relief and joy, utterly ignored.

Eager boys led the horses away and the townsfolk gathered the weary, chilblained warriors into the warmth of the zal. A youth in furs, his top lip struggling to produce a moustache, came to Gerlach and greeted him with a nod as the demilancer dismounted. Other townsfolk grouped around, puzzled by the sight of a stranger holding the rota banner.

The youth held out his hand to take Gerlach's reins.

'What is his name?' he asked.

'He called Byeli-Saksen,' Gerlach answered in broken Kislevite. 'Take care him of good.'

The youth nodded solemnly, and led the tired troop-horse away with the rest.

The townsfolk grouped around Gerlach.

One of them, a thin, elderly woman, looked into his eyes. 'Why does Mikael Roussa not the carry banner?'

'Is dead he,' Gerlach said.

The woman frowned, as if this was not an answer. 'I know he is dead. Where is he?'

'At Zhedevka place, fell he,' Gerlach answered, wishing his fragile command of Kislevite was less basic.

The woman nodded at this, very matter-of-fact, and turned away. Other townsfolk closed around and put their arms around her heaving shoulders.

Beledni appeared. He took Gerlach by the sleeve and led him through the huddle of onlookers into the zal.

The sudden heat was shockingly fierce. Gerlach thought he would pass out. The hall was packed with the people of the stanitsa, many of whom were joking and laughing with the lancers, and feeding them hot staya as they helped them strip off their heavy travel garments.

Beledni took Gerlach to the end of the zal, and up onto a hardwood platform above the fire. This was the stage from which the village ataman presided over his people. The ataman himself, a middle-aged man with long, shaggy hair and the heavy upper body of a woodcutter, stepped up to join them with his esaul, who carried the ataman's bulava, the small mace that was his statement of power.

The ataman looked at Gerlach with a curious frown. Beledni turned to the assembled people and raised his stout arms for silence.

'This is Gerlach Heileman, of Talabheim!' he roared in Kislevite. 'The rota has braved much in this dark year, and lost many of our comrades. When Mikael Roussa fell down to his death, this brave man saved our banner, and for that duty, Beledni rotamaster has made him rota bearer!'

The townsfolk cheered out their approval.

Beledni tried to shush them a little. 'He is one of us now. He is of Yetchitch krug. Embrace him as a brother. We have called him Vebla!'

The people cheered again, though this time the applause was mixed with great laughter.

Gerlach looked at Beledni 'You make words kind, rotamaster,' he said, as best as he was able.

'Vebla deserve as much,' Beledni said, switching to his unpolished Reikspiel. 'Vebla deserve praise of krug. Now… Vebla give back rota banner to ataman.'

Gerlach turned to face the ataman and hand him the banner. Just before he let it go, Gerlach pulled it back and kissed the haft. The ataman took the banner, and carefully slipped the tip of its shaft down through a hole in the wooden stage so that it stood upright, watching over the zal. Then he crushed Gerlach to his chest in an enthusiastic bear-hug.

The people cheered again.

At the esaul's urgings, kvass and salt were brought out for the toasting. Gerlach made sure he knew where the nearest seat was.

II

THEY FEASTED WELL, slept and feasted again. The storerooms of Yetchitch, loaded with salt meat and cured pork from the autumn slaughter, yielded a plentiful supply of food, and there was a never-ending provision of kvass and koumiss.

Through the long nights of feasting, stories were traded. The lancers recounted the details of their adventures, their deaths and losses, their victories and escapes. The townsfolk and the families returned the favour with tales of the harvest, of animals sick or lost, of births and deaths and marriages. Music was played on the horsehead fiddle and the tambor.

Vitali proudly introduced Gerlach to his aged mother. Vaja showed off two little children he didn't look old enough to have sired. Mitri had Gerlach meet his plump, beautiful wife.

Kvetlai, nervous and hesitant, took Gerlach to meet the girl he was betrothed to marry. She was stunning and shy and, like Kvetlai, little more than a child. Her name was Lusha.

She had three sisters, and insisted they were all prettier than her. Her only brother, older than all the girls, had been Sorca.

When she saw the look of pained surprise on Gerlach's face, she told him, 'I have mourned him already. I mourned him when he went away.'

Mitri's wife, Darya, wanted to know why Gerlach did not shave his hair like the other warriors.

'A topknot and a moustache is so much more fetching,' she insisted.

'Men here, they not shave,' Gerlach said, pointing to the ataman and some of the other male townsfolk.

'They are not warriors!' she clucked.

III

THE WINTER PASSED by. Maksim led a small band of men out from Yetchitch to recruit warriors from the other villages in the territory, hoping that the rotas of other stanitsas would be up to strength for the thaw.

Five youths from the Yetchitch krug had reached the age to join the rota. The men and the townsfolk spent one riotous, drunken night initiating them. This involved lewd drinking games, and the ceremonial shaving of their heads down to a tuft.

Beledni performed this duty with the sharpened tip of his own lance.

'Vebla not understand,' Gerlach said to Vitali, as they watched the shaving pantomime.

'We shave before battle, all of us,' Vitali said.

'This Vebla know. Vebla understand it nyeh.'

Vitali grinned his small-toothed grin. 'Before battle, we sharpen our swords and speartips. Make them trusty and sure. Then we shave our heads and cheeks and chins. If the rotamaster finds any men with stubble, he knows their edges are not battle-sharp.'

Gerlach sighed at the simplicity of it.

Heads pale and bare – and, in some cases, bleeding – the shivering, gawky supplicants stood straight as Beledni inspected them. Then he had each one touch the hem of the banner cloth on the stage and utter an oath of allegiance. Proud mothers wept.

The five boys were called Gennedy, Bodo, Xaver, Kubah and Valantin. Kubah was the youth who had come out on their arrival to lead Saksen away. He was, Gerlach learned, Beledni's own son. He could see it now. The familial similarity. Add a good few pounds, a few years and take away the front teeth…

Beledni then explained the philosophy of the last battle. Every battle, he told the boys, was the last. It was the one that would steal their life. If they treated any combat less seriously, they would surely die. A man of the rota fought every battle as though it was his very last.

Then Borodyn brought out their wings. Each one was fletched with the feathers of birds the youngsters had killed. Crow, crossbill, magpie, jay, kestrel. More illustrious plumes – eagle and hawk – would come later, once war skill had been tested.

These were the wings a rider needed to carry him up into the heavens to be with Dazh.

The laughter had died away. Everyone trooped out into the cold night, pulling on their outer garments and furs, and walked to a lamp-lit plot behind the zal. The snow had been cleared and five open graves were exposed, cut from the black earth.

The people of the stanitsa stood round as funeral prayers were said for the five boys. Their mothers and sisters cast dried summer flowers and the boy's shorn hair into the graves, and cried brokenly with loss. The boys were dead now, dead and passed away beyond the bosom of the family. They would be grieved now so that the grief could be set aside. No one would wait out the length of the year to hear news of their boy's fortune. They were dead, and gone to the fate of the rota.

They were, forever, riders of the dead.

IV

LATE IN THE midwinter, Gerlach had a vivid dream that woke him suddenly. He was lying in the zal, under furs, and sweating. All the men of the rota slept in the zal. Their family izbas had no beds for them now.

He found Borodyn sitting nearby, watching the great hearth crackle and spit.

'Vebla had dream,' Gerlach said, coming to sit by him.

'I suspected as much. We all have. I have seen it also in the stars. What did you see?'

'Vebla see–'

'In your own tongue, Vebla. I can manage that.'

Gerlach smiled. 'I saw a battle. A great field of men. Kurgan and the banners of Kislev, opposed. I had to ride out and fight their warlord.'

Borodyn horse master nodded. 'This I have seen, we all have seen. Dazh has written it in the krug of the sky.' He looked at Gerlach, his eyes reflecting the red sparks of the hearth.

'I thought you had come to us to save the banner. The rota banner. I thought that was why Dazh and Ursun had sent you. But that was just the start. The meeting point of Yetchitch rota and Gerlach-who-is-also-Vebla.'

'And now?'

'If the gods ride with you, you will fight the champion of Khaos.'

'Archaon? I will fight Archaon? Is that my destiny?'

Borodyn shrugged. 'Dreams don't lie, but they confuse. All I know is you are the one who will do battle with a great beast of Khaos. If you win, the oblast and your great Empire will live on. If you fail, and this monster beats you, then the Old World will sink away in a sea of blood. So, yes. I believe you are the warrior who will contest with Archaon, for no greater evil lives in the world.'

'Will I win?' Gerlach asked.

'The stars do not say, and neither do the dreams.'

'But will I win?' Gerlach insisted.

'Of course. You will have the rota of Yetchitch krug at your side.'

* * *

V

THE LAND WAS crusted with heavy snow, but the skies were clear and blue. Midwinter was behind them, and they were in that static place where the fallen cold simply lingered.

Gerlach went out into the town yard, and watched the boys of the stanitsa as they broke ponies to the snaffle bit. The rota supplicants, aloof in another part of the yard for they were boys no longer, were training the horses they would ride in Beledni's company. They were riding them in circles, reinless, and beating tambors, first one side of their mount's head and then the other. Bang-bang! Bang-bang!

Gerlach stood by the town fence, and watched the circling riders as he whetted the blade of the new spear Beledni had given him. Kubah was running his horse, trying to startle it with his hand-drum. He was a fine horseman, just like his father.

The next day was to be the wedding time of Kvet-lai and Lusha. Gerlach had decided to shave for the occasion. He went into the zal, and ladled hot water out of the kettle-pan permanently fixed over the flames. Then he gingerly began to use the spear blade to shave his chin, his cheeks and his scalp, all except for his moustache and a long lock at his crown.

VI

EVERYONE GOT DRUNK at the rowdy wedding feast. The groom, his new white beshmet laced with feathers, insisted that Gerlach say a few words – a proposal loudly supported by Vaja and Vitali – and a few words was all the demilancer could manage. He spoke, in slurred, hopeless Kislevite, of Zamak Spayenya and Kvetlai's bravery, and then admired the beauty of the bride. The gathering cheered him anyway.

When he fell back into his seat, Mitri's wife stroked her hand across Gerlach's smooth scalp.

'Is better,' she decided.

The music swept up, and the feasting turned to dancing. Gerlach was dragged by the hand into the swirling bodies by Lexandra, one of the bride's sisters.

Lexandra was quite the most beautiful girl Gerlach had ever seen. As they danced, tight together, she giggled.

'You are Vebla.'

'And you are Lexandra.'

'Is not so funny. Vebla it is funny.'

'What does vebla mean? What does it mean, Lexandra? No one will tell me.'

'There is a ewe.'

'A ewe?'

'A mother sheep. It has lambs. Some are strong and big, others are small. Smallest of all, it fight hard against others, wanting milk. It... it annoying little beast, always in way, always underfoot, always begging for more, always needing care. It pushy and demanding.'

'And that is a vebla?'

'Pretty much so,' she said, and laughed so hard her head tipped back.

He whirled her around to the beat of the tambor. Her happy laughter would haunt him forever.

* * *

VII

A WEEK AFTER the wedding. The rota woke to the
sound of Maksim bashing a ladle to and fro inside
a brass potato pot.

He ignored their oaths and taunts and suggestions
what he might do to himself.

'First thaw,' he said.

VIII

ACCEPTING THE ROTA banner from the ataman, Gerlach turned and walked out of the zal into the yard.
Snow covered the ground, dense and crisp, but
there was a smell of water in the air. The sky was
greenish-blue above the pines.

The townsfolk clapped and yelled as Gerlach
emerged. Over the winter, Borodyn had worked on
Gerlach's battered, worn half-armour, and inlaid it
with gold and silver chasing. A spike replaced the
cockade of his troop helmet, and a veil of silver
mesh hung down where his lobster tail had been. A
lamellar coat clinked over his cuirass, right down to
his hips, and furs were tied around his shoulders.
Brackets on his backplate supported the frame of
the tall wing of eagle feathers. It would take him a
while to get used to the heart-shaped visor Borodyn
had attached to the front of his helm. One had to
look hard to discern that the basis of his helmet was
an Imperial demilance burgonet and not a szyszak
at all.

Lexandra ran out to him and gave him a ritual
swig of koumiss and a heavy kiss that made the
people roar. Gerlach held her close, then handed

the banner to the waiting Kubah, splendid in his lancer wargear.

He leapt into Saksen's saddle from standing, to more appreciative whoops. Byeli-Saksen, fit and well-nourished, had been freshly dyed white and red, following the pattern the boys of Dushyka stanitsa had established. His mane and the tail that had been docked and bound as per cavalry rules had long since grown out to flowing length.

Kubah passed the banner back into Gerlach's hand. He hoisted it up, and Yevni blew the call to advance.

The fifty-three men of the rota, riders of the dead to a man, turned and galloped out of Yetchitch stanista and vanished into the forest.

The folk of the krug stood and waved until long after they were out of sight.

MAZHOROD

I

In the Kislevite tongue, it was called Mazhorod, but the Kurgan knew it as Khar'phak Aqshyek, for a great battle significant to them had once been fought there in a distant time. In summer, it was possible to walk the land thereabouts and find old arrowheads, shield bosses, bridle rings and other trinkets the ancient conflict had left behind in the soil. Mazhorod marked a decent fording place in the River Urskoy, a wide bank of shingle that slowed and lowered the old, broad river as it turned.

On either side of the crossing lay the spare, open country of a great plain, thinly populated with bent trees, gorse and steppe thistle. A high ridge of young mountains lay to the west, and a circuit of lower, rocky hills to the south-east.

It was barely spring. Snow still lay thick and heavy on the ground, and it would for six weeks more. But the thaw was on the land. The sky was a clear blue-white, and the air was clean and fresh. The Urskoy thundered along at its highest annual measure, swollen with melt water and riddled with shards of ice.

The year was still breathlessly young, but the fighting season had begun.

The rota's journey back down across the steppe to Zoishenk took three weeks longer than anticipated, even though Maksim's nose for the signs of thaw had got them into the saddle early. The snow that had drifted on the steppe during midwinter in the storming gales now formed deep dunes like a white desert. The riders had to wade many miles on foot, leading their mounts through cold, knee-deep snow.

When they reached Zoishenk, they found the Sanyza pulk had already formed and gone. Fyodor Kurkosk, the Boyarin, had successfully used the winter to amass a considerable force four times the size of the diminished remnants that had gathered on the Tobol the previous summer. He was joined presently by the Uskovic pulk, also now of great size. Not wishing to delay any longer, and fritter away the early start they had got to the year, the Boyarin had led his army south.

In the oblast that lay several hundred leagues west of Kislev itself – a land that had suffered under the predations of the Norscya hordes – the Boyarin's force had encountered the roaming army of Okkodai

Tarsus. The High Zar's cold, hungry mass of warriors was spreading west, summoned, it seemed, by Archaon, to support the crucial war now under way on the far side of the Middle Mountains.

The High Zar's horde was nearly twice the size of the Boyarin's combined pulks. They met outside a thorn-wood at Krasicyno. For a while, it seemed as if the pulk's escape from Okkodai Tarsus on the salt-pan the previous year had been but a postponement of their destruction by his hand.

Until, that is, another army arrived. Moving up out of the south, an Imperial army from Stirland closed in on the High Zar's heels. Caught between Kislevite and Imperial armies at Krasicyno, the horde of Okkodai Tarsus was crushed, broken and put to flight in a battle that lasted two days.

Large portions of the Norscya horde, including the High Zar himself, survived and quit the field, but their further operation as a viable force was extinguished.

Jubilant, the combined army of allies turned west. They were one of the first forces from Kislev and the east to sweep back towards the Empire's heartland at that dark, needy time.

Others, led in part by the tzarina herself out of Kislev, were close behind.

Beledni's rota caught up with Fyodor Kurkosk's army at Mazhorod, bringing with them other late arrivals from Zoishenk. The mood was ebullient and confident.

Gerlach was not. That very fact enraged him. At last... at last! They were striking back and avenging the cruel wounds inflicted the previous summer. Everything he had been wishing for was now happening.

But now his midwinter dream, the memory and obscure meaning of it, was in the way.

'You be look happy, Vebla?' Vitali admonished him as they rode along together.

'Yha,' Vaja agreed. 'We war at ride. This what Vebla keep want, all through time. Ride at war, rota, Vebla say. Ride at war me with. Why you not ride at war me with? Like echo in cave. Now we ride at war you with and… hello! Vebla, he look like man who find piss in his cup.'

'I am content,' Gerlach said to them in their language. 'I am content we ride at war. Vebla just…'

'What Vebla just?' Vaja asked.

'It's the dream you had, isn't it?' Vitali said in Kislevite. 'The dream we all had.'

Gerlach nodded.

'It will come when it will come,' Vaja said sagely. He turned his hand, as if letting dust sprinkle out of it. 'Is of no matter.'

'I think,' Gerlach said, 'it might be of some matter.'

II

At Mazhorod, just before the crossing, scout riders ran back to the pulk. They had seen a great mass of the enemy coming eastwards towards them. Mazhorod would be their meeting point, their place of battle.

The Boyarin camped the great pulk in the rocky hills south-east of the crossing. From there, they could see the whole plain, and the winding river. As night fell, they were able to view the torch fires of a massive Kurgan host on the far side of the Urskoy.

'Tomorrow, we fight,' Beledni told the rota as they gathered around the spitting fire of the krug. He had been summoned with the other company officers of the pulk to a meeting with the Boyarin, and now he brought the import of that audience back to his men.

'They will try for the crossing, probably at dawn. The Boyarin orders we take them as they come across. The river is deep. They will be vulnerable.'

The men cheered this. The skins of koumiss passed around the circle as men toasted victory. Beledni ordered them to shave.

Gerlach left the krug and walked out onto a jutting headland of rock. Around him, in the snowy gloom, the fires of the Boyarin's great pulk flickered in the dark.

A few leagues away, on the other bank of the Urskoy – the river invisible now in the night – the fires of the enemy camp blazed on the plain.

'You are not shaving as I ordered,' Beledni said, appearing out of the night behind him.

'I will, rotamaster. Dutifully, before I sleep.'

'You have a trouble in your mind.'

Gerlach looked at the heavy, old rotamaster. 'You know about the dreams?'

'I have had them myself.'

'I find this frustrating,' Gerlach said, gesturing down at the lights of the Kurgan host. 'Dazh has told me I am to fight the great beast of Khaos, and that the future of great nations rests in my hands.'

'Yha.'

'Archaon, damned be his name, is the great beast, surely?'

'Beledni rotamaster would imagine so.'

'Well… he's not down there, is he? We have to break this host of Norscya tomorrow. And even if we win–'

'We will win, Vebla.'

'Of course. But even then, this great effort is just a step on the way for me. How many more armies must we break before I get to face the beast? How strong do I have to be?'

'Strong enough.'

Gerlach ran his hands back over his smooth, bald head and straightened his braided topknot. 'I hope so. It just seems I shouldn't be doing this. I should be somewhere else, where it matters.'

'This matters, Vebla. This matters. This, and then the next thing, and the next. It is a journey. And the journey is a–'

'Circle. I know. But how could my journey ever turn full circle and end up where Dazh says I should be? I've never met Archaon. I've never met any beast of Khaos. I think perhaps my journey is a straight line, whatever the Kislev philosophy thinks. And this fight we are preparing for is in my way.'

'You are Vebla,' Beledni said, switching to his broken Reikspiel. 'You nag and annoy. You worry at things. You not give up. You will find out the way your circle closes.'

Gerlach smiled. 'Can I tell you something, rotamaster?' he asked.

Beledni nodded.

'When I was a young man…' Gerlach began. 'Last year, in fact,' he added, making Beledni laugh. 'I believed I could single-handedly change the whole world. I rode out of Talabheim, so full of piss and vinegar, I was going to take on the night and over-throw it, all on my own. Be a champion of the Empire. Turn back the entire Norscya hordes with one flick of my blade.'

Gerlach looked up at the stars for a moment. 'My time spent with you, with the rota – out on the steppe – it changed my outlook. The wide oblast made me realise how small I was. How insignificant. Just a lone, little man in a huge world. It was… humbling.'

'The steppe is humbling to all,' conceded Beledni.

'Yha. And it was a long overdue lesson for a Vebla like me. Know my place. Be not so arrogant.'

'Whole year has not been wasted, then?' Beledni chuckled.

Gerlach laughed. 'But now, Dazh tells me I am not a little man after all. I am everything my puffed up ego had me believe. So Dazh says.'

'Dazh, he shows us things that are significant,' Beledni nodded.

'Well, I have this destiny suddenly. One I'd cast aside because it was stupid. To be the man who single-handedly saved the world. To be the man who could face the beast of Khaos. To matter – really matter – in the scheme of things. And it's come too late, just when I realised I didn't matter after all.'

Beledni sat down on a rock. 'Dazh can really be a bastard like that,' he admitted. That made Gerlach laugh again.

'Every man matters,' Beledni said. 'How he lives, how he dies, what he does. The way he conducts his life, the manner of his passing from it. The krug turns and we take each day as it comes to us. If Dazh says you will find your beast of Khaos, you will find it. He will turn the world so it happens.'

'Will he?'

'Your dream was not a prophecy to make sense of. It was Dazh, warning you what was going to happen.'

III

THE WARBANDS OF Surtha Lenk's host massed on the west bank of the Urskoy as dawn came. They had been seething up into a frenzy since midnight, as the shamans blessed and praised them and screeched war-prayers amongst them.

In the weak, chilly light of dawn, the crossing seemed immeasurable. The Urskoy ran hard and frothy, glinting with broken pieces of ice. The horses would shy and refuse.

Carnyx horns blew loudly in the half-light. Though warriors in the warbands were disquieted, the zars and Hetzars were in no doubt. Archaon had ordered this. The Lord of the End Times had sent word to Surtha Lenk, ordering him east to deny the armies of the steppe. Archaon's eastern flank was exposed. The Lenk's horde was the measure of its urgent defence.

Those zars chosen by Surtha Lenk to lead the attack congregated on the foreshore of the crossing. Zar Herfil, Zar Skolt, Zar Bellicuz, Zar Narrhos, all massing horsemen, some nine hundred between them. Behind them advanced the foot troops, two thousand all told. In the feeble light, they could all see the Kislevites and the Sigmarite Imperials assembling to meet them on the other bank.

Zar Azytzeen led his horsemen up through the thick clot of readied warriors on the west shore. They parted as he approached at the head of his horse troop. He frightened them all. He was a stark figure, his arms wrapped in trophy rings, his head encased in a spiked gold war-helmet that some said had been taken from the barrow at Chamon Dharek. Others said it had been purpose-made to fit his head by the priest-smiths at that forbidden place. Whatever the truth, it was a chilling visage. The helm, beaten of white, Scythian gold, had only one eyeslit – on the right side. The rest of the half-visor was fashioned in the bas relief shape of a snake-fringed eye, with blue jade set into its pupil.

'We will make blood flow this day, Zar Azytzeen seh,' Yuskel said, spurring his braying black and white striped horse forward. The standard of Azytzeen's warband fluttered, upright in his thick hands.

'We will that, Yuskel seh,' said the zar.

IV

THE CARNYX BLEW. The Lenk's host charged forward into the water, stumbling headlong through the heavy flow. Infantry came first, lifting high their shields and berdish axes. Behind them, the first of the horsemen dared the cold, fast river.

The great pulk waited for them, arms ready.

Kurgan men were swept over by the freezing melttide, their bodies washed away down stream. Horses fell numb and followed them, their riders tumbling and swirling after them.

But Surtha Lenk's force persevered by dint of sheer weight. The first foot warriors scrambled up on the east bank, and ran towards the patient enemy. Shortly after, the first of the riders made it across. Zar Herfil's band. Zar Skolt's.

The pulk waited until a significant mass of the enemy was across. An enemy that now had the river at its back and nowhere to run to.

Bone horns and clarions sounded. The pulk moved forward. The Stirland pike wall formed up to meet the attackers, while Imperial archers, on both sides of the river bend, punished the enemy that had cleared the crossing with a deluge of arrows. Men fell, left and right, impaled.

At the same time, a vast company of horse archers rode up along the bank from the south, and pelted the Kurgan struggling across the water. The effect was considerable. Hundreds of Kurgan died midstream, hailed on by a mass of Kislevite bows. Zar Herfil himself fell with an arrow through his skull, and Zar Skolt lurched off his whinnying horse, two Kislevite barbs sticking through his torso.

The great pulk sent up a huge roar of triumph, goading the enemy. The river and the pulk had combined to inflict terrible loss on the Kurgan.

On the western bank, Zar Azytzeen cursed aloud the names of the enemy gods, and blamed his own for their lack of support. Even his staunchest comrades blanched at this blasphemy.

'Tchar! Changer of ways! Why do you forsake us so?' Azytzeen bellowed into a dawn sky that was as blue as the eye of snakes. He took off his golden helmet so his sacred, ruined eye could glare up at the face of his god.

Perhaps Tchar was listening to his favoured son, or perhaps great Surtha Lenk had made similar entreaties, with his sorcerous power. Whatever the cause, the sky grew darker suddenly. Marbled clouds of storm weather slid across the firmament and robbed away the daylight. Snow fell, at first, then hail too, ringing off the wargear of friend and foe alike. A savage chill cut the air, and the temperature dropped away sharply.

And the Urskoy at Mazhorod crossing froze solid.

The Kurgan yet to deploy from the west bank hesitated in bewilderment. The water had frozen so abruptly, so unnaturally that the warriors and horsemen still midstream were locked into it, some crushed by ice, others trapped and screaming. The eager spirit of the great pulk faltered and dimmed at the abnormal spectacle.

'Now! Now!' Zar Azytzeen roared, clamping his helm back over his head. 'Now, in the name of Archaon and Tchar!'

Hzaer blasted his carnyx, and the sounds wa
enthusiastically picked up and amplified by the
hornblowers of other warbands. The bulk of the
Kurgan horse horde thundered forward and clattered across the thick raft of ice, their hooves
splintering fragments into the air like sapphires.
Behind them, the foot warriors, the spearmen and
the axemen, poured forward.

Azytzeen's warband was first on the shore. They
charged through the scattering survivors of the first
wave. At the sight of him, the front line of the Stirland pike wall broke in panic. The company of
horse archers led by Dmirov, son of Gaspar, brother
of Antal, was closest to the Kurgan horsemen. They
had been harrying the Norscya who had made it to
the shore. Dmirov turned his men and rode them
full tilt into the oncoming riders.

Kislevite bows cracked and hissed, and arrows
tore at the Northers. Warriors were struck from their
saddles or fell with their slain or crippled
warhorses.

The Kurgan had drawn their own bows. Berlas,
Lyr, Diormac... every man including the zar himself, drew and shot, not once, but again and again,
loading to the cord from the clutch of spare missiles
they held between the fingers of their bowhands.
Black shafts hailed into the oncoming Kislevites,
volley after volley.

In seconds, dozens of them were down, rolling
and flailing. By the time the two horse companies met, more of Dmirov's men were dead than
alive.

Their arrows mostly spent, the Kurgan drew lades as they came level with the galloping steppe archers. Horses flashed past all around, but the heavy, armoured Northmen had much the better of it. Efgul took Dmirov's head without even slowing down. Sakondor slew the archers' banner bearer.

Then they were coming around and into the flank of the pulk, breaking it before them.

They were not alone. The other mounted warbands followed their Zars into the charge and drove into the facing and right-hand lines of the pulk. This sundering impact had scarcely been delivered when the Kurgan infantry followed.

The battle, so nearly won outright in its first moments, was now pitched and locked.

And fortune, in a manner that would please the eye of Tchar, was changing.

V

THE ROTA OF Yetchitch krug had been stationed on the right of the pulk, ready to sally out around the pike wall, when the river froze and the change began.

Beledni rose in the saddle and turned to the men. 'This is the last battle, remember! The only battle! Fight now as if it was your last stand, and it will not be so!'

At Beledni's fierce command, Yevni blew the charge, and the rota turned out, racing fast, lances couched. Two other rotas rose with them. It was a fine sight, a glorious sight. The gold and silver warriors, their tall wings fluttering, hammered through

the snow cover with their banner tails flying fror
their lance tips.

A section of Kislev partisans, foot troops raised
from the oblast, had just been split wide by the warband of Zar Kreyya and a wedge of Kurgan axemen.
The galloping lancers came up into them like a
golden tide.

None of foul Kreyya's men, armed as they were
with axe and pallasz, had any reach to match the
Kislevite lance. Spear-shafts shivered in lancers'
hands, and they recoiled in their saddles and stirrups, as the long weapons cut into the Kurgan.
Lances snapped and splintered on impact. Not a
single one failed to wound or kill outright.

In one jarring moment of collision, the five new
riders of the dead were baptised in battle, and
claimed the honour of their first war-kill.

The zar's surviving men tried to break, but they
were hemmed in by the now panicking infantry axemen around them. Kurgan began to kill Kurgan,
involuntarily at first, as maddened horses trampled
infantry. Kreyya, in his effort to ride clear, killed
footmen in his path. Some of the terrified infantry
turned their axes on the horsemen in a sick desperation to stay alive.

Most rota lances now had been dropped or broken. A few riders managed to keep hold of theirs
and used them as they drove the charge home. Mitri
left his, finally, through the chest of Kreyya's hornblower.

They took out their javelins, the shorter, throwing
lances, and hurled them into the thick press. Vaja,

st ahead of Gerlach, loosed his first javelin with
ch force it went through the shoulder armour of
the fleeing zar. Kreyya screamed out, and fought to
keep his warhorse upright. He managed to turn, in
time to take Vaja's second javelin between the eyes.

The rotas had slaughtered Kreyya's warband and the
infantry around it. Yevni blew his bone horn to raise
the tempo again, and Beledni swung the krug around.
There was another Kurgan warband closing in ahead.

And this one was already at full charge.

VI

YUSKEL HAD SIGHTED the rank position of the Kislevite Boyarin, and yelled the fact to his zar. Roaring,
Azytzeen pushed them forward. This was the kill he
most wanted. The Boyarin's head would be placed
at the summit of his first skull stack to watch with
burned-out sockets as Chegrume gave Zar Azytzeen
his first victory mark. Then it would be cased in
gold and set on the warband's standard.

Most of all, it would win Azytzeen favour with the
High Zar. Then there would be no doubting the
identity of Surtha Lenk's new favourite. He would
be Hetzar Azytzeen, chief of chiefs.

A single line of Kislevite lancers stood between
him and the Boyarin's trabanten. The winged horsemen had just come through one fierce melee, and
their lances and javelins were mostly spent. He
would demolish them, take their heads, and cast
the plucked feathers of their ridiculous wings into
the hailstorm.

* * *

VII

AT FULL STRETCH, without hesitation, the warband
Zar Azytzeen and the rota of Yetchitch krug came
across the snowfield at each other, and met head
on.

VIII

'GREAT DAZH AND Sigmar preserve us all…' Gerlach
gasped as he saw the beast that rode at the head of
the enemy warband. The golden, one-eyed helm
was wretched enough, but some obscene blue fire
seemed to glow out from it, through the gold where
there was no eye-slit. A daemon-thing, a creature
stalking abroad, loosed by the otherworld. Gerlach
could not imagine what foul hell had spawned that
warrior.

But the blue and the gold had been shown to him
by Dazh in his dreams, and he knew with utter certainty he was in the right place after all.

IX

THE WORLD BROKE, as if struck by a hammer. Kurgan
warhorse and Kislevite chargers tore past each other.
Confusion was all around them.

Confusion, and death.

Berlas loosed the last of his arrows. Mitri crashed
over into the snow, his arms flung up, a black shaft
slammed through his chest. Beledni rotamaster
left Diormac dead in his wake, with a sword blow
cleft through his helm. Maksim received a wound
in his thigh from Efgul's axe blade as they swept
past each other, and then met Sakondor face to

...ce. Sakondor's pallasz took feathers from Mak-
...im's wing. Maksim's sword took Sakondor's head
off entirely.

Gennedy, youngest of the supplicants, hurled his
last javelin but missed his mark. He screamed,
briefly, as Lyr's sword felled him and his horse
together.

Fegul One-Hand closed with Ifan, and they traded
sword cuts, their horses turning around each other.
Both landed wounding blows, but Fegul One-
Hand's northern power broke Ifan's guard and split
him through the chest. Fegul was whooping his victory when Kvetlai, with tears of rage in his eyes,
rode by and silenced him forever with his shashka.

Vaja and Vitali, as ever a pair, flanked Gerlach as
they came through the thickest part of the charging
Kurgan line. Their swords hacked Northers off their
mounts. They were closing tight on the foe's
hideous standard and the brute on a striped horse-
thing that carried it. Yevni and Kubah were hard at
their backs.

Yuskel saw them coming, and raised his
broadsword. Hzaer and Lyr plunged past him in
defence. Hzaer thrust forward to reach the rota banner and kill its bearer, but Vitali locked with him
and fought him saddle to saddle.

'Ride on!' Vaja shouted. 'Ride on, Vebla!' He was
fending off Lyr's bill-tipped sword, his horse
wounded and bleeding. Gerlach lurched Saksen on,
trying to avoid the milling fighters around. Yevni
and Kubah streaked past Gerlach and went straight
for the enemy bearer. Kubah's sword tore through

Yuskel's neck as he and Yevni flew by. Yuskel
striped beast brayed and kicked as Yuskel toppled
from its back, and then ran. The warband's standard
fell.

Yevni turned back, his horse's hooves slithering in
the red-stained snow, trying to take the enemy standard as a trophy to break their morale.

Hzaer, in a hate-rage, wounded Vitali and broke
off, covering the short distance to the fallen standard at a mad gallop. He struck Yevni off his mount
with his first blow, and then hacked down into the
head and shoulders of the fallen man as he tried to
get up. Efgul appeared, took up the standard, and
rode it clear.

Vaja saw all this as he stabbed his sword through
Lyr's heart.

X

ZAR AZYTZEEN SAW the fluttering banner and the
bearer on the red and white gelding. The Horse-of-
Karl-Azytzeen shrilled as rowel spurs dug into its
belly. It bolted forward. This was the one, Azytzeen
knew. Even without the banner, this was the one.
The inner sight Tchar had blessed him with was
showing him that.

Gerlach saw the flash of gold and heard someone
– Vaja or Vitali maybe – yelling his name in warning. The beast, the Khaos beast, that he had lost
sight of in the mayhem of the horse fight, had reappeared now, and was riding him down.

That blue fire. Just the sight of it froze Gerlach's
blood. As blue as the single blue eye he had seen in

is fever-dreams. Not a prophesy at all. Just Dazh
warning him what was coming.

His sabre was in his hand, his old demilance
sabre. It did not seem weapon enough to fell a beast
like this.

Gleaming riders suddenly rushed in and interposed themselves between the Khaos beast and the
rota bearer. Beledni and Borodyn, rotamaster and
horse master, side by side, confronting the charging
zar. Neither one seemed remotely afraid.

Perhaps they should have been.

Zar Azytzeen's sword wounded Borodyn's mare so
badly that it started to bolt, and then fell dead,
throwing him to the ground. The fall, even onto
snow, was so violent that Borodyn did not rise.

Beledni's shashka rang against the zar's pallasz.
Sword masters both, they traded savage blow after
blow, looking for the weaknesses in each other's
guard.

Beledni found it, and struck in. His shashka broke
against the warrior rings that cased the zar's right
arm.

Zar Azytzeen swung his sword.

'Beledni!' Gerlach screamed. The rotamaster
swayed for moment, then slipped gently out of his
saddle.

Gerlach hurtled Saksen forward, screaming
Beledni's name. He needed his sword now, and he
needed his other hand on the reins to ride at such a
rate. Without hesitation, he threw the rota banner
into the snow and went straight at the murdering
zar.

Azytzeen blinked at him. What he saw was a warrior, armed only with a cavalry sword, too deranged by anger and grief to be thinking clearly. It would be no effort to fend him off and kill him. That foolishly small sword...

A demilance sabre.

Karl-Azytzeen stared at the oncoming rider, and fixed him with the inner sight of Tchar.

He saw him, and knew him.

Gerlach Heileman. Why, of all the things Tchar had revealed to him, had this strange vision been left so late?

His great and bloody pallasz, rose in his hand for an easy kill. But he hesitated, for a second.

Gerlach's sabre, held at the charge position across his howling face, ripped down, tip-foremost, and ran through the zar's trunk, so deeply and so soundly the blade was snatched out of Gerlach's hand.

Gerlach pulled Saksen around for another pass. He drew his dagger in case the Khaos beast showed any signs of fighting on.

The zar lay on his back in the snow, dying it red. His golden helm had tumbled off.

The blue light had faded away completely.

He was dead.

Gerlach halted and gazed down. The zar's twisted face, ruined by scars, was somehow familiar to him.

Insanely, like the nonsense of a fever-dream, it was the face of Karl Reiner Vollen. But it was not. It was something that had once been called by that name. What had he become? What would he have become if Gerlach had not ended him here?

Gerlach shuddered, numb. If he had known for a moment the identity of his foe, perhaps he would have hesitated...

The sky was clearing as suddenly as it had gone black. In the wide plain, the great pulk, with renewed effort, was breaking the horde of Lenk and driving the remains of it back across a river that was in flood again.

Gerlach ignored his surroundings, caring little who won or lost now. He gathered up the fallen banner of the rota and walked to where Beledni lay. Borodyn, injured and in pain, knelt beside the rotamaster.

Gerlach crouched down too. There were tears in his eyes.

'Vebla not mourn. Is no time for grief,' Beledni sighed. 'Beledni rotamaster being dead for many years.'

Gerlach tried to stop his tears, but he could not manage it.

'You kill him, Vebla,' said Beledni. 'Like Dazh show you.'

'It was a circle, after all,' Gerlach said.

'Yha. Beledni rotamaster tell you this. But Vebla let banner fall.'

Gerlach shook his head and shrugged.

'Is of no matter,' he said.

PYRES

I

THEY BURIED BELEDNI and the other dead in the open steppe. The laden horses galloped away towards Dazh's fire. Gerlach hoped that when they ran out of earth to ride on, they would have wings to carry them onwards.

II

LATE IN THE spring, at Chamon Dharek, the last of the warband, who had fought to recover the body of their zar before fleeing the field at Mazhorod, laid him finally to rest.

They placed him in the golden mound, his wargear around him. Berlas laid a bow, unbroken, at his side.

The dauntless Horse-of-Karl-Azytzeen stood watch outside, its body stiff with fresh-hewn stakes,

as the grave fires were lit. Hzaer blew a last, lon
blast upon his carnyx and Efgul shouted out th
name.

'Azytzeen!'

III

THE SNOWS DEPARTED. The war across the world
ground ever on. In the oblast, the spring freshened
the land and clouds of mosquitoes rose from the
melting ice. The rota lodged at Olcan Stanitsa to
heal their wounds and recover their strength.

Gerlach had been unsettled for days. He was tired
and longing for something he could not name.

Late one afternoon, as he stood in the yard and
looked out across the steppe towards the reddening
sky, he saw a cloud that looked like lambs suckling
around a ewe, and knew that it was his time. That
cloud had gone round the circle and now he had
seen it twice. His journey was done.

He prepared Byeli-Saksen and put on his wargear.
Vaja and Vitali sensed what was going on, but did
not protest. They helped him don his gear. Gerlach
gave the rota banner to Kubah.

'Guard him well,' he told Vaja and Vitali.

Then he rode out of the gates and into the steppe.
Twilight was closing. Behind him, at the gateway of
the stanitsa, Vaja and Vitali suddenly began shouting his name, as if they had changed their minds,
and now hoped he would not ride away after all.

'Vebla!' they shouted, 'Vebla, yha!' over and over
into the fading light. Gerlach did not look back. He
rode towards the embrace of fate, and kept riding,

til it was dark and the men, and the sound of
their voices shouting his name, had faded entirely
into the endless steppe.

ABOUT THE AUTHOR

Dan Abnett lives and works in Maidstone, Kent, in England. Well known for his comics work, he has written everything from Mr Men to the X-Men in the last decade, and currently scripts *Legion of Superheroes* for DC Comics and *Sinister Dexter* and *Durham Red* for 2000 AD.

His work for the Black Library includes the popular strips *Lone Wolves* and *Darkblade*, the best-selling Gaunt's Ghosts novels and the acclaimed Inquisitor Eisenhorn trilogy.

More Warhammer from the Black Library

THE GAUNT'S GHOSTS SERIES
by Dan Abnett

*In the nightmare future of Warhammer 40,000, mankind
is beset by relentless foes. Commissar Ibram Gaunt and his
regiment the Tanith First-and-Only must fight as much
against the inhuman enemies of mankind as survive the
bitter internal rivalries of the Imperial Guard.*

The Founding

FIRST AND ONLY

GAUNT AND HIS men find themselves at the forefront of a fight to win
back control of a vital Imperial forge world from the forces of
Chaos, but find far more than they expected in the heart of the
Chaos-infested manufactories.

GHOSTMAKER

NICKNAMED THE GHOSTS, Commissar Gaunt's regiment of stealth
troops move from world from world, playing a vital part in the cru-
sade to liberate the Sabbat Worlds from Chaos.

NECROPOLIS

ON THE SHATTERED world of Verghast, Gaunt and his Ghosts find
themselves embroiled in a deadly civil war as a mighty hive-city is
besieged by an unrelenting foe. When treachery from within brings
the defences crashing down, rivalry and corruption threaten to bring
the Ghosts to the brink of defeat.

The Saint

HONOUR GUARD
As a mighty Chaos fleet approaches the shrineworld Hagia, Gaunt and his men are sent on a desperate mission to safeguard some of the Imperium's most holy relics: the remains of the ancient saint who first led humanity to these stars.

THE GUNS OF TANITH
Colonel-Commissar Gaunt and the Tanith First-and-Only must recapture Phantine, a world rich in promethium but so ruined by pollution that the only way to attack is via a dangerous – and untried – aerial assault. Pitted against deadly opposition and a lethal environment, how can Gaunt and his men possibly survive?

STRAIGHT SILVER
On the battlefields of Aexe Cardinal, the struggling forces of the Imperial Guard are locked in a deadly stalemate with the dark armies of Chaos. Commissar Ibram Gaunt and his regiment, the Tanith First-and-Only, are thrown headlong into this living hell of trench warfare, where death from lethal artillery is always just a moment away.

SABBAT MARTYR
A new wave of hope is unleashed in the Sabbat system when a girl claiming to be the reincarnation of Saint Sabbat is revealed. But the dark forces of Chaos are not oblivious to this new threat and when they order their most lethal assassins to kill her, it falls to Commissar Gaunt and his men to form the last line of defence!

GRAPHIC

Warhammer graphic novels from Dan Abnett

The dark worlds of Warhammer are brought to grim reality in Dan Abnett's series of awesome graphic novels. From the evil dark elves to the thundering behemoths of Titan – carnage and mayhem are just a page away!

Available from all better comic shops and book stores or online at: *www.blacklibrary.com*

NOVELS

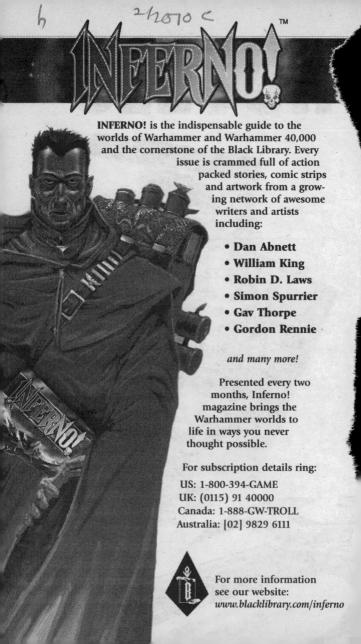